Jack Maggs

Jack Maggs

PETER CAREY

Alfred A. Knopf   New York   1998

THIS IS A BORZOI BOOK
PUBLISHED BY ALFRED A. KNOPF, INC.

www.randomhouse.com

Originally published in Great Britain by Faber and Faber Limited, London, in 1997.

Library of Congress Cataloging-in-Publication Data
Carey, Peter.
Jack Maggs / Peter Carey. — 1st American ed.
p.   cm.
ISBN 0-679-44008-9 (alk. paper)
1. Great Britain—History—Victoria, 1837–1901—Fiction.
I. Title.
PR9619.3.C36J33   1998
823—dc21   97-36893   CIP

Manufactured in the United States of America
First American Edition

Think of yourself as a magnet, with your arms and especially your hands as the two poles. Touch the patient by placing one hand on his back and the other, in opposition, on his stomach. Then imagine magnetic fluid circulating from one hand to the other . . .

Question: Should one vary this position?

Answer: Yes, you can place one hand on the head without moving the other, always continuing to maintain the same attention and having the same will to do good . . .

Question: What is an indication that a patient is susceptible to somnambulism?

Answer: When, during magnetisation of a patient, one notices that he experiences a numbness or light spasms accompanied by nervous shaking. Then if the eyes close, you should lightly rub them and the two eyebrows with your thumbs to prevent blinking . . .

Question: Are there different degrees of somnambulism?

Answer: Yes. Sometimes you can only produce drowsiness in a patient. Sometimes the effect of magnetism is to cause the eyes to close so the patient cannot open them; if he is aware of everything around him he is not completely in the magnetic state . . .

Question: How does one bring a patient out of a magnetic state?

Answer: . . . it is by an act of your will that you awaken him.

Question: You mean you only need to will him to open his eyes in order to awaken him?

Answer: This is the principal operation. After that, in order to connect your idea to its object, you might lightly rub his eyes, while willing that he open them; and the effect never fails to occur.

Du magnetisme animal (1820)
by Armand Marie Jacques de Chastenet,
Marquis de Puységur

Jack Maggs

1

It was a Saturday night when the man with the red waistcoat arrived in London. It was, to be precise, six of the clock on the fifteenth of April in the year of 1837 that those hooded eyes looked out the window of the Dover coach and beheld, in the bright aura of gas light, a golden bull and an overgrown mouth opening to devour him—the sign of his inn, the Golden Ox.

The *Rocket* (as his coach was aptly named) rattled in through the archway to the inn's yard and the passengers, who had hitherto found the stranger so taciturn, now noted the silver-capped cane—which had begun to tap the floor at Westminster Bridge—commence a veritable tattoo.

He was a tall man in his forties, so big in the chest and broad in the shoulder that his fellows on the bench seat had felt the strain of his presence, but what his occupation was, or what he planned to do in London, they had not the least idea. One privately imagined him a book-maker, another a gentleman farmer and a third, seeing the excellent quality of his waistcoat, imagined him an upper servant wearing his master's cast-off clothing.

His face did not deny the possibility of any of these occupations; indeed he would have been a singular example of any one of them. His brows pushed down hard upon the eyes, and his cheeks shone as if life had scrubbed at him and rubbed until the very bones beneath his flesh had been burnished in the process. His nose was large, hawkish, and high-bridged. His eyes were dark, inquiring, and yet there was a bruised, even belligerent quality which had kept his fellow passengers at their distance all through that long journey up from Dover.

No sooner had they heard the coachman's *Whoa-up* than he had the door open and was out into the night without having said a single word.

The first of the passengers to alight after him saw the stranger take the porter, a famously insolent individual, firmly by the shoulder blade. He held him there for a good moment, and it was obvious from the look which appeared on that sandy-haired individual's face, that he held him very hard indeed.

"Now pay attention to me, Sir Reverence."

The porter was roughly escorted to the side of the coach.

"You comprennay-voo?" The stranger pointed with his cane to a large trunk on the roof. "The blue item. If it would not inconvenience your Lordship."

The porter made it clear that it would not inconvenience him in the least. Then some money changed hands and the man with the red waistcoat set off into the night, his cane tapping on the cobblestones, and straight up into the Haymarket, his chin up and the orbs of his eyes everywhere reflecting an unearthly flare and glare.

This light had shone all the way from the Elephant and Castle: gas light, blazing and streaming like great torches; sausages illuminated, fish and ice gleaming, chemist shops aglow like caves with their variegated vases illuminated from within. The city had become a fairground, and as the coach crossed the river at Westminster the stranger saw that even the bridges of the Thames were illuminated.

The entire Haymarket was like a grand ball. Not just the gas, the music, the dense, tight crowds. A man from the last century would not have recognized it; a man from even fifteen years before would have been confused. Dram shops had become gin palaces with their high great plate-glass windows, their engraved messages: "Gin at Three-pence—Generous Wines—Hot Spiced." This one here—it was like a temple, damned if it was not, the door surrounded by stained panes of rich dye: rosettes, bunches of grapes. The big man pushed his way up to the bar and got himself a dram of brandy which he drank in a gulp. When he turned, his face revealed a momentary confusion.

Two children were now tugging around his sleeves but he seemed so little aware of their presence that he walked out into the street without once looking down at them.

All around him was uproar, din, the deafening rush, the smell of horse shit, soot, that old yellow smell of London Town.

"Come on, Guv, come with me."

"Come on, Sir."

A young woman with a feathered hat had placed her hand on his elbow: such a handsome face, such short legs. He tugged himself free, walked on a yard or so, and blew his great hawk's nose like a mighty trumpet. As he carefully refolded his handkerchief—a bright green Kingsman of an earlier time—he inadvertently revealed the stumps of the two middle fingers on his left hand, a sight which had already excited curiosity aboard the *Rocket*.

His Kingsman safely put away for the moment, he started along the Strand, then seemed to change his mind, for a moment later he was heading up Agar Street, then cutting up to Maiden Lane.

In Floral Street, he paused before the now illuminated window of McClusky's Pudding Shop. He blew his nose again, whether from soot or sentiment the face gave no indication, and then, having entered that famously lopsided little shop, emerged with a syrup dumpling sprinkled liberally with confectioner's sugar. He ate the dumpling in the street, still walking. What he began in Floral Street he finished back on St Martin's Lane. Here, just a little south of Seven Dials, the stranger stood on a quiet dark corner, alone, free from the blaze of gas.

It was Cecil Street he had come to, a very short street linking Cross Street to St Martin's Lane. He dusted down his face carefully with his kerchief, and then set off into the darkness, peering to find what street numbers he could see—none.

He had almost arrived at the great river of Cross Street, with its noise and congestion of gigs and post-chaises, hackney cabs and dog-carts, when he came upon a single phaeton stopped in the street. It was a most expensive equipage, that much was clear even in the dark, and indeed, once he had crossed the street, there was sufficient light to make out a gold coronet emblazoned on the shining black door. From inside he could hear the sound of a young woman weeping.

A moment later, he would have been in Cross Street. However, the door of the carriage opened and a matron in a long dress descended from the coach and addressed the person still seated inside. "Good night, Mum," she said.

Hearing this voice, the stranger stopped abruptly in his tracks.

The phaeton drove off but the stranger stayed very still in the shadow

of a doorway whilst the matron opened the gate leading to a high narrow house directly opposite him. A feeble yellow light showed through
the fan light above the front door.

Then he spoke: "Excuse me, Missus, but is this Number Four?"

"If you've come for tablets, come back tomorrow."

"Mary Britten," he said.

He could hear her rattling a big bunch of keys.

"You come back tomorrow," she said.

The stranger stepped into the middle of the street.

"Get a lamp, Mary."

"Who's that?"

"Someone you should recognize, Mary Britten."

She remained with her back to him, still busy with her bunch of keys.
"It's dark. Come back tomorrow."

"Someone you should recognize covered with soot."

Finally, she found the right key. The door swung open, and the feeble yellow light—there was an oil lamp burning in the hallway of the
house—revealed a tall, handsome woman in a long dress: blue or green,
very fancy-looking, shimmering like silk. She hesitated a moment, an
old lady, all of seventy years, but such was her carriage and her bearing
that she would pass, in this light anyway, for fifty.

"So this is Cecil Street," he said. "I thought it would be posher."

She hesitated, peering into the night, one hand ready on the door
handle. "What you doing here?" she whispered. "You're a dead man if
they find you."

"That's a nice home-coming."

"Don't bring your trouble here," she said.

"You got respectable."

"You come to put the bite?"

"I'm doing well myself," the stranger said. "You going to ask me in?"

She made no move to offer an invitation, but her tone did become
more solicitous. "They treat you bad?"

"Bad enough."

"How'd you know I was here?"

"I saw your puff in the newspaper."

"And now you've come home to play the old dart, you varmint."

"No, Ma. I'm retired. I come here for the culture."

She laughed harshly. "The operah?"

"Oh yes," said the stranger seriously. "The opera, the theatre, I got a lot of time to make up for."

"Well, I must go to bed, Jack. So you must forgive me not inviting you in to have a chat."

"Perhaps I'll look up Tom."

"Oh Jesus, Jack."

"What?"

"You bastard," she cried with real emotion. "You know he's dead."

"No! No, I never."

"God help me, Jack, God save me. I ain't so green as that. I know who you paid. I know how it were arranged and all."

"I didn't pay no one nothing, I swear."

"What do you want, Jack?" said the old woman, and this time her voice quavered. "What're you doing here in London?"

"It's my home," Jack said, raising his voice and revealing the fiercer character which the porter at the Golden Ox had briefly glimpsed. "That's what I want. My home."

"I still got my Bilboa, so don't think I wouldn't use it."

The stranger shook his head, and laughed. "You worried I might have a bone to pick with you, Ma?"

"Aren't you worried someone's going to hang you, Jack?" Having made this bitter speech, she stepped inside the house and closed the door behind her.

"I'm coming back, Ma."

There was no retort from inside the house, merely the heavy clanking of some chains which seemed to amuse the visitor.

"I'll be back tomorrow morning. We'll have a proper chat when I come back."

There is no doubt that Jack Maggs planned to keep his promise, but the morrow held events he could not foresee. Three weeks would pass before he would call at Cecil Street again.

2

Great Queen Street had once been home to the pugnacious Lord Herbert of Cherbury. Lord Bristol had lived there. Also Lord Chancellor Finch, and the Conway and Paulett families. But on that damp Sunday morning when Jack Maggs came marching up from Long Acre with his silver-capped cane tucked under his arm, all that remained of the Golden Age were some pilasters and other ornaments still clinging to the façades of a few houses on the west.

There was now a tobacconist in Great Queen Street, a laundry, and a narrow little workroom where glass eyes were made for dolls and injured gentlemen. Actors lived in rooms at Number 30. A retired grocer from Clerkenwell now had the leasehold to Number 29.

But it was Number 27 which seemed to take Jack Maggs's close attention, and he stood across the street and stared at it very hard. It was a handsome house—four storeys, a high iron fence, a pretty gate leading down to the servants' entrance. It had a bright front door, a brass door knocker, a fan light, and such was his excitement to behold this property that the left side of his firmly sculpted face was soon visibly quivering.

A dog cart came travelling pell-mell down the street towards Long Acre with its driver, a young man no more than twenty years, standing upright in the seat. All the visitor's attention was on the house, until the moment the driver cracked his whip.

Then Jack Maggs jumped out of his skin. He stepped out into the road, and raised his stick as if he intended to chase the offender and punish him, but a moment later he was a perfect gent, presenting himself on the doorstep of 27 Great Queen Street with his distress reduced to a small flickering on his left cheek.

Jack Maggs Esquire removed his hat and grasped that brass knocker. He knocked quickly, firmly, but politely.

When there was no immediate answer, he knocked again. And then, a minute later—Rap-rap-rap.

It was not possible that there was no one home. The caller was well-informed about the residents of 27 Great Queen Street. There was a butler in this house, a housekeeper, a cook.

He stepped back onto the edge of the roadside so he might look up at the high windows. He observed their dark and curtained aspect with agitated eyes, then, turning impulsively, he opened the little gate leading down to the servants' entrance.

It was at this moment that Mercy Larkin came to the parlour window of the house next door. Mercy was the kitchen maid, by title, but being the *only* maid in that confusing household, was presently arranging her employer's small library of books where he liked them set—upon the little cedar dresser with the oilcloth square atop it.

She saw the man she would soon know as Jack Maggs descending the steps to the servants' entrance of Number 27. He had come, so she imagined, to take Mrs Halfstairs's examination for the post of footman. The moment she saw him, she knew he was the one. He had the right size, the right legs, but was at the wrong address.

Then Jack Maggs turned and caught her eye. It was not really a footman's face, or no footman she had ever seen. She stood at the parlour window, her duster in her hand, and shivered.

Jack Maggs had not the least knowledge of Mercy Larkin, Mrs Halfstairs or the rest of Mr Buckle's chaotic household, but as he shut the area gate behind him he saw the maid was still staring at him. He saw her pale skin, her pretty ringlets spilling out from under her cap. Had you asked him his impression of her appearance, he would not have heard your question. He had been spotted. He felt the rough rope of Newgate round his neck.

He descended the last steps, escaping her gaze. With his broad back pressed against the wall, he could look into the kitchen. It was his profession to recognize an empty house when he saw one, and this house was like a grave. And yet he knocked, tapping and scratching against the pane.

"Excuse me down there."

He resisted the urge to flatten himself further against the wall, but rather stepped out where the maid could inspect him.

"All's well," he smiled. It was an easy smile, and his teeth were very good and regular. "I'm expected."

"They've gone," the maid said, staring at him very hard. "No one home but draughts and mice."

"Gone?" he said hoarsely.

"You've come to see about the footman's position, am I right now?" The stranger smiled.

"It's Mr Buckle's residence you were wanting," she suggested.

"Gone where? Where have they gone? I am expected." He ascended the stairs to the street.

"Gone to Calais," she said. "The Spanish Main. How would I know?

The gentleman didn't have the manners to inform me of his destination."

The stranger was now at the top of the area steps, and Mercy could see that he had a twitching palsy in his cheek. He put his hand to it.

"Sometimes," Mercy continued, "they send a servant in a coach, but no one stays for long."

"So they are not gone totally?" he asked.

"As I said, they come and go." She paused. "I really thought you were come to be our footman. Mrs Halfstairs is most particular about the height of our second footman. She is sitting in there with her ruler."

"Footman?"

"You're the height, and all. It's a right shame you're not a footman. You're not a footman?" she repeated.

He watched her say it, like you watch an auctioneer raise a hammer, but in truth he had already decided what he was to do.

"I'm *their* footman," he said. "I'm Mr Phipps's new footman."

"So you *are* a footman," she said, smiling. "I knew you was a footman."

"Of course I am the footman, girl. I am a footman to young Mr Phipps who has all my papers," Jack Maggs said to the maid. "My letters of recommendation, all locked inside. What is a man to do now?"

"Perhaps you were late."

"Late?" he cried, thumping his stick on the footpath. "I am never late. I was first footman to Lord Logan who perished in the fire in Glasgow."

"Mercy Larkin," said a female voice from downstairs at Number 29. "Come down from there immediately."

"It is a footman," the maid explained, "most tragically positioned."

3

Mr Percy Buckle was the owner of a gentleman's residence at 29 Great Queen Street, but he was no more a gentleman than the man who was presently entering his household in disguise.

A year before he had been a humble grocer in Clerkenwell, and for years before that time he had been well known, around the tap rooms and penny gaffs of Limehouse, as a seller of fried fish.

Then, on a brisk autumn morning in 1836, Percy Buckle had "my little visit from the solicitor," as a result of which good fortune he became, in two short months, the master of a household in Great Queen Street and the owner of the Lyceum Theatre on Holborn Hill.

Having spent a lifetime laboriously elevating himself from fried-fish man to grocer, this inheritance came as a great shock. He was at first rather feverish and dizzy, and could take nothing stronger than the toast and broth brought to him by the daughter of the mad woman he employed to scrub his stairs. For days he tried to follow the dark and slippery lines of blood and law that had led from the body of a deceased stranger to his door in Clerkenwell. He lay in his newly pressed night shirt, in his freshly laundered sheets, and looked at the small square of neat sunshine as it passed across his bedroom wall.

Then on the third morning—Guy Fawkes Day, in fact—the fever lifted. Percy Buckle looked around his little room and knew he never had to weigh a pound of flour again in his life.

I can read all day.

Even as a grocer he had been a bookish fellow. All his life it had been the same—even when he was too tired to manage more than half a page of *Ivanhoe* in a night, even when he smelt inescapably of sprats and mackerel, he had been a member of a lending library, and a regular attendant at the Workingman's Institute.

He sat up in bed and smoothed his neat little moustache, and those mild blue eyes began to show a heat that could normally only be induced by learned men discussing anaesthesia or mechanics in a draughty hall.

Within a week he had given the contents of his grocer's shop to the Parish. He had found a tailor. He had been to Fletcher's Bookshop in Piccadilly and purchased the complete set of Gibbon's *Decline and Fall*. He had moved to Great Queen Street where he was pleased to employ his charwoman's daughter as a kitchen maid. Indeed, he was already exceedingly fond of Mercy Larkin and would have made her housekeeper had not he discovered the household overrun with servants who were still waiting to have their wages—not paid on the last quarter day—settled by the Estate.

It took a week or so for Mr Buckle to understand that he had inherited not only a house, but a bibulous and senile butler named Spinks, two footmen, a cook, and a housekeeper who had made herself queen over the butler. Sometimes it seemed to Mr Buckle that it was too small a house to have ever held so many servants, but his benefactor, it seemed, had been as fond of them as of his cats, and Mr Buckle was prepared to be fond of them as well.

He allowed the cats—there were five of them—to come and go through the open window of the drawing room. He saw no harm in them. Indeed he was soon accustomed to having both a marmalade and a tabby asleep on his chest, purring.

He also saw no harm in letting the red-nosed butler snore in front of the silver plate, although—to be quite clear on this matter—he lacked the nerve to tell the pompous old man to stop his tippling. He was a little frightened of the housekeeper, but as she bought her bacon at sixpence the pound he comforted himself that she was capable. There is, he told himself, no point in having a dog and barking too. By which he meant that it was best to leave the running of his domestic affairs to those who were most experienced in that field. He ate kippers for his breakfast and spent his days away from the house, at the library, the museum, and the theatre.

It was into this household that Jack Maggs was brought by Mercy Larkin. The newcomer found the smell of cats to be rather strong at first, but the claret which he was shortly sharing with the butler pushed that matter from his mind. He lunched on cold roast beef with the upstairs and downstairs servants, and was then brought into the presence of the housekeeper, a Mrs Halfstairs.

Mrs Halfstairs had herself seated in her office, a peculiarly placed room, neither of the basement nor the ground floor, but located like a hunter's hide in the branches of a tree, reached either by ladder from the cellar, or a set of steep little stairs from the kitchen. Here she sat in state, surrounded by all manner of mementos relating to her brother, a Captain in the 57th Foot Regiment who had fought in those long-ago battles of Vittoria and Nive. Here, she had opened her housekeeper's journal and set about interviewing the latest candidate.

Jack Maggs was not a footman. He could not produce a letter of reference. But he was the right height, and he stood before Mrs Halfstairs with his legs astride, his hands behind his back, the scarred stumps of the two middle fingers hidden in his folded hand.

Mrs Halfstairs was a bully and a tyrant to all who came under her rule. Jack Maggs saw that and did not care. He explained to Mrs Halfstairs how it was that his references had been locked away by Mr Henry Phipps, and when he saw how ready she was to believe him, the last of his agitation left him and he began to feel a little sleepy.

Part of this drowsiness was produced by the reprieve from immediate danger, but the greatest soporific—one he had been prone to since his earliest years—was the distinctive aromas of plenty: hanging hams, barrels of apples, beeswax, even the smell of turpentine.

Mrs Halfstairs was a round-faced little woman with tightly wound grey hair. She was not quite fat but was solid and clumpish with thick wrists and narrow, distinctively pointed fingers which she now extended to pick up a rather ill-used-looking quill.

"Height?" she demanded.

Jack Maggs woke himself enough to reply that he was a little under six foot.

The little soldier beetle made a fast, irritable entry in the back pages of her journal.

"A little under?" she said. "With respect, that is exactly what I would expect from someone in Mr Phipps's employ. A little under!"

"An inch," the applicant submitted.

"So I must do my own subtraction. But can you swear to an inch, or is it really an inch and a quarter?"

"I'm afraid I couldn't say, Ma'am."

"Did Mr Phipps's housekeeper not measure you?"

"No, Ma'am, she did not."

"I think Mr Phipps's first footman is rather stunted," she frowned. "I really can't imagine what he had in mind. I'm sure he did not have a *prank* in mind. A tall one and a short one, eh? That would be like him, from what I have heard. Japes and high-jinks. Do you think that was his plan?"

"I would not imagine so, Ma'am."

"But who would?" said Mrs Halfstairs. "Who would imagine what the gentleman ever had in his mind?"

Jack Maggs sensed, even before Mrs Halfstairs pulled the bell, that he was to be employed. She put down her quill, clasped her little hands, and gazed at his sturdy legs with undisguised satisfaction.

"Maggs," she murmured to herself.

When Mercy Larkin answered the bell Mrs Halfstairs did not allow herself to be distracted from her contemplation of the applicant's anatomy.

"Fetch Constable," she said.

"I think Mr Constable is still indisposed."

"Fetch him," said Mrs Halfstairs, "immediately." Then, returning to Jack Maggs, she offered the following appraisal: "My impression is, you are five foot eleven and a half inches tall, and with your hair soaped and powdered, it will raise you to six feet. There is nothing more calculated to ruin a carriage or a dinner table than mismatched footmen. Where is that fellow?"

No sooner had the question been asked than the low door opened and a man of most un-footman-like appearance entered the room. His hair was wild, his eyes red, his wide high cheekbones coloured with what appeared to be ashes. He was dressed in breeches and braces and a white shirt which—being unbuttoned at the neck, and flowing at the tail—gave him a wretched and tormented appearance. When he saw Jack Maggs he bestowed upon him a look of intense malevolence.

"Back to back," said Mrs Halfstairs.

It was not clear to the applicant what the little woman meant, but the wild man with the blackened face seemed to understand for, with an obedience that belied his wild expression, he turned his back and stood erect.

"Bookends," said Mrs Halfstairs. "Bookends, if you please Mr Maggs."

It took a moment to get her meaning, but then he saw it: he was to stand back-to-back with Constable.

When the humiliating little act was duly performed, it produced in Mrs Halfstairs an almost touching degree of satisfaction.

"Oh my goodness," she said as she surveyed them. "Oh my goodness dearie me."

Her round, small face was stretched tight by a smile which displayed, for the first time, very short lower teeth of quite remarkable regularity.

Behind his back, Jack heard Constable sniff.

"Very good," said Mrs Halfstairs. "Very good indeed. Mr Spinks will indeed be pleased, as will our master." She took up the quill and, dipping it in the ink-well, composed a few lines. Having blotted them carefully, and sealed them in a long thin envelope with all the formality one might expect in issuing an invitation to a ball, she instructed the applicant to deliver the missive to the butler, Mr Spinks, and to remind that gentleman that the new man would need to be "kitted out" for the dinner that evening.

Jack Maggs ascended the tight little stairs to the kitchen, knowing himself to be hired without the bother of having forged a reference. As for what transpired between Mrs Halfstairs and Mr Constable in his absence, he heard only the very beginning of their conversation.

"Enough, Edward. We cannot have another day of this."

This was followed by the sound of Mr Constable weeping.

4

That evening Miss Mott must cook dinner for seven gentlemen. When Mr Quentin had been master, this would have seemed a trifle. Then it had been ten courses every night, pheasant and guinea fowl, three different puddings to choose from. But Mr Buckle, although he had acted kindly towards his household, had not been conscious of his social obligations. He was a bachelor of an oddly private disposition, and often wanted no more than a little cheese and pickle for his tea. He hid upstairs in his snuggery with his book, his glass of porter, his round of Cheshire, and whether the housekeeper was housekeeping or the butler awake, he did not seem inclined to either notice or inquire, so long as he could have the cheeky little maid to wait on him.

Now there was finally to be a Grand Occasion, the fruits of his poor leadership were everywhere: one inebriated butler, one footman mad with grief, one untrained kitchen maid who was grating the suet so slowly that the cook could not bear to look at her.

Miss Mott worked on her apple pie. She prayed to God to speed the maid, to force Mrs Halfstairs to put her tiresome ruler away and engage a new footman. When Jack Maggs returned to the kitchen, she did not lift her head, but she had that capacity, commonly found in the short and shy, for peering up whilst seeming to look down.

When she saw no tell-tale envelope (the object of her curiosity being already in the inside pocket of Jack's waistcoat) she assumed the worst—it was a well-known fault with her—and the little woman shivered like a dog with an itch that cannot be scratched.

Miss Mott was lean and sinewy and there was nowhere much for such a violent shiver to hide itself. Consequently it went right up her spine and disappeared inside her little white cap and then, just when it seemed lost, it came out the other side and pulled up the ends of her thin mouth in a grimace.

"I'm done for," sighed Peggy Mott, but to no one she imagined would care or listen.

She gave the fellow a slice of short-bread and poured him a cup of tea.

Jack Maggs added four heaped spoons of sugar to the tea and stirred. He sipped. He seemed to close his eyes, but all the while he was assessing his new home. He watched the cook's agitated little face as she sucked and blew and pursed her lips continually. She had the appearance of a sad and sorry bird, and he wondered about the nature of the cage that had made her so.

At the same time, Mercy Larkin watched Jack Maggs. She had no idea that she was observing an oyster working on a pearl, nor could she guess at the size of the upset contained inside the shell. Indeed, there was more than a little in Jack Maggs's manner to suggest a man used to being well-treated at the table. He sat himself comfortably with his big legs apart, his hands resting loosely on his belly. He yawned.

"Very good," he said to no one in particular.

He rested his chin upon his chest and closed his eyes a moment. Then a moment longer.

"Cook!" said the maid. And then, when Miss Mott did not react: "Look, ssh."

"What is it now, Mercy?" said Peggy Mott, but she looked in the direction she was bid.

"Sssh. He's asleep."

"These hares is not hung long enough," said Miss Mott nervously. "Not near long enough."

"Come and look." Mercy pushed her suet aside. She kneeled beside Jack Maggs's great thighs.

"Mercy Larkin!" said Peggy, turning from the stove to see the bold girl with her face so close to the stranger's. There was no doubt about it: the fellow was sound asleep.

"I don't think he's a footman at all. Don't he look ever so distinguished?"

Peggy Mott looked at the hard face for a moment and gave another little shudder. "He looks like a murderer."

"I think he's a butler," said Mercy. "Do you think we might have him instead of Mr Spinks? Do you think that might be her final plan?"

"Hush, Mercy. She has not engaged him."

"Oh but she has, Mum. You are mistaken."

Miss Mott began to rearrange the pieces of hare. "Mercy, you were never in service before. Someone should take you in hand, my girl, before you are properly spoiled. It does not help you that your dear Mother brought our master broth when he was ill." She turned from the stove. "What are you doing? What are you doing?"

Mercy slid her small white hand into the sleeping man's waistcoat and pulled out the long white envelope. "Hush, Mum. I am fetching you your heart's desire."

Mrs Mott stared at the envelope. She blinked and sucked her lips in around her teeth.

"Oh, I do give thanks." She held out her hand for the envelope. "I do give thanks." Then, quickly, her mood changed. She gave the envelope back and spoke: "Nice and lively, Mercy. Please present Mr Maggs to Mr Spinks."

"First we must wake him up," said Mercy, slyly.

"Shake him, Mercy. Tap him on the shoulder."

"I'll not touch him, Mum. It wouldn't be proper."

The cook picked up a hand of flour and sprinkled it across the table, communicating, as she did so, a growing, almost uncontrollable tide of irritation.

"Mercy, I have seven gentlemen for eight o'clock. I have Mr Oates himself, God help me. Mercy, please be so good as to wake Mr Maggs and take him—and here, take this too, the envelope—to Mr Spinks, wherever it is that Mr Spinks is presently engaged."

"And we know where that is, don't we, Mum?"

Cook sighed. "Yes, Mercy, we do."

It was as if the price was finally high enough, for now Mercy patted Jack Maggs upon the shoulder, and the new footman opened his eyes.

"We are to visit Mr Spinks," said Mercy, "so as you may be officially employed."

Jack did not understand exactly what she meant, but he felt her warmth, like a plate just removed from the warming rack. He reached in his pocket for his envelope before he noticed it in the girl's hand.

"You dropped this," she said, and handed it to him.

He knew he had not dropped it, but he took the envelope and followed her. She had a very pretty sweep to her back, and a soft white neck.

5

There was a peculiar little passage-way—its ceiling low and heavy-beamed, its walls crammed with bottles of preserves—which led from the kitchen, down a step, along a chalky white wall, and then round a corner to a heavy green door which, as Mercy opened it, revealed the butler's parlour.

This was a surprisingly pleasant little room, with a window overlooking a budding old pear tree, and a big old-fashioned country fireplace in whose deep niches and sooty crannies Mr Spinks was in the habit of hiding his claret bottles. Along one wall was a mammoth oaken dresser in which was stored the household's treasury of silver plate and before which the butler now sat. He was sound asleep with his heavy brass poker across his knee, his cadaverous old skull thrown backwards, and his little mouth wide open. The pages of the *Morning Chronicle* lay scattered on the floor beside his stockinged feet.

The new footman showed no interest in this spectacle, but turned his eyes on Mercy instead.

"You picked my pocket," he said very quietly. As he spoke he laid his hand against his quivering cheek.

"Sir?"

"You had your hand in Jack Maggs's pocket. That was very brave of you."

She could not tell if he were pleased with her or angry.

"I'm not so brave," she said.

As she knelt to gather up the newspaper she felt his presence all around her. She had a fancy—more, a kind of vision, a picture of herself laying her head against his manly chest. However, when she looked at him she found him staring at old Spinks.

Mercy did not like Mr Spinks—he was a bully and a snob—but when she saw the dried white spittle in the corner of his mouth, she was sorry that he should have lived so long as to let himself be seen like this. She folded the pages of the *Chronicle* and placed them carefully by the sleeping man's feet.

"Our master is a good man," she said. "He does not judge a human weakness."

"Not even pick-pocketing?"

"Please don't be angry with me. I done it just to stop poor Mottle fretting."

"Oh, so you done it for her, did you? That were generous of you."

"Well, yes, it was. I knew you were employed, because I saw your paper in your pocket, see. But Miss Mott, she didn't see, and she was in a state on account of us being a footman short of what we should have. Tonight we have Mr Oates—Mr Tobias Oates—coming to our house to dine." She looked at him as she said the famous name, but his features did not soften. "It is Mr *Oates*," she said. "Mr *Tobias* Oates. You'd pick a pocket for Tobias Oates, I know you would."

"I'm afraid," he said, stiffly, "I don't know no Tobias Oates."

"Oh Lor." She did not mean to laugh. "Where have you been?"

"I was with Lord Logan," said Jack Maggs, a little gruffly, "in Glasgow."

"You have surely heard mention of Captain Crumley?"

"Captain Crumley, perhaps I did."

"Or poor Mrs Morefallen."

"I've heard her mentioned."

"It is all Mrs Halfstairs lives for—to see what Captain Crumley does about his son in prison. And now it is he who is to be our guest. This is a great day for Mr Buckle."

"Mr Buckle—he is a friend of Captain Crumley?"

Mercy began to laugh, but something in the other's eyes made her stop herself.

"Mr Buckle is your new master," she said very seriously. "He has a famous author to come to dine with him tonight. It is because of this he has been in bed these last three days."

"Your master is ill?"

"He could not bear to become ill at such a time."

"He is sleeping?"

"He would like to sleep, but it is everything he can do to keep his poor brain from boiling over. No, he stays abed so as he don't fall sick. He would not miss Tobias Oates for the world."

"So do tell me, Miss . . ."

"My name is Mercy Larkin."

"Did your master also make a friend of Henry Phipps?"

"The gentleman next door? Oh, Sir, you must forget *him.*" Her almond eyes were almost grey and very still. "Now you're going to stay with us."

He held her gaze. Even when there was a great crashing in the kitchen, he did not look away.

"That's how she calls for me," she said. She thought his eyes angry. "She drops things."

"Then you should go to her," he said.

Mercy did not move.

"You should be more careful, girlie," he said.

"It's for you to be careful," said Mercy. "If I was you I would be very careful indeed."

"What do you mean by that?"

She did not exactly know, but she felt passionate and irritated. "They will be likely to have you dusting, and it was the dusting that so upset he who came before you."

"He gave his notice?"

"Aye, with a gentleman's duelling pistol. He blew his brains out."

"On account of dusting?"

She was not sure she liked his features any more. "He could not tolerate it," she said.

He raised an eyebrow.

"Beg your pardon?" she inquired crossly.

"My pardon?"

"Beg pardon, Sir," she said, "but I thought you was making a comment."

"No," he said, "nothing."

"Oh yes," she insisted, "something."

She saw him hesitate.

"Did you ever *see* Mr Phipps?" he asked at last. "How was he? What sort of man was he?"

Mercy turned to face him. She was in a funny kind of passion she could not explain and Jack Maggs, seeing her face, somehow understood that she had become his opponent. He stretched to grab her wrist, but he was too slow. She giggled, turned, flipped the brass poker out of Mr Spinks's lap so that it spun and clattered onto the tiled floor.

Mr Spinks sprang to his feet and found, before him, a stranger holding a long white envelope.

6

At five o'clock on Saturday Jack Maggs had been a man of substance, speeding towards London on the Dover Rocket. Now, at five o'clock on Sunday, he entered a stuffy attic which was, it seemed, to be his home awhile. It was not three paces from the squeaking door to the soot-stained dormer window, and he was across them in a trice, heaving up the stiff sash and thrusting his big head inquiringly out above Great Queen Street. Here he found no more interesting view than the melancholy apartments across the way and, in the immediate foreground, the slate tiles of the house next door to Mr Buckle's. The latter, however, was obviously of particular interest to him, and had he been a master tradesman, sent to inspect their condition, he could not have examined the tiles more closely. They were grey Devon slate, with almost half of their visible surface covered with a thin coating of yellowish moss. They seemed to be, for the most part, well secured, although he noted a loose piece of lead flashing and a dormer window carelessly left open to the weather.

So intent was his inspection that he became only slowly aware of a distant percussion. It was not until he had squeezed himself back into his room that he discovered someone was hammering on his door and crying, "Open up!"

He stood before the door a moment with his brow quite markedly contracted. It was not at all clear that he would "open up." Indeed he soon retreated to the window and looked out at the narrow strip of roof that might have afforded an escape. But finally he did as he was bid.

In the open doorway he was accosted by a being with hard white sculpted hair, a creature so resplendent in his yellow velvet jacket and soft doeskin trousers, that it took a full minute—during which time the impatient visitor entered the room and got himself deep into a large oak wardrobe—for Jack to realize that he was in the presence of the very same wild-haired Tom O'Bedlam with whom he had, less than an hour before, played bookends.

Edward Constable was of a lighter build than Maggs. He had fine wrists and large expressive hands which he had, in his recent dementia, been prone to wring. He had been a good-looking youth, and it was all still there: the high cheekbones, the well-shaped red lips; even the slight ridge on his aquiline nose did his case no damage. Of his recent madness there was, if one excepted the rather dangerous aroma of his master's cognac, no remaining sign.

Now, without offering an explanation, he withdrew from the darkness of the wardrobe various items which he then laid out, with a somewhat theatrical tenderness, upon the little crib. Here he set a pair of doeskin breeches from which he picked a little smut. There a white shirt, just so. Beside it a lace cravat which he must move, an inch, no more, to accommodate a yellow velvet coat, the mirror image of his own, and from whose lapel he removed a single long blue thread. To this magnificent arrangement he added two long silk stockings and a pair of black shoes with silver buckles.

The two men stood side by side regarding the objects so assembled.

"I am to try these for size?" suggested Maggs.

"Tsk," said Constable.

"I'll take that as yes," Maggs said, undressing with as much modesty as the cramped space permitted, aware all the time that he was the subject of the other's censure.

"Now look here," said Maggs, finally gaining the security of the breeches, "I know this was your mate's kit, and he was your good friend and you miss him worse than air itself. I am sorry"—Maggs paused to tuck in the shirt, but did this in such a way that his witness raised a thin, sarcastic eyebrow—"I am sorry to remind you of the good comrade you have lost. I wish it was otherwise, but you see there is naught else I can do, in the circumstances, but wear his clobber."

In response to which explanation, the footman hissed.

"No, good fellow. I really do not think it fair for you to hiss at me. For as I said, none of this business is my fault and I would rather, just like you would, that they would send me to a tailor and have the business done fair and square. But here we are." Maggs slipped the jacket on. "The shoes are tight, but the coat fits well enough, and I am sure I can limp as far as pudding if you'll be of some assistance to me."

"Assistance. Is that so?"

"It is so, my fellow," said Maggs, moving his bulk closer to the foot-man, who immediately began to back away. "And if I might start with what comes first—you can assist me with my hair."

From the recesses of the commode the footman produced a saucer with a bar of white soap, a round box, and a large powder puff. These were duly offered, and declined.

"Still, old fellow," said Maggs, "a cove needs more in the way of as-sistance than a saucer and a box."

"Oh, a *cove* does, does he?"

"He does, yes," insisted Maggs.

"You must excuse me," shrugged Constable, "for it is quarter past the hour, and with Mrs Halfstairs it is eat when she says or never."

"Mr Constable, I am asking you to render me assistance."

The footman laid his hand upon the wooden door knob. "Mr Maggs, I am refusing it."

Maggs's hand snapped around the other's wrist. Thus, even as the footman's silver-buckled shoes scuttled out the open door, the upper part of his body was yanked smartly inwards. Maggs leaned across his prisoner's flailing arms and drove the bolt home in the door.

"Now Thingstable," he said. "You are about to place us both in peril."

"Oh fie . . . ," said Constable in a tight, disdainful voice. He held his free hand to his neck. "I tremble-Kemble. You'll kill me? Is that what you have in mind? By God, I think it is. He wants to kill me."

Softly, softly, thought Jack Maggs.

"Please, Sir, go ahead. No, no really, I do beg you, it would be a plea-sure to be done away with by someone so nicely fitted out."

"Fellow," said Jack Maggs calmly, "you mistake me."

"But this is rich, Mr Maggs. This is too rich for you to understand, but my friend, Mr Pope, with whom I stood and served for fifteen years—we were boys together in Lineham Hall—has done himself in. In this very room. Here, where we would chat after our day's labours. And she, the meddling duchess, has me dress you in his very clothes, and now you say you wish to kill me . . . oh, please, you really have no notion what a pleasure it would be."

"No one said anything about killing, my dear fellow."

"I am no one's dear anything," said Constable, and burst into tears.

"Well, I must say then, I am sorry."

"Sorry you wish to kill me? Or sorry to know such a thing has happened?"

"Don't never try to beat me in the game of sorrow."

"You think to match me?"

"I will sink you," said Maggs gravely.

The pair of them stood opposite each other like two horses at a fence.

"All I require is that you assist me with my hair."

"Assist?"

"I do not know how to achieve the correct effect with the hair."

"Ha-ha," said Constable, pushing his long finger against Maggs's chest. "What are you? A toffee-twister, a dimber-damber?"

Jack Maggs took the finger, and held it hard inside his fist. Then he pulled the finger's owner closer to him. "Listen carefully, fool. You do not have the devil's notion who you're dealing with."

The pale blue eyes wandered over Maggs's face.

"Who am I dealing with?" he asked at last.

"If you are very lucky, you are dealing with a footman."

"A footman?"

"Hurry up, man. Before I change my mind."

The stranger's left cheek twitched violently.

"I'll fetch the water," Edward Constable said. "You'll want it warm."

When he was gone, Jack Maggs sat heavily on the crib, pushing his hand hard against the place on his cheek where the tic was centred. This tic pulled long cords of pain which ran from his left eye down to his back teeth, a pain now so intense that not even the thought that the footman might be on his way to call the police could rouse him from his seat.

Some time later, when the attack had finally begun to subside, Edward Constable returned. He brought a steaming copper kettle to the wash-stand.

"Now soak it," he said.

Maggs looked up bleakly.

"Hair," Edward Constable said. "You must remove your shirt and soak your hair."

The big man bent slowly over the basin in his woollen singlet.

"Singlet off."

"Singlet stays on."

Constable put two fingers against Jack Maggs's scalp and pushed his head into the bowl. The water was hot. Maggs cried out.

"Hotter the better," said Constable. "Let it soak one minute by the clock."

Then Constable cried, "Towel," and Maggs was subjected to his first lesson in the footman's trade as Constable, standing behind him, lathered his hair with soft soap and then applied the oddly perfumed powder with a puff. Sleepy Jack regarded the process in the mirror.

Constable combed the white sticky mess backwards with a comb, and then, like a baker icing a birthday cake, scraped off the edges with a wooden spatula.

"Just look at you," he said. "It's enough to make a cat speak."

7

Some time after midnight Jack Maggs would begin to record the events of his first evening as a servant.

By six o'clock that evening, he had been transformed into a footman good and proper. He ate his tea sitting at a long deal table in the company of the other servants. At half past seven he was ready to make his first entry to the dining room, and he picked up a scalding hot tureen of eel soup and prepared himself for the steep ascent to the ground floor.

His shoes pinched him. The plaster-hard white hair felt like a steel clamp on his brow.

In the upstairs hallway mirror he saw his private anger showing plainly in his eyes, but by the time he entered the dining room his manner was more that of a publican than a footman, and he came amongst the gentlemen smiling in a very jolly way, until, that is, the powdered Constable hissed instruction in his ear.

"No smile."

Edward Constable then ushered the novice towards the table, forcing him, with the subtle insistence of his shoulder, to walk around the table towards the chair where the person known as Tobias Oates was already seated at his place as guest of honour.

Constable removed the lid from the tureen.

"Stay," he whispered. He took the lid and placed it on the sideboard.

Jack Maggs watched the guests. He saw that the visitor was no more than twenty-five years of age. He was short—they all were short—but Oates was also slight and his face, were it not for his lopsided smile, might have been described as cherubic.

"Up," hissed Constable.

"Up?"

"Soup up. Hold up."

Jack Maggs held up the tureen. There was something very queer about this gathering: old fellows with bald heads, red beards streaked with grey, men whose noses showed too much attachment to the brandy bottle, the host with his poor man's teeth and hair combed thinly over his white pate, every one of them giving his full attention to Mr Oates, a young gent decidedly undistinguished in manner.

Tobias Oates did not seem, to Jack's mind, to warrant any of the excitement his name had stirred in Mercy Larkin's imagination. He was sharp, like a jockey. He wore a waistcoat like a common busker, or a book-maker, bright green and shot through with lines of blue and yellow. He was edgy, almost pugnacious, with eyes and hands everywhere about him as if he were constantly confirming his position in the world, a navigator measuring his distance from the chair, the wall, the table.

So unsettling was this character to Jack Maggs that he later devoted almost one hundred words to describing him:

> Oates watched close as his eel soup was ladled into his plate. Straightened his silver. Stared at me. Stared at me again. Then told a strange tale of a "Thief-taker" by name of Partridge who he claimed could find any man in England. In the case in point he did track a housebreaker from Gloucester all the way to the Borough, at which pt he made a citizen's arrest in v. touchy circumstances.

Jack Maggs circled the table with Constable, holding the tureen while Constable ladled. He watched everything, but he watched Tobias Oates most of all. When the writer was assured of the table's complete attention, his jerky limbs stilled, and he bestowed upon his audience a singular stroking kind of charm, relating his unlikely tale with the air of a man who is accustomed to not being interrupted.

Three times Mr Buckle put his spoon down and opened his mouth to speak. Three times he seemed to lose his courage. When he did finally talk his guests immediately turned their heads in his direction.

"The fact is"—Mr Buckle paused to acknowledge his guests' interest with a small nod of the head—"the fact you have left out—am I right, Mr Oates?—is how this Thief-taker got this intelligence which evaded the police. That is the point of your tale, or am I wrong?"

"It is I who am wrong," replied Tobias Oates. "I began the story and then realized I could not politely tell it in the company of Mr Hawthorne here."

The bald-headed, black-bearded man named Henry Hawthorne was, as Jack Maggs knew from Mercy Larkin, the chief actor in Mr Buckle's Lyceum Theatre. It was through his good graces (and doubtless for his personal advantage) that all these strangers had been brought to sit at Mr Buckle's table. He was a barrel-chested gentleman with a deep, resonant voice.

"Oh Lor," said Henry Hawthorne, buttering his bread, shaking his head, generally affecting to be much put out. "Are you not weary of your Hob-bee Hor-ss?"

"Sideboard," whispered Constable. "Put tureen."

Maggs placed the tureen on the sideboard, and took the claret bottle which Constable placed in his hand.

"No drips."

"It is Animal Magnetism," the author was explaining to the gentlemen, who all leaned most earnestly towards him, "which my friend is calling the Hobby Horse."

"Get thee to a knackery," cried Henry Hawthorne, pushing out his wine glass so Maggs might more easily find it.

"The Thief-taker," said Tobias Oates, "is not some rogue like Jonathan Wild but an educated, modern man who obtained his information by making mesmeric *passes*"—here he waved his hands mechanically up and down in front of Hawthorne's unblinking eyes—"by making mesmeric *passes* over the four witnesses the police had already interviewed, he put each into a condition of Magnetic Somnambulism. This Thief-taker, whose name is Wilfred Partridge, obtained by this method a full description of the suspect from those who *imagined* they had not seen him clearly."

"Yes," said the host. He spoke, this time, very quietly, as if to himself.

"The Cerebrum," said Tobias Oates, looking from one to the other of his listeners, "is a vessel that never leaks. It holds everything, remembers everything. And if Mr Hawthorne likes to think of Animal Magnetism as a scurrilous parlour game, it is only because he has not read his Villiers or Puysegur."

"Did you read about the Russian gentlemen in the *Morning Chronicle*?" Hawthorne asked. "Come all the way from Sebastopol to learn Magnetism in London? You read it? No? Write for it, but don't read it. Pity. They plan to use your noble art to seduce young ladies."

"Sideboard," whispered Constable. "Bookends."

Jack Maggs stood at one end of the sideboard, his hands behind his back. Constable stood to the other.

"It is pretty clear by now," said Oates, "that no mesmeric act on earth will have anyone perform an act against their moral temper."

"The report of King Philippe," cried Mr Buckle suddenly, "well, I have to say—it was of a different opinion."

"You are a student of the Royal Commission?"

"My word yes," said Percy Buckle.

Mr Buckle looked down at his own place, a red spot showing on each pale cheek.

"I must caution our host," said Henry Hawthorne, showing a glimmer of a smile beneath his large moustache. "My friend Oates has become such a secret Magnetist that I heard him—*I heard you, Oates*—try to persuade a King's Counsel that he should be magnetizing criminals in the dock."

"But Hawthorne, my old fellow, you have not taken my point."

"You have more points than a fork, Oates," said Henry Hawthorne, and turned back to his bread and butter.

"The Criminal Mind is as susceptible to Magnetism as any other," said Oates, his pale blue eyes now showing bright little flecks of brown.

The new footman listened to this most intently.

"Now come, Oates," said the fellow with the quivering chin. "No hard-hearted villain is going to give his secrets up in a court of law."

"Even the lowest type of renegade," said Tobias Oates, "has an inner need to give up the truth. Look at those gallows confessions they are still selling on Holborn. It is what our fathers called "conscience." We all have it. For the criminal, it is like a passion to throw himself off a high place."

The footman's down-turned mouth betrayed his opinion of the matter, and so obvious was the expression on his face that it would soon have been observed, had his passions not stimulated the grizzling little palsy in his cheek to its fullest fury.

As usual, he had no warning of the attack.

The pain slapped his face like a clawed cat. It flooded like spilled lemon juice behind his eyes. It hit so hard that he could not help himself but cry out, and the bottle of claret which he had been in the process of bringing to the table fell from his hand and lay spewing its contents onto the oriental rug.

Typically, it was Tobias Oates who was first to help the fallen man. While the other guests held back, he kneeled beside Jack Maggs's contorted face and gently, firmly, pried his large, hard hand away from his cheek.

"I see it." With the cool handle of the spoon he touched the victim's contorted face. As the spoon touched the flesh a tic, fast as a pulse, darted beneath the surface of the skin.

"*Tic douloureux*," said Toby Oates, offering his ink-stained hand and pulling the heavy footman upwards. With Henry Hawthorne's help, he got Jack Maggs into a dining chair. "Have you heard that name before? *Tic douloureux*?"

But the new footman was barely aware of anything except the pain and the horror that always accompanied these crises. It was not a horror of anything, or about anything, but a horror so profound that a certain time elapsed during which he hardly knew where on earth he stood.

"Look at me," said Tobias Oates insistently. "Look into my eyes I can take away this pain."

Maggs peered at Oates as if through a heavy veil. The little gent began to wave his hands. He passed them down, up, down.

"Watch me," said Tobias Oates, and Jack Maggs, for once, did exactly as he was told.

8

J ack Maggs woke to find himself still seated in the doorway on a straight-backed chair. Opposite him Tobias Oates was also seated, so close that Maggs could smell the eel soup upon his breath and feel his neat little knees brushing lightly against his own silk stockings.

"So," said the young man, "where is your pain gone, Mr Maggs?" In his manner he was solicitous and kindly, and about as trustworthy as a Newgate Bird.

"Come, Jack." He reached his finger out and touched Jack Maggs softly upon the knee. He smiled. He had long lashes and soft speckled eyes.

Jack Maggs moved his knee away.

"Come, Jack, you really are obliged to speak to me."

Someone sighed, and the footman's shoulders rose an inch.

"One moment the fellow is making speeches," said a man behind his back, "and now he is silent as the grave."

"Eh, Jack," the writer-cove said softly. "What say you now, Jack?"

"Excuse me, Sir, what speeches have I made?"

Tobias Oates grinned broadly, and looked away and over Maggs's shoulder. Maggs followed the direction of the other's gaze, and found himself, like someone waking from a dream, in a familiar place he could not quite explain. The dinner was now abandoned. The unsmiling guests crowded behind him, peering down at him as though he were a prisoner in the dock.

"You have been asleep," Tobias Oates explained. "I asked you questions and you answered them."

"Did I answer loudly, then?"

"Well, very *clearly*," smiled the young man. "But come, Jack, is your pain gone or no? That is what the gentlemen are waiting to hear you say."

But Jack Maggs had more serious things than pain to concern him. "I was asleep?" He stood. "I said my name was Jack?"

Tobias Oates stayed seated, his legs crossed, smiling that queer lopsided smile.

"Asleep but not asleep."

"I was talking in my sleep then, is it?"

"Mr Oates cured you," said the duck-legged master, now placing himself between the Mesmerist and the subject. "And now it is time for you to help cure my guests of hunger."

The footman did not even look at him.

"Please," continued Percy Buckle, who was, as usual, uncomfortable about giving clear orders to a servant. "I must ask you to at least temporarily be a footman."

In saying "temporarily" he meant only to soften his directive, to suggest that the man must labour for the present, but that shortly he might have his rest.

Jack Maggs heard *temporarily*. He thought he was soon to be dismissed, or worse. When the master put a hand upon his arm, he felt himself in danger.

"Speed," hissed Constable, the master's dog, who now came to shepherd him away. "Out. Down."

The two footmen walked shoulder by shoulder out into the hall and down the narrow stairs.

"For Jesus' sake. What did I say?"

"You were a great turn, Mr Maggs. You were a great thrill for the gentlemen, but by God neither the rug nor the flounder will forgive you for it."

"What did I say? Tell me, cod's-head."

"Oh, go back to Borough, why don't you."

Maggs's face darkened dangerously. "I spoke of Borough? What else?"

"Here he is," cried Constable gaily to the kitchen. "The right height, and no question about it."

The little cook looked up at Maggs and clicked her tongue. Then she shook her head and looked away. "Mercy, take the skin off the sauce and then warm it. We will sauce the fish in the kitchen."

"Miss Mott!" protested Constable.

"There is no choice," cried the little red-nosed Mott. "The poor dear flounder is all dried. There is nothing else to do. We will serve it by the plate and you will carry the plates up to the gentlemen already sauced. Please, Mr Constable, would you be so good as to fetch the Trafalgar Doulton. We will have to warm them with water from the kettle."

In another place, Jack Maggs's presence would have brought a hush of respect, but here, in this steamy little room, they rushed about him, ignorant of who he was. Indeed, Maggs himself moved to one side as Constable rushed past and Mercy stirred a light pink sauce.

"What did I say?" he repeated when Constable finally returned with the plates.

"How on earth would I know?" cried Constable carelessly. "I was cleaning the blessed rug."

"Then how did you learn of my connection with Borough?"

"Oh Larry," cried Constable. "Where else would you be from? Edinburgh?"

Maggs did not even have the space to be angered by these people. It was the man upstairs who was the focus of his animus. He was burgled, plundered, and he would not tolerate it.

9

As the two footmen carried the remnants of the puddings down the staircase to the kitchen, Jack Maggs asked if Mr Oates was in the habit of calling on Mr Buckle, but what with the clatter of their heels and the rattle of the china, the question seemed to go unheard. It was not until his fellow footman had rested his burden upon the kitchen table that Jack Maggs saw the snob had heard his question very well.

"Mr Maggs was just inquiring," declared the Knight of the Rainbow, "does Mr Oates come calling regularly?"

This produced a great squeal of laughter from the scullery.

"Regular?" cried Mercy Larkin, poking her white-capped head around the curtain. "Oh no. We usually have the King on Tuesdays."

Jack Maggs stood in the middle of the kitchen, red-faced, glowering. "For Jesus' sake," said he. "You don't know what you're mucking with."

"Language!" cried Miss Mott, but even her pinched little face was smiling at his question.

"Beg pardon, Ma'am." The big man spoke very quietly. "All I am endeavouring to get clear is . . . will the writing cove likely call again?"

"Oh, we are a *most* fashionable household," said Constable, splashing a little of his master's brandy into a tea cup. "There is not a coster or a crossing sweeper who is not laying plots to dine with our Mr Buckle. As for authors, why they are forever knocking down our door."

"You'll mind your manners," said Maggs in that whispering little voice which had always, in rougher places, had such chilling effect.

"Mr Maggs is such a theatrical type of gent," said Constable blithely. "I can't decide if he should play a footman," and here he patted the newcomer upon his plastered head, "or a footpad."

There were at least two men still living in London who had reason to remember that Jack Maggs did not like his head touched, and Edward Constable might then have learned a similar lesson—but the bell from upstairs began ringing for Jack Maggs's services.

He limped up the breakneck stairs to discover that all the gentlemen

(Tobias Oates amongst them) were standing at the open doorway exclaiming over the rain which had just begun to fall.

"Topcoats," hissed Constable as he passed out into the rain to call the coachman from his room in the mews.

Maggs did make some effort to do this duty as it were normally done, but he was preoccupied with Tobias Oates whom he feared would escape at any moment. When each guest had been roughly reunited with his garment, Maggs positioned himself by the open door, and here he remained with the rain blowing in his frowning face.

Oates stood out of the weather, vigorously shaking Percy Buckle's hand.

"It has been an honour, Sir," said Percy Buckle, his cheeks showing their red-hot spots once again. "Quite inconceivable to me, unimaginable. A year before last Christmas, I would not have dreamed that I would ever shake so illustrious a hand."

Oates looked very pleased to be so dubbed. "I smell a mystery."

"Oh, you are being polite, Sir. You know my good friend Mr Hawthorne and so it follows that my life can be no mystery to you. You know I had my little shop in Clerkenwell, right on Coppice Row. A most humble business, Sir, as I'm sure you've heard. I made it no secret from your friend. All the actors are aware of my beginnings."

"A wonderful story," agreed Oates, smiling. "A scholar and a grocer."

"A very poor type of scholar, I'm afraid."

"With a set of German scales on the counter and the cheese in a glass case labelled 'Pastry.'"

"Dear Lord," said Percy Buckle. "Who told you that?"

"My secret," said Oates, continuing to shake Percy Buckle's hand, "is that I once bought cheese from you, never imagining we would meet in these circumstances. It has been a wonderful evening for me, Mr Buckle, to see you so comfortably ensconced here with your servants and your Gibbon."

"Bless me. I hope you found satisfaction in the cheese."

"Indeed," said Tobias Oates, his hand still held but now retired from shaking. "Great satisfaction, for I went straight across the road to the baker's window . . . he had a sort of serving hatch with . . ."

"Mr Freepole . . ."

"Mr Freepole's is it?"

"Dead now," offered Percy Buckle.

"Indeed, dead. And bought a little loaf of bread and made myself a small picnic in that old church yard in Cutter's Close off Saffron Hill."

"We remember everything, eh, Mr Oates!"

"Indeed," said Tobias Oates, finally excusing himself the handhold. "It has been," he said, using his free hand to indicate his host, the grim footman, the open door, "a night to remember . . . and goodnight to you, Jack Maggs Esquire."

"Goodnight, Sir," said Jack. And had no choice but to stand like a fool as the man who had robbed him walked away undamaged.

But then Jack Maggs had the good fortune to be dismissed to bed.

He rushed up the stairs into his attic and, upon entering, extinguished his candle. He rushed to the dormer window. He opened it, and poked his coiffed head out into the rain.

"By Jove," he heard a familiar voice float upwards. "I'll tell you this, Hawthorne. You are mistaken, most grievously mistaken."

Jack Maggs lifted his window sash as high as it would go, and when it jammed half-way he would not be stopped but squeezed himself like a python through the opening, his shiny buckled feet first, then his stomach, then (painfully) his shoulders, until he was standing on the steep and mossy slates three giddy storeys above the street.

Keeping his hand on the window ledge, he looked down over a thin line of guttering and confirmed with his eyes that which his ears had already told him: there, forty feet below, was little Tobias Oates, standing in the rain.

"I may be mistaken about what has occurred in private," said Hawthorne. (He had his foot on the steps of Mr Buckle's coach, but did not seem inclined to enter.) "But I am not mistaken about the Unholy Passion in the air."

"I am sure you are mistaken."

"I have ob-served," said Hawthorne, "how the two parties are *besotted*."

Jack Maggs released his hold of Mr Buckle's window ledge and then edged his way across the slick roof tiles until he reached the partly open window of Mr Henry Phipps's dormer.

As he hooked his fingers under the sash, he heard the noise of steel rolling along cobblestones. He looked down and saw the carriage moving away with Edward Constable standing ramrod straight on the footplate at the rear of it.

Tobias Oates, however, was walking. He was crossing Great Queen Street diagonally, heading east.

Mr Phipps's dormer window yielded, opening sweetly to its full extent.

Jack Maggs entered. He bumped into a wash-stand and sent the water jug crashing. He cursed and, in a sudden fit of temper, kicked at the pieces. He found the door and then the stairs. He ran down two flights in total blackness but on the first-floor landing fell over an abandoned trunk from which silver sugar bowls and tea pots rolled, together with the intruder, all the way down to the hall below, where they lay about him on the carpet, their round forms hidden in the dark.

He stood slowly, feeling the pains in his back and ribs.

For this he laboured? To stand in Henry's hallway like a thief, his breeches smeared with London soot?

He unlocked the front door slowly and set off after Tobias Oates, hobbling north along Great Queen Street in his pinching shoes.

10

I may be mistaken about what has occurred in private," Henry Hawthorne said in his great booming voice. "But I am not mistaken about the Unholy Passion in the air."

"You are mistaken."

"I have ob-served," said the actor, grasping Tobias Oates's shoulder and squeezing it very painfully, "I have ob-served how the two parties are *be-sotted*."

"My hat is off to your nightmare fancy, Nuncle."

Tobias could not walk away for fear this would cause Hawthorne to speak even louder. He could only hope that the other guests, impatiently waiting inside Mr Buckle's coach, might imagine that the "passion" so discussed somehow related to the dinner just ended.

"Really, Hawthorne, you do not give either of the parties any credit."

"My dear Tobias," the actor said fondly, swinging from the coach with one arm. "I give *you* every credit."

"Good." Oates tipped his hat abruptly. "Then you will see me tomorrow at Rules."

And then he fled, or so it felt, into the wet night with his coat drawn around him tightly, whispering to himself as he scurried round the corner from Great Queen Street, "Good God. Great good God."

Tobias Oates was twenty-four years old, and for twelve months past he had been the head of a family which now consisted of his wife, Mary, his son, John, and his wife's younger sister, Elizabeth. Having come from no proper family himself, or none that he could remember without great bitterness, he had for all his short, determined life carried with him a mighty passion to create that safe warm world he had been denied.

So it was that he was now the husband of a rosy-cheeked and broad-hipped wife who in no way resembled that pinched and worried woman who had brought him so resentfully into the world. He was the father of a babe just three months old, a boy, whom he doted on as his father had never doted on him. And if he had no more than a florin in his pocket, he was also still the master of a substantial house, a place of books and laughter, of colourful rugs, of mirrors, these last being desired for their light: he would not have his son grow up in dreariness, or darkness. He had a long dining table that could welcome his wife's aunts and uncles, and there was a splendid alcove in the parlour big enough to accommodate a twelve-foot-high fir tree at Christmas. It was towards this pleasant house in Lamb's Conduit Street that he now walked briskly, but not quite directly. He could not arrive there yet. He was too agitated by this conversation which had set his heart beating wildly in his chest. Instead he set off down to Lincoln's Inn Fields—the long way home—to calm himself.

His secret had been seen.

This secret pressed at him all day long, and as he set out through the dark streets towards the place where the secret had its nest, it was with the most perplexing mixture of feelings. He walked briskly—some would say fiercely—with his shoulders back, a fast sort of duck-toed march as if he were intent on Moscow, as if he could escape his secret, which was that he was in love with his wife's sister.

This had never been his intention, and had begun through no other enthusiasm than their mutual concern for his wife, who had been confined to bed in the last months of her term. This confinement, coinciding with their moving into Lamb's Conduit Street, brought Tobias and Lizzie intimately together, necessitating the shouldering of small domestic offices which a husband and wife might more properly have performed together. The final act of their tragedy had been completed by no other agency than a heavy counterpane which they had folded together, halving, quartering, until they were, by reason of their honest household labour, brought into temptation.

No one who knew Tobias, not even the old actor who thought he saw the "thunder," had any understanding of his unholy thirst for love. He had not known it himself. He did not know the curse or gift his ma and pa had given him: he would not be loved enough, not ever.

He never really knew this truth about himself, not even when the fame he craved was finally, briefly, granted him and he travelled from city to city like a one-man carnival act, feeding off the applause of his readers. Even when it was thrown in his face, so to speak, he did not see it.

In 1837 he had even less idea of his own character. She was eighteen years old, he defiled her. *Toby, Toby*. He had been at church an hour before he did so. Now he would have abandoned all hope of Paradise for her.

Afterwards, they knelt side by side and made solemn vows to God, which vows they soon broke, once, then twice, and again, in the little garden, in the rain, in his study at three in the morning. She was a child and he was a fool, worse than a fool. He was worse than the father whom he would never forgive, and only minutes after having escaped the wine-stained Henry Hawthorne, he was thinking of her again. He gave his florin to a beggar in Lincoln's Inn Fields.

11

Jack Maggs was famously fast upon his feet, but now he was half-crippled by his dead man's shoes. God damn, but they cut him. They squeezed his toes in their vice. They cut his heel with their hooks. He took them off, but then suffered another wound on account of this: so he had no choice but to stop and put them on once more. With all this fuss, he almost lost sight of Tobias Oates, and had the writer not begun to sing so free and careless, he might have disappeared into the fog. But then, by Jesus, there came that fine tenor voice, not twenty yards ahead. "Sally in our Alley." It was a filthy song.

He had the bastard. He had him easy-peasy. He limped along behind him to Lincoln's Inn Fields with his shoes torturing him at every step. It was only pain, or so he told himself. He had suffered worse.

As the song arrived at that place where "Nature's soft stream was flowing" they came to coal-dark Carey Street. By then they were but fifteen feet apart.

In Chancery Lane a great lurching galoot of a link boy came rushing up the pavement holding his blazing faggot high into the night. The link boy, all of fifty if he were a day, was providing light for two young gentlemen, who were, in turn, attempting to escort a little whore, and all three of them as drunk as Captain Harry's horse.

As Tobias Oates turned to look at the link boy, Jack Maggs stepped back into the doorway of the Great High Court where he found a second whore busy at her trade and not pleased to have the interruption. A moment later Jack Maggs was out in the street again, making himself one of the party with the puffing link boy, boldly sharing the smoky light as far as Theobald's Road. He was just in time to see Tobias Oates turn off into the darkness.

Jack Maggs hobbled across the path of a hackney cab, then hip-hopped along Lamb's Conduit Street. For reward he saw Tobias Oates step up onto the front step of a house. He arrived outside this door in time to hear a heavy bolt slid home into its hasp.

Then a sudden light flooded through the fog behind him, throwing his own massive shadow on the door.

"So," said the man with the lamp. "What's up here?"

At first Maggs thought it was a soldier behind the lamp, but it was a bobby, an esclop, a frigging peeler with a fancy coat. Jack Maggs had not seen this type of coat before.

"You would not want to swap your uniform with mine, for all the tea in China," said he cheekily. "They give me shoes, the shoes don't fit. They send me out to walk behind my master, and not even a topcoat to bless myself with."

The peeler was a big strong fellow with a face like a potato. The look in his eye, as he held up his lantern, was the same one you see in a policeman who would like to harm you badly, if only he could do it at no risk to himself.

"Where's your master?" he demanded.

"Just went in."

"Went in where? I didn't see no one."

The peeler ran his lantern over Jack Maggs again and there revealed the damage done by the journey across the roof, the tumble down the stairs, the subsequent excursion through the drizzle. The Knight of the Rainbow was in a sodden, speckled state.

"Just went in," Jack Maggs said, suddenly very sharp indeed. "Right here. Mr Tobias Oates. The author of the tale of Captain Crumley."

The esclop pushed his hot lantern a little closer to Jack's nose.

"Captain Crumley?"

"That's the one."

The bobby paused. "Get on home," he said at last.

There was no choice. Jack Maggs opened the gate, walked down the steps into the area. There, below street level, he pressed himself flat against the kitchen door, but Mr Peel's man was not so green. He held up his lantern and peered down after him.

It was Despair made Jack Maggs try the kitchen door handle, and Fortune decreed it be left carelessly unlocked. He entered Tobias Oates's house and slid the bolt behind him. Through the kitchen window he could see the bobby's legs as they walked back towards the front door.

The village pony was not satisfied—it seemed he was going to knock up Tobias Oates and ask him questions about his footman. Jack Maggs therefore crept up the dark stairs into the hallway, ready to flee out the back if the policeman knocked.

At first he stood hard and still as a log of wood, but when it was clear that the policeman had walked on, he relaxed. Still he did not move, but stayed exactly where he was, breathing deeply.

Elsewhere in the household he heard a flurry of whispering and the fast shuffle of bare feet, and then, not too much time after, the old familiar music of a squeaking bed.

12

In the place Jack Maggs had most recently come from, the houses had been, for the most part, built from wood. They strained and groaned in the long hot nights, crying out against their nails, contracting, expanding, tugging at their bindings as if they would pull themselves apart.

Tobias Oates's house in Lamb's Conduit Street was built from London brick. It was newly painted, newly furnished. Everything in it glistened and was strong and bright and solid. This was a house that would never scream in the dark, nor did it reek of sap or creosote. Its smells were English smells—polished oak, coal dust, Devon apples. The intruder breathed these strange yet familiar odours for as long as it took the master to get himself to bed.

Then he crept up the stairs and, on the upper landing, drew his long arms around his chest. It was an action such as the Devil might make when surrounding himself with his cape. It might also have been by a mortal man wishing to cloak himself in Night, and if the latter were the case, Jack Maggs might be said to have succeeded, for a moment later he appeared, a slow and smudgy phantom, in a small room off the landing. Here he stooped over the small wooden crib in which lay Tobias Oates's first-born son.

Maggs's inky shadow flooded the crib. He leaned very close, so close indeed he might have bitten the child. Instead, he brought his wide nostrils almost up against that soapy skin and, with his arms clenched behind his back, inhaled John Marshall Oates's breath. This act he repeated three times, and when he was done he straightened himself and placed his hands deep in his pockets. In the next room, the child's father turned in his bed and coughed a most wide-awake cough. The intruder removed his hands from his pockets and moved slowly back into the shadow by the tall cupboard, and there his breathing became very slow and deep.

In other circumstances, Maggs had been known to act violently, but in Tobias Oates's house he was a sloth. His heavy limbs bled into the darkness and as the clock ticked loudly in the downstairs hallway, he seemed to flow from room to room as slow as a moon-made shadow.

He stood above the bed of a young spinster. The vigour of her dreams had served to push her night cap from her head. Her hair was loose, floating like seaweed around her sleeping face. One bare white arm was flung out across the sheet, the other held between her knees beneath the covers. Beside her bed was a dresser where the intruder found a piece of jewellery, a necklace. He picked it up and ran it through his three fingers, before quietly laying it down again.

Two o'clock found him in another room, his severe hawk-nosed face an inch away from Mary Oates's small down-turned mouth. He stood over Tobias Oates who was sleeping on his stomach in a perfect imitation of his son.

As the hall clock struck the quarter-hour, he reluctantly retreated to the kitchen. There he took a draught of cold water, and splashed a little on his face. The extreme agitation which had hitherto marked his face and body was no longer to be seen.

He sat himself at the kitchen table with his glass of water, and rested his eyes.

He woke with a great start to find a woman, an older big-bellied woman with strong forearms and large hands, standing over him.

She had the oil lamps lit. She was in cap and apron. "Did he tell you to wait?" she said.

"He did, Ma'am," said Jack Maggs, automatically smiling and showing her his strong straight teeth.

"Said he was going to fetch you a shilling? Said you were to tell him your story, is that so?"

He stood and stretched. "So he said, Ma'am."

The cook—for he assumed her to be so—shook her head and went about readying the kitchen for breakfast, riddling the grate, throwing in the coal, getting the great kettle back in its place on the cold black top.

"He cannot help himself. He saw your livery, and thought: there's a chap with dirty livery. Just what you would think or I would think, but Mr Oates, he can't stop there—he's thinking, how did that fatty-spot get on his shoulder? He's wondering, in what circumstances were the stockings torn? He's looking at you like a blessed butterfly he has to pin down on his board. It is not that he hasn't got a heart. Indeed, I'm like as not cold-hearted in comparison. But he is an author, as I'm sure you don't need telling, and he must know your whole life story or he will die of it. There's a boy from Tetley's with a porcelain eye, he left the poor little mite waiting half the day. Miss Lizzie found the little tyke crying on the doorstep when she was going walking with the missus."

"Well, I'll be on my way then," said sleepy Jack, noticing for the first time his torn stockings. "For to tell you the truth, Ma'am, I must be explaining myself to my own master."

"Sit up all night and not get your shilling? No, no. You must go up."

"I've a long way to travel, Ma'am, and a household to attend to."

"You can't leave now. He's left you sitting for hours. You go up and tell him. He's a fine man, a good man. You won't find a better one."

"Just the same," said Maggs.

"Just the same, my aunt. You go, Sir, or I'll bring him down myself."

"But surely he's asleep."

"Asleep? He never sleeps. It's half past five and he's in his room. Come, I'll show you where it is. If he's writing in his book, don't mind. Just say, here I am and John's my name and I am here for to get the tip you left me all night waiting for."

So Maggs ascended the stairs a second time. It was just as well, he thought. *If 'twere done, 'twere best done quickly* . . .

13

Tobias Oates had an obsession with the Criminal Mind. He found evidence of its presence in signs as small as the bumps upon a pick-pocket's cranium, or as large as La Place's *Théorie analytique* which showed the murder rate in Paris unchanged from one year to the next.

There was a little shop in Whitechapel, the province of a certain Mr Nevus, where Tobias was in the habit of purchasing what he called "Evidence." Here he had recently paid a very hefty sum for the hand of a thief. With the exception of the tell-tale little finger, which was malformed, the fingers of the hand were long, thin, very delicate; sadly in opposition to the skirt of skin which trailed back from the harshly butchered wrist. This hand floated in a large wide-throated jar of formaldehyde identified by a brown discoloured label, on which was inscribed a legend in Arabic the meaning of which was not, as yet, available.

He had many such secrets hidden in his study. There, in that cubby hole labelled "M," were the notes he had made on his visit to the Morgue in Paris. There, on that very high shelf up against the ceiling, was a parcel wrapped in tissue paper and tied with black ribbon—the death mask of John Sheppard, hanged at Tyburn in 1724.

There was much of the scientist about Tobias Oates. The study, with its circular window and its neat varnished systems of shelves and pigeon holes, was ordered as methodically as a laboratory. There was not a loose piece of anything here, not a nightingale feather or an unbound sheet of paper: everything was secured in its own place, tied up with ribbon, or tucked away in labelled envelopes. In these corners Tobias Oates stored not only his Evidence, but also experiments, sketches, notes, his workings-up of the characters who he hoped would one day make his name, not just as the author of comic adventures, but as a novelist who might topple Thackeray himself. And it was this ambition, always burning bright within him, which brought him to his desk before dawn on that day when Jack Maggs came knocking on his door.

The sharp, demanding nature of these knocks announced a visitor who was unfamiliar with his household. Tobias swiftly slid the jar into the corner of his desk. He placed an open encyclopedia in front of it, and picked up his quill. He opened his chap book. He appeared, as he turned his head towards the door, rather as he does in the portrait Samuel Laurence painted of him in 1838. That is, he looked towards his visitor as at a bailiff, or some other person with the power to knock him off his perch.

"Enter."

The door swung open to reveal Percy Buckle's footman.

Tobias Oates took in the splashed stockings, sooty knees, damage to the powdered hair.

"Is this bad news?" he asked.

The dark eyes stared back at him balefully.

The writer reached for the golden cord which tied his gown, pulled it loose, tied it once again.

"The pain returned?" he guessed, but he was very confused by such a visitor at such an hour.

The fellow took a half-step into the room.

"What happened to your stockings?"

"I fell," the footman said curtly, blinking and looking hard around him.

"For heaven's sake, man, it is five in the morning."

"The hours are hard, Sir."

"You were dragged out from your bed? Does that mild man really send his servants out at such hours?"

For answer the visitor clenched his two hands and held them out strangely from his sides. This gesture was queer and unexpected, suggesting more power than any servant had a right to assume. It was then Tobias began to feel afraid.

"Some wrong has been done you?"

"I've been waiting all the night, since you finished your pudding."

The footman took a further step into the room. Toby picked up the only weapon available, his paperweight. It was a two-pound weight belonging to the kitchen scales.

"But where, dear God? All night?"

"In the street." Jack Maggs closed the door behind him.

"This street? Outside my house?"

"And then most recently, I was conveniently inside your kitchen."

"Man, you're shivering."

"I know it."

Tobias did not relinquish his two-pound weight, but he offered the chair he had been sitting on. "And what is your true purpose, old fellow?"

Jack Maggs had sat himself in the chair but immediately stood up again, folding his great arms across his chest. "What was it you did to me at dinner time? To be blunt, Sir, that's what's on my mind."

"Ah, so that's it. The pain has come back!"

"Tell me what you did to me."

For answer Tobias attempted to lay his hand against the servant's cheek, but Jack Maggs jerked back his head, curled his lips and showed his gums.

"You pried into my secrets."

"No."

"That's why those gentlemen were looking at me so strange when I woke up."

"You deserve an explanation," said Tobias carefully, "but you'll not get it by glowering at me. Here, I'll take this stool, and you have my chair again. No one wishes you ill, you have my word. What you call 'strange' was human sympathy. They are gentlemen, perhaps, and you are a footman, but they were moved by you. You are filled with Phantoms, Master Maggs. It is these Phantoms who cause you such distress. Did you know that? Do you know what hobgoblins live inside your head like beetles in a fallen log?"

"But how did you make me speak?" cried the visitor, sitting forward again in the chair, his hands upon his spattered knees. "In all my life I never have spoke in my sleep, not never."

"Last night you were a Somnambulist."

"Whatever it is called, it is a terrible thing, Sir, for a man to feel his insides all exposed to public view, a thousand times worse than to come before you with my stockings in this state."

"Would you rather keep the pain?"

"I would have it back ten times over, if my secrets came with it."

There was a long silence.

"Do you read?" Tobias asked at last.

"I am not an ignorant man, if that is what you're thinking."

"You might like to read that little chap book by your elbow. There, that's the one. Turn to the third last page. The date is the sixteenth of April. There you may read exactly what secrets you have given me."

Jack Maggs stared at the book but did not touch it. "Oh Sir," he said, very quietly. "I do really wonder whether that were wise of you."

"Open it. Read."

The footman shivered so violently that Tobias Oates was reminded of Pharaoh, a race-horse belonging to his father whose freckled flanks would twitch and shiver at the onset of the saddle. Then, as Jack Maggs slowly and carefully read the two pages of handwriting, Tobias Oates hatched his scheme.

"This is all I said? Naught else besides?"

"That is all."

"Then I was drunk, Sir, if you'll forgive my French."

"But this Phantom lives within you," said Oates earnestly. "You have a creature who wishes you harm, who lives within you like a worm lives in the belly of a pig. It is the Phantom who hurts your face."

"I ain't acquainted with any Phantom, Sir. I never heard his name before."

"I believe that I can remove this pain of yours for ever."

"Oh, I have had the pain for many years, Sir. It is an old friend by now."

"Was it friendly to be so attacked in public?"

Jack Maggs closed the little chap book and placed it carefully back upon the desk. "I am happy as I am, Sir."

"But what if I should take the demons from your heart where they are causing you pain? What if I write them on paper and then place the pages in this box here? When we are done, we can go to this fireplace, Jack Maggs, and we can burn them together."

"But what is it to you, Sir? It is my pain after all."

"I am a naturalist."

"I heard you was an author."

"Yes, an author. I wish to sketch the beast within you. If you were to continue with this experiment I would not only attempt the cure, I would pay you wages."

"I do not want money, Sir."

Tobias laughed suddenly, bitterly. "Good. What other inducement might I offer you? Not to cure your pain? You are fond of your pain."

"I don't need nothing."

"An introduction?"

The footman hesitated. Oates felt that hesitation, like the dull pressure of an eel on the end of a baited line.

"What mean you by introduction?"

"I was imagining you might like an introduction to a superior household . . ."

The footman waved this away.

"It was some other type of introduction that you sought? Speak up."

"Well, I had planned to ask you, Sir, if you had visited the house again. It took my attention when you spoke of it."

"Ask now."

"There are still Thief-takers in business," the footman began. "Is that what I understood you to have said?"

"You were robbed?"

"You mentioned a Thief-taker at dinner. Partridge. Him who can find any man in England."

"There is someone you want found?"

"It's a family matter, Sir."

"So that could be our bargain?" Tobias Oates leaned forward on his stool and put out his small square hand to shake on it.

"I never said I wanted it." Jack Maggs folded his arms across his chest. There was a pause. "But if I were inclined that way, when would you deliver him?"

"Directly."

"Today?"

"No, no. Good heavens. There would have to be value in the bargain for me. Four weeks, three."

"No, no," the footman stood, shaking his head and knocking his knuckles together. "I could not wait four weeks."

"Three," said Tobias Oates, also standing.

"Two," said Jack Maggs. "Two or nothing."

"Two then. Can't say fairer than that."

The footman put out his hand to shake and Tobias Oates imagined he could feel an equal but opposite enthusiasm in the other's violent grasp.

14

"Then this is how we will proceed," said Tobias Oates, turning his back so that his great excitement could be hidden from the subject. "I will send a note to your Mr Buckle, explaining the present circumstances."

"He'll dismiss me from his service."

"On my word, he will *not* dismiss you."

"He will."

"By the Lord above!" Tobias turned. "Mr Buckle will do exactly as I wish him to."

"If I am dismissed, where will I have my crib?"

"Your master is a student of Mesmerism. He will be pleased to make you available for science."

Jack Maggs's eyes narrowed, his hawk-nosed face turned hard and shiny, just like, Tobias thought, a peasant with a pig to sell.

"I never said I were available to science."

"Nonsense. You made a bargain."

"No. You will get me to the Thief-taker. That is the bargain."

"Yes, I undertake to introduce you to Mr Partridge and do everything in my power to make that meeting a productive one for you. You, for your part, will do what I ask of you."

But the fellow was now staring down mulishly at his hands.

"You never said nothing about science."

"For God's sake, man," cried Tobias Oates irritably.

"Don't shout at me, Mr Oates. I know what I heard."

"What is there to be unsure about?"

Jack Maggs opened his hands so that the stumps of his fingers lay plainly displayed upon his knee. "I won't have nothing written down."

Tobias feared he was about to lose his subject. He had played his hand too obviously. The man had seen his need.

"That's a pity, Master Maggs, because the deal is done and good enough to stand up in a Court of Law. I am going to make these movements," he said, keeping his voice as stern and solemn as a magistrate. "They are called 'passes.'"

"No."

"You look me in the eye," cried Tobias Oates. He began to pass his hands before the footman's malevolent, heavy-lidded eyes. "Watch my hands, fellow."

Finally, Jack Maggs did watch. He watched warily, sitting a little sideways in the chair, as if the square white hands might do him a damage. And yet, by the time night had lifted from the misty little garden, his unshaven chin was resting on his chest.

"Can you hear me?" Tobias Oates asked.

"Yes, I can hear you."

Tobias blew out his red lips in silent relief. He reached across to his desk and picked up, first his note book, then his quill.

"Are you comfortable?"

The footman shifted his backside, a little irritably. "Yes, comfortable."

"Is the pain there?"

"Leave me alone."

"Now you and I, Jack Maggs, we are going to imagine a place where there is no pain. Can you find a place like that?"

"Leave me alone. The pain is always there."

"Then we are going to make a picture, like in a fairy tale. We are going to imagine a door so thick, the pain cannot get to you. We can imagine high walls made of thick stone."

"A prison . . ."

"Very well, a splendid prison, with its walls twenty feet thick and—"

The Somnambulist began to move his arms about violently. "No!" he shouted. "No, damn you!"

"Quiet," hissed Tobias. "Do you hear me? Quiet. If you don't like a prison you can have a blessed fortress. A castle with battlements and flying flags. It can be a house. It does not matter."

"A house."

"Yes. A good sturdy house with double walls of London brick, and oak shutters on the windows."

"Morrison Brothers on the doors."

"Very good. Indeed. The locks and latches are made by dear old Morrison Brothers. Now we are standing on its threshold. Where is the pain?"

"Damn the pain. It always follows me."

"In a shape? Is it the same shape? Like a man? Like an animal?"

"I'm trying. I'm trying."

"Good. Good man."

"When I look at it, it changes. Now there are two of them."

"A man and an animal."

"No, no, leave off, leave off of me. Leave me alone."

"Very well. Is the pain there?"

"Yes, of course. I told you. It is always there. I have to stop. I have to stop this now."

"We can stop it by going inside the house and locking the pain outside."

"Must I?"

"Yes, you must."

A pause.

"Where are you now?"

"God help me, I have done what you told me to. I have gone inside the house."

"Where is the Phantom?"

"You know the answer."

"Is he inside or outside the house?"

The Somnambulist placed his hands over his ears.

"Inside or outside?"

"How can I see when you are talking to me all the time? Let me alone if you please." The footman paused, and frowned. "There are people everywhere. I can't see him."

"There are people inside the house?"

"Ever so many."

"Who are they?"

"I don't know them."

"What sort of people?"

"Gentlemen . . . and ladies."

"What are they doing?"

"Walking around, spying on things. They are opening the drawers and the cupboards."

"What of the Phantom?"

"Looking in through the window, most agitated."

"Because locked out?"

"Yes, locked out."

"And the pain is gone?"

"No, the pain is bad. They should not be there. It is my place, not theirs."

"Yes, it is your place. Yours alone."

"They don't want me owning it. They'll take it from me."

"No, it is yours, Jack Maggs. You know it is yours. You must expel everything that agitates you."

"They won't listen to me, Sir. I am not a gentleman."

"But have you tried?"

"Yes, yes," Jack Maggs cried passionately. "A hundred times over, I have told them, but they will not listen to me, and I must do what they say."

"What shall we do? What might persuade them do you think?"

"Oh, Sir, that sort . . . that sort should pet the old double-cat."

"The double-cat?"

"The double-cat. The thief's cat. It has a double twist in the cord."

"You mean the cat-o'-nine-tails?"

"The double-cat is heavier."

Tobias Oates had been sitting with his legs crossed, writing diligently in his court reporter's shorthand, but when he heard this comment he looked up sharply. "Perhaps we could open the door and simply ask them to leave."

"Oh, that's a joke." The sleeping man twisted his mouth into an ugly shape. "A very good joke, that is."

"Well, if you would like to try a joke, my man, see what I am doing to them now."

"I can't see." Jack Maggs contorted in his chair. "I can't see you doing anything."

"Oh yes you can. You can see exactly what I am doing. I am sending them to sleep. Can't you see that?"

"I'm not sure."

"Of course you can. Can't you see their eyes closing? You know I have the power to do that, don't you?"

"I think they are dying."

"Some are falling down, but it is only sleep that causes it. They are falling asleep."

"Now what will I do with them?"

"We are going to get your Phantom to carry them out."

"He won't do that."

"He will do it if I tell him to. I am telling him to remove these people from your stronghold. Look at him. How is he today?"

"He has a nasty look about him, Sir. He keeps staring at me."

"Yes, but he will do as I say, and he is strong enough to carry out the sleeping people. Some of them are quite large, aren't they? Do you see a woman with double chins?"

"No, I don't think so."

"Surely there is a woman there in a black dress with a great deal of jewellery?"

"I think I see her now."

"Is the Phantom dragging her?"

"No, he has picked her up. He is picking her up and carrying her out of my house."

"You must be feeling a deal better."

"Yes, I am."

"Is there any pain?"

"Everything is much better. Much better, thank you, Sir. He is going to stay outside the door now, Sir?"

"When he has carried everyone out."

"He has, Sir. He's a such a jolly old bullock, ain't he?"

"He has removed them already?"

"He's a regular dervish, Sir."

"And outside now?"

"Yes, outside."

"Then I am locking the door. You are in your house. You are all alone. Nothing can harm you. You are going to the window now. You are looking out of the window?"

"Yes, I am looking out of the window."

"What do you see? Any street numbers? Shops?"

"Nothing, Sir."

"You can't see anything?"

"Pitch black, Sir."

"Come, Jack Maggs, there is the lamplighter, now look—it's as bright as day."

At this, the Somnambulist became extremely agitated, rolling his eyes and striking himself upon the breast.

"I am not permitted to tell you."

"You must."

"No," cried the footman and threw out his arms, one of which struck Tobias Oates a grazing blow upon his temple.

"Cease!" cried Toby. "Be still!"

But Jack Maggs groaned and flung himself violently back in his chair.

"Be still there, that's a fellow. Down now." In this style Tobias continued to soothe his angry subject, talking very low, as to a frightened beast.

When peace was finally established, Tobias Oates stood and gazed down at Jack Maggs. He would be the archaeologist of this mystery; he would be the surgeon of this soul.

His youthful face was flushed, and the flecks in his pale blue eyes had turned as bright as mica. He picked up the stool and moved it over to the desk, and though it was too low for such a task, he sat upon it to compose his letter.

"*Dear Mr Buckle*," he began, "*one sometimes hears a servant described by this or that lady as a 'treasure.'*"

With his prisoner's breathing whispering in his ear, he continued— three drafts before he had it exactly right.

15

It was Edward Constable who informed Mrs Halfstairs that her new footman was missing. He presented himself triumphantly in her parlour door at six o'clock on Monday morning, knocking in that brisk way—*one, two, one two*—that was at once so characteristic and so insolent.

She bade him enter.

"Yes, Constable."

"It's your man, Ma'am . . . He's bolted."

Her stomach tightened. She lay her quill down on the blotter.

"Which *man*, Mr Constable? If it is Mr Maggs you mean, he has likely gone on an errand for the master. Did you inquire of the master?"

"It is my belief, Ma'am, that Mr Maggs was never in his life an upper servant. He seems to be some kind of rascal."

"You are not a parson," said Mrs Halfstairs, "and were not employed to have beliefs. Did you check with the master?"

"You think the master harmed?"

She had thought no such thing, but now she thought it—she saw again the dreadful death of the previous footman, his skull half blown away and all that *matter* on the oaken dresser.

"I came first to you, Ma'am," said the footman. "I did not think to wake the master."

"Then go now, if you please, Mr Constable, and check the silver."

"The silver, Ma'am?"

She caught his bright hard eye.

"Not the master, Ma'am? The *silver*?"

"Do as I have asked you," said Mrs Halfstairs. "And pray do not disturb Mr Spinks with this news until I tell you to."

She climbed the stairs with a heavy heart, wishing for the old days when Mr Spinks had ruled the household. Constable would not have behaved this way then. Pope would not have dared to kill himself. As she walked heavily up the stairs—her breathing came hard to her—Mrs Halfstairs was convinced already that her master had been harmed. Her mood was therefore much elevated when she peered round Mr Buckle's partly opened door and found him safely snoring in one corner of his enormous bed.

As she returned to the ground floor a knock came on the front door, and she answered it herself, to Mr Oates's messenger.

By the time Constable came to inform her that the silver had not been stolen, she had carefully examined the contents of Tobias Oates's letter and knew that Jack Maggs was to be a source of glory not of shame.

She gave the envelope to Mr Constable so he might take it to their master.

"I heard the door bell, Ma'am."

"Yes, Mr Constable. It was this same letter."

"Perhaps Ma'am, could I ask, that I be permitted to answer the door, as is my duty?"

"I am always pleased for you to do your duty, Mr Constable. And your master will be pleased to receive this letter at your hand."

That gave him pause a moment. But then he came at her from a different quarter.

"And did you notice, Mrs Halfstairs, when you was answering the door, did you happen to notice that the next-door servants were about again?"

"No, Mr Constable, I did not."

"I also went to the door, Ma'am."

"No need for you to have done that, Mr Constable."

"And found them all everywhere about the street."

"I did not notice, Mr Constable."

"I wonder, did it occur to you, Ma'am, that perhaps Mr Maggs has run away with them?"

"Run away with them, Constable?"

"He has an interest in them, does he not? He said he was to be their footman, although I doubt he was, but he had a very fierce interest in that household, and asked us many questions about Mr Phipps himself. Seeing all this activity, Ma'am, I naturally drew it to Mr Spinks's attention, and he thought that may explain your man's departure."

"Mr Constable, did I not request you to wait until you informed Mr Spinks?"

"Ma'am, you know it most improper for a footman to go having secrets from a butler."

Mrs Halfstairs took a breath. "Take this letter to the master," she said at last. "And when you are done with it, present yourself down here."

And then she went to find Mr Spinks and see if she might restore some order to that poor old wandering mind.

16

At half past nine the absent footman limped in through the kitchen door. His eyes were wild and red, his hair most queerly disarrayed; a great smudge of black disfigured his smart yellow livery; and yet there was, for all his hobbling, nothing in the least apologetic in his demeanour.

"Can a cove get a cup of something?" he demanded, sitting down at the long deal table and glaring at Mercy Larkin who was busy cutting the rot from the day's potatoes.

"Yes, Sir," said she, but no sooner had she set her knife down than Mrs Halfstairs, always alert to the creak of the kitchen door, came clattering in from her parlour on her heavy heels and—without one word about Jack Maggs's disgraceful livery—escorted him straight away upstairs to be brought before the master.

"Can a *cove* get something?" said Constable mocking Jack Maggs's hoarse voice. "That *cove* is about to get his marching orders."

"I never heard of such a thing," said Miss Mott. "It is the butler's job to dismiss him. I can't imagine what Mrs Halfstairs is thinking of— taking him before the master."

"At Lineham Hall," said Constable, complacently stirring his third teaspoon of sugar into his tea, "he would have his livery removed at the gate house and be sent off in his undervest."

"Mr Constable!" cried Miss Mott.

"Or worse," said Constable, who had a fondness for shocking the cook. "I once saw a page boy put out in the frost with nothing but a pair of old hessians on his feet." And he then went on to describe, in some detail, the cruel ways in which various servants had been dismissed from his previous establishment.

Constable had a long repertoire of such incidents but was cut off in his first chapter not only by the return of Mrs Halfstairs and Jack Maggs, but also by the arrival of the butler himself. Mr Spinks entered the kitchen with a long brass poker which he had, perhaps absentmindedly, carried away from Mr Buckle's snuggery. He stood with his back to the dresser, swaying slightly, seemingly unsure of why he had come. Observing the distressing confusion in those cloudy eyes, Constable turned all his attention on the miscreant.

"Oh hello Maggs," said he conversationally. "If you had slept the night at home you would have woken to the sight of your friends next door galloping in and out of their front door."

Jack Maggs jerked his head towards his informant.

"A stranger would have thought them thieves," continued Constable, as if unaware of the effect he was having on his listener. "Sugar bowls. Tea pots. You should have seen the *plunder* they carried off."

"Mr Phipps is returned?" asked Maggs, fixing upon Constable a gaze both fierce and hungry.

"If you had been back a half hour earlier, you might have had your old job back."

"We have no interest in that household, Mr Constable," interrupted Mrs Halfstairs.

"Young Mr Phipps was there?" Maggs asked again but to no effect. Mrs Halfstairs was staring malevolently at Mr Constable and so Maggs repeated the question to Mercy, who answered him gently.

"Not Mr Phipps. Just his carriage, and two of the upper servants."

"You saying he is back?"

"No, Mr Maggs. I'm afraid he ain't returned."

Mr Spinks banged his poker. "Sit!"

"Sit," echoed Mrs Halfstairs. "What is it that you are thinking?"

Jack Maggs did not sit. "I am thinking that if Mr Phipps is home, it is time for you and me, Mrs Halfstairs, to say farewell."

Mr Spinks cleared his throat.

"Did not Mr Buckle welcome you back into the fold?" said Mrs Halfstairs, turning incredulously to Mr Spinks. "Did you ever hear so generous and Christian a speech? No, no, Mr Maggs, it is Mr Buckle who is your master now."

"He's not sacked?" cried Constable, indignantly.

"You skate on very thin ice, Constable," hissed Mrs Halfstairs. She turned back to Mr Spinks. "It is true that he has behaved in a most improper manner, but on the other hand he has found favour with Mr Oates. That is true, is it not, Mr Spinks?"

"Oates likes him?" Constable demanded. "Oates has an interest in him? Oates will visit? This Hopping Giles has become a social ornament? Is that what I am witnessing?"

"As any crossing sweeper would know," said Mrs Halfstairs, "it would be a distinction to the household to have a connection with so up-and-coming a gentleman as Mr Oates."

"But this rascal," cried Constable, "he never even heard of Captain Crumley."

Mercy saw that this last intelligence reached Mrs Halfstairs with a certain force. The housekeeper blinked her little eyes. "Still, we will not release him to Mr Phipps," she said at last.

Constable appealed to the butler. "He could not do his own hair. I did it for him."

"Mr Maggs has agreed to be the subject of Scientific Experiment. Is that not so, Mr Spinks? It is your brow?" Mrs Halfstairs suggested to Maggs. "Mr Oates wishes to measure it?"

"Surely, Ma'am," sneered Constable, "you measured it already."

"You have pushed my patience, Mr Constable."

"It is a light enough load, Ma'am."

Mrs Halfstairs looked hard at Mr Spinks.

"The point," began Spinks, "the point, Sir . . ."

"The point is about service," said Mrs Halfstairs. "And I cannot see that you can require Mr Constable's any longer."

There was now a great silence in the kitchen.

"Quite so," said Spinks at last. He tapped the brass poker on the floor between his shoes, then turned a stern unflinching gaze on his footman. "Quite so. Not require him."

It was obvious Constable had not expected this turn of events. He began to rise from the table, a teaspoon still in his hand. His handsome face was stricken.

"Mr Spinks . . . Sir? Mr Spinks, Sir, do you know me?"

Mr Spinks tapped the poker on the floor. "I know you, Sir."

Constable held himself erect, but Mercy could see—anyone could see—that his cheeks were hollowed and his eyes desolate.

"Sir . . . you are dismissing me?" His proud demeanour was contradicted by his trembling voice. "Mr Spinks, have you forgotten? May I remind you, Sir, about the problems with my letters . . ."

During all of this dispute Jack Maggs had seemed to be occupied with his own thoughts, but now he took two paces forward and stood beside Edward Constable.

"Mr Constable and me," said he. "We are a pair."

Then, much to Mercy Larkin's surprise, he smiled at Mrs Halfstairs.

"We are bookends, ain't we, Mrs Halfstairs? Can't have one without the other."

17

It is no easy matter to ride the footplate of a phaeton, to pose like a piece of German porcelain, to float like one of God's angels above the mud and ordure of the London streets.

Yet when the two footmen walked out to the mews the following morning—that is Tuesday, April the eighteenth—Jack Maggs did not request instruction, and he rode without anyone having shown him how to keep his knees a little loose, to hold his chin high, to alight before the coach was finally still. Even Edward Constable, who was of a habitually critical frame of mind, was impressed by the performance.

Their first appointment was the Patent Office Library on Chancery Lane, and although there was no more momentous business at hand than their master's wish to peruse the plans of the latest donkey engine, they proceeded towards this destination at desperate speed, cutting in ahead of pony carts and hackney cabs, in a style at once so reckless and arrogant that even the most belligerent of London drivers—and that was the grand majority—gave way to the handsome blue phaeton with the gold lion emblazoned on its door. Having watched Maggs survive this desperate charge it was obvious to Edward Constable that his benefactor had, not to put too fine a point on it, a "gift."

At the Patent Office, Constable opened the coach door, guided his master past a puddle, and watched him scurry up the steps. The very sight of Percy Buckle Esq., with his sunken cheeks and bandy little duck-legged walk, would normally have been enough to put him in an irritable sort of mood, and indeed it was a constant trial to him to wait in attendance on so low-bred a master, but on this particular morning, Edward Constable had almost no interest in Mr Buckle. It was his fellow footman who preoccupied him, and in this regard his skill on the footplate was a very small item indeed.

The two servants stood side by side on the footpath of Chancery Lane. Only inches separated them, but the newcomer affected a distance which Constable, much burdened with his own feelings of guilt and gratitude, soon found intolerable.

"You are a puzzle of a fellow," he began.

Maggs turned, briefly presenting him with the blank wall of his face.

"If I was unfriendly to you," Constable persisted, "—and it is not even 'if' for I know I was . . . "

"It's past, mate. Forget it."

"My friend is dead. It makes me bitter, and when I'm feeling bitter I say things I regret."

"Say no more then."

"But I must say more," cried Constable. "So help me, Mr Maggs, I must do more. I am a man that always pays his debt."

"The old dame was whipping you, and I took a great personal pleasure in stopping her. But if you want to thank me . . . do you know that fellow driving our coach?"

"Foster."

"You know him a good while, no doubt?"

"He was with Mr Quentin when we were at Bath."

"You've done him some favour in your time?"

"We know each other, Mr Maggs. What do you want? Say the word."

"Tell him that Jack Maggs begs the use of the titty he is sucking on."

"Mr Maggs, I want to oblige you."

"Then here's the answer. Ask him."

"But Mr Maggs, you ask the one thing I cannot do."

"Your wooden leg ain't broken, is it? Go tell that dozy old farmer that his brother the footman wants to dance with his sister Miss Flask."

"I enjoy a gin myself, Mr Maggs, but a footman in his livery cannot be seen drinking from a flask."

"You said yourself—I am a scoundrel, not a footman. A Knight of the Rainbow may not get a thirst, but a scoundrel . . . Come, Mr Thingstable, I have the pain back in my face. Would you rather I went into that little dram shop yonder? I do not doubt they would be pleased enough to have my money. It is a funny thing about a dram shop, they have a great fondness for we rascals. We are patron saints to them."

"I'll speak to Foster, Mr Maggs."

The lanky coachman, a West Country man, stayed in his seat with a rug around his knees, and from this high throne engaged Constable in a long and dogged negotiation. Finally terms were agreed on, and he handed across his "drop of the doings."

"You had to pay him?" Maggs inquired.

"It is my pleasure." Constable looked up and down the street which was, at that moment, free of servants. "Now. Drink it now."

Alas, it was at that very moment, as Maggs tipped the flask up to his lips, that Percy Buckle came skipping down the steps of the Patent Office.

"Where to now, Sir?" shouted the coachman, but not before Percy Buckle saw what he was not meant to. He frowned and clapped his gloved hands together. "Well, do you know," he said, looking from Maggs to Foster very suddenly. "Well, do you know, today I'm going to try a new one."

"A new patent, Sir?" cried Foster, perhaps worried he would lose his silver flask for ever.

"A new book shop," said Percy Buckle. "The largest shop in London."

Constable opened the door for his master. "That would be Bowes & Bowes, Sir," he said nervously.

"Now there you are wrong, my man," said Mr Buckle, fetching an addressed letter from his side pocket. "It ain't. It's Lackington's Temple of the Muses."

"Never heard of it, Sir," said Constable.

"Well you don't know London like I do," said Percy Buckle. "It's in Finsbury Square."

"Up Holborn Hill?" The coachman groaned.

"'Fraid so," said Percy Buckle. "'Fraid it is precisely up the good old Holborn Hill."

At the foot of Holborn Hill, Maggs and Constable were dispatched to run alongside while the groom applied the whip to the horses' backs. Thus it was a hot and weary Maggs who finally helped Percy Buckle dismount at Finsbury Square.

"Give it," said his master.

"Pardon, Sir?"

"The flask," said Percy Buckle, thereby causing one red spot to appear on each of his cheeks.

Constable watched Maggs. He saw how fiercely he looked into Percy Buckle's eyes, and how his master twitched and jerked in the gaze of his servant's attention. But then, to his great relief, he saw Jack Maggs take the coachman's silver flask from his back pocket and put it into his master's hand.

18

A footman caught drinking in the street might consider himself fortunate to keep his job, but to Jack Maggs, who was not a footman, the confiscation of the coachman's flask brought—*Jod's blood*—a most ungrateful passion rushing along the capillaries of his face.

When he returned to the house he was still out of sorts, and it took everything in him to accept the polishing rags and beeswax which Mrs Halfstairs now presented to him. She put him in a dark little cubby at the back of the house. And there, with no view of the street at all, he was compelled to polish the bindings of Mr Buckle's books. *Frig me for a blind man.* He had not come to London for this indignity. *Damn me for a horse.* He had come to meet with Henry Phipps. That gentleman might be arriving this very minute and he would not know.

At supper time he took the chair with the best view of the street, and never once took his eye off it. He drank his pint before the grace was said. He repulsed Mrs Halfstairs's questions about the mysteries of Mr Oates's experiments, bolted his shepherd's pie, refused his bread and butter pudding, and—without being dismissed or excused his labour— went up the gloomy staircase leaving the silent servants sitting, rather fearfully, in his wake.

Once in his room, he drove the bolt home in the lock and changed from the doeskins and white stockings into the darker, sturdier garments he had arrived in.

He had had little sleep the previous night and his heavy-lidded eyes were now sunken and red-rimmed, and his hair was speckled with London smuts, but he had no mind for his powder puff. He opened the tight little window, pushed his body out, and stared down into the street. Once or twice he sighed, and once it seemed that he might climb out the window, but he remained in this tight, uncomfortable pose for over an hour, listening to the carriages and voices in the street.

Then, suddenly, he heaved his bulky body out through the window.

He had one hand on the sill and began to edge his great leg out in the direction of Henry Phipps's house, and there he was—splayed out like a spider—when he heard, above the noise of carriage wheels on the street below, a sound more alarming and more intimate: "Hsst."

Under the moonless sky he moved, sloth-like, back in the direction from which he had come.

"Hssst."

He got his hand back on his window sill. Then he allowed himself to turn and look back along the roof line. He was not sure what he could see, but there was an uncertain dark shape at the third dormer window of Mr Buckle's house.

"Constable?"

There was no answer, but he watched in horror as a shadow poured from the window, sliding, then crawling across the slates towards him.

He saw the hair, the skirt, the maid.

"Go back, for God's sake."

For answer she gave a startled cry, and slipped. He leaned out towards her but the stupid biddy skittered towards the guttering, her skirt ballooning out like a spill of ink, her pale hands flapping fish-like against the tiles.

Jack Maggs did not save her, but something did, for here she was, alive and crawling up towards him.

"Get to the blazes," he hissed. "Go back."

"Cor," she said. "Those tiles is slippery as a Christmas pig."

He took hold of her sleeve for she was still being most careless of her safety. She hooked her hand into his belt. "What you up to?" she inquired. "What's a footman doing crawling round the roof at night?"

"None of your damned business, Judy."

"My name is Mercy, Mr Maggs, as you very well know." She brought her face close to his. He had suspected her drunk but now he discovered that her breath was sweet with sugared tea.

"Get back inside."

"I may," said she, "or I may not."

"If you don't want nothing bad to happen, Judy, you'll go, and quick and lively and forget you ever saw me here."

She considered this threat. "Then may I please go in through your window?"

"No."

"It is an awful way back into my own. I'm afraid I'll fall."

"Christ!"

"You're not very polite, are you."

"I'll give you polite." He helped her through into his room, and then climbed in himself and locked the door behind her. And then, with his heart pounding uncomfortably in his ears, he returned to the roof. A minute later he entered Henry Phipps's house through its unlatched dormer window.

Once inside he calmed considerably. He went carefully down the stairs, gathering blankets from the bedrooms as he went. In the gloomy drawing room he dropped the blankets on a settle and then emptied the contents of his jacket onto a pale yellow walnut bureau—a sheaf of paper, twine, a bone-handled clasp knife, a fat creamy tallow candle, a long yellow quill, a little apothecary's vial which would later reveal itself to be filled with a queer kind of ink. Lastly from his trouser pocket he removed a small silver-framed enamel portrait. He was about to place this on the desk but then changed his mind and returned the miniature to his pocket.

He next dragged the desk across the room so it stood beneath the windows. He removed his shoes. He picked up a blanket, then stood on the desk top. With the advantage of this height he was able to hang the blankets across the curtains. He used the knife to cut the twine, the twine to tie the blankets to the rods. He worked swiftly but neatly, and when he was finished there was—for all the makeshift quality of the arrangement—a workmanlike symmetry to it.

He came down from the desk, restored it to its previous position, then lit the candle, which first sputtered, then gathered strength as it revealed the sparkling nests of gilt everywhere adorning the handsome room: chairs, mirrors, picture frames, even on ceiling mouldings far above his head.

Here he settled himself, a massive man in the centre of a jewel box, carefully arranging his quill and his paper. He picked up the blue apothecary's bottle, and was about to remove its ground glass stopper when he heard a footstep on the upper stairs.

He snuffed the candle, standing quietly in the smoky dark, his heart beating very slow. He knew it was the man he sought. He knew without seeing him, without being told of his return, and when the footsteps came down into the hall he coughed first to give a decent warning.

"It's me," he said. "Jack Maggs."

"I know it's you," said Mercy. "Who else would it be?"

19

Mercy Larkin's father had been a mechanic at the Woodwell pickle factory in Wapping, and had provided for his family handsomely. Mercy's mother had done a little of the lace work in the summers, and Mercy had for a while attended Mrs McFarlane's School where—if you put aside the blots and smudges—she did not disgrace herself as a scholar.

But one balmy night in May when Mercy—aged thirteen—was sitting on her front step cutting the patches of rot from the taters, she saw a strange procession of men walking down the steep and narrow street.

There was a crowd of them on either side of a dray which was drawn by a pair of skittish chestnut mares. The men were whoaing and shouting for fear, it seemed, that the beasts would slip and fall. At first she thought the men actors in a theatre troupe but when they stopped silently before her she looked into the back of the dray and saw her pale-faced father lying on a bed of straw, with his bloody bandaged arm across his pale blue smock. It were no one's fault, the men said, for Horace had been clowning and had fallen backwards into the main drive. It was only a broken bone, but it flopped like an empty sock when the foreman himself lifted Horace Larkin and carried him inside to his bed. It was only a broken bone, yet what woe it brought, all so quickly: gangrene and death, penury and eviction, and on a hot May day in 1829 there were no crowds of men, only one workmate to help move the widow and her daughter from their little cottage in Finsbury. Their departure was early so no one would be awake to see their shame. They walked up the cobbled street on foot, then rode a dog cart to a damp and crumbling slum at the back of Fetter Lane. There Mercy and her mother attempted to set up a little business as the bakers and street vendors of plum duff.

This occupation proved taxing, and only erratically rewarding: more than once her mother came home with signs of damage on her clothes or person. Marjorie Larkin had always been quiet, but then, her husband had been noisy. He had taken up all the space and so her quietness was a relief, or at least could pass unnoticed. Now, in widowhood, her quietness seemed darker, deeper, more alarming, and when she cut her black hair so queerly short, she had nothing but silence to answer the questions of her weeping daughter. She sawed at the hair with the same knife they used to cut the plum duff into ha'penny slices.

During the day, Mercy was imprisoned in their steamy little room with the foul smells of the fried-fish sellers drifting up in the hot air of the court below. Her mother would not say where she went or what she did or how much money she had. Her eyes seemed to sink back into her head and no one would guess that she was a young woman and had once been beautiful.

Then she began to take the duff out at night, loading her little cane basket and covering it with a cloth. Then she locked Mercy in the room with chains and a great black padlock. She was sometimes gone only a short time, but at other times she would be gone so long that Mercy began to fear her mother dead, and that she herself would die before anyone would find her.

They were dreary nights and days spent locked away above the gin-soaked little court. Mercy was not by nature a passive girl and she would never forget that hellish summer when she passed the hours pacing up and down the dreary room, praying to God to prevent her nibbling at the precious supply of duff-flour, to stop her dipping her wetted finger one more time.

Then one Sunday, without explanation, her mother began to work upon a pretty dress for her, sewing blue ribbon on its bodice, and adding layers of crêpe de chine which she hung from the waist. It was not a usual kind of dress but no one could deny that it was very gay, and although the girl was alarmed by its want of fashion, she was most encouraged by the fact that it was not black. Despite the fact she did not ask, she clearly understood that the mourning was now over.

No plum duff was cooked upon this long day, and the room was cooler and dryer on account of it. Finally mother and daughter set out, just as the bells began to ring for evensong. Neither of them had eaten all day long, but Mercy, although a little light-headed, was far too excited to think of food.

They walked down into Fleet Street, the mother in severe black, the daughter like a bird of paradise. They paraded, their heads high, amongst the quality along the Strand, and from thence on into Haymarket, at which jolly scene they arrived just on nine o'clock. There was a grandfatherly old fellow with a dented stove-pipe hat who had set himself up a coffee stall, and it was here, with the charcoal smoke blowing in their eyes, and the appetizing odours of coffee and chicory in their nostrils, that the two women finally paused.

The young girl's dress certainly drew attention, and there was nothing in the eyes of those who looked at her to suggest that it was—as she had been most certain—out of the fashion. It was the hottest part of summer and the crowds were heavy everywhere.

They had not been standing on their pitch more than a minute when a tall gentleman with a red set of whiskers doffed his hat to her mama, and talked to her with such solemn familiarity that Mercy supposed him to be an old employer of her father's. When, minutes later, her mother pushed her towards the man, and said, "Go with him," she went willingly.

That was when the storm started, not in the still, humid street that was their destination, but in Mercy's mind; years later, the confusion of her memory still blew dust and soot across that street and curled up into the evening sky.

She had set off in innocent expectation of being bought an ice, or tea; and indeed her stomach gave a most unladylike growl when they passed Reilly's Chop House. Instead, she and her companion went to the back of a casino, and stopped beside a door from behind which there emanated a great clattering of crockery, and the smell of onions cooking in butter.

The gentleman had barely spoken to her, and when he took her arm, she still thought him shy. He then called her "Lettie" or "Lassie." His diction was not clear, and it occurred to her later that he had been the worse for drink. He helped her into the doorway, and she took the door knob, expecting it to open. When she found it locked, she did not have time to turn before she felt the stranger's arms around her waist, and then he was squashed against her back with all his great weight, holding her clamped, talking to her all the while he lifted the back of her dress.

She felt the air upon her skin. She did not know what to do.

What happened then happened, and like a broken plate was soon all pieces, most of them missing in the dark—the pain, the onions cooking in the butter, the smell of pipe tobacco on his whiskers, the wetness on her legs.

When he put some money in her hand, the coins dropped and rolled out into the lane and he—red-faced now—stopped and chased them, and brought them back to her, and doffed his hat.

"Thank you, Miss." He looked as if he might cry.

"Thank you, Sir," she said.

He hesitated, then turned back towards the coffee stand. She stepped down from the doorway and walked away from him. She sought out the dark corners of the lane, places where the wetness she could feel would not show up in the light.

She walked back through those boisterous crowds. Men sometimes spoke to her. She did not know how long she walked, or where she went. A tall severe woman, eyes glaring beneath her hat, handed her a small square of white paper: REPENT FOR THE KINGDOM OF HEAVEN IS AT HAND. She was still holding the paper when she found, at last, the coffee stand. Her mother, upon seeing her, slapped her daughter across the face, then immediately began to weep.

When the little fried-fish seller introduced himself, the mother stopped her tears and turned all her powerful upset on the stranger. She called him "coarse" and "vulgar." She said he had a "low understanding" of their situation.

"You don't recognize me, Ma'am?" said Percy Buckle, who had emerged from the confusion of Haymarket with the smell of fried fish heavy about his person. He was not "vulgar" as Marjorie Larkin said, but had, in fact, "a betterly appearance" with his brown surtout jauntily buttoned up to his black satin smock. He had his tray of fish slung by a leather strap about his slender neck.

"You scram. You skedaddle," cried Marjorie Larkin, so loudly that a small crowd began to gather round them, and the owner of the coffee stall began to shout at them to move away.

"I am your neighbour, Ma'am," said the earnest little man. "And I am this girl's neighbour too, and with your permission I am going to take her to her home."

But the mother did not understand his offer, imagined in fact that he was making the very offer that she had already solicited, and now the poor wretch turned—her eyes so dark and haunted—to the owner of the coffee stall, and asked him please to chase the fish seller away.

The coffee-stall holder, a large coarse man with a big voice, then began to shout. He called Marjorie Larkin a hoo-oor and other things, and splashed the slops from a cup across the cobbles at her.

"I am your neighbour," the fried-fish man said quietly to the young girl.

"You are the Devil," cried Marjorie Larkin.

Percy Buckle ignored the jeering crowd and repeated: "I am your neighbour."

Only when he opened his fishy little purse and put a silver florin in her hand, did Mercy's mother deign to notice him, and then she followed him, as he indicated she should—he did not touch her in any way—out of the Haymarket and back down along the Strand.

The sad little party made its way back into the unnamed court at the back of Fetter Lane where, the Larkins soon discovered, it was their benefactor who was responsible for the bad fish smell which daily filled their little room, his accommodation being just one floor below theirs.

That night the earnest little man cooked them a fish and potato soup, and then, having made them promise not to leave their room until they saw him again, he returned with freshly fried fish for their breakfast.

And that was the start of Mercy's long friendship with Percy Buckle who, even when he had ten fried-fish men working for him, always had time to sit and read the girl a bed-time story.

He was, as Mercy often said, the kindest, most decent man in all the world, and she would—as she later told Jack Maggs—as soon cut off her own arm as lose his kind opinion.

20

I know it's you," said Mercy, emerging from the dark of the stair, her glistening eyes holding the pin-point reflection of his candle. "Who else would it be?"

Jack Maggs was thus exposed at his secret work: he had a dark blue apothecary's bottle in his hand, a tartan blanket wrapped around his broad shoulders.

"Christ, Judy, you have a taste for trouble."

A half-wit would have known it wise to pretend no curiosity, but here she was making obvious note of all the clues to the mystery before her: the quill, the paper, the blankets he had tied up so neatly across the curtain rails.

He had begun to hide the bottle in his jacket pocket, but what was the point?

"Ain't you afraid of me?"

She raised her eyebrows mockingly. "Oh, I know you would not harm me."

He snorted. "You is just a little mite, Judy. Your ma should be reading you fairy tales in bed."

"My ma is a mad woman."

It would be a lie to say the answer did not shock Jack Maggs but he continued speaking as if he had not heard her.

"Now," he said, "why don't I give you one more shy at the coconut? Why don't you go back to your bed, and mum's the word."

"If you are such a fiercesome villain," said she, "how come you saved Eddie?"

"I don't know no Eddie."

"Mr Constable, the footman. Him you had sworn to murder in his bed."

He sat wearily on one of the gilded chairs which were arranged in a ring in the centre of the splendid room. He rubbed his face, smearing smuts amongst his stubble.

"I am an old dog," he said, "who has been treated bad, and has learned all sort of tricks he wishes he never had to know. You are a young woman with all her life ahead of her, Judy."

"Mercy," she insisted.

"Mercy then."

Said she, "I am an old dog too."

"Mercy, I am too old a cove for you to fancy . . ."

She put her hand over her mouth but could not stop her laughter. "*Fancy?* Lor, oh dear, Mr Maggs . . ."

He folded his arms angrily across his chest but said nothing.

"What are you planning?" she asked him.

"What am I planning?"

"Aye, what are you planning in Mr Phipps's house?"

"What I am planning . . ." He walked to the desk and began to shuffle through his pile of papers. "What I am planning, little Miss Muffet, is to find my letters of recommendation which was left in this household."

"But you don't have no letters. Eddie swears you don't."

"Is that so?"

"He had to learn you how to fix your hair."

Jack Maggs began to answer her, but—*Christ*—she held up her hand to quieten him. "Shush. Listen."

Now he, too, heard—a carriage. His first and only thought was Henry Phipps. He limped to the windows and peeked cautiously between the deep folds of blankets.

"It's only Buckle," he said, "come home from his Correspondence Society."

"Oh Lor." Mercy leaped to her feet. "Dear Jesus—home so early."

"He cannot need you now, at this hour."

"No, no, I have to go. Oh dear God save me."

And she turned and ran off up the stairs.

Maggs followed, but at a more leisurely pace. By the time he arrived at the dormer window, she was already outside, slipping and sliding her way across the mossy tiles in her stockinged feet. He did not doubt her ma had been a mad woman.

21

In the early morning, by the light of four bright candles, Jack Maggs finally dipped the great albatross quill into the apothecary's bottle.

He wrote, *Dear Henry Phipps*, in violet-coloured ink.

He did not write these words from left to right, but thus:

Dear Henry Phipps

He wrote fluidly, as if long accustomed to that distrustful art.

He paused, staring up at the gilded ceiling while the ink faded to a pale, pale lilac. Then he continued:

> I did arrive on the date of which I had advised you and found you absent from these premises.

He watched these fresh lines fade, first to lilac, then to white; until, that is, they became invisible.

He continued:

> I had hopes you might return tonight, perhaps having mistook my hastily written 23 for a 28, but I have waited these long hours on the settle, and now at your very handsome walnut desk in vain.
>
> It is a most melancholy business to be solitary in the place in which I did invest such High Hopes, but I do trust my disappointment will be brief. I have a messenger who will soon fetch you. If you now read this letter it can only be because you have met up with him, the Thief-taker, and he has told you how to make these words visible. I hope he has remembered to tell you that you must BURN EVERY-THING when it is read. Many of the events I tell you are from a long time ago, but I fear they may still be used against me by my Enemies.
>
> The Thief-taker has given you the mirror. If it be any cheap mirror, know that this is not the same as I gave him, for I am a wealthy man, and it was my pleasure to send the best mirror that can be obtained in London. If you are acquainted with the hallmarks of the

great silversmiths, you will read a distinguished story on the mirror's handle.

Well, Henry Phipps, you will read a different type of story in the glass, by which I mean—mine own.

You will forgive me for being too much the bull at the gate in my previous correspondence. It was written in a great rush in a Dover Inn, soon after landing. I dare say that my words were not as well chosen as they might have been and that I revealed things that made you fear a Criminal coming to harm you.

Henry Phipps, you were raised to have a tender heart and to obey the laws. This was always so clear in your loving letters, and it is no stretch to imagine that you were frightened to hear Jack Maggs was finally on his way into your polite and educated life.

I had many years to prepare you, and I did not. But what is done is done and you now give me no choice but to put my life before you all at once, to make you privy to information that could, in the wrong hands, have me dancing the Newgate Jig.

You have known for many years that my name is Jack Maggs, although Maggs was not my father's name, but a name given to me by my foster mother who believed I talked too much. What my father's name was I cannot tell, for when I was just three days old I was discovered lying in the mud flats 'neath London Bridge.

I was picked up by Mudlarks. I do not recall this, but have so oft been told of my Good Fortune that for many years I saw them in my dreams: wraiths pulled up from the stinking mud of the Thames. These half-starved scroungers found the strength to fight for my shawl and bonnet with such a passion that it was always said by Silas Smith—my Benefactor—that it was a wonder I was not torn in two like the child divided thus by Solomon.

Now pay attention to this Silas Smith, for he will come into the History later. It was he, that lanky thief with the long face and claret nose—a parson's son—who paid the Mudlarks a ha'penny each for my naked body and then another ha'penny to carry me to a place where I might have the stinking mud washed off me.

He asked the moochers, did they know the whereabouts of a midwife, but they were slow of wit, and begged his pardon for never having heard of such a thing. Silas then asked them who it was attended

when the babies were to be born. But the Mudlarks never lived inside a house and never saw a baby born and could not think how to
get the money until the oldest of them thought that Mary Britten
might answer the description.

—Then take me to her, Silas said.

He followed the shivering little river rats up Pepper Alley Stairs.
He walked through that stinking rubbish strewn street—no longer
there, so I have been told. He ducked under a rotting trellis, came
into a court strung high and low with drying washing, its gutters
spilling over with soap suds. He was always one to play the left-
handed fiddle, but he could never have imagined that he would finally prosper from this adventure.

As the party came into the court, the baby was crying and the
Mudlarks were growing most reluctant to proceed. The one holding
me nodded his sharp little head down a passage-way that opened in
the furthest wall of the court, but Silas would not give the ha'penny
until his guides had walked before him through the shadowed portal.

He held the ha'penny. The Mudlark still held the child. There was
but one doorway at the end of the dark passageway and Silas knocked
with his cane until the door was opened by a big-boned woman with
wild red hair. Her shoulders were bare and her skin glowed white in
the gloom.

—Madam, said Silas Smith.

Mary Britten did not even note the shining red nose. She told me,
often enough, that her only observations were of me, and she did not
want me. She heard the weak cry of a starving babe, the stink of cold
& unwashed skin. She began to threaten with the bricks she had for
the purposes of discouraging the rats.

—You take your rubbish somewhere else, she said. Take it to the
foundlings hospital, she said, imagining Silas Smith a clergyman.

But then Silas did what was, for him, a most peculiar thing—he
opened up his sovereign case.

Was it his heart he opened thus? I cannot say for sure, only that
he was a thief, and receiver, what we called a "Family Man" and normally very cagey with his money.

—I'll not see you disadvantaged, he told Mary Britten.

He gave her his calling card. Mary Britten curtsied to him and
placed her brick bat on the floor.

Said she—I'm sorry, Sir, for how I spoke, but that is what becomes of us down here in Hell's Doorway. Sitting here, said she, looking at the Devil's thieving ways etc. etc.

Silas threw the boys a ha'penny and removed his tall black hat.

Mary opened wide her door, and invited me and Silas into her life.

I grew up being told these stories, and I never liked them even as a child. I heard a hundred times how I was starved and thin and wrinkled like a rag etcetera, how she washed me, wrapped me in a piece of clean grey blanket and persuaded me to take a little barley water.

And meat, always talk about meat. Mary Britten could not tell a story without a little meat in it.

—It's meat he'll be needing, she said. It's the lack of meat that makes them slow. In that we have been blessed, she said, for my boy Tom Britten is a finder down at Smithfield. There is always meat in my house, she said, and always has been.

—Now lookee here, said Silas Smith, you are a poor woman, but you will soon be richer for your kindness.

And then, bless him, he gave her the sovereign. He, who had more schemes than knaves in a Magsman's deck, gave away a sovereign to a poor woman.

As for Mary, this was the first sovereign she had ever touched in all her life.

—It's the meat he'll be needing, she said. Neck, scrag end, belly—that's what's missing.

And here the first entry ends.

22

At a quarter before the hour of eight the following morning, there was a boy knocking on the door at Great Queen Street with a long letter in Oates's hand wherein he apologized for the early hour, but begged Percy Buckle to be sponsor to an event which will "satisfy your humane and inquisitive nature."

Percy Buckle, as was his eccentric habit, was waited on at breakfast only by the maid, and thus, his footmen being absent, he had to ring for

Jack Maggs in order that he might read aloud to him the letter requesting his attendance at a Magnetic Experiment.

Jack Maggs listened only fitfully, for he was more concerned with Mercy Larkin, and the mischief he imagined in those sleepy eyes.

"He wants us now," cried Percy Buckle, pushing away his buttered toast.

"I cannot go now, Sir."

"Yes you can, Sir," winked Mr Buckle. "I would not miss this for the world."

"You're coming with me, Sir?"

Mr Buckle stood, slurping down his tea. "Wild horses couldn't stop me." Mercy Larkin made a hand signal Jack Maggs did not understand.

"Your kippers are done, Sir," he said.

But there was no time for kippers. No time for horses either. Down the hallway Buckle marched, his confused footman hard behind him. On the front step, the master paused to issue, sotto voce, the following instructions.

"Now Maggs, I'm sure you've been a footman longer'n I've been a master, but seeing as how your legs are so long and mine, well, call a spade a spade—I'm duck-legged—then I'd ask you to watch your step and stay back a little as we walk, not come down upon my heels. If ruffians call out, and they do, they do, you turn a deaf'n to them and don't feel you have to stand up for my honour. Doubtless it is some mistake yet in my wardrobe, and that will be attended to directly. But for now, old fellow, it is off we go. Three paces behind, if you could be good enough to manage it."

Thus Percy Buckle, a passionate Chartist in his private life, emerged as a high Tory on Holborn. He marched east along that great thoroughfare in a top hat and waterproof travelling cloak that reached almost to the pavement and which he had, from time to time, to raise above the mud. His footman followed him three paces behind, coiffed, powdered, gloved, in bright yellow livery and smart doeskin breeches.

Who can say exactly what it was that made passers-by smile to see them?—the slight roll to the fart-catcher's walk, the anxious perambulation of the little master, the hundred little clues, perceived by the brain but not so easily named, to the counterfeit they were so earnestly enacting.

At Lamb's Conduit Street, Percy Buckle's inquiring knocks were answered by the master of the house. They felt the enthusiasm of his approach before they saw him and then Tobias Oates was standing before them—flash as a sharper in a bright green waistcoat.

"Splendid! Capital!" the writer said, reaching out his bony little hands to prod Jack Maggs—a finger point against each shoulder. "Come in, come in. We have a splendid fire, carefully guarded."

Thus Jack entered Tobias Oates's home a second time. He was guided into the front room which had, indeed, a crackling fire, and was now set up as for a lecture, with its bowl of apples gone, its large red chaise pushed back against the wall, a straight-backed chair upholstered in green velvet set up in the middle and some four or five assorted dining chairs arranged like pawns in the defence of a beleaguered king.

It was in this upholstered chair that Jack was left while Buckle and Oates whispered together in the hall. He was most apprehensive and was not calmed when he heard female voices in the hallway. He inhabited the chair as if it were a place of execution.

Then Mr Buckle entered, followed by tricky little Oates and two young women.

The first of the women was Mrs Oates, who was plump and plain with a slightly injured cast to her features, or perhaps she was merely tired by the babe she now carried at her breast. The other was a fresher daisy altogether, not merely in that she was a good five years younger, but that her manner was less put-upon. Neither were great beauties, but this younger one—Maggs heard her called Lizzie—had a hungry little mouth and big inquisitive eyes.

While Mrs Oates hovered indecisively by the doorway, this girl sat straight away in the chair closest to the footman.

Are all of them to spy on me?

Oates did not start the Magnetism immediately but fussed with the firescreen instead, touching it in that peculiar way he had earlier touched Jack's shoulders. So busy was he with this operation that he left the other three not much else to do except stare at the victim in the chair.

Maggs stood this well enough at first, but as the staring went on and on it became pretty near intolerable. He had no wish to be impertinent but what was his choice?

"So, Sir," he called to Tobias Oates, "it is my good fortune, Sir, to have an audience. Have I become a fellow in a penny gaff?"

"Mark my words, Jack Maggs," said Oates, still staring at the fire-screen, "there never was a penny gaff of such importance." He then spun suddenly, and all eyes in the room turned to him. "Look at what we have today."

Tobias Oates tossed two shining discs of metal in the air and caught them behind his back.

"What's that?" said Jack, now thoroughly alarmed. "We never spoke of that."

"Conjuring," exclaimed Percy Buckle. "Very good, Sir."

"Magnets," said Oates, holding out his open palms so that Mr Buckle could examine the discs. "We'll drag the demons out of Master Maggs with these."

"In front of everyone?" said Jack Maggs. "You never said it were to be in public, Sir."

"Old chap," said Oates, widening his eyes to look at him. "Do not do this to me now."

Maggs was chilled to perceive the hard eyes behind those pretty lashes.

"You will get your introduction to the Thief-taker . . ."

"I need to talk to him, Sir."

"Yes, we will talk to him. As we agreed. Thirteen days from now. It seems to me, Mr Maggs, that this bargain is all in your favour."

"It was never to be in public."

"This is not *public*. This is my wife, her sister Miss Warriner, my little son, who is the soul of discretion I assure you. Now, shall we proceed? Or shall we abandon the bargain? You tell me, but tell me now, for all time."

"We shall proceed."

"Good man."

Oates pulled over a small piano stool and, having spun it until he had the height right, sat himself close against his subject. Then he began to pass the magnets around the other's worried brow.

"With these little magnets we shall cure you. Look." He showed how he had secured a magnet between each finger. "Look carefully."

He began to make slow passes in front of that hard resistant face.

Maggs for his part felt himself a monkey in a sailor's cage. He looked at the young lady who quickly averted her eyes.

"Keep your eye on me, Sir."

He watched the slow pass of the hands. He watched the glint of silver caught between the fingers.

He had made himself immune to the magnets, or so he thought. When Oates asked him, "How is the pain today?" he imagined himself quite normally awake.

23

Toby had always had a great affection for Characters, reflected Lizzie Warriner: dustmen, jugglers, costers, pick-pockets. He thought nothing of engaging the most gruesome types in Shepherd Market and writing down their histories in his chap book. The subject of this Mesmeric Exhibition did not know it, but he was likely to appear, much modified, in Toby's next novel. There he would be Jack Muck, or Jock Crestfallen—a footman with a coster's voice and a chest like a strong man in a circus.

Since Lizzie had experienced a very unhappy morning so far, she sat herself down with the expectation of forgetting all those fearful apprehensions that had so bedevilled her recent days.

Mary Oates was also present at the Exhibition, although it was obvious to her sister that she would really rather not be there. Poor Mary came in order to please her husband, then succeeded only in providing further evidence that they were tragically ill-suited. She had grown up, as Lizzie had, in a house of books, but unlike her sister she had never pretended any interest in their contents. Mary would rather sew than read, and it had been embarrassingly revealed, on more than one occasion, that she had never grasped the point of *Captain Crumley.*

Now, with this grizzling baby on her hip, it was clear just how little patience she had for either science or literature. She called the Exhibition "an entertainment," asked blunt questions about the noise that would be made, and how soon the business might be over. If she had any intimation of her husband's genius, she was careless of revealing that genius was a quality she did not value highly.

While her older sister gave all her attention to the baby on her lap, Lizzie shyly observed the subject of the demonstration. He leaned backwards in his chair and patted his hands upon his stockinged legs. He looked for all the world, she thought, like a Cockney King settling down to watch a dance.

Then his gaze settled on her and she glimpsed his dark and hostile spirit. She turned her head away, only to see her dear fine Toby step forward to engage the fellow.

"Watch me, man," said Toby.

As he held up his hands, Lizzie felt a chill of fear grip her womb; they seemed very delicate instruments with which to master such a beast.

Yet the footman must have recognized some greater power, for as he considered the writer's hands, a strange criss-crossed frown erupted on his brow. He jerked his head sharply away, across the room, then stared fiercely at Mary and her baby.

"Keep your eye on me, Sir," said Toby.

But the footman now rested his frightening eyes on Lizzie Warriner, who shuddered.

Then Toby spoke again: "Jack Maggs, I command you."

The fellow subjected his reluctant attention to the other's gaze. Once he closed his eyes, but soon after he opened them again, and before too many moments had passed, the footman's head began first to nod, and then to loll. As that alien body finally surrendered, Lizzie Warriner felt an unexpected stirring of her own blood.

"Can you see our Phantom, Mr Maggs?"

The answer was very clearly spoken. "He stays mostly behind me."

He raised his head. His eyes were open. If Lizzie had not known the footman was mesmerized, she would have judged him to be fully awake.

"We are going to chase him away. What do you think frightens him?"

"I don't think my Phantom is frightened, Sir."

Toby now put his hand into his jacket and produced a shortish horse-whip which he had had, all that time, concealed upon his person. He dangled it in the air, so its end waved inches above the Somnambulist's head. This was very good, Lizzie thought, very good indeed. Toby was a fine actor. He had played Sir Spencer Spence at the Lyceum, and loved to amuse his friends and family with skits based upon that pompous old sawbones. Indeed, he had a great talent for all kinds of dialects and voices, tricks, conjuring, disappearing cards, pantomime performances.

Now, as he raised the whip, Lizzie patted Mary's arm consolingly, for Mary was, as usual, fearful, squeezing tight her eyes, clutching her poor babe tightly to her.

"Do you imagine our Phantom might fear the double-cat?"

"No, Sir."

For reply, Tobias swung the whip. It brushed the ceiling, and slapped against the settee. He brought it back again and down, producing a loud thwacking noise. A brass candle-stick leaped off the mantel and rolled across the floor towards the window.

The babe woke, bawling. Mary stood up, holding her hand protectively around the soft little skull. Now, too, the footman was rising. He pulled himself up slowly from his chair as if constrained by invisible chains. His face contorted pitifully.

"Oh no, not flog him!" he cried. "You mustn't do that, Sir."

"Toby, dear . . . ," Mary whispered timidly.

"Remain seated, Sir," said Toby. He waved at his wife, making pushing motions with his hands towards the door.

When the creaking door was finally closed behind the bawling babe, Toby silently indicated, for the benefit of the others, the footman's physical distress. He pointed at his restless limbs, his twisted mouth.

"Yes, perhaps we should flog the Phantom?" he said loudly.

"Oh God no, please . . ."

"Do you think he would like that?"

"No. Let me wake up."

Toby mouthed to his audience: *Watch.* Then, adopting a jolly, kindly tone, he spoke again to his subject: "Why are you so agitated, Jack? No one will harm you. It is your enemy we are to deal with today. He who is causing you pain. Can you see the place where we are going to deal with him?"

"I am used to the pain, Sir. It is an old friend."

"I asked you another question. Did you not hear it?"

Jack Maggs began to beat his fists upon his chest. He was truly like a wild animal, and Toby his expert trainer.

"Can you see the place where we are going to deal with him?"

"Leave him alone, I beg you."

"You are attached to your torturer, Mr Maggs. Can you see the place?"

This last question was accented by one more crack of the whip.

"Yes, yes," said Maggs, visibly cowed. "I can see it."

Mr Buckle stood, his arm raised as if to protest.

"Please, everyone be calm," said Toby. "Master Maggs, we must see where it is he is going to be taken."

"Please, Sir, I can't bear to watch a flogging."

"What would you watch instead?"

"The sea, the river."

Toby now approached his subject very close. He brought his hands up to the fellow's mouth and it seemed as if he were about to draw the poor man's demon from him, dragging it back in his splayed fingers. "Now you are going to tell me. What is the river like? Do you know birds, Jack? Can you see birds?"

"Oh yes, Sir, hatfuls of birds."

"Pelicans, no doubt."

"Pelicans, Sir. Oh yes."

"You can give me a pelican? Good old Jack."

"I can, Sir. By golly there's a handsome fellow."

"Paint him for me, Jack. Give me a picture."

"Oh he's a big one."

"Do me a sketch."

"It has a great chest, and a great scoop of a beak. It comes in like a man-o'-war. It is a beautiful thing, Sir, the pelican."

"Any other birds?"

"Is the Phantom to be whipped, Sir?"

"Tell me about the birds. Are there parrots?"

"I can't look for parrots. How can I look for parrots when you have that damn triangle set up like that?"

"Tell me about the parrots, man."

"I'll not watch it, God damn you. I'll not watch it. You can't make me. You don't know what you're dealing with."

"Is the pain still there?"

"Yes, yes, damn your eyes, the pain is always there. God damn it."

"You will be calm, Jack, and keep a decent tongue in your mouth. There are ladies present."

"Then damn you for bringing them to so damned a spot."

"Old Sir, do please rest your mind. No one will be flogged today."

"No flogging?"

"None."

"Oh God, Sir. Thank you, Sir. I could not have borne it."

"Don't cry, old chap, it is too beautiful a day. Can't you feel the lovely sun on your face?"

"That sun could kill you, take my word."

"Indeed, Jack, it is fearsome hot."

"Blistering, Sir."

Percy Buckle leaned forward and patted Lizzie Warriner on the elbow. He pointed over Jack's shoulder, out the window where cold rain had begun falling once again.

"I'm so thirsty, Sir."

"Remove your jacket if you wish, your shirt."

"But the ladies . . ."

"The ladies are gone."

Lizzie, confronted by a man about to undress, found herself most seriously discomfited. She stood. But her brother-in-law fiercely shook his head, and she sat down again, her eyes averted.

"I can't take my shirt off."

"You must."

"Captain Logan won't allow it."

"There are no regulations here," said Tobias.

Jack Maggs shed his jacket, then his silk ruff and shirt, then the coarse wool singlet, and stood before them, naked to the waist.

Lizzie Warriner sat in her seat, her eyes lowered.

"Turn," said Tobias.

The footman turned. As Lizzie Warriner raised her eyes, she gasped at the sea of pain etched upon the footman's back, a brooding sea of scars, of ripped and tortured skin.

"You will stand," said Tobias. "You will stand perfectly still. You will not go anywhere. Do you understand?"

"I am too hot."

"Here it is shady," said Oates. "You are comfortable."

And then he quickly escorted Lizzie Warriner and Mr Buckle from the room.

24

Tobias Oates locked the door to the front parlour. Then he looked from Miss Warriner to Mr Buckle, his mouth twisted in a peculiar smile.

"I got the rascal."

"Dear Brother, what are we to do?"

Tobias Oates waved Miss Warriner and Mr Buckle towards the staircase with little motions, like an old woman driving chickens into a coop. He ushered them upstairs and into a small cabin which, Percy Buckle realized, must be the sanctum sanctorum. The little grocer was consequently unable to refrain from touching the desk, from running his curious hand over the smoothly varnished surface of a pigeon hole. Here, he reflected, the prodigy wrote his novels. Here was the birth-place of Captain Crumley and Mrs Morefallen.

"Mr Buckle, you could have been murdered in your bed."

Mr Buckle took his hand away from the desk at once. Tobias turned his attention to his sister-in-law.

"Did you not wonder at my intuition, Lizzie? I guessed he was a bolter from New South Wales."

Miss Warriner took him by the sleeve of his jacket. "Dear Brother, what will he do to us when he finds himself exposed? He is a singularly large man, Tobias, and I do not doubt he will be very angry."

"He is mesmerized," the young man said impatiently. "I doubt he will remember anything."

The young woman drew her shawl tightly around herself.

"It was when he described the pelicans, Lizzie, I knew the theorem was proved. Do you see what I have now? Do you see what I have been given?"

"I see, Toby, that you have brought a very dangerous man into your family's presence."

"He will not wake up until I release him, Lizzie. Don't you see what I now possess? A memory I can enter, and leave. Leave, and then return to. My goodness, my gracious. What a treasure house, eh, Buckle? You can hear the cant in his talk. He has it cloaked in livery but he wears the hallmarks of New South Wales."

"You cannot keep him here," cried Lizzie. "He is not some nasty hand you can store in a bottle."

"I will visit him in prison."

"With respect, young Sir," said Percy Buckle.

"Yes, Mr Buckle?"

"I am very aware, Sir, that it is a privilege for me to be . . ."

"Now, Mr Buckle, come, come."

"I don't mean to embarrass you, Sir, and I am grateful to have been called to witness such an unusual experiment."

"Mr Buckle . . ."

"But in my opinion, Sir, and it seems that I differ from you here . . ."

"Please continue."

"We do ourselves no credit in judging him."

Oates snorted. "Did you not see his *back*, man? He is a scoundrel."

"Well, we saw a page of his history," said the little grocer stubbornly. "Whatever his offence, anyone with half a heart can see that he has paid the bill. I could not send him back for more."

"I'm sure you don't wish to return with him to *your* household?"

Mr Buckle became silent.

"To be robbed? Or murdered in your bed?"

Percy Buckle brought his mild eyes up to meet those of the young host's.

"He has not hurt me yet."

"Mr Buckle," said Tobias Oates, laying his hand upon the other's bony little shoulder. "I fancy that a grocer, who is every day concerned with serving honest citizens, does not see the things a journalist sees."

"With respect, Sir, I think you forget something of my history."

"I forget nothing," said Tobias proudly. "I can name the flowers growing beside the path on my fifth birthday."

"I was one of those poor beggars you see selling fried fish in Seven Dials. I was witness to things there, Sir. You and I might trade cruelty for cruelty, but we would know it best not to frighten Miss Warriner with that which we would rather forget ourselves."

"No one forgets. It is all in there, Buckle. This Australian of ours holds his life in his cerebrum. He carries pelicans and parrots, fish and phantoms, things the Royal Botanist would give a sov or two to hold. When he mentioned the double-cat . . ."

"God love me, Sir. The name itself."

"When he mentioned the double-cat on our previous encounter, that was the clue to his secret. It is a punishment invented in New South Wales."

"Did you never imagine yourself in his position? I *felt* that damned thing. Forgive me Miss Warriner, but damned is the right word for it."

"Buckle, dear Buckle. It is my business to imagine everything."

Percy Buckle's mouth had become small, his cheeks pale and sunken. He stared hard at Tobias Oates before he answered.

"Is it, Sir? I suppose it is. As for me, I had an older sister who suffered transportation to that same cursed place. I had the honour of standing in Newgate and seeing the Judge pronounce the words. I held my mother, Sir, when the poor old lady fell away. Excuse me crying, Sir. My sister was not an angel either. Lord knows what became of her."

"Surely you heard eventually."

"How could I have heard?" said Percy Buckle tersely. "She had no letters. How could I have heard? Put yourself in her place—how could she get word to those who loved her? She was a plucky thing, our Jenny. She thought me such a sad item with my fried fish, but I never did forget that day, God help us all, that Mother England would do such a thing to one of her own."

"I think you a fine man, Mr Buckle. A Christian."

"I do hate to keep disagreeing with you," said Percy Buckle, looking down at the floor, and speaking in such a low voice it was difficult for his listeners to make him out, "but I am not a believer."

"But surely you would not wish this fellow back inside your household."

"I do not see I have a choice."

"But what of your safety? The safety of your other servants?"

"I would like a better choice, and that's a fact, but I can't rightly see any. Shouldn't we, Sir, not stand here talking when he is left there by himself all alone and who knows what terrors he is going through, imagining himself still alone in that dreadful place?"

Tobias Oates smiled. "You are a brave man, to take a lion into your home."

"Not brave. Ask anyone. I am as timid as a dormouse. I wish I were brave, for it would make this business easier."

Tobias Oates measured his distance from the wall. He ran his hand through his hair. He produced a tortoise-shell comb and rapidly combed himself. "Then I will maintain my interest in the case," he declared. "I will not give him up."

Percy Buckle cocked his head. "You were about to give him up to the Law."

"Ah yes, but seeing that you insist we keep him—"

"That *I* keep him," corrected Percy Buckle.

"But Toby," Lizzie said, "we cannot let him go free."

Tobias ignored her. "At night, Mr Buckle, I walk the city. I walk down past your old shop in Clerkenwell, down into Limehouse, back up through your dreadful Seven Dials. Wally Duke's. The Hopping Toad. The Sheaf of Barley. I have them all here inside my cranium. But what you have brought me here is a world as rich as London itself. What a puzzle of life exists in the dark little lane-ways of this wretch's soul, what stolen gold lies hidden in the vaults beneath his filthy streets."

"I don't follow you, Sir?"

"It's the Criminal Mind," said Tobias Oates, "awaiting its first cartographer."

25

Each night, behind the double curtains, Jack Maggs impatiently roamed Henry Phipps's rooms, inquiring deftly into drawers and dressers, running his large square-fingered hands over damask and lace. Here he slept fitfully on the settle, alert to every noise that might signal the return of the man he had come to meet. Here in these rooms he continued the letter which he intended the Thief-taker to present to the house's absent tenant.

Each morning, by dawn, he was back in Mr Buckle's house, and as the clock at St George's rang for Morning Prayer, he would wearily present himself at Tobias Oates's front door. On being admitted by the taciturn house-keeper, he would carry a cup of tea up to Mr Oates's study where he would, at eight fifteen precisely, be mesmerized.

By *mesmerized* he understood that he was made the subject of magnets, and that these magnets in some way tugged at his Mesmeric Fluid, a substance in his soul he could not see. He understood that, under the effect of magnets, he was able to describe the demons that swam in this fluid, and that Tobias Oates would not only battle with these beings—

named Behemoth and Dabareiel, Azazel and Samsaweel—but also, like a botanist, describe them in a journal where their host might later see them.

At first the convict had been astonished to read Dabareiel's flowery speech—he could not believe that such an educated being might exist within him—but he accepted it soon enough, and with all the various explanations Oates constructed, it never once occurred to Jack Maggs that these "transcriptions" had been fabricated by the writer to hide the true nature of his exploration.

There were, as in all crooked businesses, two sets of books, and had Jack Maggs seen the second set he might have recognized scenes (or fragments) more familiar to him: a corner of a house by London Bridge, a trampled body in a penal colony. But even here the scenes were never very clear. For the writer was stumbling through the dark of the convict's past, groping in the shadows, describing what was often a mirror held up to his own turbulent and fearful soul.

This second set of notes was entered in a red leather volume, Tobias's daily work book. This journal contained many notes for novels, essays, and rough drafts of sketches for the *Morning Chronicle*, but from the twenty-first of April, 1837, six days after Jack Maggs's arrival in London, it was almost exclusively devoted to his hidden history.

During lunch at The Sergeant's Inn on April the twenty-third, Henry Hawthorne found the writer pale but very lively and voluble. He polished his knife and fork with his napkin and drank three glasses of claret before his soup was done. He asked nothing about Hawthorne's *Lear*, which had opened to hostile reviews the night before. He blithely likened himself to Thackeray. He said he was like an archaeologist inside an ancient tomb. He invited Henry Hawthorne to secretly observe one session, and witness him pushing into the musty corridors of the Criminal Mind.

Alarmed by his young friend's mania, Hawthorne did indeed visit on the next day, and was astonished to see the seated footman, in full livery, cry out and curse so murderously. Perhaps it was the role of Lear that made him think so, but Hawthorne was convinced that he would find the footman gone mad on wakening. Indeed, Hawthorne did not leave the house when he said farewell, but hid in the nursery with a brass poker in his hand. Here he waited until the criminal had been escorted from the house, only then revealing himself to his astonished friend.

26

On the night of Tuesday the twenty-fifth of April, having started awake from a troubled sleep, Jack Maggs took himself once more to the walnut desk in Henry Phipps's drawing room, dipped his quill into the apothecary's bottle, and penned the following:

Look, Henry, whether you like the sight or no, read these words and imagine what it was to have, not your life, surrounded by a ring of golden chairs, but mine.

Come, please, and meet *my* great Benefactor—Silas Smith. This is what passes for a Kind Man in my history. He has a long red nose, and an old-fashioned turned-up collar, and he comes into the gloomy court where I am playing at some boyish game of bones.

—Now Jack, says he, you and I are going to do your lessons.

And there is Mary Britten (whom I called a mother) and her big red-boned son—Tom with his long jaw and his lonely little eyes. He had such big hands, did Tom, but never held a pen. When Silas Smith came knocking on the door to take me to my lessons, it was me he came for, not Tom.

Tom felt this very keen. He sat on the floor in the corner with his cheek resting on his bony knees, and sulked. As for me, I would have given up all lessons if I could have had Mary Britten love me, and call me Son.

Mary was young and handsome then. She had had her Tom when still a girl and could not have been more than twenty-three when she first took me in. She was a very dervish of a woman, always scrubbing and cleaning, and angry too, never at peace, never able to sit down and have a moment free of agitation, but if I could have chosen, she is the one I would have wished to claim me as her own. She was a force of nature, the Ma—her long arms, her wild hair, her skin always smelling of snakeroot and tansy. She could fill a space. She could stand her ground. She was the Queen of England in that little white-

washed room, delivering our neighbours' babies, serving soups, examining the bones and offal on the rickety pine table.

If she was gruff and fierce with me, if she would clip my chil-
blained ears as soon as look at me, she also did her duty by me in
those early years. She grew me up.

When I was four years old I would walk beside her great skirts,
across London Bridge and up to Smithfield—an hour's walk, never
once was carried—to where nine-year-old Tom was working as a
"finder," which is a polite way of saying that he were a thief. He
worked the filthy slippery floors amongst the sawdust darting like a
rat, a cat, and here a breast bone, there an end of chop fat, there a
kick up the keyhole for his trouble. It was not till he had been scoured
in the cold bath that we saw which was his blood and which blood was
that of beasts.

She had such a belief in the virtues of meat, the Ma. Had you seen
her on market days, coming home from Smithfield with her lads pale
and close around her great grey skirts, you might not have guessed
how we regarded that bounty on her back. It was our future she saw
in those stolen scraps. It was lack of meat she believed made all of
those children in Pepper Alley so slow and listless. She liked to point
them out to us as if they were strangers to our eyes—Billy Hagen,
Scrapper Jones, sitting there by the lime-green musty wall playing
with the bones. They never knew the name of the country that they
lived in, never knew anything but the names of the Hagens and the
Smiths.

Yet I do fancy that Tom, himself, was a little slow of wit. But that,
as she would say, is not the question of discussion.

Each market night, Ma Britten carried the bag of bones back to
our little home. This was not as simple as it sounds, for all the poor
streets we passed through were somebody's territory. On our side of
the bridge it were the Hagens and the Smiths. They and their friends
and allies were in a state of war. It was a dangerous matter to be
unaffiliated.

But Mary Britten was her own person. She carried a great military
sword, disguised from official eyes with old newspaper and hat ribbon, and more than once she drew it. One summer's evening on London Bridge itself, she cut a slice down a young man's arm so you could
see the shining blue white of bone from his elbow to his wrist.

She liked me "be-in' useful" and I therefore urgently made myself a useful little chap, as if my life depended on it. At five I was a scavenger for the coal which was often washed up on the river bank. Sometimes I lost this coal in fights, but if I could bring it home to her, she would pick me up and hug me, and I did so like the feel of her strong arms, that grassy herby smell which hung about her, I would have done anything to get it.

At five years old I could scrub a floor as good as any char. By six I could wash and sort the bones and offal, placing them upon the table in the manner she liked—a gruesome sight to your gentle eyes I'm sure—but it was nothing for me to arrange the innards in the way she found them most useful, and I fancy I had the knowledge of a slaughterman when it came to identifying the otherworldly shapes and colours of the organs of dead beasts.

Some she selected for soup, some were sold, and others she mixed with tansy, savin, snakeroot, to make her "Belly-ache" sausages which she hung from the ceiling and for which women paid her a tanner. At that age I had no knowledge of the great upset they caused inside their wombs.

I was, as I said, in no way her favourite, and yet I was the younger, and it was me she took with her when she went down to Kent for the hop-picking in the summer. Tom got left behind, he cried to be so abandoned, but she would not bend no matter how he pleaded. Tom felt his feelings very deep, and when we returned at the end of August he ran around the kitchen roaring and breaking her windows with a broom.

It was after this last adventure that Silas first came to fetch me for my lessons. It was to mark a new stage in his association with our household which had, until now, been most irregular.

He arrived with a suit of clothes, and he and the Ma watched closely while I dressed in them. These clothes were so filthy, they stuck to me like they were made from treacle and smelt so foul you would think I had been rolling in the river mud.

—Very good, said Silas, just the trick.

The Ma was a demon for being clean, and I never thought she would allow me to dress like that. But she nodded her head, and turned back to her stove. As she lifted the lid, the snout of a pig rose slowly to the edge of the battered old black pot.

Said she—You bring him back.

Said Silas—Don't you fret. We ain't travelling far.

But as I found out, this was not so, for we began by going onto London Bridge.

When we were standing in the middle of that mighty thorough-fare, Silas turns to me and says—Now lookee here whipper-snapper, you cannot walk aside me. I must use the footpath and you must run along the street. You must follow me, see, and not be run over. And do not lose me because we shall be going at a fair old clip. If the runners stop you, you are to say you are on an errand for Mr Parkes, the chimney sweep.

Said I—I don't know no Mr Parkes.

Said he—Oh yes you do. And he gave my ear a twist to help me understand him. Said he—Mr Charley Parkes of Ludgate Street who has called for you to help him on a particular job in Kensington.

I asked was that place far away?

—Not so far, said he. You'll follow me and when you see me walk into a stables, you'll walk down the alleyway beside and wait outside the door and in a moment, why, then your Uncle Silas will come and let you in.

I asked him what would happen then.

—Then you'll begin your lessons.

Thus all the time I followed him along the busy streets, dodging the hooves of horses and the wheels of mighty drays, I was imagining I was about to go to school.

Silas had told me about school before. He was an educated man, and once walked beside the sea with Mr Coleridge, or so he claimed. In any case, he could recite whole scenes from Shakespeare, and often did, sitting in our room at Pepper Alley Stairs.

It was by now September but the weather was still warm, and the sky blue. The rush of vehicles along the bridge was fearsome. Four-horse coaches, great omnibuses from which elegant cads cried "Kensington! Chelsea! Bank! Bank! Bank!" I trotted amongst the starved old horses of the hackney cabs, trying all the time to keep my eyes on Silas, who strode along amongst the quality, taking me further and further from the London that I knew.

I thought I was tasting what my future would be, and I was most pleased with what I saw about me.

The footpaths were filled with men and women in fine clothes. The houses were often very grand indeed. I saw footmen in plush breeches and neat white stockings riding on coaches, and men in grand livery waiting outside great doors with brass knockers on them, and I puzzled at why Silas should have put me in such filthy clothes, and rehearsed me in this cock and bull story about the chimney sweep.

Yet I was, as I recall, most light of heart and happy to follow. It was only when we came into the Mall that I, feeling myself very small, nearly lost my nerve. Such a fine wide space ahead and, at the very end, gates that might have been the ones that Peter guarded, so brightly did they seem to shine, even at that distance.

Yet even as I approached Buckingham Palace, no one inquired as to my purpose. They saw a Climbing Boy and understood, better than I did, what my business was meant to be.

I walked beside the King's south wall. No one stopped me. I ran my hand along the bricks and as I did so my mind flooded with dazzling pictures of the school that Silas had selected for me. I wondered whether there would be a place to sleep or if I would have to take this journey every day.

It was dusk as we neared our final destination, walking along a street of very grand white houses, then down a lane filled with shining black coaches and carriages, and men busy with harnesses and reins. Here was the stable yard of which Silas had spoken, and now walked boldly into, stepping daintily in his shining shoes while I, dressed in my rags, followed down the mews until I found a small odd-smelling alleyway. There I found a door with many silver horseshoes nailed onto its bright black surface.

In a moment this strange door opened and I passed inside.

I waited to see where my desk would be, for Silas had often described to me the school at Westminster Abbey where he had learned his Latin, but there was no desk here, rather a tall gloomy room with the strong smell of leather and linseed oil, and many different sets of harness hanging on the walls.

There was a ladder on the wall which led up to a kind of loft. Up this ladder Silas went, nimble as a spider in the dark.

I followed, and soon found him at a window looking out at the night. He had taken off his coat, and when he saw me beside him, he climbed out onto the roof of the house next door.

He held out his arms to me. Said he—Go very careful, and keep your head down.

It was only then, as I followed him across the roof tops, that I understood I was not to go to school. Yet when he presented me, fair square, with a chimney, I did not fully understand my situation.

Silas carefully lifted off a chimney pot and placed it on the roof. Said he—All right, young whipper-snapper, down you go.

Said I—What for?

—What for? He brought up his eyebrows in a show of great surprise. What for? She didn't tell you?

—If you mean Ma, said I, the answer is no, she did not.

—How forgetful of her, said he, but it is no matter, it is a simple enough errand. Slip down this here chimney and unlock the back door of the house. That's all there is to it.

I asked what would happen then.

Said he—I will come into the house.

I said that I would likely fall and break my bones.

—Nonsense, said Silas. Get in.

I said I was too frightened to.

—Nothing to be frightened of, said Silas, grimacing as he picked me up. You'll find it easy enough. It's like walking down the stairs.

And so saying, he picked me up, and slid me in, as simple as dropping shot into a cannon.

27

I soon had reason to doubt that Silas had ever seen the inside of a chimney. First it was tight as a pipe, and the walls were caked with soot so many inches deep that I was held by soot, swaddled by soot, and had I not got given a great push on the crown of my head, I would not have fit at all. But push I got, and there I was jammed in like a cork in a grog bottle, some foot below the top, coughing and wailing and choking myself with fear.

Then there came another great push on my shoulder—a boot most likely—and I was edged down further still, and there the cork was stuck fast in darkness. I was very afraid, and imagined I would die.

When death did not come, I kicked with my boots, and squirmed my shoulders and, in trying to climb back up towards the sky, slid even further into the pit.

I have no idea how far down the chimney I was stuck, but in any case I was caught there a long time.

Then a great sheet of soot gave way, a thick lump of it, and I shrieked out in fright as I fell. The chimney was widening. In my alarm, I scratched at the walls, thus bringing down more filth into my panicked lungs. I coughed. I choked. I might have fallen to the grate below had I not, like a babe, jerked out my arms and legs and thus gained purchase on those protuberances which Silas had doubtless referred to when he said the inside was like a staircase.

By this stage I must have been about half way through my descent, and while surprised to be still alive, I was also very frightened, for it was dark in there, and I was forever coughing and choking on the falling soot, sure that the chimney must soon become too wide for me to hold on to in just this way.

I looked up towards the sky, but could make out nothing but the faint colour of the night. I had thought to see Silas looking over me, but although I called out his name I never had a reply except the constant dropping of soot.

I began to cry. I fancy that I cried a good long time, and that Silas must have already become most impatient waiting for me to appear at the back door, and even when I did begin to move again it was with great timidity, and I might have been a good hour in my descent had I not slipped and fallen.

I landed in the hearth with the wind knocked out of me, and I lay there on the cold hard grate gasping like a mullet brought up onto the dock.

When I had my breath back, I found, to my great surprise, that I was not dead. My legs hurt a little, and there was a large bump on my head, but nothing to stop me stepping out of the high fireplace and peering around the room I had so abruptly entered. My eyes were used to darkness by now and thus I could see better than you might think.

And what a place it was I had arrived at.

It was the smells that first of all impressed themselves, the smell of apples and oranges, and what may have been cinnamon, but in any case something sweet and strange. There were no smells of drains either, and it was this I'm sure that made the other smells the sweeter and gave me a feeling of almighty comfort.

It was a long double room with great glass doors which, I soon discovered, could be shut across the middle to make it into two separate rooms, but for now the doors were open, and the resulting space was bigger than Mary Britten's quarters. In that damp, low-ceilinged little place, we shared one bed and two chairs between the three of us. Here there was enough upholstered seating to accommodate half the population of our little court. All around the room there were armchairs, sofas, chaises, love-seats—none of which I could have named for you, never having seen such things before. In my enchantment, I sat on each of them, each one, and it is only now, all these years later, that I reflect on the sooty mess I must have left behind.

But the door—I had Silas waiting for me at the door.

It is easy enough to say, open the back door, but he had not told me where the back door was. He did not know himself, of course, not from the inside—it was half a flight down from the kitchen, which was itself down a long and narrow staircase off another hallway.

Finally I found my way there in the dark, guided by Silas's nervous whistle. But even having found the door, my work was not done. I was six years old, no locksmith, and I was at the chains and catches some five minutes with no other instruction than Silas's curses on the other side of the door until the last chain fell away. Then the door swung in, and the knob knocked me in the middle of my forehead, and I was momentarily made insensible.

I woke to discover Silas slapping me around the head and pulling my ears, asking did I want him sent to America? I said I did not, and that I had done as well as I could, and that I had nearly died inside the chimney. Such was my upset that he soon was quite civil, even giving me a handkerchief to dry my tears. Then he lighted a little dip he had carried in his pocket, and told me to follow him and I would learn something which I would thank him for.

By now he had several workmates with him and they, having rushed in while I was insensible, were busy elsewhere in the house. Silas took me down beside the kitchen to a grand room which he said was the butler's and there he held his dip in the air and whistled.

In the spluttering light I saw first his enormous grin, and then the reason for it: three grand dressers as massive as galleons all bursting with silver plate, like so many moons—tureens, salvers, candlesticks, great trays as big as shields—all glittering behind their locked glass doors.

—There, said Silas, speaking very gently. There you are my little darling.

I thought he spoke in this affectionate tone to me, and it was a moment before I saw that it was the silver he was addressing.

Said he—There you are my fine cold little beauty.

He approached that plate like a man coming up towards an altar.

—It is Uncle Silas, come to take you dancing up the City Road.

He kept on talking, ever so gently, as from his sleeve he withdrew a long steel jemmy which he must have had up his sleeve all the way along the Mall.

—My lovely little bitch, said he. And set upon the dresser in a most brutal fashion, jemmying and levering and cursing between his crooked teeth, until the first dresser gave up its secrets with a terrible screech as the brass hasp separated from the oak.

—Hold the dip, said he, hold it high.

The dip was a little thing, just a bit of wick dipped into tallow, and it burnt my finger and splashed hot wax down my arm. I held it gingerly as Silas swung the door of the dresser open.

Above my head in another room, I heard glass breaking.

—Hold it here, over here.

I held the dip closer as he took out a great silver salver.

When I turned to look at him, he made me gasp. He had fitted a monocle on his left eye, and now it grew and swam before me like a fish.

He saw my face, and chortled.

Said Silas—Now lookee here, you coal-faced rascal, and I will show you a set of hallmarks that you will remember when you are an old man with children of your own. *Selvit Arbus est*, said he, *Servus et Cuccina erbe wit*, or words to that effect.

Of course I came close to see so wonderful a thing but Silas already had the plate wrapped up in a rag, and was adding to the contents of the sack which I had carried all the way from London Bridge.

This sack now turned out to contain nothing more valuable than soot, but amidst this acrid substance he now carefully packed those pieces of silver which took his fancy. Many a fine-looking piece of plate he lay aside, and more than once picked up an object—a plain-looking little cruet, say—that I, with my child's eye, would have imagined of no value.

Thus, most slow and careful, he filled the sack, and when he had washed his long white arms and spent one last moment inquiring of the contents of the dresser drawers, he lifted the entire load onto my bony shoulders and had me follow him out into the summer's night.

Thus we returned the way that we had come, with me staggering along the roadway amongst the shit and carriage wheels, and Silas striding with the quality on the footpath of the Mall.

The sack sawed at the flesh on my shoulder, and at times the pain was so v. bad I had no choice but stop and shift my load, though I dared not tarry for fear of losing sight of Silas.

Of course the old dodger must have kept a nervous eye upon his precious goods but he gave nary a sign of that to me, and once we were in the West End I had the dickins of a time making out his green coat bobbing and ducking through the crowds. And although I now say "the West End," at the time I had no idea of where on earth I was, and I imagined myself at risk of being forever lost to Mary Britten and Poor Tom, who now seemed to me the dearest people in the world.

The journey was all the worse for me not knowing where it might end. Even when we finally reached a cat-infested lane-way beside a net-maker's—it must have been in Wapping—and Silas took the heavy sack away from me, I could not be sure that I was permanently excused my burden.

I followed him up a rickety wooden staircase, although I would rather not have—it was attached to the crumbling brickwork as pre-cariously as a beanstalk tied onto a cane. At the top, Silas stooped and carefully unlocked some heavy chains, and there we entered a small, low-ceilinged room which my nose told me had, not so long before, been used for drying fish.

This, it soon turned out, was where my patron did rest his head, and I was most surprised to find it a more humble place than my own.

He laid the sooty sack inside the doorway, and when he had lit one more of his stubby little candles, I saw a movement amidst a pile of rags in the far corner. At first I imagined rats, but then saw a thin white arm, and then a pair of large dark eyes, as the creature—it was a little girl, about my own age—gazed sleepily up at us.

—Papa.

She extended her arm from her dark nest, and Silas, answering to this most unlikely title, knelt beside her and stroked her head. I was—I can still remember—most astonished by the tenderness exhibited by the man who had made me carry this cruel weight; now he was fussing amongst the tangle of bedding and dragging out a rag doll with long dark hair just like the little girl's.

The girl, however, was looking not at the doll, but at me.

—Is that Jack?

Silas admitted that it was.

—Poor Jack.

She held out her hand to me, and I, having looked to Silas for his approval, offered my own sooty paw. Thus she returned to sleep, still holding my hand with a determined grip.

Silas left me there, holding the girl's hand, and took his candle over to another corner where I heard him lifting floor boards.

—Come here, young 'un.

I freed myself from the little hand, and went to where Silas was kneeling over the floor cavity, his stooped form silhouetted in the light of the sputtering candle. What I expected, as I crossed towards him, was to be shown some treasure he had hoarded away, and I was not mistaken. It was a small black volume with words stamped on it in silver letters, and when Silas gave it to me it was with such reverence that I imagined it must be the Shakespeare he so often liked to quote. But when I asked if it was poetry, he laughed and said it was, after a sense, and that I should memorize a line or two and it would improve my prospects no end. And then, saying he would be back in a minute, he left me alone, and as I heard his light, slippery feet descend the wooden staircase, I tried to take my mind off the fact that I was left in a very strange place, and turned my attention to the book.

I soon deduced that it was not poetry, but a peculiar collection of odd signs, with handwritten annotations attached to almost every one. Thus:

There were many pages of this type of thing, row after row of little punched shapes: squares, escutcheons, trefoils, bifoils, and inside these shapes were lions and chalices and crowns and the likeness of a man I took to be a King. I gazed long at these mysteries, trying to establish what they might mean, and when I heard Silas's foot upon the stair, I imagined myself on the brink of being admitted to an important fellowship.

Yet when Silas returned, he seemed to have lost all interest in my education. Indeed, rather than explain the marks to me, he took the book from me and returned it to its place in the floor. Whatever it was he had gone to fetch, he did not tell me, although I could smell fried fish and see a bulge in his jacket where he had a little parcel hidden.

If he intended to share his fish, it was not with me. Instead he produced a handsome little silver spoon from his pocket and said I was to give it to my mother. —Tell her I am coming tomorrow so she can cook my sausage in her pan.

I was too afraid to ask him to tell me the way home, and so I set out, running along the dark rough streets, trying as best I could to follow the route that had brought us here. Walking along the crooked lanes, trying to keep the evil-smelling river to my right, I was often lost and always frightened. Once I was chased by a drunken man who promised to cut off my ear and eat it, but I was also befriended by a man I took to be a sailor who walked me all the way to London Bridge and gave me a penny to go home with.

And how pleased I was to be home. Mary Britten, who was, for all her excitements and passions, normally a distant sort of mother, came rushing up and hugged me to her, soot and all. When I produced the penny and the silver spoon, her green eyes lit up and she took me by the hand and led me to the table, and placed a great bowl of soup beside me, while Tom sat on the bed whittling a wooden fish hook with his clasp knife.

—He stinks, he said.

Ma Britten turned that spoon over in her hands.

—He's been *use-ful*, said she, and to my nose it's a *use-ful* sort of smell.

I ate the soup hungrily. She had dished me a good-sized bowl and put the ladle deeper into the pot than was usually her wont, so the broth was thick with meat and barley, a fact not lost on Tom when he came to the table to watch me eat.

—He looks like a nigger.

—Aye, black as a nigger but carrying the King's silver.

She had the silver teaspoon sitting on the table, and she turned it over and over with her finger in a way that made me think of a cat playing with old knucklebones.

—Did he show you his book? asked she.

She peered down at the spoon with her handsome head cocked to one side.

I said he had.

—Did he learn you the marks?

—No, Ma'am.

—He will learn you the marks. She turned the spoon through another ninety degrees. Said she—You will be able to read a tea pot better than a vicar reads a Bible. And you will do very nicely on account of it.

It was then Tom leaned over to take the spoon, but as he got his hand to it, Mary saw him. She tried to snatch it back with the result that the precious object was knocked flying across the room and landed with a clatter beside the bed.

Ma Britten rose screeching to her feet.

—He did not mean it, I cried. Tom was already cowering with his raw hands around his ears.

Mary said he did not have to mean it, and kicked him in the backside. He did it, said she, and that's as good as meaning.

By now she had the poor fellow by his ear and was dragging him towards the bed—Where is it? Where is it?

—It's there, it's there.

Mary Britten saw the spoon and picked it up. She began to polish it upon her apron.

—Why can't I learn the marks too? Tom cried. I want to do nicely. I should do nicely. I'm not the mud rat. I'm the son.

His long pale face was now an unusual shade of red and I realized with a shock that he was crying. I think it surprised his mother too, for she softened in a way I rarely saw her do, and she clasped the bawling boy to her breast and stroked his hair.

—You are the man, said she. You are the man that gets the meat.

This stopped the tears and I soon found Tom staring at me from the comfort of his mother's stomach.

—I hate him, said he.

I looked at his eyes and somehow understood not only that he was jealous, which was a surprise to me, but that he was also frightened. When his mother tried to disentangle herself from his grasp he did not want her to let go.

—I'll kill him, said Tom. I'll drown him.

Mary Britten did not attempt to contradict her son's passion. She was now standing on tip-toe on a chair, hiding the stolen teaspoon up above a rafter.

—He does hate you, she said to me. It is true, and natural enough in its way, just as it is natural that you be feared of him, but I must tell you both, you are each lost without the other.

Then she turned to Tom and said—You may kill him, but you may as well cut off your arm, for it is this sooty fellow who is going to take you out of this pit. It was what he was raised to be. It was what you carried home his meat for.

It is only now I write this down for you, I allow myself to feel what I must have known all those many years ago. At the time I felt a buzz or hurt, but I was tired, and full of soup, and once I saw I was not to be murdered, I wanted nothing more than sleep.

It is only now I feel the fury in my furnace: that the bitch would make this speech before a little nipper, letting him know that he had been raised for a base purpose like a hog or a hen.

28

The clock at St Giles had long ago struck midnight, and still Jack Maggs remained at his desk, his heavy lids lowered so his eyes might better see the little whitewashed room in Pepper Alley Stairs as it had been so long ago. So deep was he in this reverie that when he heard the footsteps above his head, he imagined them—for the merest moment—to belong to Ma Britten.

But when he heard the fast patter on the last landing, he knew that it was the mad woman's daughter once again.

He frowned and laid the quill down.

It had been four days since her first passage across the slippery roof, and by now he was familiar with her habit of staring at him when she thought him unaware of her. He had thought her pretty on first sighting, but now he was concerned only with the dangerous consequences of her spying. She was a chatterbox, a gossip. She and Miss Molly Constable were for ever whispering and raising eyebrows at each other.

Now she entered his drawing room, as urgently as any heroine onto a stage. She wore no shoes, no cap. Her dark curls spilled down her shoulders.

"Mr Maggs," she said, "your secret is known."

This gave him a fearful jolt, though he did not show it. He dipped his quill once more in the ink and began another sentence. His visitor, in no way discouraged by his coldness, came to stand beside his shoulder, and he quickly realized that she was trying to read what he had written. He caught her at it, but like a cat snaffling scraps from off the table, her appetite was greater than her shame. She read until the last lines of the letter faded from lilac to white.

"Very clever," she said.

Jack Maggs then spoke in that quiet voice he used when most severely agitated. "I'm pleased it meets with your approval, Madam."

"But if it is intended to hide a secret, it is no longer worth such trouble."

"Someone has been talking to Mr Phipps. Where did they see him?"

"Now whoever made you imagine such a thing?" She spoke in cadences more suitable for addressing a small child. "Whatever did I say to make you think of Mr Phipps? What I said was, *your secret is known.*"

What the girl meant, Jack Maggs did not know, but he stood and tidied his papers. He rolled his letter up and tucked it inside his coat. In short, he prepared himself for flight.

"You are a plucky girl," he said severely. "And you are a pretty one, as well you know, and I dare say the young drakes is very forgiving when you tease them, but I am past these games, comprenay voo? It is bad manners for you to come talking to your footman like this."

"Bad manners!" she exclaimed angrily. "I took a great risk to bring you this news."

"Then give it."

"My master, Mr Oates, his wife, they know your secret."

"That I am here in this house?"

"Not that."

He reached for her arm and she, misunderstanding him, gave him her hand. This he held with a pressure so firm as to be almost cruel.

"You heard them say that my soul is full of ghosts and goblins?"

"Yes."

He snorted and released her. "They are my guests in their curiosity for six more days."

"They say," she murmured, pulling her shawl around herself, "that you are a convict from New South Wales."

"Damned if they did!"

"They say you told them so."

"When?"

"I did hear it this very hour, although when *he* heard it I cannot say."

"Him?"

"The master. He reads to me. He would be reading to me now but I said I was ill and must go back to my bed. I'm for it if he finds me gone."

Jack Maggs fetched his boots which he had left standing by the hearth. They were not the dead man's shoes, but his own comfortable hessians, which had been made by an old hunch-backed cobbler in Paramatta.

"Are you going to bolt?"

She was a nosy little mite. He tied the green-hide laces tight and double-knotted them. Then he turned so he might privately slip his dagger into its nesting place beside his right ankle.

"Don't bolt," she said. "You are safer here with us."

Jack Maggs took the little creature by her wagging chin. He held her hard, his thumb and forefinger clamping her around her jaw bone. "They sent you here to delay me while they fetched the peelers."

Now she saw what sort of man he was. He had her in his clamp, and her eyes were urgent in their plea.

"Think clearly, Sir. Why would I delay you when I knew you would delay yourself, when I knew you would sit up here all night dreaming in this very chair?"

He let her go, but not happily. He stoppered his ink bottle and dropped it in his pocket. He picked up the quill then threw it down. He was in no way certain about how he should proceed.

"Mr Buckle had a sister," she said, "who he loved most dearly. This sister was transported to Botany Bay."

On hearing this, the quality of his attention changed. She seemed to see this. "He wept to see your injuries. And he wept again when he told me. He could not read me another word of his *Ivanhoe*. He was so upset by what you had suffered."

Jack Maggs then sat down behind his desk. Mercy Larkin sat simultaneously, in a gilt chair whose seat was embroidered with a hunting scene.

"We wept together," she said.

"Did you, girlie?"

"Your secret is safe," she insisted.

"Being known only," he said bitterly, "to the master and the household staff?"

"I am not the household staff. They call me a maid, but that is not my true position in the household. I have known Mr Buckle since I was a child. He has read to me for ever so long a time."

"You are shivering."

"It isn't right that you frighten me."

"I ain't going to hurt you." He offered her a blanket—the grey one under which he sometimes slept. "But you must tell me the truth. What is it that the gentlemen have said about me?"

"Mr Oates used the Magnetism," she said. "He has little magnets the size of pennies."

"That much I know."

"The magnets are attached to your soul. They are like a poultice . . ."

"This I know."

"And with the magnets he dragged your soul to the other side of the world and persuaded you that it was summer and so you took off your shirt in the presence of a lady and cried out to see a fellow who was to be flogged. You described a foreign bird. You were often angry and cursed God. You gave yourself away and now they know you are a convict escaped from New South Wales."

"The bastard."

"You are wrong. He is as decent a master as you could ever find."

"Not him, the other. The smarmy bastard hid this from me."

"They dared not tell you," cried Mercy. "They thought they would be murdered in their beds. Mr Oates has a wife and a child, and now it

seems that if you have escaped they also have broke the law for arbor-
ing you."

"Harbouring."

"Yes. It is a very dark secret. Mr Buckle himself could be sent to
Newgate."

He did not know what he should do with her. She seemed aware of
this, for when she spoke again she leaned out and touched his sleeve.

"You can depend your life on us," she said. "We are your friends."

He was sick at heart but he let her go without damage or threat. He
escorted her up the stairs, and locked the dormer window closed behind her.

29

Outside the house, there was a great wind storm. In the dim drawing room of Jack Maggs's dream, a man in uniform was sitting in
the shadows.

Is it you?

It is I, answered the Phantom.

Maggs rolled himself tight inside his tartan rug while his dreaming
eyes attempted to make out the fellow's regiment. The Phantom, as if
sensing his intention, lit a gas lamp which flared so brightly that the
sleeper brought up his hand to cover his eyes.

It was a uniform made to protect the King himself. The jacket was
ultramarine, the trousers black, and underneath his arm he held a bell-
topped shako.

I am in the 15th Hussies, said the Phantom.

Hussars, said Jack.

Hussies, insisted the Phantom, opening a great-coat to reveal a naked
female form, a soft bush of hair and such sweet little breasts with soft
rosy nipples.

Very funny, said Jack, smiling in his sleep. He knew it was a dream.
He knew the breasts would not be there if he reached for them, but
might remain if he were still. He was very warm and comfortable. The
bright light of the gas warmed his cheek.

That gas is a bleeding marvel.

No gas here, said the Phantom.

Jack looked to the lamp. It was still burning bright. Behind it were trays of fishes, their scales gleaming in the artificial glare.

I thought it was gas.

No gas here.

It then became very dark. Something was brushed lightly over Jack's face. He could smell the leather. He knew what it was: a horse's bridle.

You like to ride, Jack?

The bridle crossed his face again.

Yes, Sir.

I'm heading up towards Mount Irwin. You can use a theodolite, I think?

Is that Captain Logan?

In his dream, Jack Maggs saw himself still smiling. When he stepped forward to look at the Phantom's face, he saw he was the spitting image of Captain Logan.

I thought you was dead.

Not me, said the Phantom, who no longer looked like Logan. His hair was fair. He was much younger. But the uniform was the 57th Foot Regiment and the bridle was not a bridle.

We're going to do a spot of mapping, Sir?

But Jack felt the cold empty terror in his gut. There would be no mapping. This was not a bridle.

One hundred lashes, cried Captain Logan, and lay them on until I see the bone.

Maggs was standing, then he was falling. He could not bear to be seen in such a state. He walked past Parker's Hut. Ahead, at the archway of the prisoners' barracks where the cursed triangle stood, Rudder, the flogger, was standing at attention.

Weeping, Jack Maggs turned to the Phantom, and begged him to show mercy. Then the Phantom turned away, leading his horse by its bridle along a path, and Jack picked up a great round rock and brought it down upon the Phantom's head. The Phantom fell and the dreaming man lifted the rock high and flung it down onto the head so it split like rotten fruit. This action he repeated a good long while.

In London, the wind shook the windows in their frames.

30

Percy Buckle did truly wish he had a better choice than to give shelter to the convict. This is not to say that his resolve to harbour Jack Maggs weakened, but that it was a resolve bought at the cost of the peace which had finally come to him with his inheritance.

Now Mr Buckle could no longer sleep and, sadly, it had become normal that, one hour after midnight, he should still be needful of the company of her whom he called My Good Companion.

Mercy, still wearing her maid's apron but not her bonnet, sat herself at her master's feet. He was distracted, fretful, forever putting down one volume to pick up another. Tonight it had been *Ivanhoe* first, then that long piece of Hazlitt's, the one about the young lady which brought him such discredit at the time, and then—for the Hazlitt made Mercy most impatient—the French novel by Madame Valli which was called, by its English publisher, *Imogene*.

It was at that point, when he had finally arrived at the French novel and thereby gained his Good Companion's rapt attention, that he imagined he heard the footsteps on the stair.

"Hark," he cried, and leapt up, his hand at his ear.

"'Twas nothing," said Mercy. "Read on."

"It's him," he said, and laid aside the book.

"Lord," cried Mercy, "do you fancy he roams the house all night plotting ways to murder us? If that is so then he must be very feeble-witted because he has had a whole week and neither of us has suffered so much as a scratch."

"Shush, there he goes."

"This is even worse than Hasluck."

"Hazlitt!" said Percy Buckle. He set down the gaudy blue novel and strapped on the short sword which had been part of the general jumble of his inheritance.

Mercy stared helplessly at the open pages of the discarded book. After a short while she managed to unlock the mysteries of the word *ballroom*.

"'Tis the wind," she said.

"Not the wind," said the little man, retying his smoking jacket and drawing the short sword. "Snuff the candle."

Mercy, most reluctantly, did as she was bid.

Ever so slowly, Percy Buckle opened his bedroom door, and stood silently in the dark, trying to make out the noises of the house.

He was a man of small stature, no more than five foot and two inches tall. He had a weak chest and some arthritis in his hands, but in his occupation as a seller of fried fish, he had known no choice except to stand up to those who would rob, steal and otherwise bully him. Now, with his heart beating so hard he could barely hear another thing, he descended the stairs in the night with his sword drawn.

"Who's there?" he cried.

No answer.

The night was not completely dark. The clouds scudding over London sometimes revealed the moon and it was by this erratic illumination that Mr Buckle found his way into his hallway, and then down the little breakneck stairs into the kitchen.

It was darker now and yet he was aware, half-way down those stairs, of the presence of another.

"Who's there?" he cried.

He heard a small sound—not the wind or the window—which produced, in his mind, the picture of a dagger handle knocking against a dresser.

He stared down into the darkness towards a place where the blackness was knotted hard together, like ink poured into ink. It shifted as he stared at it.

"I see you," said Mr Buckle. "Defend yourself, for my sword is drawn."

"Begging your pardon," said a familiar voice.

"Maggs?"

"Yes, Mr Buckle. It is I."

This answer did not appease Mr Buckle in the slightest. The hairs on his neck straightened themselves once more, and he felt that deathly prickling sensation all the way down his spine. "Maggs, what are you doing in my kitchen?"

"I am eating a cheese sandwich," said the voice. "For I am very hungry to have missed my dinner. I had no meaning to frighten you, but your Mrs Halfstairs had me deliver your parcel to Mr Hawthorne at the Adelphi Theatre. I had to wait for him an hour, and when I was back the dinner was all done."

"But we would feed you, man," cried Percy Buckle. "Good grief, we do not mean to starve you. But we do not like you to creep around the house like a thief."

"Now I am like a thief?"

"Why did you not light a candle?"

"I can see in the dark."

Mr Buckle said nothing.

"Because I was a thief. Did you know that?"

"No, Maggs, I did not."

"Are you sure?" inquired the other, in a very low voice that made Mr Buckle's skin creep.

"Yes, very sure. I swear I did not."

"In any case, I would not have broke your lock, Mr Buckle."

"Thank you, Maggs, that's very decent."

"I would not have broke your lock on account of—it would not have been worth my while."

"Well, yes, I'm sure," said Mr Buckle, quickly. "But a thief could not know such a thing from the street."

"He would need only look into your kitchen window."

"My kitchen window? And what would he see there?"

"The Trafalgar Doulton."

"The Trafalgar Doulton?"

"Trafalgar Doulton in the kitchen dresser. I would know that I would not find valuable silver plate and Trafalgar Doulton in the same household. But I can see I have frightened you. I am sorry. I can make a light now. Would you like me to light a candle now?"

"You know that about the Doulton?"

"Oh yes, Sir. It would be a rule."

"And they have those . . . rules, in that line of work?"

"Would you like me to find a candle for you?"

"I have dined in houses, with most distinguished gentlemen," said Percy Buckle, "amongst the most wealthy type, and they are all for the Trafalgar Doulton."

"Perhaps things have changed in my absence. I was abroad, Sir, as you may have been told."

A long silence.

"A chap might guess it, Maggs, that you had been abroad." Percy Buckle stared into the blackness. The denser part of it was moving. "What are you doing?" he cried.

"I am putting the cheese away."

"Yes, good," said Percy Buckle. "We can talk about your travels at another time. But for now, get you to your bed quickly, Maggs, for tomorrow we will need your good strong arm around the household."

And thus he made his rapid way up into his sanctuary and there he bolted fast the door.

The room was now in darkness. He found his way into his bed, and into the sleepy arms of his Good Companion.

"Was it him?"

"Hush, talk in my ear. Yes, it was he."

"He did not murder you?"

"He may not be a murderer, but he admits he is a thief. He told me, as bold as brass. He said, I am a thief and a very good thief too. He told me all the business of thieves, what they steal and what they will not."

"Then he is an honest man."

"He was drunk. I have been too soft with him."

"And what great crime was he committing?"

"Hush, Mercy. He was making a cheese sandwich."

"Do you wish your own sandwich?"

"You are a dear girl," said Percy Buckle, and was mostly quiet for a minute or so. Then he gave a little sigh.

"Like so?" said she.

"Turn over," said he.

"You should say, *Turn over, my pretty one.*"

"Yes," said Percy Buckle, busying his face in all that coal-black hair. "Turn over my pretty one, and raise your sweet white bottom in the air."

And thus for some little while the master did manage to take his mind off the Trafalgar Doulton, and the possibility that a creature other than a cat could see in the dark.

31

Said Mary Oates: "Your father says you are snubbing your old friends in Fleet Street."

Her husband was surprised to hear her say such a thing, not least because he had entered the dark bedroom imagining that she was finally asleep.

"He says you imagine that the Press is now beneath you."

"Mary," he whispered, "it is after midnight."

"He says that you never reply to the *Chronicle* when they telegram you."

"For God's sake. My father is a fool."

"So you often say, dear."

Toby turned to the rattling window and looked down into Lamb's Conduit Street. The wind, which had been blowing from the east in the earlier part of the night, had now changed quarter to come howling down from the north, driving an empty barrel right down the centre of the road.

"When did you talk to my father?"

"He came this afternoon to take the painting."

"What painting?"

"The Maclise."

"Good Lord," he cried.

"Shush. You'll wake John."

"Mary, you did not let my father steal our painting?"

"No, no," she said, sitting up in the bed. "He is to have it cleaned by an old fellow down in Whitechapel. It is all the smoke from the fireplace at Furnival's Inn. He has spoken to you about it."

"Oh dear God."

"Toby, don't go on so. I'm sure he'll bring it back again."

"Then you know better than I," said Toby, much irritated. He had been counting on being able to sell it himself. "My father will tell any untruth to get his hands on money."

"But it is not untrue that the *Chronicle* has been asking for you, Toby."

Tobias was not happy to hear mention of the *Chronicle*. On two occasions, in the first weeks of their marriage, Mary had offered opinions about his business dealings, and he had very firmly insisted that a husband's work was his own affair.

"The *Chronicle* is very eager that you write for them."

"And I am too busy to oblige them."

There was a silence then. He felt her hardening in the dark. This capacity for hostility had shown itself repeatedly of late. Indeed, as she now turned violently in the bed, he felt he must revise his understanding of the maternal character he had presumed to know so well.

"Too busy playing knucklebones," she muttered.

"My dearest," he began. In spite of all the irritation that had seized him, Tobias put his hand gently upon her plump shoulder. "My dearest, I did not play knucklebones. Is that what you imagined? That I was playing games with Jack Maggs?"

"You told me yourself."

"Then you misunderstood me, dearest. It was a game of knucklebones played in the last century, in Pepper Alley Stairs. I found it in my Somnambulist's memory. He could play the bones and describe the very floor he played it on. I have just finished recording all this in my note book. Money will come of it, you must believe me. Entwhistle will pay me good money for this serial."

Still she persisted. "But you said yourself you do not have a story."

"That is so, Mary, but the story will come."

At last, she took his hand. "You never needed magnets before. You used an ink and pen. You made it up, Toby. Lord, look at the people you made. Mrs Morefallen. Did you need magnets to dream her up?"

"Has not the money always come, Mary? Have I not looked after you? Do you not like your new home?"

"Lizzie likes it."

"And you?"

"I dare not like it."

"Why not?"

"I know we will have to leave it."

"What nonsense, my darling. Do not say that. If we leave it, it will be to a better home still."

"But what am I to say when the butcher will not even give us tripe until something is paid off the account?"

"Oh please, dearest, it is after midnight."

"And the grocer, Heaven help me, they will not see me in the shop. Please Toby, will you go to Brighton?"

"Brighton?"

"Yes, for the *Chronicle*."

"Lord help me. How did my father know this?"

"It is five pounds and expenses, and it will only take the day. Please, Toby. You could write in the coach as you did coming back from Leeds."

"Mary, you have been reading my telegram."

"It was lying open on your desk. What am I to do? Surely you could abandon your magnets for one day."

"You think I have no idea of money?"

"No, my dear, I know you have a very good idea of money. You are very clever with money, but we have none."

While it did not please Tobias that his wife should talk to him like this, he liked it even less that she was right. He could not possibly tell her that he would do as she had asked and so, even as he went to his office to pack his yellow attaché case for Brighton, she did not have any idea that he had capitulated; the young woman stayed in the dark room with her eyes wide open wondering what meal could be made from sago and potatoes.

32

Jack Maggs opened his eyes and saw, as he did every morning, the mortal stains which the attic's previous inhabitant had left upon its melancholy walls.

The late Mr Pope's room was a depressing little hole, and so far removed from the mansion Jack had left behind in Snail's Bay that he was angry and insulted before he was properly awake.

He stirred his bellicose bulk inside the bed, but when he finally swung his heavy stockinged legs free of the blankets, he was rewarded with the sound of an empty grog bottle crashing to the floor. BLACK SEAL SPECIAL SCOTCH WHISKY, courtesy of Mr Buckle's cellar. He sat with his head in his hands and watched it roll beneath the washstand.

Late the previous night he had gone in search of a second of the same, and had been caught by the master of the house. Drunk, he had insulted his host's Trafalgar Doulton. Belligerent, he had as good as confessed himself a crook.

Now he rose from bed, seeing clearly to what degree his safety depended on the other's good will. Thus, very wearily, he managed to make himself a footman once again. He shaved with cold water in the chipped pudding bowl provided. He sponged his livery as best he could, that is to say, not well at all. He wet his hair and tried to make a new order of it, finally resorting to a great deal of powder which did little to hide the damage to its architecture. All this time it was on his mind that he must smooth things over with his benefactor, and so he limped off down the stairs wishing with all his heart to make himself agreeable.

As he came down the back stairs he saw Mercy Larkin leave the dining room. He crept along the hallway a little, then hesitated.

"Jack Maggs? Is that you, Jack Maggs?"

It was the master calling from the dining room.

"Yes, Sir," he answered. "Coming, Sir." But when he came into Percy Buckle's presence, he was dismayed to find him now very icy in his manner.

"Stand over there," said Percy Buckle imperiously. "Against the wall."

This, no matter what the stakes, was a very hard sort of order for Jack Maggs to take.

"I was on my way down to the kitchen."

"I dare say you were. Against the wall."

Jack Maggs moved back, but he could not make himself go all the way to the wall.

"What else, Sir?"

Percy Buckle chose not to notice the resistance. "You will see I am eating," he said. He did not address Maggs directly; and indeed, had he not raised his papery voice a little, he might have given the impression that he was speaking to himself. "You will see I am eating my kipper from the poor old Trafalgar Doulton."

There was then an exceptionally long silence during which it became clear just how insulted Mr Buckle felt himself. He should not have been insulted, Jack thought: the silver on the breakfast table accurately fulfilled his prediction of the night before. That is, it was not worth the trouble stealing. Of this low quality, however, Percy Buckle seemed to remain as ignorant as ever. He sat at his table sipping milky tea, occasionally feeding a pinch of kipper to the marmalade cat which whined round his legs.

At length he announced, "You will not be visiting Mr Oates this morning."

"Oh. Why's that, Sir?"

"That ain't your affair, Jack Maggs."

Now Jack Maggs did not wish to argue again. He wished only to be agreeable, but just the same he was rattled to find his mesmerism cancelled. He could not waste a day.

"With respect, Sir," he began.

"Respect, Jack Maggs, now there's a thing."

"Aye, it is. It is a great thing, Sir." If his smile was strange, it was not his intention that it be so. He wished only to demonstrate good will. "But I have a bargain with Mr Oates and I had hoped he would respect it. Here I am, aren't I? I am waiting for him."

"A gentleman of leisure."

"Oh, I know I ain't a gentleman, Sir. I am a servant and I don't have no leisure as it were, but I exchanged him two weeks of my life, Sir. That was my bargain with him. If the gentleman is not to call me for two days, it must be at his own cost. I am going to count those days as taken."

"But what of your bargain with me?"

"I got no quarrel with you, Sir. You are as fine a master as ever were. My bargain was with Mr Tobias Oates."

Percy Buckle then made a great show of adding sugar to his tea and stirring it. When this was completed to his satisfaction he solemnly laid his spoon upon his saucer.

"Jack Maggs, you wear my livery."

"Yes, I do, Sir. Proudly, Sir, and that's a fact."

Percy Buckle patted at his moustache with his napkin. "Then I would require the respect a man in your position should show to one in mine."

"A good point, Sir, but what exactly do you mean?"

"A man in your position," began the master.

"That's it," interrupted Jack Maggs. "What mean you by that part? Let's call a spade a spade, Sir. Let's admit it: you saw my back."

But Mr Buckle could not admit any such thing. Indeed, it now appeared that he could not say anything at all. Instead he began to spread butter on his previously abandoned crusts. He devoted a great deal of attention to this task and when he finally spoke he was still at it, laying on the butter like wet mortar on a brick. "Our *bargain* is that you are my footman. And for my part, I would like your respect, Jack Maggs."

"Yes, Sir."

"That is satisfactory to you?"

"Oh yes, Sir. It is."

"And seeing as how you now have free time today, I would like you to clean my silver."

"Yes, Sir."

"You will find all the necessary rags in Mr Spinks's little parlour. Mrs Halfstairs will direct you."

"Meanwhile, Mr Buckle, you have what I might call my little *secret*."

But Mr Buckle would not tangle with that question.

"Everything is kept where it should be, Maggs. You need not fear."

"What do you mean by that?"

Percy Buckle finally looked up and, for the first time in their entire transaction, held his footman's gaze.

"I mean," said he, "you need not fear."

And on the uncertain strength of that assurance, Jack Maggs departed.

Two hours later, Constable found him in the back parlour, with all the tarnished plate set out in front of him but not a piece yet touched.

"Good day," said Constable, sitting himself down.

The other nodded sullenly, and began to brush some Oakey's on a very dumpy looking Georgian tea pot.

Constable rested his sharp elbows conversationally upon the table.

"You are not a servant, Mr Maggs," he said. "You make yourself miserable in acting like one."

Jack Maggs listened carefully.

"You came to Great Queen Street with an 'attachment' to Henry Phipps. When he was not here, you decided to stay and watch for him."

Still Jack Maggs stayed silent.

"I can find your man, if you should like me to."

"*You* can find Henry Phipps?"

"Dear Mr Maggs, it is not something I would recommend."

This was said very gently, with the utmost consideration, but it had the most obvious effect of offending Jack Maggs.

Said Constable, "May I inquire about the nature of your 'attachment' to the gentleman?"

"Personal," said the other coldly.

"Then I would abandon that attachment."

"Oh, you would, would you, mate?"

Constable did not quite sigh, but his shoulders dropped a fraction and he lapsed into a rather melancholy silence which was not without a certain power.

"You know him well?" Maggs finally asked.

"I know friends of his, yes."

"They can take me to him?"

"One would not just *drop in* on the gentleman, Mr Maggs."

"Then you can deliver a letter to him?"

"It is quite probable."

"Your friends would bring me Mr Phipps's reply, or take me to him?"

"If my friends can find him, they'll deliver your note. I can't say more than that."

"It is more than a note. Tell your friends to say that Jack is waiting. Tell him that I continue to wait. No, not that. Say only that they have certain papers for him—I'll give them the papers before they set off—and that they will wait while he reads them. Would they wait an hour, your friends? I'd pay them well."

Constable smiled wanly. "My friends are my friends. They will not require payment, Mr Maggs."

"You are in touch with them directly?"

"I shall meet with them on Monday." The footman rose wearily. "On my day off."

But Monday was three days away. It was impossible that Jack Maggs should stay three days.

33

Typically, Mercy had managed to overhear a great deal of the conversation between Mr Buckle and Jack Maggs, and although she had not re-entered the dining room until the latter had been abruptly dispatched to clean the silver, she knew that Jack Maggs had carelessly disclosed the information she had passed on: that is, that the scars on his back had been seen.

As she set a fresh tea pot upon the cluttered breakfast table she knew that the master could be in no doubt as to the identity of the gossip. He was a generous man, but very spiteful when crossed, and as she took his empty cup from him she feared she was in danger of being cast out of the house.

She was a proud young woman, and extremely particular about who she waited upon and why. Yet when it came to retaining her benefactor's good opinion, she was prepared to jettison self-respect completely.

Her only hope in the present instance was that Mr Buckle might show the full blaze of his temper, and plainly charge her with her crime. Then she might, if not deny it, at least beg his pardon. She would lick his boots, and like the taste of it. She would make herself a worm and crawl into his ear. She would slide along his very veins and curl up inside the red wash of his angry little heart. But when she set the cup of tea before him, the master brought his cold, strange cat eyes to bear on her, and then she saw he would not lose his temper. He would not even name her misdemeanour.

He said it was a very nice sort of day.

It was not a nice day at all. It was grey and drizzling.

He said he had had quite enough to eat. He pushed his chair back and, having given her another thin-lipped smile, left the room. The wretched condition of the kipper on his abandoned plate confirmed the severity of his upset.

Mercy had always loved this dining room with its great round table and its amber and violet stained-glass windows. Sometimes, when she waited on the master, she liked to fancy that the day had come when she was finally Mrs Buckle. When the world outside was very wet or windy, there was a particularly deep pleasure to be had simply in standing behind that unbending little back and, with her hands hidden behind her, making a firm circle where her wedding ring might one day be.

Now, as she stacked the cutlery and china on her tray, she remembered the slum she had inhabited in Fetter Lane. The thought of being destined for such a place once more produced a dreadful feeling in her bowels. She would rather die than return to that life, and while she could not undo her indiscretion, she knew she must straight away explain her personal situation to Jack Maggs. He must never place her so at risk again.

In the scullery Miss Mott was cutting up the liver, but Mercy barely noticed her. She began to wash the dirty dishes, then abandoned them. She could think of only one thing: she must tell Jack Maggs to keep his mouth shut. If he revealed her visits across the roof, she would be undone for ever.

She therefore hurried off down the passageway to the room where she knew he was engaged. She came around a dog-leg and found the moon-faced housekeeper counting the preserve bottles in the passageway.

"Yes, Mercy?"

"I've come for lemon skins. For the brass in the dining room, Mum."

Mrs Halfstairs gave her two very mouldy halves of lemon rind. Mercy could not think of a story which would get her round the housekeeper, and now she was a victim of the story she had already invented. She must return to the dining room and do the brass.

In the dining room, she discovered that Mr Makepeace was now set up with the master at the table. Mr Makepeace was the lawyer who had brought Mr Buckle his Great Good Fortune, and now it seemed it had been Mr Makepeace's Great Good Fortune too, for his accounts were constantly being dropped through the letter box by his hobble-legged boy. He himself was a young man, in his twenties. As to what his features were, it is hard to say, for the distinctive quality of mouth and chin and nose were swallowed in the sea of his great corpulence. Even his voice seemed affected, for all that escaped the gravity of the body was an exhausted high-pitched whisper which made him rather hard to hear. Mercy set the lemon skins aside, and moved closer to the conversation.

"Luck or fortune," said Mr Makepeace, "but in either case, it seems I have found your felon in the very first volume."

There were crumbs on the floor below the table, and Mercy, having no whisk or pan, now counterfeited those implements with her hands.

"It is Maggs with two *g*s," whispered Mr Makepeace. "There is a Mags with one *g* in 1813, but he is a forger from Sheffield."

Good Jesus, thought Mercy.

"I do not know about the *g*s," said Mr Buckle, "but he is a Londoner, no doubt about it."

"Then I have the rascal," said Mr Makepeace.

Mercy looked up across the top of the table to see him place a large leather-bound volume on the reading stand.

To discuss Jack Maggs with a man of law seemed, to Mercy, a very dangerous thing. To her, a lawyer was of the same species as a judge, and the judge the same genus as a policeman, and a policeman the same thing exactly as Harold Hoban, the hangman at Newgate Prison. So agitated was she by this conversation that she quickly withdrew into the hallway. Here there were a great many small engravings, each of which she now vigorously dusted and straightened, until this upsetting intercourse had finished and the visitor departed.

When Mr Makepeace had gone, Mr Buckle did not call for her. This confirmed her fears: he was very angry with her.

She therefore began slowly to edge her way back into his presence, as though compelled by the requirements of her labour. She arrived finally at the hall-side door, and there she was, attacking the brass door knobs, when the cause of all her trouble came thundering up the stairs and burst into the dining room.

"This is wrong!" cried Jack Maggs, waving a tin of Oakey's silver polish in the air.

It was only at this moment that she saw clearly what a dreadful liability he had become. She watched her master take the can of Oakey's and peer down at the label.

"If it is silver . . . I," began Percy Buckle.

"Who gives a frig for silver? You have not been straight with me."

The master then produced his icy smile. "*I* not straight with *you*?"

"Now I hear my history is known to Mr Constable."

Dear Jesus, here's trouble.

"Do you have *him* in the room when I am naked? And her?" He pointed a finger to the doorway where Mercy was rubbing the lemon round and round, feeling the blood fill her neck and ears whilst the brass shone bright and yellow.

"Do you invite *her* in to see my shame?"

"Sit down, Maggs."

"Stand or sit, you'll get me hanged."

"Hanged? Ah, there you are wrong, Sir."

Jack Maggs sat, not on the chair indicated by Mr Buckle, but on the table. He rubbed his face with both his hands.

The master did not respond to this impudence, but sat himself in his chair and opened the hefty volume that Mr Makepeace had brought him. "I took the liberty of engaging my friend Mr Makepeace of Lincoln's Inn."

Oh Lord, this is worse.

Mr Buckle calmly placed his reading glasses on the end of his sharp nose and began to peer very closely at the pages of his book. "We have this morning, together, examined your sentencing and Mr Makepeace has made himself well acquainted with the law as it pertains to your situation . . ."

"My situation is my own damn business."

"There is a Jack Maggs of London transported for life in 1813. Might that be your situation, Sir?"

It was heart-wrenching to witness the effect this announcement had upon this manly man. His shoulders slumped. He shook his great head slowly.

"I'm a vermin, ain't I?" he nodded towards the book.

"A vermin?"

He stood up from the table, his jaw a little slack, his eyes dull. "Don't it say so?"

"No it does not."

"I am a cockroach, isn't that so? It was very clear what would happen to me if I were to ever set foot in England again. I was transported for the term of my natural life. Weren't those the words? Did not his lordship wish to crush me with his heel?"

"There are no cockroaches here," said Percy Buckle, speaking very rapidly. "But it does say that one Jack Maggs received a conditional pardon in Moreton Bay in 1820. And we have concluded that if only you were to remove yourself again to New South Wales you would be, to all purposes . . . well, no one would wish to hang you."

"I *know*. God damn. I do know, Sir. But you see, I am a fucking *Englishman*, and I have English things to settle. I am not to live my life with all that vermin. I am here in London where I belong."

"Respect," said Percy Buckle, now obviously angry.

Jack Maggs paused.

"You give me respect, Jack Maggs, and I'll give respect to you. I'm the one that saved your skin. Now I am prepared to be your agent, to sell your property."

"How do you know about my property?"

Dear Jesus, he is staring at me.

"It was I," said Percy Buckle, "who yesterday discovered that Jack Maggs is the owner of a freehold . . ."

"Who was it gave you the idea to look that up?"

Again he looked at Mercy.

"How could it be me?" she cried. "You never told me nothing." And to the master she insisted, "He never told me nothing, Sir, I swear it."

"I will shelter you, Jack Maggs, and then convey you to where you will be safe."

"But God help me, Mr Buckle, I have just arrived. I came into the country with the most careful plans. I had a man at Dover in my pay, and when my papers were presented, he turned the other eye. Everything was as it should be. Everything was on the wink, but now there is a household full of busy-bodies all wanting to talk about my life."

"It was you who came to us, not we to you."

Jack Maggs shook his head slowly. It was true. It was not, looked at that way, their fault, and he looked from Mercy to Buckle with a countenance that was infinitely sad.

"What am I to do with you all?" he said. "That is the question."

34

Mary Oates was most surprised to hear her husband's footsteps on the stair, and learn that he was off to Brighton to write about the recent fire. She should not have been surprised. Money was a subject always on his mind. One can see the evidence on all his manuscripts—their margins marked with calculations headed £—s—d.

Tobias Oates knew exactly the price of pork and bacon. He knew how much they owed the butcher, the grocer, the tailor. When he caught the Mail Coach at St Martin Le Grand, he had planned his costs and revenues as carefully as the owner of a factory. On his return from Brighton he intended to sit inside and write through the night with candles burning, but as the coach rattled out of London, he was alone atop—tuppence ha'penny the mile, half the cost of being inside.

By Clapham Common, there was a light drizzle. Toby wrapped himself inside his Petersham coat, turned up his velvet collar and stared ahead into the wet dark, adding and subtracting, multiplying and dividing. The horses' hooves rang. The harnesses rattled. He added the unpaid accounts from the plumber, the boot-makers, the stationer. Glimpsing the terrifying size of the totals, he then hid certain larger debts from himself, either setting them aside or putting them against possible windfalls.

On the credit side he entered the value of the painting his father had stolen: ten guineas. To this, he added a further sum of fifty pounds, this being payment for the unwritten story of Jack Maggs.

While it was true that he had never been paid so large a sum for any piece of writing, and that as yet he had no actual drama for his Magsman to act out, he was emboldened by the hard ache behind his eyes. He knew this pain of old. It was the exact same sensation he had when he first glimpsed the comic figure of old Captain Crumley. It was the distinct twinge behind the eyes, the tension in the tendons of the hands. When he entered the soul of Jack Maggs, it was as if he had entered the guts of a huge and haunted engine. He might not yet know where he was, or what he knew, but he felt the power of that troubled mind like a great wind rushing through a broken window pane.

Dawn found his eyes resting on the soft green of the Sussex Downs, but his thoughts were still inward. So immersed was he in this hidden landscape that by the time the coach horses were changed at the Half Moon, his eyes, despite the early hour, were bright and hard and alive with calculation.

In this way he continued all the way down to Brighton, and when he finally arrived at the Old Ship Inn he was inhabiting a kind of trance which he could not totally abandon. He took a cab directly to Hawke & Sons, the undertakers in Gibbons Lane.

While other writers might have begun to report the tragedy from the site of the fire, or from the bed-sides of surviving children, Tobias chose to begin his inquiries in a mortuary. As to why this was, he could not have told you, although it was doubtless anchored somewhere in his habit of confronting the things he feared the most, which pigeon-hole would, by the by, accommodate his fascination with Jack Maggs.

The death of children had always had a profound effect on him. When the young victims were also the children of poverty, it produced in him a considerable rage, which the editor of the *Chronicle* had reason to expect would be much to the newspaper's benefit. For Tobias had been a poor child too, and he was fiercely protective of abused children, famously earnest in defence of the child victims of mill and factory owners.

In Brighton, where a cheap-jack builder had laid a gas line to murderous effect, it now took no more than a touch of the undertaker's hand to bring all his passions to the surface.

"You wish to view the deceased?" asked the younger Mr Hawke. He was a tall sandy-haired fellow whose turned-down mouth expressed his habitual disapproval of the living. "You wish to physically inspect them?"

"Yes. I will leave it to *The Times* to describe the damage to the hospital," said Tobias Oates. "I am sure their man is already kicking round the ashes as we speak. *The Times* has not been here, I warrant."

"No, Sir."

"The *Observer*?"

"You are the first to think of such a thing."

"I have come to write about the children, Mr Hawke. I warrant I will be the only one."

Mr Hawke turned his back and opened a chapel-like doorway through which he poked his beakish nose. "Mr Threadle," he called. "Corporation key!"

An elderly gentleman shuffled out holding a large brass key which Mr Hawke took from him. Without speaking a word to Tobias, Mr Hawke then walked out of the office. It took a moment for the writer to realize that he was being invited on an expedition. He therefore followed Hawke's high stooped back out into a lane-way, and thence into a smaller lane, and thence into an alley. He could smell a peculiar sweet smoke in the air but, the dull red walls about him being high, he had no way of knowing if it was the hospital he could smell or something far more innocent. Finally, they entered a narrow cul-de-sac and addressed a heavy door which, after some jerking, answered to the brass key. They proceeded immediately down some worn stone steps where the light was poor, and the air damp and very earthy.

They came to a small wooden vestibule and from thence passed into a very large and vaulted basement. Tobias was to learn later that it was the basement underneath the Town Hall, but at the time it felt as if he were in a catacomb. His emotions were stirred by what he saw—achingly small coffins, spaced at regular intervals on the uneven brick floor.

Mr Hawke bent over the first coffin. "There," was all he said, but when he turned towards the writer his face revealed considerable feeling.

Tobias kneeled beside the coffin. It was a little girl, no more than eight, with a small posy of bluebells clasped in her hands.

"Suffocated," said the undertaker.

Her eyes were closed, but even so, Mr Hawke had managed to give the dead girl an alert and very grown-up manner.

"You would not recognize them," he said angrily. "They ain't nothing like what they was when first I got them."

The coroner's report said her name was Mavis Crofts, an orphan, and she lay there in her little box with all the solemnity of a matron at the communion rail. Tobias felt a burning behind his eyes. As he steeled himself to describe this determined little face, all the fierce subterranean passion which had accompanied his journey to Brighton suddenly found a home in the mortuary.

"This is murder," he declared.

Mr Hawke nodded fiercely, and then turned to a single coffin which, unlike the others, was covered with a white muslin cloth.

"We may best pass over Thomas Griff, Sir."

Tobias stared down at the muslin, the same material as Lizzie's night gown.

"It weren't just the smoke, Sir."

"Lift the cloth, Mr Hawke."

"You don't need to see it, Mr Oates." Mr Hawke folded his hands across his chest.

Tobias reached out his hand towards the cloth. The muslin felt exactly as it did when it clothed his sister-in-law's young body. He pulled it aside, and thereby confronted a sight so unnatural that he did not at first comprehend what it was that he was looking at. It was a human being, wet, bubbled, like meat, the blue-white bones broken through the charred and blistered skin.

"Oh my dear Lord!" He turned away, distressed, his hand across his mouth.

"Thomas Griff," said Mr Hawke. "Carpenter's apprentice. He was a father to his young brother."

"Dear God," said Tobias Oates, resting his forehead against the cold damp brick of the nearest wall. "Dear Lord forgive them all."

Mr Hawke replaced the muslin cloth. He walked past the writer and opened the door to the street.

"You'd do better to see the correspondence at the corporation," he said when Tobias had joined him in the lane-way.

"Correspondence?"

"The matron wrote many letters about the gas. You might look back to the second of January."

Tobias wrote *January 2, 1837* in his notebook, but in his mind's eye he still saw poor Thomas Griff—the black skin, the horrid blue-white of the bone. He bid the undertaker good-bye and walked directly to the site of the fire. There, in the company of a young constable, he spent an hour tracing the path of the gas line. He went next to the offices of the corporation, and inspected the matron's correspondence. By three o'clock he had returned to the site, this time in the company of the head of the building firm responsible for the leaking gas line. Thomas Griff's body was before him all the time, and he interrogated the builder in the smoking ruin until both their shoes were smouldering.

He interviewed the weary red-eyed nurses. He collected stories about the children who had died. He brought boiled sweets to the survivors who had been evacuated to St Stephen's church hall. Here he produced pennies from behind ears and made a scarf appear inside a patient's sling. He was a good magician, and would have entertained them longer had his attention not been distracted by a weary young resident who was obviously waiting for him to finish. This was Dr McAlpine, a Scot. He had been sent to ask the writer if he would please be the guest of the hospital doctors at dinner.

Tobias did not hear him. He stared at the distressed young resident, but it was poor Thomas Griff's face he saw.

God save him, *this* was how Jack Maggs would end. He did not know how he knew this, or why this appalling spectre forced itself into his mind.

"Doubtless it's been a hard day for you, too," said the doctor. He placed his hand comfortingly on Tobias's shoulder, and a fire exploded in the writer's mind. "Unless you have another obligation?"

Tobias's freckled eyes stared back at his questioner, but he saw instead this horrifying vision: Jack Maggs trapped inside his burning house, a whirl of fire blazing all about him.

"No, no," he stammered. "Not at all."

He turned away and watched the disturbed beetles and spiders running away across the burning floor. He had glimpsed the ending of his book.

35

The reader of Tobias Oates's novels will be well aware of the role of doctors in his work: how time and time again they betray his heroes, abandon them, act snobbishly and capriciously towards the poor. None of this can prepare us for the fact that when Tobias finally realized he was being invited to dine with surgeons, and that these distinguished men not only knew his name but were professed admirers of his comic novel, he immediately decided that he was too exhausted to travel back to London until the morrow.

Of course this meant that he would lose a good four hours of labour, but while this would have been unthinkable only that morning, it did not seem to matter to him now. He would take the dawn mail. He would lodge at the Ship Inn. He sponged his own shirt collar so he would not have to tip the maid.

It was spring, the evening fine and clear. He might have breathed in the ozone on the esplanade, but instead he lazed inside his hotel room, hands clasped in his lap. He gazed out of the window at the lane-way, occupied with no other labour than a vague and pleasant daydream of his ultimate success.

At five minutes past the appointed hour, he presented himself at the imposing doors of the Hippocratic Institute. He was greeted by a butler and then relegated to a footman. As he followed this ornate fellow up the wide marble staircase he caught his own reflection in a mirror and wondered if he had been mistaken in accepting the invitation. He was bright, but rumpled, sponged, but damp. The left side of his jacket sagged with the weight of his note book.

A door opened before him. He entered a grand room whose high-arched windows afforded a view of the grey silky sea. Here he discovered eight elegantly dressed gentlemen waiting for him. Those with knighthoods wore the ribbons of their rank.

They were taller than he was. They had been to Oxford and Cambridge, had grown up with Greek and Latin, with Plato and Aristotle. And if they had admired their guest's novel, they were obviously having great difficulty accepting that this was the same chap who used the English language like a lyre. He felt their disappointment even as he shook their hands.

Sir Stephen Wall later wrote a memoir in which he recalled the evening, particularly how the "red-lipped Cockney" had sat at table and cleaned his cutlery with his napkin. Sir Stephen describes how Tobias repeatedly rearranged his wine glass, his water glass, every single piece of cutlery, "thereby presenting himself to Medicine as a sufferer from neurasthenic agitation."

Yet if Tobias felt momentarily disadvantaged, he would not be cowed. He solemnly gazed upon the surgeons, one by one, as if he had been appointed to sit in judgment on them. There had been a long tense moment when first he took his place at table but then, without preamble, he began to tell the story of a chance meeting with Mr Thackeray. The tale went against him quite considerably, though it soon had his audience laughing very merrily.

Next he introduced them to Percy Buckle. He gave them the fried fish, the "Great Good Fortune," the mewling cats twining round the dinner guests' legs, the pair of footmen with their yellow livery. He gave them, in the rough, a draft of that piece which was later so often anthologized: "A Grocer in Great Queen Street."

By then the wine had done its work, and they became, altogether, as rowdy a group as students on the last day of term. Tobias ate roast beef pooled in blood. It was very tasty. He said so. *Tasty* was too low a word. He feared it revealed too much of his childhood, of his mother's bread and dripping sandwiches. But when he saw his hosts were charmed completely, he glowed within the enclosure of their love.

As the custard boat was passed around, Dr McAlpine revealed to the company that, last winter at the Orpheum in London, he had seen Tobias Oates play the part of that preposterous saw bones Sir Spencer Spence. The resident was able to recall several of his lines.

In fact he chose the only lines which Toby himself had not written. But this was not exactly literature in any case, merely a sketch in which he had parodied the manners of the Regency Surgeon Sir Herbert Catswaler.

Now, in Brighton, at the end of this long disturbing day, he was pleased to put all of his energy into "doing" the entire part for the assembled doctors.

He began, at first, with the voice alone, using no more props than a pudding spoon and a glass of port, but soon the pompous old windbag had a life of his own, and he was waddling up and down the room, grilling the surgeons, abusing them as "damned wretches" and "dunderheads."

My God he made them laugh and roll about in their seats, and even the most proper of them, a very tall and sallow gentleman named Pepperidge, laughed so much that his beard was soon wet with tears.

For three hours Tobias felt prosperous, wise, celebrated. Then, a little before midnight, the surgeons rode off into the night, and all the writer's well-being evaporated.

He stood on the footpath outside the Hippocratic Institute and suddenly saw that he had not behaved like a man of letters but like a common conjurer, a street magician. Would Thackeray have acted thus? Never. *Never.* He had been Jeremiah Stitchem, Billy Button, taking sixpences from the footmen on Blackfriars Road. He was Toby Oates, son of John Oates, a well-known scoundrel.

He walked first along the promenade and felt the clean salt air in his face, but then he took himself back to the Ship Inn and, with an unseasonable fire built for him in the little room, he set out to cleanse himself completely, to make himself everything that he had so far failed to be. He closed his eyes, contorted his face. He was not vulgar; he was not a buffoon. He took his quill once more unto the well.

36

Tobias arrived back at Lamb's Conduit Street with a full and detailed expectation of how the morning would proceed. As it was a Saturday, he knew his wife and child would have already departed for her mother's house where they would stay until after the child's mid-day sleep. Mrs Jones would already have her large kettle boiling on the stove and he would, within ten minutes of returning home, wash all the grime and smoke from his travel-weary body. By half past ten he would be towelling himself dry. At a quarter to the hour, he would perform his callisthenics. He would then don his long silk gown and, as the hall clock struck eleven, he would watch from the sitting-room window as Mrs Jones walked up the area steps with her marketing basket under her arm. He would then walk down the back stairs and bolt the kitchen door, upstairs again, and bolt the front door. The house would then be empty of people, with the exception of Lizzie Warriner in her room.

He turned the key of 44 Lamb's Conduit Street, thinking of his sister-in-law, and most particularly of that little clasp which must be undone to remove her precious necklace.

Imagine, then, his chagrin to step into his hallway and see, through the open doorway of the sitting room, the retired grocer he had described so humorously the night before, sitting bolt upright on the red sofa by the fireplace.

The traveller dropped his case beside the hall-stand, and picked up what mail had accumulated in his short absence. He advanced towards the visitor, flicking through the letters in order to hide his irritation, although he achieved, of course, the opposite effect.

"You'll excuse me, Sir," said Percy Buckle, rising from the sofa. "But I felt I should tell you before I acted."

"What is it, Mr Buckle?"

"I'm sure it is my own fault, Sir, and no one else's."

"Mr Buckle, what on earth has happened?"

"I am talking," said Mr Buckle, whose cheeks were now bearing the badges of his great emotion—florin-sized red spots, one on each cheek—"I am talking about our Jack Maggs. Not to put too fine a point on it, Sir, he has gone mad."

"Sit down, Mr Buckle. If he is mad I'm sure it is not you who made him so."

"He knows."

"Sit. There, I'll sit too. You'll excuse me, Mr Buckle, but I have a most pressing engagement. We will need to deal with this matter of yours rather quickly."

"Now, Sir?"

"Now."

Mr Buckle then spoke in a voice so low that Tobias Oates had to strain to hear him above the thunder of a passing dray. "He knows we saw his scars."

"Very well," said Tobias Oates. "This is not so bad."

"He is certainly a bolter, Sir, and therefore he thinks it *very* bad. He reckons himself to be in mortal danger."

"He has my word: I will keep mum. Tell him that."

"Yes, Sir," said Percy Buckle, worrying at the brim of the sealskin hat which was balanced on his knees.

"So," Tobias said briskly, "that is that."

"Well, Sir, it is and it isn't. There is also the kitchen maid. She is also a party to his secret."

"The *maid* knows he is a bolter?"

Percy Buckle squeezed his hands together.

"You told the maid?"

"Not a great deal, Mr Oates."

"And she told him," asked Tobias, his voice rising, "that you and I had been staring at him with his shirt off?"

"She meant well," whispered Percy Buckle.

"Very well," said Tobias Oates. "Your Jack Maggs is concerned . . ."

"Oh, I would not say *concerned*," interrupted Mr Buckle.

"What would you say?"

"I would say, he was in a rage."

"With me. Is that it?"

"He has the maid held hostage, Sir."

"The *maid*?"

"He has her locked up in my snuggery. He says it is to stop her gossiping to the servants, but God knows what depravity he practises on her there."

Tobias Oates looked up, at that moment, and saw the figure of his sister-in-law standing in the open doorway in a long white muslin dress. She smiled at him.

"You are home, Mr Oates."

"Indeed, Miss Warriner." He half-rose.

"You will be attending to that clock?"

"Indeed, indeed yes. Very soon."

She retreated, smiling.

"Now, Mr Buckle."

"He has taken my sword, Sir," said Percy Buckle. "He held it against my throat." And here the little fellow pulled his collar down to show a red bruise on his chicken neck.

Tobias Oates looked at the little grocer and despised him for his broken teeth, his dirty little smile. "Mr Buckle," he rose, "we should discuss this at greater length this afternoon."

"He believes that the maid has gossiped to the other servants—Mr Spinks, Mrs Halfstairs, Miss Mott. He ordered me to instruct them to stay indoors."

Tobias sighed, and sat again. "And you did as you were bid?"

"Mrs Halfstairs is to go to her brother's tomorrow, and it would cause a great upset if she were stopped. I tried to point this out to Mr Maggs. I cannot cage her. But when I told him this he flew into a rage with me, and that was when he did the damage to my throat. As for the maid, he will not let her out of his sight. She must sit locked in the snuggery, from dawn to . . ." He stopped, and turned away.

"For God's sake, man, please don't cry."

"I'm sorry, Sir. I did not wish to trouble you, but I thought it best I tell you before I went to Bow Street."

"Bow Street? But you have been harbouring a felon. You cannot go to Bow Street. Are you mad?"

"Well, you was going to call the police yourself."

"No, no, Mr Buckle. It is too late for that."

Percy Buckle then began to shake his head like a horse refusing the bridle.

"Then take him, Sir," he cried. "Please come and take him. Bring him to your house."

"You undertook to keep him," said Tobias sternly.

"You can't make me," said Percy Buckle.

"Tell me," Toby smiled, "did you ever have a book dedicated to you, Mr Buckle?"

"What's that got to do with the price of eggs?"

"Mr Buckle, please be calm—if you will return to Mr Maggs and tell him I will personally undertake to keep his secret within four walls."

"He won't believe me."

"Tell him I will quarantine the household. Tell him no one will leave or enter. Won't that make him happy?"

"You'll lock up my housekeeper? My butler? Sir, with respect, you're going to make things worse."

Tobias had no idea how he would do what he was suggesting, but he had unlimited confidence in his ability to do it.

"If you will deliver this message to him, then this book I'm now writing will one day bear your name."

Mr Buckle paused. "Bear my name?"

"Yes."

"Where?"

"Where?" cried Tobias incredulously. "Are you *bargaining* with me, Sir?"

"Why shouldn't I bargain with you?" cried the tearful grocer. "You have made me break the law."

"It would be at the front of the book, before the title," said Tobias Oates more quietly. "It would say, *'To my friend Percy Buckle, a Man of Letters and a Patron of the Arts, without whom this book could not have been written.'* How is that? Is that not handsome?"

"I was christened Percival."

"Yes, yes, Percival." Tobias put his hand on the grocer's bony elbow. "I will come to your house by evening. You tell him that. As for the dedication, I will write it out for you so you may study it. We may discuss the choice of words together."

Percy Buckle permitted himself to be escorted to the door, then he found himself gently guided out into the street.

Tobias Oates quietly bolted the door after him. Then he walked downstairs to the kitchen and, having confirmed that Mrs Jones had left for market, locked the area door, and hurried up the stairs to Lizzie.

37

M r Buckle had a shop-keeper's manners. That is, he usually appeared timid, almost obsequious, yet when he discovered that Jack Maggs, in addition to holding his Good Companion prisoner, had also taken possession of his bureau, he was filled with a fury that was all the more intense for being incommunicable.

He looked down at Mercy, examining her closely for signs of damage, yet, finding none, he was not mollified.

"You take the ottoman," she said.

"I'll stand, thank you very much."

She laid aside her knitting. "I ain't tired."

"Sit," Mr Buckle ordered.

And then, his raw hands folded in front of him, he leaned against the wall and waited for Tobias Oates to make his promised visit.

Soon enough, thank the Lord, the bell did ring. There was a murmur of voices followed by the distant tread of Constable's feet upon the stairs. As they arrived outside the snuggery, Percy Buckle moved impatiently towards the door but was pushed violently aside by Jack Maggs, who proceeded to interview the footman, while he, the master of the household, was left to stare at his assailant's sweat-stained back.

Upon hearing that the visitor was a doctor, Maggs let out a curse, then returned to the bureau, a delicate piece of furniture which he nevertheless proceeded to *punch* with his bare hands.

Mr Buckle felt he had no choice but to pretend this act of violence was not occurring.

"Is it Dr Krone?" he asked his footman.

"No, Sir," said Constable, and it was to his professional credit that he also displayed not the least reaction to the explosive situation in the snuggery. "It is not Dr Krone. But the gentleman speaks oddly and I did not catch the name."

"Then I'm not at home to . . ."

"See him," interrupted Jack Maggs. "We don't want no one thinking anything is up."

"See him?" Mr Buckle's voice had risen almost to a screech. "You are in such a panic lest anybody talks to anybody. Why should I see him?"

The convict ignored Mr Buckle and addressed Constable instead. "You go with him. See no one gives the game away."

Said Mr Buckle, "Constable is to stay here with Mercy."

"Go with your master," Maggs continued. "See there's nothing said about Jack Maggs."

To this vexing exchange, Mercy Larkin pretended not to listen. Mr Buckle, however, saw through his Good Companion's counterfeit, and when he saw how she affected such great concentration on her pearl and plain, he understood she was ashamed for him. He left the room with Constable, feeling angry and humiliated.

His visitor turned out to be a very strange one: a portly gentleman in a Regency frock-coat who stood with his back to the empty fireplace, his legs apart, holding a great leather bag against his stomach.

The master of the household advanced with his hand outstretched. "Percy Buckle Esquire at your service."

"Send him out."

"I beg pardon, Sir?"

"The servant. Out."

"Perhaps I might be . . ."

"Out, out," the doctor cried, making shushing movements with his hands while Constable took long careful steps backwards like an odd and long-legged marsh bird.

"Now look here," cried Percy Buckle, who was by now tired of being pushed about by others. "I take this very ill."

"Ill?" The doctor poked him in the ribs with a short square finger. "I'll give you *ill*, Sir. There is Contagion in Great Queen Street and I am here to have you act with the greatest expediency to avert a catastrophe for all concerned."

38

A short time later, Edward Constable was recalled to the sitting room. Now only two candles were burning where before there had been six. These candles being at the far end of the room, by the curtained window, the room was now so very gloomy that the footman could barely see the visitor at all. Then, from the murky shadows of the master's wing-back chair, came a foreign wheeze.

"Ah there you are, fellow. Now bring me a nice wedge of Cheshire and a glass of port."

"I'm not sure we have Cheshire, Sir." The candle light made the peculiar visitor's skin look smooth and waxy, like an effigy. "We do have a very good double Gloucester."

"Is this fellow your only footman, Mr Belt?"

"Buckle, Sir." The master rose from the gloom of his own adjacent chair.

Oh please, Sir, do not stand for him.

"Mr Buckle, is this the only footman?"

Sit. Sit, Mr Buckle.

"No. I have a pair."

"Then send me the other," cried the doctor. "I don't like this one at all."

"Oh no. We don't need to push it quite so hard."

"Send him to me. I'll have to see them all in any case."

Constable had already stood for a quarter of an hour with his ear pressed very tight upon the drawing-room door, but all to no avail. So although he now did what he was bid, and called Mr Maggs to stand attendance in the sitting room, he could not explain the nature of the doctor's business.

"It smells fishy," said Mercy. "When he has you there, Eddie, why would he want Mr Maggs?"

"He is what they call 'eccentric': meaning he is rich and has no manners."

Maggs turned to Constable. "Go look in the street."

"What would I look for?"

"Go look in the damned street. See who's lurking."

"Would it be too much of an imposition," asked Constable, feeling his voice tight inside his nervous throat, "for you to say *please*?"

The convict turned his hard and private eyes upon him.

"Please," he said.

Constable looked for evidence of mockery. Satisfied there was none, he went out into the drizzling night where he discovered nothing more than a passing whore with a cane basket and a boy with a lantern holding a horse. He returned to the house, and tip-toed past the drawing room. On the stairs he found Jack Maggs in the process of hiding a rough-looking dagger in his boot.

While Constable described what he had seen outside, Jack Maggs listened intently, his jaw set hard, his eyes hidden in the shadow of his brow.

"Very well," said he abruptly. He returned to the snuggery, where he took the sheaf of papers from his master's desk, rolled them up and tied them with a ribbon. He slid these papers into an inside pocket.

"If 'twere done," he said, " 'twere best done quickly."

Mercy began to plead not to be locked up again. She spat in her palm and crossed her heart; she swore she would die before she betrayed him.

Consequently the two footmen came down the stairs two steps at a time, leaving Mercy Larkin in the unlocked snuggery. As they entered the gloomy sitting room, Constable's heart was beating very fast. He recognized a tangled skein of shadow—the doctor—rise out of the wing-back chair. The doctor held his hand out to Jack Maggs. There was a flash of silver.

"Come, man, put out your tongue."

"Why would I do a thing like that, Sir?"

The doctor held a silver instrument high in the air. "Because," he cried, "there is Contagion in the house."

Maggs took the doctor's wrist, and thereby wrung from him a high and sudden cry of pain. A metal instrument clattered to the floor.

"Jack Maggs," cried Buckle, fluttering around the two men. "Jack Maggs, I order you."

But what he "ordered" he did not say, and now Jack Maggs was dragging the doctor, squirming and flapping like a great fat-bellied moth, into the far corner of the drawing room.

"God save me!" cried the visitor.

Jack Maggs manacled both the surgeon's wrists with his left hand, thus freeing his right hand to pick up one of the two remaining candles. He then forced the visitor down to the floor.

"You bleeding dromedary! I'll rip your bleeding throat out."

"Stop at once," wailed Percy Buckle. "It is Mr Oates."

Constable turned expectantly towards the doorway but was puzzled to find it empty.

Maggs held the candle close upon the fellow's upturned face and there revealed: grease and powder, a kneeling Tobias Oates staring wide-eyed at the light. "I know the dog," he snarled.

"Listen to me, man," cried Percy Buckle urgently, and while the big man maintained his hold of the terrified doctor, the master whispered into his ear.

39

J ack Maggs followed the doctor to the kitchen, where he watched him conduct a lesson in the correct way to wash the hands. One after another Sir Spencer Spence made the servants and their master follow his example; no one was pardoned from this exercise. When Mr Spinks claimed exemption, the doctor lashed him with such irascibility that the old man began to tremble.

Finally, when the butler's hands were washed and dried to the doctor's satisfaction, the latter set a large black bag upon the deal table. Opening it, he took out a long object which, when its wrapping of black velvet was removed, turned out to be a cruel serrated knife.

"Oh dearie," said Miss Mott.

The doctor then produced a second instrument with a long curling tail like a corkscrew. He toyed with this while he spoke of the "organ of secretion" and how it changed its colour when weakened by Contagion. The organ, he said, as a consequence, became large and flatulent like a great blue balloon, and he held the corkscrew as if intending to puncture everybody immediately. Finally, to the relief of all, both implements were put away.

But the ordeal was by no means over, as the doctor now announced that he would examine the members of the household individually, inside the scullery.

Although the scullery curtain was drawn, those who waited in the kitchen could hear every scrape and rustle. Mrs Halfstairs was first. Next was Mr Spinks. One by one, the victims coughed, gagged, and spat into a little silver bowl. They walked out of the scullery with hot cheeks and downcast eyes.

Jack Maggs was last of all. Entering the tight little alcove, he knew the power of Tobias Oates to be greater than he had suspected. This doctor, with his twisted red mouth and wild bright eyes, was incredible, ridiculous, and yet he *existed*, given life by some violent magic in his creator's heart. The jerky little writer was thus made invisible. A glaring demon had taken his place, and this being took Jack's jaw in its dry square hands and made as if to thrust a metal spatula down his throat.

When Jack Maggs grasped its wrist, the creature did not yield. Rather it raised its coal-black eyebrows, and brought its soft little mouth to whisper mockingly in Jack's ear.

"You wish to hang?"

Peering around the curtain, Jack Maggs saw what he was meant to see: that herd of dangerous gossips gathered in the kitchen, staring back at him.

"Sputum," cried the doctor, and thrust the spatula down his throat.

Five minutes later, the house was declared to be in a state of Quar-

antine. Thus, for the cost of a sore throat, Jack Maggs had precisely
what he had wished: the dike was plugged; the gossips were contained.
But as he set out to secure his territory, the convict's heart fell prey to a
new anxiety—a blood-dark feeling in his gut—that he had become the
captive of someone whose powers were greater than he had the wit to
ever understand.

40

T he minute Sir Spencer Spence had left the house, Maggs took
himself down into the cellar where he found a rusty hammer and
a paper bag of nails.

He drove in the first nail, two inches above the lock of the front door.
He hammered it in on a good angle and felt it bite into the oaken frame.
Each hammer blow helped ease the knotting in his gut.

"My house," cried Mr Buckle, appearing suddenly behind him.

Maggs drove in the second nail, three inches below the lock. "It's
what your doctor ordered."

"He said nothing of the sort. Stop! I order it. You must not hurt my
house."

Maggs stood on tip-toes to place a third nail at the top of the door.

"You're splitting it."

Maggs drove the nail home. He turned the handle of the door and
tugged on it.

"That's what I call a Quarantine."

"Look what you are doing. Look at how it splits. Please stop this, now.
I order you. This is not a Quarantine. This is not what Mr Oates meant
at all."

But Maggs was already half-way across the drawing room. He tied
back the heavy maroon curtains and stood, briefly exposing himself to
the night while he drove in nine more nails in fast succession.

"You misunderstand the meaning of the word," said the master of the
house. "I'll fetch the dictionary. Hold off my windows while I get the
book. I order you!"

But Jack Maggs would be no one's servant any longer. He retrieved a
chair from the dining room, and, with a spray of six-inch nails poking
from his mouth, moved across the three windows—bang, bang, bang.

"Here—" Percy Buckle re-entered the room, the dictionary open in his hands. "There's no hammering mentioned under Quarantine."

But the drawing room was done, the curtains drawn, the windows already pinned at top and bottom. Maggs replaced the chair in the dining room, and lit the candles.

Percy Buckle laid the heavy book upon the dining-room table. "This is my house," he said.

But Jack Maggs was already on his way to the next floor.

41

When the house was finally snug, Jack returned the nails and hammer to the cellar. This room, being beyond Mrs Halfstairs's territory, was a rancid labyrinth of passage-ways formed by high piles of coiled rope, abandoned scenery, and hanging costumes which must have begun their life in the late Mr Quentin's theatre. Jack had not been in the cellar a moment when he heard the upstairs door open and saw candle-light shadows moving down the stairs. The maid's soft voice called out for him.

"Here," he said gruffly, lifting his oil lamp.

They met, not without some confusion, in a corridor of ancient costumes: long ballgowns with mildew creeping up their ruffled sleeves.

"You nailed my bedroom window shut," she said. Her voice seemed slow and sleepy.

He admitted that he had been into her room and quarantined it.

"Why not Mrs Halfstairs's, then?"

Had she been crying? In the gloom, he glimpsed her slightly swollen upper lip.

"You think she might be scampering out across the roof?" he asked sarcastically.

"As I'm sure you know, she's come down with Contagion."

Jack knew of no such thing. The odours of dark and dirt had always had libidinous associations for him; now this smell surrounded him and for a moment he knew of precious little else.

"Of course," Mercy said. "It ain't really Contagion, no matter what the doctor says. It's that Metzmetric Fluid, as you know yourself. The poor old cow has got the fluid in her chest."

Maggs raised an eyebrow.

"Oh, so you think me ignorant?" she said.

"No."

"Then for your information, Sir, I went with Mr Constable to a Metz-metric Concert in Great Windmill Street at Christmas. That was an education I can tell you. There was a lady they made dance and sing and then she shook all over. It was done by using magnets on her Fluid. That's what he done to you with all that waving of his hands. It were the same, exactly. It's how he stopped your face hurting. You think I don't know what's going on?"

"What's *that* got to do with Mrs Halfstairs?"

"You think I don't know that weren't no doctor? It was Mr Oates with all that powder on his head."

Quietly he asked, "The others know it was Mr Oates?"

She snuffed her candle and dropped it in her pinny pocket. "They wouldn't know their nose if it sneezed at them."

"But you set them straight?"

"Not yet, no."

"Then come with me," said Jack, taking her by the arm.

"No! Let me be!" She pulled away.

"God damn," he exclaimed, grabbing her by the waist so suddenly her cap fell off. Her hair brushed his face, releasing the faint scent of soot into the air.

"I'll not be locked."

"God damn me, you will."

She was fast and lithe, but he pinned her, took her, her feet kicking six inches above the floor, carried her up the stone stairs to the ground floor while the ancient oil lamp, which he had kept hooked in his bad hand, swayed dangerously against her skirts.

At this hour the ground floor was empty. He set her down and the pair of them regarded each other, breathing heavily.

"Lock me," she burst out. "I don't care."

"Yes."

She shook her hair and brushed it from her eyes. "I don't mind."

"Good."

"Lock me up all night."

In silent agreement they proceeded upstairs. A light was showing underneath the master's door. They crossed to the back stairs, and thence upwards to the attic. Three times Mercy's black skirts brushed against Jack's knees. He felt this so acutely it seemed to him she must also know his knee through the medium of the fabric. When she entered her room, he was hard behind her.

It was a very pretty little home she had made for herself, with many embroidered cushions and a framed painting of a young girl sitting below a windmill with a rag doll on her knee.

"How old are you?"

"A lady don't reveal her age."

He passed her the lamp, which she stood on tip-toes to hang carefully from a hook at the apex of the attic ceiling. While she was so occupied, he removed the key from the door. Hearing the metal scrape in the lock, she spun around.

"No!"

But he had already stepped outside the door.

"Good night," he said, and locked her in before he could change his mind.

A minute later, he climbed across the roof, carrying all his turbulent emotions with him to the abandoned house next door. Here he wrote page after page, pouring all his feelings into that secret history. He slept two hours on the settle, and when he woke he began again: *Dear Boy* . . .

At six o'clock, he recrossed the slippery roof to Mr Buckle's house. When he unlocked the maid's door, she was dressed and waiting for him.

42

Mercy Larkin applied her "nurse-maid's rouge," pinching her cheeks, tweaking them spitefully, all the time contorting her face and letting out small cries of *ooh* and *ouch*. This cosmetic recipe she had learned from her mother, who had applied it enthusiastically before launching her daughter out into the Haymarket.

Now, waiting for her door to be unlocked, Mercy set to work on her upper lip. She had no mirror with which to appraise her handiwork but when the tingling in her lips and cheeks told her the effect had been achieved, she sat upon her three-legged stool with her hands resting in her lap. The face she turned towards the door now showed those swollen, slightly bruised features that always produced so amorous a response in Mr Buckle.

When the door at last swung open, she should have recoiled from him who stood before her: Jack Maggs with red-rimmed eyes, unshaven cheeks, his hair spectacularly disarrayed.

"You going to put me in the snuggery?" she said.

For answer he held open the door so she might pass before him. As they walked together past the master's partly open door, Mercy's lips began to itch—an omen, as she was well aware, that they would soon be kissed.

They descended the stairs together to the kitchen, where she saw Mrs Halfstairs's small blue eyes appraising her features. Had she pinched too hard? The housekeeper opened her mouth as if to reprimand her but then, most unexpectedly, sighed and lowered her braided head into her hands.

In the sudden quiet that followed, Mercy donned her apron, then took the pan of kippers from Miss Mott, turning her face so the cook might not see her lips.

A moment later Miss Mott was sitting at the table. This was unusual: Miss Mott never sat down, not even to drink a cup of tea. Yet it took a good long moment for Mercy to realize that no one was thinking of her lips, that her amorous expectations were not an issue with the other servants. They were sick: Miss Mott, Mrs Halfstairs, Mr Spinks.

As Mercy buttered their toast she heard the butler cough. She listened to the gummy Magnetic Fluid bubbling in his chest. It was Contagion, no doubt about it.

She ate quickly then went, as usual, to set the table for the master's breakfast.

She had not been at this task a minute when Jack Maggs arrived at the doorway of the dining room; she felt his eyes upon her back. Knowing the master might arrive at any moment, she prayed to God to not let nothing happen here. She finished setting the table hurriedly, and allowed Jack Maggs to escort her back to the room they had occupied all day yesterday.

Inside the snuggery, she turned urgently to face him. Her mouth was dry, her heart agitated.

She saw his dark eyes hesitate. She thought he was going to smile, but then he walked past her to the bureau. Disappointed, she watched him select one of the new goose-feathers in the master's drawer.

"He won't like you doing that," she said.

Jack Maggs winked at her. He cut three inches off the feather's top, cleared the barrel of its scurf, and made six fast cuts. Having thus manufactured a new quill, he set back to writing.

"It must be most important."

"It is."

"A good friend, no doubt."

"I hope so, yes."

Thus, to all intents and purposes, he abandoned her on the ottoman. There was nothing to do but knit and wait, and see what might happen. From time to time she secretly freshened her complexion, but with less hope as to the consequences.

The entire morning passed without further conversation, and she had naught to do but wonder at the passion which drove that strange hand. Some time in the early afternoon, however, Maggs stopped abruptly. A floor board creaked outside in the hallway. Then he put a finger to his lips and carefully laid the quill down. He rose, moving towards the door.

Then she saw it: a *dagger*. She had never seen one in a man's hand before. It was at once deadly strange, and quite familiar—an ugly black blade with a hook at its pointy end. It should have made him repulsive to her, but it did not, and instead she watched how very graceful was his movement toward the door.

There was a low moan out on the landing, then a great crash as Jack wrenched the door open. She rushed to see.

"Jod's blood," cried Jack Maggs, and pushed her roughly back into the snuggery, but not before she had seen the heaving prostrate body of Mr Spinks.

The key was then turned in the lock; she was left alone listening to Maggs's heavy tread ascend the stairs to the servants' floor.

It was only then she realized he had left his secret letter sitting on the desk.

43

Silas and Ma Britten [Jack wrote] had a very original ambition: to do a series of clever burglaries without never laying fingers on the goods. And once they got Sophina and me properly trained-up to the art, it was, so Silas said, like having ferrets, except that he was excused the bother of carrying the cages.

Looked at from his way, it was a very pretty little dart. First Yours Truly would climb down the chimney—a journey I now made as easy as jumping out of bed—and then I would light my candle and inspect the locks on the dressers and cabinets. If need be, I would then unlock the kitchen door and whistle for the lever man, a great half-wit pugilist called Wexall whose brain had been jolted in its box one time too many. Wexall had nothing more to do than break the locks and then scarper, a service for which he was pleased to receive a silver sixpence. Then Sophina would enter, always carrying a little posy of flowers—I know not why this was—and wearing her good hat. It was she who was trusted to select the most valuable pieces of silver plate, and I, her black-faced companion, who would pack the treasures in the sack of soot. We went about our work as happy as eight-year-olds, magging to each other all the while.

Silas, meanwhile, had arranged for an old dustman by the name of Mr Figgs to come to pick up the sacks which I placed outside the door. Silas told me that Mr Figgs thought himself to be carrying naught but dust and ashes, and was happy to deliver the sacks to his net loft in Wapping for a penny each. This must have been a lie, but I believed it then.

In the summer of 1801 we did over twenty of these "errands." We did so well that before the fireplaces of London were hot again, we had abandoned the rotten little court by London Bridge and moved, with Silas and Sophina, to Islington. We took a whole floor above a tobacconist's in Upper Street and from this address Ma Britten kept herself as busy as ever, making her sausages and ministering to her female visitors. Whereas once she had received her callers in a curtained little area beside the stove, now she saw them in a small room above the yard at the back.

No one went to Smithfield any more. Ma Britten would send me with a note and half a crown to a proper butcher's shop where a number of red-faced men, all named Mr Ayres, would wrap me up some lamb chops or a piece of liver.

Thus my life improved all at once. Tom was rarely there to twist my wrist or otherwise hurt me. I ate great meals of roast meat and roast potatoes. And if we were forbidden to play with the respectable children, Sophina and I had each other for company. Silas, to give him credit, often took us to the park, where we played hide and seek, and hoop-a-penny and blind man in a sack.

Alas, life was not so merry for Tom, who suffered much from home-sickness. Each Sunday he left his master's house in darkness, arriving in Islington before the church bells had begun to ring. I would wake to the sound of his big heavy boots upon the stairs. Once inside our door he would run to our mother's room, climb up into her bed and cry.

Tom did not like Silas or Sophina either. This was to my advantage because he seemed to lose his old dislike of me. Indeed I was now his ally, and on these Sunday visits he took to walking out with me, sharing confidences about his hopes and plans.

One September morning, before it had become properly cold, he took me all the way down into St James's Park. He bought me a glass of milk from the stalls where they had the cows. There were a great many servant girls drinking the milk, which was said to be good for their complexion, but Tom paid the girls no mind at all.

It was me he watched. He was always watching me. His long bony face was alert and slightly angry.

—Does Silas buy you milk?

In fact, he bought us milk on many occasions, but I knew enough to say he never had.

—The brute has you all tied up in the harness, said Tom. He is riding on your back. He is taking all the money and won't even buy you milk.

I ventured that Silas had taught me a great deal.

—We have no need of strangers sleeping in our house, said he.

I thought, at first, that he was referring to one of Ma Britten's female customers who had recently spent the night vomiting and groaning in the small room at the back. I agreed that I did not like it.

—We should kick him down the stairs, he said, and take his clever Latin with him.

—Who?

—Silas, you little mutt, who did you think we were talking of?

I reminded Tom that it was Silas who had orchestrated our good fortune, that if not for him we would still be living in that room by Pepper Alley Stairs.

—We was happy there, said Tom. Before he came and stuck his big red nose in. You and me and Ma, we had good days. We didn't have no porker snoring in the night.

—Still and all, Tom . . .

—Still and all, we must get rid of him.

—Sophina is my friend.

—I never said nothing about her, said Tom. You want my opinion, she's a giddy goat, but I ain't got no quarrel with her. It's him we must get rid of.

—How would we do that, Tom?

—I ain't talking of hows just at the moment. All I'm talking of is the fact of the matter and all I am telling you is—and here he pushed his raw face close to mine—Silas is a cheat and a liar and he is not a part of our family.

Tom frightened me that day. As we walked back up Haymarket I thought I had liked him better when we were enemies.

He walked so close. He was forever bumping into me, and as he walked, he talked, his mouth pushed close over towards my ear. He told me that we could get a great deal of money and run away to Bristol. He told me that his master had a steel closet with gold bars in it, and that I should come with him and climb down the chimney and unlock the door.

As I write this now, I see what I did not see then: Tom was not right in his mind. Perhaps he was ever thus. Or perhaps it was the strain of being forbid his mother's company that finally unhinged him. Certainly that day I could make no sense of him but thought it was my own fault, that perhaps I was as slow and stupid as he said. When I pointed out that he was already in his master's house and did not need me to come down the chimney, he flew into a rage and did not quiet until I had agreed to come with him to Bristol. This promise, fortunately, he soon forgot.

He came back in the middle of that week. I do not know how he got into the house, only that I woke to find him shaking me. He told me I must get dressed quickly without a sound. His big mouth was close to me again, his breath smelled bad.

I slipped out of the bed which I shared with my play mate, and he led me out into the back yard. And there we stood, in the shadow of a pear tree, with his hard hand shackling my wrist, shivering, saying nothing.

I asked him what it was we were waiting for.

For answer he clipped me round the ears, then put his finger to his lips. After we had stood there a good half-hour, I heard a great loud knocking and much shouting, and then a candle was lit, and soon I saw, at the window, all manner of men with lanterns and candles. It was the police.

—That'll teach the smarmy clack-box, he said.

We then returned to our rooms, wherein we found Silas gone and Ma Britten pale and quiet. She looked at Tom very thoughtful like, and asked him how it was he was here so early of a morning.

I went in to comfort poor Sophina who was crying most piteously.

—Jack, Jack, she said, Jack, they took my da. Who will take care of me now my da is gone?

44

It was hot and close in the snuggery, and whenever he stretched Jack Maggs released a great manly smell like bed linen in the warmth of early morning. Sometimes Mercy thought she could not bear another moment of it, being confined so close with him.

For his part though, he hardly seemed to notice her, and yet she had felt his keen interest on other days, feeling his stare when he thought her ignorant of his attention.

If she was now unattractive to him, he had heard the gossip in the kitchen. He knew she was a chipped and mended cup in a rich man's dresser. It was clear to him, clear to anyone who looked into her eyes, that she was stained brown from use.

He was also rather stained and used, but this did not make him the least unattractive to her. Indeed, it was the knowledge of his ill-usage that stirred her heart so painfully. Why then could he not extend the same charity to her?

She had imagined his scars most vividly. She had thought of his back with particular clarity. She would have dressed it with unguents and lotions, but he was busy writing letters to his beloved and did not care for her anyhow.

The bureau had always fitted the master very well, but it was not made for Jack Maggs. She watched how those immense thighs jammed beneath the dainty little desk and, when his feelings ran away with him, how they lifted the desk clear off the floor so that the cedar top tilted like the deck of a ship at sea. Throughout all this turbulence he would keep on writing, back to front like a Chinaman, until Mercy thought she saw a kind of glow, from behind his neck and shoulders, like the light from a furnace door. As he wrote his thick lips moved, and his eyes screwed almost shut.

It was not until the middle of the second long day, as he left to carry Mr Spinks up to his bed, that she had her chance to look:

Tom did not like Silas or Sophina either

she read, but then the whole page vanished, and although she peered very close at the paper and held it up to the light, it kept its secrets to itself. So it was with each and every page.

She heard his tread on the stair and immediately sat down upon the ottoman.

He entered without glancing at her, but stared down at his papers for so long that she began to fear that she had somehow marked them. He had been carrying some items in his arms, though she could not make them out until he laid them down: three lemons, some twine and rough brown paper, and a splendid silver mirror.

"How is Mr Spinks?" She tried to sound conversational, but her voice quavered.

He looked at her, severely.

"Ailing." He held out the mirror for her to take. At first she thought it a gift and her hand trembled when she took it.

"It's ever so pretty," she said.

"He was a clever old cove what made it. Dead now."

He held out his hand and she understood she was to give the mirror back. He began to wrap it in brown paper.

"It's a gift?" She smiled to hide the sickness in her heart.

He continued folding his brown paper.

"Here, let me do it. She'll think you've bought her a flounder if you wrap it up like that."

She smoothed out the paper, and carefully wrapped the mirror. She felt him watching her; she imagined his breath upon her neck.

"You want me to wrap the lemons, too?" she said lightly.

Unsmiling, he placed the lemons in front of her.

He was standing next to her very close, and she felt his attention on her while she made a neat little parcel of the lemons. After she had completed this task, she wrapped the letters themselves. Finally, when the three parcels had received their kiss of sealing wax, she placed them, one atop the other, in the centre of the desk. She felt all her hair to be on end. She had to speak, no matter what it made him think of her.

"I don't mind you lock me," she began.

There was an odd agitation showing in his eyes.

"I never did tell a soul about you," she said.

Then he leaned down and kissed her. Upon the forehead, like a bishop or an uncle.

"How did little Buckle nab you? It don't make sense, the pair of you."

"It makes sense."

"Did you lose your papa?"

"What?"

"Did you lose your papa?"

His eyes were soft and brown, all their hardness gone, just as they had been last night in the cellar. She looked at him, trying to understand what it was he felt, and then he lifted his poor misshapen hand and stroked her hair.

"Lost your da?" he said roughly. "The poor thing lost the da."

Then she wept against his musky shirt and she felt how he pitied her. He did not embrace her, but he continued gently to stroke her hair, and she might have stayed there for ever, so she felt, had not the inevitable knock come, so soon, upon the door.

He stepped away from her.

"It is Constable," he said. "Come to collect the parcels."

It was not only Constable but also, alas, the master; and this latter person now rushed into the room looking intently at her from under his raised eyebrows. The poor frightened man had strapped his sword around his dressing gown and it clanged against the doorway as he entered.

"Everyone still well?" he asked, staring all the time at Mercy.

Jack Maggs did not seem to notice him. "Now listen here, Eddie, you reckon your mates can find this Henry Phipps." And so saying he thrust the three parcels into Constable's arms.

Mercy thought: *not love letters*.

"Tell them Mr Phipps must squeeze the lemons in a bowl, and then brush the juice across the paper. Then he is to use the mirror. They should tell him it is a good mirror as he will find mentioned in the first letter. They should tell him there is more to the story, but he better come and hear it from my lips, soon, for I cannot stay here in this house a great deal longer. Can you remember all of this?"

Mercy blew her nose.

"Lemons, brush, mirror," said Constable. "More to tell."

"They should tell him—to suggest a place where we can meet in private. He can write me a note"—Maggs turned to Mr Buckle—"and then you will be free of me. I will be gone from your life."

"No, no," said his host, but Mr Buckle's earnest little ferret face was obviously relieved and Mercy saw him as she had never seen him before. She wished it were not so, but her saviour had begun to cut a pathetic figure in her eyes.

45

In foul-smelling Floral Street, Edward Constable alighted from a hackney cab and carried his three parcels to the door of *Mafooz & Son, Importers of Dates and Coffees*, this drab business being distinguished by a small lantern which had been left to burn, carelessly it seemed, throughout the night.

It was a little after dawn as he pulled on the bell, but in far less time than might have been expected at such an hour, the peep-hole in the door was opened, and his business was demanded of him.

The answer being satisfactory, he was admitted into a dim, smoke-stained corridor where a faded individual with rouged cheeks and pouchy eyes was pleased to take his hat and gloves.

This was Magnus, as much a landmark for a certain caste of Londoner as the new column in Trafalgar Square. Magnus was the subject of many anecdotes, most of which devolved from the extremely handsome figure he had cut early in the reign of George III, the period from which his present wig most certainly dated.

This club was an institution in Covent Garden at that time. It was certainly well known to the costers that a certain type of gentleman (known in their parlance as Foreman's Friends) frequented these rooms above Mafooz's shop. The costers themselves, when they were finished with their brandy at the Dog and Whistle, had been known to beg admittance, and then there would be all sorts of fun and dancing into the small hours, particularly on Saturday night and often continuing well into Sunday morning, sometimes even at the hour when Edward Constable arrived to inquire after Mr Henry Phipps.

Neither by word nor by manner did Magnus allow that Mr Phipps might be presently upon the premises, but he did not deny the possibility either. Rather, he ushered Constable into a small room with its title LORD STRUTWELL blazoned boldly on its door. The room was decorated in most masculine style, with various flags and battle standards, and armchairs upholstered in Moroccan leathers.

Here, Constable sat himself down and waited with his parcels on his lap. He displayed no appetite for the bound engravings which filled the book cases, engravings which, in a happier time, might have produced in him a state of almost damnable desire. He waited half an hour with his back turned to the book case, and when the door behind him opened, he stood.

It was apparent from the moment Henry Phipps entered the room that he was drunk. He sat himself down heavily with his long legs stretched out and the contours of his manhood immodestly displayed beneath his doeskins.

He was a tall, well-made young man of conventionally handsome appearance. He had straight fair hair, long side whiskers, a good straight nose, and clear blue eyes, but it was the mouth which was the most expressive aspect of his physiognomy: being one moment utterly persuasive of its charm, and the next distinguished by its churlishness.

Now he squinted up at Constable. "Are you not that fellow from Great Queen Street?"

"I think you know me well enough, Sir."

"The racehorse, eh?"

Edward Constable's mouth tightened.

Henry Phipps was not too drunk to note the expression.

"Oh Christ," he said as he closed his eyes, "please, don't play the footman with me."

"I am a footman, Sir, as you might have reason to recall."

Henry Phipps opened his eyes sufficiently to consider Constable.

"My name is Edward Constable. It was my friend who died . . ."

Phipps then leaned forward, speaking more quietly than he had hitherto. "As I told you before, I will have no more discussions relating to that affair." He made as if to rise.

"Stay, Sir. It is some other business."

Mr Phipps sighed. "Perhaps you wish to blame me for the rain last night. I am, Sir, a tall fellow. Perhaps I caused it."

"That is not my purpose."

"For the sky does love me, eh, and then the rain does fall, and poetry being poetry, why"—he lay back heavily in his arm chair—"then I am to blame."

"Mr Phipps, it is not that business, it is another . . ."

"Not involving my supposed obligation to you?"

"No, Sir, to another."

"Oh Lord, this is very boring."

"I am here on a message from Mr Jack Maggs."

"The Devil you are!"

"I am, Sir."

Henry Phipps's manner now changed completely. He removed himself to the arm of the club chair, folding his large hands upon his lap, and regarded Constable with earnest attention.

"And how is he? How is Jack Maggs?"

"I would say that he was pining for you, Sir."

"Pining for me, you say? How odd. But sit down, Edward. Tell me, what is he like? A ruffian, I warrant."

"He is very comely, as a matter of fact."

"Oh he is, is he? A racehorse?"

"A little grim at times, but the ladies are most taken with him."

"The *ladies*?"

"There is a certain aspect to his manner which does betray his past, and yet you would not know the tortures he has passed through if you did not witness the scars."

"He has scars?"

"He has been flogged, Sir. Yet for a man so abused, I think you will find him of a very decent disposition."

"The thing is this, Eddie, old chap, I really do not think I will have an opportunity to 'find' him at all. I am called away."

"You were 'called away' once already, were you not, Sir? Mr Maggs believes it was his imminent arrival that was the cause of your departure."

"Now I am called away, let us say, further."

"Abroad?"

"Further than it is your damned business to inquire."

"In any case, Sir, he has asked me to deliver these little packages to you."

And here Constable offered the three parcels to Henry Phipps.

The gentleman did not immediately reach for the gifts but rather peered at them.

"What's this?"

"I believe one of the objects to be a mirror."

"A mirror? Is he sarcastic then? What in the deuce does he mean by giving me a mirror?"

"And this one on the top contains three lemons."

"Lemons?"

"And the largest of the three, so I understand, is a certain document which Mr Maggs would have you read."

Constable then held out all three parcels.

"A legal document?" asked Henry Phipps, unable to hide his growing excitement.

"No, I think not."

"Not the title to a house, for instance?"

"I imagine it is a sort of letter."

"A letter?" cried Henry Phipps, suddenly angry. "Do you think I could correspond with such a one as he? And do you not consider the doubtful position you place yourself in? You are breaking the law to know his whereabouts without disclosing it. He is a dangerous man, Mr Racehorse, a man condemned to banishment, for ever. If you wish to reveal my presence to him, I swear I will make you wish that you were never born."

"Sir, my information is that he sits up half the night writing in order to explain himself to you."

"He said this?"

"Please, Sir, he thinks only of you. If ever he did you harm, I am very sure that he is sorry."

For the third time, Constable attempted to deliver Jack Maggs's gifts.

"He says it is necessary to squeeze a little lemon juice upon the pages. And then to read them through the mirror image." There was a pause. "He is very fond of you."

"But I am not fond of him. Tell him that I find the very notion of him vile."

"Can I give him no comfort?"

"Yes: you may tell him that I am well aware of the obligation he has placed me under, and that he can therefore rely upon my silence for the moment."

And with that the interview ended, and Henry Phipps strode from the room.

46

Constable, searching the house high and low, found Jack Maggs in Mr Spinks's bedroom, at which doorway he remained unannounced.

The Australian sat aside the butler's sick-bed. His back was to the door, and he was offering a spoon of broth to the old man.

"You should never look a pooka in the eye. The eye is the strong point of all these dark magicians."

He moved the spoon closer. The butler turned his head aside. The spoon withdrew a little.

"Every creature has its strong point," continued the big man. "With a pooka it is in the eyes entirely. Were it not for the eyes they would be helpless as a new-hatched chicken."

Mr Spinks knocked the spoon aside, and some liquid fell upon his counterpane.

Jack Maggs patiently set the soup bowl and spoon upon the side table. The feverish butler withdrew as far as he was able, until he was sitting up straight and hard against the bed-head, far too preoccupied to notice the footman standing in the doorway.

"Don't look at me like that, old chap," said Jack Maggs. "I'm not the pooka who put the spell on you."

Mr Spinks folded his arms across his chest.

"His name is Oates."

"Pooka!" croaked Mr Spinks sarcastically.

"So you can open your gob when you want."

He offered another spoon of broth, but the butler's mouth stayed firmly closed.

"Very well then." Maggs took the old man's unshaven chin and dug his thumb and second finger in at the hinge, between the gums. "This is how I drench my sheep in New South Wales."

"Mmmph," cried Spinks.

As he struggled to avoid the broth, the butler's rheumy eyes alighted on Constable. The footman smiled encouragingly. Spinks began to speak, but as his mouth opened, so the soup slid in and Maggs clamped his horny hand over the old chap's mouth and nose. There was no choice but to swallow.

"Fight fluid with fluid."

In his distress, Mr Spinks pointed to the door.

Jack Maggs, seeing Constable, immediately set down the bowl upon the side table. "He squeezed the lemons? He understood the mirror?"

While Mr Spinks escaped back beneath his covers, Mr Constable held up the unopened packages, then watched as the other inspected them, checking each and every untied knot along the way.

"Apparently he is not known of."

At this point, Mr Spinks began to snore. Jack Maggs busied himself covering the old fellow's withered shanks; when he finally showed his face again, his eyes were completely expressionless.

"If the man will not be found," said Constable sympathetically, "he will not be found. There is no better place to hide than London."

Jack Maggs showed no further interest in the topic.

"Mercy is doing for the women," he said. "I said I would do for the Bishop here."

"You have new linen," Constable offered. "If you lift Mr Spinks I'll do the changing."

Constable then removed his jacket, and draped it carefully across a chair. While Jack Maggs lifted the butler, he swiftly stripped the bed and laid a cool clean sheet upon the old man's ancient mattress. In all this, he was as efficient as a guardsman, but the effect of seeing Spinks's ruined body cradled in this way by his companion was to make the winds blow stronger, to flood his mind with Christian images of the type celebrated in the stained-glass windows of the little church of St Mary Le Bow. From here he was carried, in a great swirl, to turbulent visions of Maggs's scarred body, his massive strength, producing in him such a mighty want, not to nurse bullying old Spinks, but to *be* nursed himself, to have Jack Maggs take his head and lay it in his lap, to stroke him with that hand.

He now felt a dangerously strong desire to confess that he had indeed discovered the whereabouts of Henry Phipps, that he had thereby foolishly revealed Maggs's whereabouts to a man who did not wish him well.

He knew it unwise, but he had a passion to unburden himself, to disclose that he too had known Henry Phipps, known him in the most personal and private sense. He had been flattered and led astray by that gentleman.

He had gone next door to deliver an invitation to tea with Mr Buckle. There he was engaged by the young master in talk of the West Country and its charms. He was taken upstairs to see a small oil painting of a storm off Bristol which, as it turned out, was not hanging where its owner had advertised it. He was then persuaded to stay to wash the young master's hair, to towel him dry, to hold his head against his breast. He heard his soft promises; he had heard himself called Angel; he had taken his manhood deep inside of him.

And thought himself, for cursed truth, a princess.

For two weeks in 1836, Edward Constable had been drunk with Henry Phipps, dreamed of Henry Phipps, had been reamed, rogered, ploughed by Henry Phipps so he could barely walk straight to the table. He had been invited to take a tour of Italy with Henry Phipps, and upon acceptance, he had confessed the circumstances of the invitation to dear Albert Pope, who had been his honest friend and intimate companion during fifteen years of service.

The next day Albert blew his brains out with that horrid little pistol.

He could have told Jack Maggs how badly Henry Phipps had behaved after Albert's death, but he held his secrets tight, like a fistful of
gravel against his heart.

He tried to cover Spinks but the old man again became agitated and
thrashed around, kicking the coverlet away and pulling at the neck of
his fresh night shirt as if he meant to tear it from his body.

Constable picked up the old man's dirty linen from the floor and tied
it into a bundle. Though still dressed in his Sunday best, he hoisted the
bundle onto his shoulder and carried it from the room. In the passage-
way he was surprised to find Jack Maggs still close upon his heels.

47

The May sunshine fell in a steep bright mote upon the household
linen, which was now bubbling and ballooning from the top of the
wash-house copper.

There was, for the moment, no other labour demanded of Edward
Constable and, although he had at first anticipated stealing a moment
in the sunshine, he now began to notice how closely Jack Maggs continued to cleave to his side. The dark and steamy wash-house began to
seem a great deal more appealing than the sunshine.

While his companion leaned carelessly against the ancient wall, engaged in no more productive activity than puffing on a corn-cob pipe—
the fragrant smoke of which acted as a potent tonic on the footman—Constable stirred the sheets and pillow-cases. He breathed deep
of that singular blend of soapy steam and dark tobacco.

"Pear's in blossom," he offered.

"Yes. Pear."

After which no more words were spoken. Constable felt a slight tingling in his neck and a general tension, by no means disagreeable, of
the type a chap might feel whilst dawdling beside another chap, as yet
unknown.

"I lived a long time with secrets," said Jack Maggs at last.

Constable's heart thumped in his chest.

Said Jack Maggs: "You know where I come from?"

"No."

"Doubtless you were told already by our little Miss." Maggs puffed a little harder on his pipe. "It is New South Wales I come from. There. Now you hear it from my own lips."

Constable looked down into the confusion of the steam.

"Why do you tell me this, Mr Maggs?"

"Three years of that time I had the misfortune to be in a hell called Moreton Bay. There a man might be killed on account of knowing another man's secret."

"Killed?" Constable thought of men with secrets like his own: Ensign John Hepburn, the drummer Thomas White, all those other jolly fellows who had been prosecuted and convicted and "launched into eternity" outside the Newgate walls. "You mean hanged?"

"No, no," said Maggs impatiently. "Listen to me: had you known anything as dangerous as what you know of me now, why, you'd be a risk to me."

"You can speak plainly with me, Jack."

"I am trying to, Eddie. Listen: in Moreton Bay, every man would be a spy on every other man. It was how they kept us down. If you and I were lads together in that place, then you must give me a secret of yours, should you chance to stumble over one of mine. That way we were in balance."

"Jack, are you confessing to me?"

"No. I am going to trade with you. I am going to tell you a secret."

"But you already gave me a secret."

"I need one of yours. I'll pay you double."

"I have no secrets," said Constable carefully. "What secret?"

"The one I saw on your face when you walked into Mr Spinks's room."

"You think you saw my secret written on my face?"

"Aye."

"It was in my manner? How I spoke?"

"On your face."

"That clear?"

"That clear."

"But what would you tell *me*?"

"That Henry Phipps is my son."

"Your son?" Constable hesitated. "You do mean *son*? A type of son, being like a son?"

"It is a clear enough word."

"But do you mean he is your *petit fils*? Or do you mean that you are, an older man, like a father to the younger . . . in many ways?"

"Whatever it is called, it is clear enough," Maggs said, and Constable felt himself forced to hold that dark excited gaze.

"Henry's afraid of me, ain't that it?" demanded Maggs. "Your friends saw him, didn't they?"

Constable hesitated.

"Then he must be told he has nothing to fear from Jack. I am his father. I would rather die than hurt him."

"What of his mother?" Constable asked carefully. "Where is she?"

"We never did meet."

"Then you do not mean *son*."

"Don't be so thick, man," said Jack Maggs. "I have said it plain. Now, come, come, I want your secret, laddie."

There followed then a long silence, and Constable, much confused, began to hoist the first sheet high out of the copper and lead it towards the mangle.

"My secret may not please," he said at last.

"Please or not please." Maggs came to the handle and began, slowly, to turn it. Both men watched thoughtfully as the sheet, squashed and steaming, uncoiled itself from the mangle and lay in the stone trough.

"My secret?"

"Yes."

"I am fond of you," said Constable.

The roller stopped.

"You are *fond* of me?" Maggs asked perplexedly.

"I am, yes."

"And it was that which was on your mind when you walked in. You are *fond* of me?"

"It was."

And it was at that delicate point that their conversation was interrupted by the sound of a most piteous wailing. The two men ran out onto the little yard, and looked up to whence the sounds came. There they saw Mercy Larkin, framed in Mr Spinks's high window.

"Oh Lor," she cried, "come quick, come quick. Mr Spinks is taken bad."

Jack took Constable's shoulder: "Tell me—your friends saw my Henry? He did not want to know me? That was your secret?"

Constable was not by nature a liar, and when he looked into those hooded hungry eyes he wanted, more than anything, to tell the truth. But Constable feared that if Henry Phipps were found, then Jack Maggs would be lost.

And so he lied.

"No," he said, looking him straight in the eye. "I swear. They could not find him anywhere."

48

At three o'clock on this first afternoon of May, Jack Maggs found the little grocer hidden far from the spring sunlight, in front of a sad and smoky fire in his bedroom. The curtains had been drawn and the candles lit, and Mr Buckle, dressed in an embroidered silk smoking jacket, had his pointed nose deep in a book. The unsavoury smell of cheese was strong about the room, and this smell, Jack Maggs soon saw, had its source in a yellow wedge of Stilton which, together with a glass of wine, was set up on a tray beside his elbow. When Mr Buckle finally became sensible of Maggs's presence in the room, he leapt up so quickly he almost sent this tray flying.

"Whoa there," cried the footman.

As he fled towards the fireplace, Mr Buckle's slippers flashed beneath the turn-ups of his trousers, like the prow of an oriental boat. They were queer and sparkly, and nearly distracted Maggs's attention from the war-like poker which Percy Buckle had picked up and was holding secretly behind his leg.

"Do not fear me, Mr Buckle."

"Fear!" scoffed Mr Buckle, backing himself up against the mantel.

"Please sit down, your Lordship."

Mr Buckle brought the poker out of hiding and, by way of justifying his attachment, poked the fire with it.

"Sit."

Mr Buckle sat abruptly down. "Yes?"

"It is Mr Spinks's rattle, Sir."

"Rattle?"

Maggs was surprised to see the fearful eyes become more distant, his manner harden. "You mean a cough?"

"A rattle is a rattle. There ain't no doubting what it is. We had best get a doctor to him very quickly."

"What else beside the cough?"

As Jack Maggs told the symptoms, Mr Buckle listened, his head a little to one side, his hands clasped in his lap. He appeared most sympathetic in his demeanour but it was soon clear that, contrary to all his earlier fright and agitation, the master had little anxiety on Mr Spinks's behalf.

When Jack Maggs offered to drag him to his butler's bed where he might inspect the patient for himself, Mr Buckle responded by pushing his bony little backside deeper into his chair.

"Then what of Mr Oates?" he cried. "What do we do there?"

"In what respect?"

"I would be a very foolish man to go running to a doctor without asking Mr Oates's permission."

"Why's that?"

"It is Mr Oates who should call the doctor," continued Mr Buckle. "He's the one responsible for the injury."

"He laid the spell?"

"He laid the spell. That's it exactly."

"Very well," Jack Maggs granted. "Then let me run the message to Mr Oates."

"But it was only a prank, see," said Percy Buckle, rattling the poker on the hearth. "That's what alters it. That's where you should watch your *P*s and *Q*s. What will Oates think if I say my man is dying of his prank? He will think me trying to blame him for something which I have no right to blame him for. You may not know this, but I am a student of the Law. Oates could sue me for a slander. And if he could, he would. I hear he is a fierce gent about his reputation."

"You tell him that Mr Spinks has the Mesmeric Fluid on his lung, and he will die of it unless Mr Oates be so nice as to take it away."

"No, no."

"Damn you! I'll fetch him myself."

"He may not be at home," cried Percy Buckle.

But Jack Maggs was already checking his fob pocket to find a shilling for a cab. "One more thing, your Lordship."

"I am listening," said the other, beginning to preen his moustache again.

"You will hear me drawing nails from the front door."

"Very good, Master Maggs."

"But I would have to kill anyone who left your house."

"Yes, yes," said Percy Buckle, so distractedly that Jack Maggs would later wonder whether he could possibly have been understood.

Mr Buckle, however, had heard very well indeed, and as the criminal ran down the stairs of his house, he sat looking into the fire, watching Goats and Demons dancing in the flames above the coals.

49

M r Buckle loved his house, and he celebrated his Great Good Fortune, not merely on the fourteenth day of each month (when he retired to the snuggery to re-read the will) but at almost every moment of almost every day.

He had been often observed to stand and stare off into space, in what his servants imagined was a kind of rapture. It was, as Miss Mott said, as if the master could see an angel in his hallway, but Mr Buckle saw no angels, it was his house he worshipped, and what a miracle it was that he should own that dark-green wall-paper, the stained-glass fanlight, the gloss of polish on the oaken floor.

You could have fed him rancid bacon and he might not have complained. You could leave the sheets unlaundered for two weeks at a stretch. But Heaven help you if the floors weren't polished, if the mantelpiece wasn't dusted every day. He liked his inheritance to shine. Consequently, to see the fresh injury which Jack Maggs's departure had caused to his front door was more disturbing to the owner than even he—who had seen the rusty nails first breach that lustrous black surface—might have anticipated.

He knelt before the door as if winded. The nails had been ripped out roughly. In their place were jagged wounds: gouges, dents, raw splinters. Tenderly, he laid back the splinters inside the wounds, but the hurt was too savage for such ministrations.

Back in his sitting room, he repeatedly pulled the bell for Constable. When he was not answered, he returned to the front door and picked up the horrid nails himself. He dropped them into his jacket pocket, and hurried down the breakneck stairs into his kitchen. Here he found the fire dead and a queer pink-grey mouse eating a crust of bread on the table. The three thin lines between Mr Buckle's eyebrows deepened. At first it seemed that he might strike the mouse, but then all his energy emerged in a violent shiver. He went quickly back up to the ground floor and then up the back stairs.

And there, in the snuggery, he discovered Mercy and Constable sitting side by side on the ottoman, chatting contentedly like dowagers at a ball.

He spoke to them politely. They were lazy and familiar in return.

He requested them to come downstairs to sweep up the mess of nails and splinters. He did not wait to see how this order was received, but descended straight away to the drawing room and picked up—he could have chosen anything—a recent pamphlet from the Workingman's Association. Although he made a convincing show of reading, he was far too upset to study anything. All his attention was focused upon his servants who, even as they came down the stairs, were chatting as familiarly as before.

When they had swept up the dust and splinters, they were cool enough to enter the drawing room without an invitation.

Mercy *sat* in the embrasure of the window. Constable stood. And there they stayed, busy at *waiting*, he realized, for the return of the criminal whom they seemed to expect at any moment.

"I've got to tell him, Mercy," whispered Constable. "It ain't right for me to keep this secret from him."

"Don't be so hard on yourself, Eddie. It's not fair you have to decide."

Mr Buckle did not know what secret they meant, nor did he care. He turned the page of his pamphlet.

"Who else could decide?" asked Constable. "I'm the one what knows."

Behind the pamphlet the master's face was as drained of blood as their shining countenances were hot with it. Mercy whispered something. He could not make it out. In reply Constable said, with uncharacteristic passion: "Whatever Henry Phipps has sworn, it ain't worth spit."

Mr Buckle put aside his pamphlet.

"Mr Constable," said he, "you'll not speak of a gentleman in that tone."

Mercy then presumed to raise an eyebrow.

"What mean you by *that*, Miss?"

"I was surprised, Sir," said she, just as saucy as if it were midnight and the door were locked.

"Why would you be surprised?"

"No reason, Sir."

"Answer!" he cried, and she realized, at last, how angry he was. Her tone became more sober.

"I recall you did not think much of that gentleman next door."

"You value your position, girl?" hissed Percy Buckle.

She stood up straight, putting her hands behind her back. "I'm sorry, Sir."

There was a silence then, for a while.

"I do beg your pardon, Sir," said Mercy.

"I also beg your pardon, Mr Buckle," said Constable. "I forgot myself."

Percy Buckle looked at the maid with his eyes narrow and his mouth now exceeding small. She had, finally, a frightened look about the eyes. He stroked his moustache and then folded his pale dry hands carefully upon his lap. "Did you attend to my bathroom yet?" he asked.

"Yes, Sir. I did it the moment you first asked me."

Someone in the street cried *Whoa-up*.

"Is it him?"

"No, Sir."

"What is that you have there in your apron, Mercy? What is it that you're playing with?"

"Nothing, Sir."

"Then bring your 'nothing' here."

The girl came a little closer and Percy Buckle suddenly took her wrist and wrenched her violently towards him.

"Why," he said, prying her hand open, "it is a little lock of children's hair."

"Two locks."

"Two locks," he agreed. The wool around the hair was old and faded.

"They was in his jacket pocket, Sir."

"So our convict is a family man," he said, looking into her agitated eyes. "How got you to have such a personal item, my girl?"

"Why, Sir," she said quickly. "It was very clever of me as you'll see. He had taken his jacket off to write his letters. Then Mr Spinks was took.

Then Mr Maggs left me to help with Mr Spinks. They were in a little envelope in the breast pocket. It *is* baby hair, Sir, ain't it?"

"Perhaps," Constable suggested, "it is Mr Phipps's hair."

"Don't be daft," said Mercy. "How could it be Phipps? These babes have dark hair."

The footman abandoned his post at the window, and asked if he might be permitted to touch the two locks of baby hair.

Mr Buckle could not decide if this was impertinent or not, proper or not. He stayed in his chair, watching uneasily as his footman held the locks of hair in his nimble long-fingered hands. This was how they were grouped, three of them clustered around these sad remains, when there came a sudden knocking on the front door.

50

Tobias dutifully began his report for the *Morning Chronicle*. He wrote a headline: A FIRE IN BRIGHTON. He underlined it twice, then laboured on a small distinctive flourish beneath the underline.

The ink on the flourish was still wet when his first interruption arrived: a rather chatty little bailiff with muddy boots and three promissory notes signed by John Oates on the strength of his son's good name.

Toby exchanged these three notes for one of his own, in which he promised to pay seventy-eight pounds twenty days hence.

Then he took out a sheet of fresh paper and wrote a painful letter informing his father that he could be no longer responsible for his debts. This took less than five minutes, but he then spent almost half an hour composing a more cautious public announcement to the same effect. He planned to deliver this advertisement to the newspapers when he handed in his report to the *Chronicle*, and when he had composed the announcement to his satisfaction, he made three fair copies which he placed in individual envelopes addressed to *The Times*, the *Observer* and the *Morning Chronicle*. The unexpected expense of these advertisements then led him to take a fresh sheet of paper on which he made a revised estimate of his expenditures and incomes for the following quarter. These totals were very bleak indeed, so he put aside his Brighton Fire and set out to produce a quick Character Sketch for the

Observer. This newspaper now paid five pounds for such pieces, and he was soon standing on his chair, looking for his notes for the "Canary Woman of Islington," "Old Tom Wicks of Camden Town," and other *Types* and *Characters* which he had collected for this very purpose. He finally settled on a Crossing Sweeper and sat himself at his desk where, on one more clean sheet, he began:

> *Those readers familiar with McKenzie's Chop House in Fetter Lane have doubtless had the benefit of the broom of Titchy Tate, with-out ever imagining that he who wields this instrument with such violent effect, believes himself to be the luckiest little boy in all of London.*

He would have executed both "Titchy Tate" and "A Fire in Brighton" by lunch time, except that he was pushed into a furtive conference with Lizzie (although what that conference was to be about he could not de-termine, for she had fled the room before it had half begun).

Next came his wife in a state of great distress on account of an angry red pustule which had emerged on their baby's breast. Toby was con-siderably alarmed by what he saw, but when he suggested bathing the infection in salty water his wife seemed to think this very wise advice in-deed, and he was able to return to his study, and once more take up the quill.

Whereupon Jack Maggs appeared at his doorway, demanding a doc-tor for a sick butler. He had no choice. He pushed "Titchy Tate" aside and took a fresh sheet of paper on which he composed a note to Dr Grieves of Gray's Inn Road, requesting him to please be so kind as to attend to a butler at 29 Great Queen Street. This letter he gave into the care of Mrs Jones, asking the sturdy old lady to put on her shawl and take it up to an Inn in Chancery Lane where he knew the doctor ate his lunch.

He doubted the butler's condition was dangerous, but he was a cau-tious man and, given his little joke about the quarantine, he thought it politic to be present at Great Queen Street to introduce the patient to his doctor. Thus he went to dress, and all the while he went about this business he had to endure the sound of the criminal's hectoring foot-steps pacing in the hall below.

Some minutes later, as he followed Jack Maggs back down through the drizzling streets to Holborn, he reflected that the man had as good

as stolen five pounds from his pocket. He therefore, consciously, rec-
ompensed himself.

Tit for tat, he memorized the hard shine to Jack Maggs's skin as it
cleaved close to the bones of his cheek and jaw. He would use those
bones, perhaps tomorrow. On the following day he would return for
those deeper, more painful items which must still be cut free from the
softer tissue of Jack Maggs's memory.

He was developing, with every passing hour, giddy ambitions for this
novel. *Captain Crumley* had been a comedy, a pantomime, broad
strokes, great larks, a rowdy tale of old London that had Mr Davidson
the butcher in a fever while he waited for the next instalment. But in all
of English literature there was nothing like the dark journey he now
planned to take inside the Criminal Mind. He began, as he walked, to
chisel away at its plot. He charted a course by abstract reasoning, almost algebraically. From Birth to Death, from Light to Dark, from
Water to Fire. It was with some irritation that he found the walk had
ended, and he must abandon this activity in favour of the real world.

In Percy Buckle's drawing room, he found the physician had already
arrived, and was standing with his back to Mr Buckle's fireplace. Dr
Grieves was a neat, well tailored man and in spite of being nearly fifty,
of a markedly athletic appearance. He had always seemed a quiet fellow, almost excessively polite in his manners, so when Tobias saw the
doctor's stern face, his compressed mouth, he began immediately to
apologize for dragging him from his luncheon.

"It were better you had dragged me from my breakfast."

"The patient is very ill?"

"Very dead. To put it bluntly."

In the silence that followed this announcement, Oates could hear the
most piteous chorus of wailing descending from the upper floors.

"Oh dear," said Toby.

No response from the doctor.

"A nice old chap," offered Toby.

Mr Buckle nodded his head vigorously in agreement.

"He came down quickly?" Toby inquired of Percy Buckle.

Before the master of the house could supply this intelligence, the
doctor turned to him and asked the privilege of a moment alone with
Mr Oates.

Once Mr Buckle had departed, the doctor sat himself down in a wing-back armchair by the fire. There he put his hands upon his knees, and gazed long and hard at the black and smoky logs.

"Your shirt is showing, Sir."

Tobias Oates followed the motion of the doctor's head and saw a three-inch twist of bright green shirt sticking out from his flies. He coloured furiously. Dr Grieves continued as the writer attended to his shirt.

"As to the other business, I am damned if I know what to say to you."

"Who else was I to send for, if not my own doctor?"

"Oh, dear God, Mr Oates, you cannot go around killing people."

"I assure you—"

"You cannot come into this household, Sir, impersonating a member of the College of Surgeons. How do you think it would be, for you to be charged? What would the judge say, upon hearing that you had convinced the deceased that you were a surgeon?"

"It was a prank, a joke."

"Mr Oates, the old fellow is dead."

"But not of my prank."

"Mr Oates, it is not as if you were a Balliol undergraduate . . ."

This, to Toby's ear, was only another way of saying that he was not a gentleman.

"And on account of this lack," he smiled bitterly, "I am a murderer?"

"I will write pneumonia on his death certificate, but if you really want my true opinion, it is that you bewitched him."

"Sir, you are a man of science."

"A man is known by his deeds, Sir. And you bewitched him. Just, Sir, as you bewitched the cook and the housekeeper who—although you have not asked after their health—are, whilst upset to learn of their companion's death, not in any present danger themselves."

"But surely, he was an old man. A pneumonia might have arrived in any case."

"Do not, please, tell me my business, Mr Oates. I was pleased to have you a guest in my house. I enjoyed our evenings together."

"As did I."

"But I cannot thank you for having me commit a perjury on this death certificate."

"Perhaps, Doctor, it is not a perjury. I do not say that I was not remiss, but—"

"A perjury. I cannot forgive you for it."

Tobias put his head in his hands.

"I beg your forgiveness," he said at last. When he looked up, his face showed his grief.

"But it is your God who will forgive you," said the doctor, severely. "It is with Him that you have your business to settle. I have no thirst for ruining you."

This last sentence was not without its effect.

The young man looked up at the physician, curly hair dishevelled, eyes swimming with tears. "I would do anything to undo this."

The doctor stood up. "Then you must pray. In the meantime, you may know that the death certificate protects your reputation at the same time as it threatens mine: you will understand me, I am sure, when I say that I cannot serve your family any longer."

"But what if my babe is ill?"

"Then you will take your babe to a doctor, and the doctor will cure your babe, and you will be a lucky man."

"But I know no other doctor. He had, this morning, a kind of pustule . . ."

"Mr Oates, London is a big city . . ."

"I know London, Sir. I know it perhaps better than even you do. It is an exceedingly big city, and if my babe is ill . . ."

"A big city, in which you will find many excellent doctors."

"You will give me an introduction?"

"Please, Mr Oates, how could I do that? I have already played loose with my good name."

"You are casting me out?"

For answer, the doctor stood and pulled on the bell.

"Who else would I turn to?"

It was the criminal, in all his wild and slovenly dishabille, who answered the call. Toby, in the midst of his own distress, noticed the doctor's astonishment as he asked the soiled and spotted man to fetch his coat and bag.

"If my wife is ill, who would I call?"

For answer, the doctor made a small formal bow, then walked out into the hall where Jack Maggs had his great-coat ready. He slowly donned the coat and buttoned it, then, without a word to anyone, he left the house.

The criminal closed the door behind him, then stood in front of it.

"Thank you," said Toby, meaning that he would also take his leave, but the criminal did not move. He stood unnaturally straight, with his eyes straight ahead.

"Mr Oates," said he. "I need a word with you."

"I can't think of that now . . . ," said Tobias Oates.

The criminal then stepped so close to him that Tobias could smell the rum on his breath. Then the novelist found himself being lifted from the floor and shaken so his teeth rattled in his head.

He was next replaced carefully on the floor, but still held very hard by the shoulders. The smell of alcohol was very strong again. He could see the pores of his tormentor's nose, the iron whiskers, the twitch in his cheek, the black fury in his eye.

Tobias Oates's life was unravelling.

51

Tobias had spent a dreadful year, his fourth, in a home for orphaned boys in Shropshire, where he had been bullied continually. Thereafter he lived one year in Devon, with a mother who was most loudly inconvenienced by his presence. Brought by her to London at the tender age of five, he was soon put in the care of his father, although it was a very hard kind of care he got from that gentleman, and he was pretty much forced to make his own way from there, to find his feet in a city that would as soon have trampled him into the mud.

He had been cast off but he would not be flotsam.

He had been denied a proper school but he had learned to read and write and he had made himself, by will, a sorcerer of that great city.

Now, each day in the *Morning Chronicle*, each fortnight in the *Observer*, it was Tobias Oates who "made" the City of London. With a passion he barely understood himself, he named it, mapped it, widened its great streets, narrowed its dingy lanes, framed its scenes with the melancholy windows of his childhood. In this way, he invented a respectable life for himself: a wife, a babe, a household. He had gained a name for comic tales. He had got himself, along the way, a little belly, a friend who was a titled lady, a second friend who was a celebrated actor, a third friend who was a Knight of the Realm, a fourth friend who was an author and tutor to the young Princess Victoria. He did not dare look down, so far had he come.

Until this morning, when his fun and games had killed a man.

Then the doctor had cast him out, and this *criminal*, this outcast, had felt himself free to pick him up and shake him as though he were nothing but a rabbit.

"You would best be very calm, Sir," he told Jack Maggs, although it was he, Tobias Oates, who was, by some trick of Fate, suddenly the criminal. "If you want this to end safely," he cried fearfully, "you had best watch yourself."

He disengaged himself and sought to button the jacket which had been torn off in the scuffle.

"Here's the button, Sir. Give me your coat. The maid will attend to it."

"Be *still*," said Tobias.

"Yes, Sir, I'll be still."

And the scoundrel was still a moment, although his contemptuous dark eyes stayed on the writer.

"You have pulled off my *button*," Tobias said incredulously. "Are you not a *footman*, Jack Maggs? Are you not a *servant*, man?"

For answer Jack Maggs sat insolently in the master's wing-back chair and crossed one massive leg over the other.

"I'm bogged here," he said. "Two weeks, and stuck up to my axles in the mud." He rubbed his hand over his dark cheek and Toby saw the tic moving once again. "You are bogged with me, and I am bogged with you. And every day that passes, why it gets a little worse for everyone. It was on my behalf you came up with your Contagion. You could not know it would prove a wee bit fatal."

"I can hardly be responsible for pneumonia!"

"As I said, you could not know."

In the silence that followed Tobias began to believe that he was being threatened.

"I am most eager," the convict continued, "to get along the track, but I cannot do it until I find Mr Henry Phipps. When I have him, then I'll go. It was not what I had planned, but such is life." He paused. "And as for what you done to Mr Spinks's Magnetic Fluid . . ."

Tobias Oates looked at the convict's face—the coarse black brows, the dry cracked lips—and found it vile.

"Do you imagine you can *blackmail* me?"

"I want what is owing—the name of the Thief-taker."

"To hell with you, you tinker."

That made his tic leap good and strong. Tobias saw it.

"You gave your word!"

Tobias looked into his adversary's belligerent eyes, and knew that he could not afford to lose him. "You sold me fourteen days, Jack Maggs. I have used no more than eleven of them."

"But it is two weeks from the day we agreed."

"Only eleven days have you sat for me."

The criminal raised his misshapen hand and pressed it hard against his cheek.

"Two days," Tobias explained, "I was travelling to Brighton and back."

Maggs would never beg. It was written in his body that he would not bend, that he must stand straight and hold his head high. But now he was—Tobias saw it—inexplicably, at breaking point.

"I have money." The convict tried to smile, but the tic rippled down his face again. "Twenty guineas. How's that? I'll pay you for the man's address. If you have expenses besides, I am your man."

The sheer quantity of money shocked Tobias. He gave a sharp incredulous laugh.

"You name the figure." The other man was now sitting forward on the edge of his seat. The palsy had changed the texture of his skin; it was oddly pale and crêpy. "Thirty if you must. Then I'll be out of everybody's life."

"I'm sorry, old chap," Toby said coldly, "but you must give me the three days you owe me."

"For Christ's sake, have mercy. I cannot wait three days. I cannot bear it any more."

"You are still my subject, no matter what booty you are carrying."

But Maggs barely heard him. His eyes rolled backwards in his head. He gave a groan and clutched his face in both his hands.

Tobias Oates watched his adversary as he slowly fell back into the cushions of the wing-back chair. To the maid who rushed forth from the shadows, he said:

"You may send him to my house at nine tomorrow morning. I'll treat him then."

52

When Tobias Oates returned home it was already dark and he found the entire household—his wife, his sister-in-law, the housekeeper—all gathered in a circle in the kitchen, bathing his wailing baby boy in a metal tub.

"What is it? What's the matter?"

The women did not turn, and this alone made his pulse run the faster.

"What is it?" he cried and forced himself into the circle. There he saw his infant son, his face quite pale and his little chest now hugely inflamed. What this morning had been a pustule now seemed to look more like a growth. It was red and very hard, and when his papa touched it with his fingers, the little fellow emitted a thin weak wail.

"What ails him, for God's sake? What is it?"

"It is witch's milk," said the housekeeper, laying her large broad finger tips gently on the swelling. "Set hard as rock."

"He has a fever," his wife said. "I sent for Dr Grieves. I sent the grocer's boy, but the boy has somehow upset the doctor, for he was sent away with no message."

"That boy!" exclaimed the old housekeeper, continuing to sponge the whimpering child. "He would be better back in Ireland praying to the French. He should not be here, nor neither should his mother."

"Damn Grieves," cried Oates. The three women looked at him with such alarm, that he immediately began to smile, and coo, and pat his hands in the air.

"Grieves . . . ah, Grieves," he said. "Poor old Grieves."

"What is wrong with Dr Grieves?"

He could not think what to answer them, and, saying only that he would fetch the doctor himself, he fled back out into Lamb's Conduit Street just as a hackney cab came trotting by. He hailed it before he knew quite what he was to do with it.

He looked up at the mulish driver who, in turn, glowered down from his bench, with his many-skirted coat wrapped tight around him. He was a thug-like fellow with heavy brows and great yellow teeth like tombstones in his mouth.

"So what's your pleasure, Sir?"

"I need a doctor nearby. Do you know of a doctor?"

"Doctor, Sir. Yes, Sir. Straight away."

And off they set up Lamb's Conduit Street, along Gray's Inn Road, down across to the other side of Saffron Hill, passing on the way a number of buildings with lanterns advertising doctors.

"Now listen, fellow . . ."

"Yes, Sir."

"I only have a shilling or two about me. Where were you going to take me?"

"Why, to Merton Street, to Dr Hardwick's."

"What sort of doctor is he?"

"Blessed if I know, Sir," shouted the cabby, "but he is a doctor, and well thought of, I do know that."

Tobias Oates wondered what class of person thought well of this doctor, and for what reason. But he had no choice: "Very well," he said, "to Dr Hardwick's."

Soon enough they rolled into a dismal little street in Clerkenwell. The cabby pulled up before a high narrow house, distinguished by the smoke-blackened lantern burning faintly by its door. Had it not been for the evidence of this miserable lamp, Tobias would have thought the building abandoned.

"If this is only for the shilling," said the cabby, "you best move smartly, Sir."

"Very well," said Tobias. He alighted, approaching the dark deserted pile with some uncertainty. The front gate was crooked on its hinges, and the stone stairs leading up from the street smelled as if a herd of cats had been encamped there.

He knocked on the door once, twice.

Very soon he heard a distant shuffling and then a cry of, "Who's there?"

"I have a sick baby. I need a doctor."

A male voice replied—a single word—but Tobias could not distinguish it. He knocked louder. "I need a doctor."

There followed a loud noise of chains being dropped onto a floor. Then the tall door opened a fraction, and in the darkness—for there did not seem to be so much as a candle lit inside—he saw the shadow of an old man's face, or rather, what he took to be the face of an old man, for the voice that came out of it seemed very old indeed.

"Who's there?"

"Excuse me. Are you Dr Hardwick?"

"I am, Sir, have been, and will be a good while yet. And may I have the pleasure of knowing who comes knocking on my door while I am in communion with my herrings?"

"My name is Oates, and my babe is sick."

"How old is your babe?"

"Three months."

"Then you must know it for a fact—babes are always sick. It is their nature. How is he sick?"

"He has a fever. There is a great red lump upon his chest."

"If you want to ride for a shilling," called the cabby from the street, "I cannot wait for you to sign the Peace."

"Who's that?" inquired the doctor.

"The hackney cab."

"Do you owe him money?"

"Sir, will you come with me?"

"Can you pay me?" asked the doctor. "That is always a question worth asking."

"Yes, yes, I can pay you," said Tobias Oates.

"My fee is five shillings, and has been since Waterloo."

"Please, Sir . . ."

"But I have been known to accept chinaware in its stead. More than once, a little Delft. Do you know Delft? I don't press for it, but I make it known."

"I thank you," said Tobias Oates, who had neither Delft nor dosh to pay any bill.

"I only make it known."

"And I thank you for giving me that possibility to consider." With these assurances the anguished father was able to get the doctor into the cab without actually lying about his financial situation.

The journey was conducted in almost total silence, and later Tobias could recall little else of it but the strong smell of fish, which he took to be herring, upon which the doctor had obviously been making an enthusiastic attack. It was not until they reached Lamb's Conduit Street that he had a good chance to look at his companion, and there, by the light of the candle his wife held high at the front door, he saw that Dr Hardwick was a man of perhaps sixty years of age, balding on his top, but with a great shock of ginger hair much streaked with grey. His eyebrows, which were also ginger-coloured, were a very powerful feature of his face, pressing powerfully over his cloudy eyes. His clothing was old, his great cloak actually ragged around the hem and sleeves. Mary Oates, who saw all this at the same moment as her husband, turned as pale as the wax of her candle.

"This is Dr Hardwick, my dear," said Toby.

His wife burst into tears and ran down to the kitchen where they found her, a moment later, holding the whimpering babe fiercely to her bosom.

The ragged old doctor entered the kitchen as though it were his own, dropped his scuffed old satchel upon the table, and called for water with which to wash.

When he had scrubbed his large freckled hands, he turned to Mrs Oates, who had removed herself as far away as the scullery. She was rocking her babe and talking to him in small and private whispers.

"Now, Ma'am," said he, "please give the patient to me."

Mary Oates looked to her husband who, not without serious trepidation, echoed the doctor's request. The young author then watched his son passed to the old man, recalling at the same time the case of Dr Snipes of Wapping who had killed three of his spinster patients and fed their remains to his fox terrier. He wanted only to cry out, stop! enough! But he watched as the stranger removed the swaddling from his precious son and squeezed his stomach with his knobbly jointed hands.

"Hold him. Not you, Ma'am. You, Sir."

Tobias Oates did as he was ordered. He held his son down on the table while the doctor removed a small spirit lamp from his bag and lit it. Toby looked away a fraction. When he looked back, the old man was passing a surgeon's knife back and forwards under the bright blue flame of the lamp.

"Hold him tight, Sir. Ma'am, look away."

Tobias Oates looked at the three women who were bunched, his wife at the centre, over by the scullery. The two sisters had a similar expression on their faces, their eyes wide, their lips parted.

Tobias Oates turned away from them.

"Papa's here," he said, feeling himself a liar and a fool. "Papa's here, my darling."

But as the knife approached the dear little boy's chest, the tears began to well up in his father's eyes, and as the blade came down across the swelling on the red protrusion, as the child's face contorted in outrage, as the little fellow shrieked, as the great river of pus flowed forth from the lanced boil, Tobias Oates cried shamelessly, or so it appeared to all who saw him. In truth, however, the shame was very deep, and when he saw the evidence of infection pour forth from his son's innocent body, he felt the poison to be all his own.

53

When the wound had been stitched and the old doctor had liberally swabbed the entire of little John's chest with a violently coloured purple tincture, when the patient's cries had begun at last to become less fierce, and he had been dispatched with the womenfolk to the nursery, the doctor packed away his knife and spirit lamp and snapped shut his enormous bag. Then he turned his rheumy eyes and tobacco eyebrows towards Tobias Oates.

"Now . . ." he began.

He did not have to venture any further—Tobias knew what was to come next, and he came dancing out from the crease to meet it.

"I look forward to your account."

At this, everything which had been solicitous in the old man's manner, that which had given the suppleness to his old fingers, and drawn the steel so kindly across the child's infection, was now withdrawn, and Tobias Oates saw the old man's head pulled down into the neck, the shoulders up towards the ears, his very flesh contract around his bones.

Dr Hardwick folded his forearms across his pale, discoloured waistcoat. His great hairy brows came down upon his eyes.

"I keep no accounts," he said coldly. "I am not an inn keeper. I need the five shillings, Sir, and I made that very clear when you dragged me from my dinner."

"Pray do not embarrass me," began the young man.

"Pray do not anger me," said the doctor, now very quiet indeed.

He closed his bag briskly, shrugged on his ragged cloak. Tobias, relieved to imagine the painful scene to be in its final act, followed the tat-

tered garment up the stairs to the hallway. There he found that the
stranger, far from departing, was intent on pushing his way deeper into
the family's life.

Dr Hardwick took a candle from the wall sconce and walked into the
front room where he began a close perusal of the objects on its walls
and tables. "You are just newly established here?" he asked in a manner
more like that of a customer in an auction house than a visitor in a private home.

Tobias was disinclined to answer so impertinent a question, and yet
he was weakened by his impecunious position. "Some few months," he
answered.

"What is your profession, Sir?"

"I am a man of letters, Sir."

The doctor picked up a small porcelain ornament on the mantelpiece, turned it over, then dismissed it.

"You would be wiser to have waited a little longer before you married. Until you had a little capital."

Tobias tried to laugh. "What do you know about my capital?"

The doctor held the Bluebell plate which Mary had displayed
proudly in the centre of the mantelpiece. "Only what I see. But the evidence does point all one way."

Only later, when the fellow had gone, could Tobias Oates admit how
boorish and ill-mannered Dr Hardwick had been, but at the time, during the moments he was being so brazenly insulted, he was like a man
who sees at some distance a human form falling from Waterloo
Bridge—he did not quite believe what it was he witnessed. When, at
the end of the doctor's stock-taking, Lizzie came down the stairs to an-
nounce that the babe was finally asleep, there was nothing in Tobias's
manner to suggest to her that anything improper was taking place. Indeed, he laboured to give the impression that all was well.

"I was just telling Dr Hardwick," he said, "that we were newly arrived
in Lamb's Conduit Street."

"Oh yes," she said brightly. "We were previously at Furnival's Inn."

The doctor held the sputtering candle high. "And was it in Furnival's
Inn that you received the gift of that necklace?"

"Oh—" Lizzie's hand rose to touch the necklace, an old-fashioned little confection of silver and small blue stones. "Well, yes, indeed, it was
at Furnival's Inn, although it was a rather sad kind of a gift for it was be-

queathed to me by my grandmother, a dear old lady of whom I was exceedingly fond."

"Give it to me," said the doctor.

Lizzie hesitated.

"No need to remove it," said Tobias quickly, holding out his hand for the candle. "I will hold the light so Dr Hardwick can see."

"No, no." The doctor fixed his eyes upon the young woman. "Please be so good as to take it off."

"No," cried Tobias. "You must not."

He knew full well what the doctor intended, but when Lizzie, having silently reproached her brother-in-law, raised her pretty little hands to the clasp, he did not trust himself enough to forbid her once again. He watched in dismay as she delivered the precious article—that adornment of which she was, in all the world, most fond—into those alien freckled hands.

Dr Hardwick gazed down upon his treasure, his head tilted a little sideways, looking for all the world, so Tobias thought, like a crow upon a dust mound. When he looked up again, his eyes seemed to have cleared.

"This is very beautiful," he said.

"Thank you," said Lizzie, colouring with pleasure. "I don't think my brother-in-law has ever really noticed it before."

"Elizabeth!"

"It is worth a great deal more than the five shillings," said the doctor.

"Oh yes," said Lizzie. "The Jew on High Holborn offered me two guineas without my even asking his opinion."

"Then it is worth four," said the doctor. "Would you let me, if I promised to be very careful with it, would you let me borrow it a day or two?"

Lizzie looked at the untidy old man in confusion. He smiled at her; she coloured and looked to her brother-in-law, who gave her—so she later complained—no help at all.

"I'm sure that I could have it back to the young lady by Wednesday. Would you not say so, Mr Oates?"

"Tobias . . ."

The old man continued. "You will be needing me back again. I should say, by Wednesday. Or Tuesday if the fever has not abated. In any case, you will be pleased to see me, I am sure of it."

"You will give us a receipt, of course," said the writer.

"If you have the pen and paper," said the doctor to Lizzie. "And if you will be nice enough to give the article some clear description, then I'll sign it."

"I would describe it only as my grandmother's necklace, Sir, but what do you want with it?"

"I am a student," the old man said, dropping the necklace into the deep pocket of his filthy cloak, "a student of the human body, of the human nature, and of objets d'art of all descriptions."

"Tobias?" inquired his sister-in-law.

But Tobias Oates again affected not to hear. He busied himself at the little table by the window, engaged in making a minute architectural description of the necklace and its fastening. As he wrote these hundred words, his dancing mind was once more occupied with the question of money, with how to get it and get it quickly, so that he might get this necklace safely home again.

54

As her brother-in-law escorted the peculiar old doctor from the front room, Elizabeth Warriner stayed by the lace curtains looking out into the bright moon-lit street.

While the loss of her necklace had disturbed her, this disturbance was a very small rain-drop in the storm of emotion contained within her slender frame. She watched the shadow of the peculiar old doctor passing the window, and she turned to find him who occupied her every waking thought standing before her, his dear face clearly visible in the moonlight.

"Best light a candle," he whispered.

"She is gone to bed by now."

"There is still Mrs Jones. She would think it very odd were she to find us in the dark."

"Mrs Jones is sleeping in the nursery with little John." Lizzie took the unlit candle from Toby's hand and waited for him to embrace her. "She is asleep," she insisted.

She saw his mouth quiver, his chin ripple. "I am so very sorry," he said.

She put a finger on his lips.

"Oh Toby, you silly man."

She embraced him then, but his body was stiff and unyielding with preoccupation, and when he heard a creak of the floor boards above their heads, he sprang away from her.

"We must light a candle," he insisted.

She took his hand, he held hers fiercely.

"I'm so sorry about the necklace," he said. "You will have it back tomorrow."

"Tobias, I don't give a fig for the silly necklace."

"Dear sweet Elizabeth." This time he embraced her completely, holding her passionately around the waist, pressing himself hard against her, so hard, you would imagine, he must feel everything that was agitating her heart.

"Dear sweet Elizabeth, it is your only ornament. What did I hear you tell Closter's wife about the stones? Did you not say what happiness it gave you, just to gaze upon them in their little case?"

"Now it is less important."

"It is less important because I was foolish enough to let them be stolen from you?"

"Toby, you do not mean stolen."

"You will have them back by lunch, I promise you."

"Even if they had been stolen, it would mean nothing to me. Other events have put it in a better perspective."

"Yes, little John will soon be quite well again, it seems."

She looked at his face, and saw that he had not the faintest notion of the emotions agitating her. "He was a brave little man," she said cautiously. "It is of that general subject that I wished to speak with you, dear Toby."

He faced her solemnly.

"Say it, dearest."

"Say what, dear Brother."

"Say it."

"Husband," she said, and he, hearing that forbidden word, embraced her once again, smothering her in kisses.

"Do you love me, Husband?"

"You know I do. You know it so."

"And love all that is mine?"

"The parings from your lovely fingernails."

"And . . ."

"Here, I give you a kiss for your thoughts."

She disengaged. "I am afraid that my thoughts will not be acceptable to you, my dearest."

"Oh Lizzie," he chided. "How can you say such a thing to me?"

"For my thoughts are of our child . . ."

"Sweetness, that cannot be."

"But Toby, it can, and is."

He stepped back from her.

"My God, Lizzie, what are you saying?"

"I knew you would not like my thoughts. You should not have inquired after them."

"Lizzie, do not tease me."

"I am not teasing, Husband."

"What are you imagining?"

"Imagining?" Her voice rose. "Nothing. Nothing in the least imagined. Nothing, at least, you could not have imagined on the day you helped me fold the counterpane."

They were talking thus, in low, agitated voices, when they became aware of a sputtering light making its way down the staircase. The light came towards them, like a spirit, washing over the floor outside the door, then announced a plump figure in a white night gown.

Mary stood in the doorway. The light from her candle revealed her sister still standing in the darkness by the window. Tobias was leaning against the mantel, but as his wife came further into the room, he offered his own unlit candle to her flame.

"Tobias? Are you squabbling with Lizzie?"

"It's nothing, my dear."

"But Lizzie, you're crying."

And indeed, as Lizzie saw her good dull sister come towards her, her round little face all drawn with concern, she knew she could not stem the tide of her own very great upset. Huge hot tears washed down her cheeks.

Mary put her plump arm around her shoulder. "What is it, dear little Lizzie?"

"My necklace," cried Lizzie.

"What happened to her necklace, Tobias?"

"He let the filthy doctor steal it. He let the dirty old man put it in his pocket. He did not stop him. He did not care."

"I did care," said Tobias, hotly. "I cared most dreadfully."

"He did not care," cried Lizzie. "He cares only for his own pleasure."

This last remark produced a long and peculiar silence. "Tobias, is this true?" asked Mary, finally.

"The doctor did take the necklace, but only as security against the fee."

"He was a horrible old man," said Mary. "I shall take it very hard with Grieves when next I see him, that we should put our little boy in the hands of such a . . . such a *pawnbroker*. Tobias, you must get Lizzie her necklace back."

Lizzie looked to Tobias, who was resting his elbow, rather unnaturally, on the mantelpiece. He had always appeared to her as fierce and fatherly, but now she saw how the mantel was too tall for him, and how he stretched to accommodate himself to its demands. It was a vision most profoundly discouraging, and one she wished to God she had not seen.

55

When Tobias Oates was five years old, his father was charged with killing a man named Judd in a tavern brawl in Wardour Street. John Oates was tried at the Old Bailey and condemned to death by hanging.

Toby's earliest memories of London were still locked in that fetid little death cell where his father sat writing, day and night, getting up petitions for his pardon.

The Newgate turnkeys were fond of "John the Cock" and brought him pie and beer aplenty, so it happened that Toby, on being admitted to his company, would often find him in an emotional state. Sometimes the emotion was up, and sometimes it was down, and when it was down he would fall upon his estranged wife and son, crying to them that he did not wish to die.

All this, naturally enough, made its impressions on the little boy.

Finally his father won his pardon which, as his wife said, "did his character no good," and from that time he settled in Soho, where he became a kind of celebrity amongst the jockeys and book-makers of the town.

In later years, Tobias came to believe that his father had most likely been guilty of Judd's murder. In the popular newspapers much had been made of the bulk and brutality of the deceased man and the diminutive size of the accused, and yet this disparity in strength was, as Toby knew, a prescription for aggressive action on his father's part.

John Oates believed that you must meet with what was frightening you. If it was a dark corner, you entered it. If it was a bucking horse, you mounted it. If it was a storm, you walked through it. And Tobias, who was almost exactly his father's height, also inherited his habit of confronting what he feared.

He feared poverty; he wrote passionately about the poor. He had nightmares about hanging; he sought out executions, reporting them with a magistrate's detachment. And on that dreadful day when Mr Spinks had died, when he learned that the beautiful child with whom he was besotted was herself with child, as bruised and violent clouds began to rise above the pacific horizon of his life, his strongest impulse was to go where he most feared the deluge would sweep him.

That night he slept in a low lodging house in Fox Court, very close by his home. He had been there previously to report its desperate condition for the *Chronicle*, but never had he laid his body down on one of those stinking palliasses. It was an exceedingly low sort of place, with a nest of rambling dormitories, and smaller rooms arranged around a central court which was slippery with the effluent of a drain. Here a raspy-voiced old fellow in an apron demanded a penny ha'penny, and showed Tobias to a large kind of cupboard—it had no windows—where a pair of ruffians lay amidst the smell of ale and onions.

Here the author of *Captain Crumley* feigned sleep while his room mates searched his clothes looking for valuables. They were brutish types, with heavy brows and thick wide noses, and he was therefore shocked to feel the gentle intimacy of their fingers as they searched under his pillow and beneath the thin coverlet. He felt their fingers move like rats across his body.

Then they left him alone and soon they were whispering and then, a little later, he realized they were enacting some foul business between them, groaning and cursing as they did so.

Finally they slept, and Tobias Oates crept out. This scene, or rather the specifics of its setting, reappears not only in *The Death of Maggs* and *Michael Adams*, but in almost everything Tobias Oates ever wrote. There is always the court with its *vile green skirt of slime*, the little room *like a stifling cupboard, stinking of spilt ale and raw onions*. You can find the peeling wallpaper, the porter's egg stained singlet, time and time again throughout his serials, and if that is the good he got from it, it was the only good. For Tobias Oates emerged into High Holborn with his fears not beaten, but magnified, and a great certainty that he would rather drown himself than take his family down into such purgatory.

Yet once it was known that he had betrayed his wife and ruined her young sister, who would ever wish to touch a book with his name upon its spine? As he wandered down to the Thames, then through Borough, he was, in his imagination, already that reviled creature who could never hold his head up again; he would be poor, and hated. He walked the echoing streets thinking of money like that famous miser he would one day create in *French Street*. The miser is more like his creator than his readers ever guessed. True, Tobias did not have Scotty Meggitt's wealth, but he now walked the same streets Scotty Meggitt walked in the first chapter of *French Street*, adding and subtracting, subtracting and adding, *just like another man might say his prayers*.

Yet no matter how he did his sums Tobias could not get a total above eight pounds and sixpence. It was *not enough. Not nearly enough.*

Dawn found him still abroad on new London Bridge and, as the poisonous old ink received its first wash of red from the sun, he realized that the new bridge had been built atop the warren of streets where the Somnambulist spent his early years.

Pepper Alley Stairs were gone. The remaining roof tops were all grey and pink and shining in the morning drizzle. It was beneath his feet that the venomous creatures of Jack Maggs's memories lived. Here Tom dragged his bloody scraps up those grey glistening steps which still existed in the subterranean passages of that Criminal Mind. Seeing these visions, he also glimpsed the greatness of his book. That is: he had a premonition of the true majesty of the work that he would one day write. And how did he value this portent? Why, like a pawnbroker. He examined this great novel with his jeweller's glass. He might contrive to sell the copyright of such a work, and sell it entire, today, with not a word yet written.

It was not yet six in the morning—too early to do business with a publisher—but the prospect of this radical transaction now brought some colour to his cheeks. He set off, walking briskly, anxious to snaffle every pound that might be due him. As he crossed London Bridge again, the barges of the vegetable men were moving against the tide up to Covent Garden. Yes, it was too early to call on Cheery Entwhistle, but not too early to present himself to the man who had yesterday offered a fortune for a Thief-taker's address.

Like old man Meggitt, Tobias did not yet know exactly how his money might protect him, where he might flee, what bulwark he might build against the storm, but at seven o'clock he knocked at Mr Buckle's door keen to do business with Jack Maggs.

He was received by the kitchen maid, now dressed in mourning for Mr Spinks.

"There you are, Sir," cried she, in a manner unpleasantly familiar. "I was about to come and fetch you."

And with no other explanation she led him, not to the drawing room, but up an empty gloomy staircase which, in a better regulated household, would have been illuminated by a decent lamp.

The little maid was, to judge from her voice, soon an entire floor ahead of him. "This way, Sir. It's very bad, very bad indeed."

Tobias Oates, now much confused, grasped the banister and set off to catch her up. He would simply have increased his pace but he was prevented from so doing by the treacherous irregularity of the treads.

The house was queerly empty and lifeless. It was also taller than he had imagined, and so poorly served by windows that when he arrived on the second landing, he did not see the footman until the latter had thrust a paper into his hand. Tobias started, and cried out.

"I beg your pardon," whispered Edward Constable. "I don't know what to tell Mr Maggs, Sir. I don't know what is right."

Toby peered at the paper in his hand, but could make out nothing in the gloom.

"Up here, Sir," called the maid.

Tobias turned to the footman, but found him gone. He pocketed the paper and set off again to the top floor, only knowing it to be such by the exceedingly low ceiling on which he bumped his head. Hearing a whisper ahead of him, he followed it glumly towards its source.

Dear God, another servant dead!

A door opened, and a feeble grey sort of daylight came out onto the landing. Negotiating around what appeared to be a great many rolled-up rugs, he stepped into a stuffy attic room.

He had feared to find Mrs Halfstairs or Miss Mott, but now he recognized the great lumpy body of the man he had come to get his fifty pounds from. Tobias immediately noted the queer waxy skin upon his cheek. It was that damned *tic douloureux*.

He peeled the grey rug slowly back. There, stripped of his only comfort, Jack Maggs whimpered like a child.

"Good morning, Jack Maggs."

On hearing his voice, Maggs tried to raise himself. He appeared to be fully dressed, even to the hessian boots still on his feet, but he was very sick indeed. He peered at his visitor through swollen eyelids.

"It's you, Sir?"

"It is Mr Oates."

"You'll find me Henry Phipps after all?" he asked pathetically. "That's all I need, and then I'm off."

"Fifty pounds, that's what's agreed? I'll get you to the Thief-taker."

"That's the man." He clutched at Toby's sleeve. "Then I'm away. I'll trouble you no more. Cash in your hand, and leave you in peace. God, this damned thing hurts, Sir. It's this bleeding Phantom that you talk of."

"You can get the fifty pounds today?"

The sick man tried to raise himself again, but failed. He lay back down upon his mattress with his hand across his eyes. "Give me a moment, give me a moment."

"Very well. Let us drive out the Phantom first."

Tobias was exceptionally tired himself, but he leaned across the bed and began the long process of magnetizing the patient. It was awkward to have a prone subject but they were both well-practised in the dance. Tobias made the passes artfully and Jack Maggs's head soon fell back onto the pillow.

Tobias dragged up a three-legged stool and arranged himself, knees up, like a passenger on a wherry. His stomach rumbled. He drew breath, closed his eyes. When he spoke his voice was flat, without enthusiasm.

"What can you see?"

"Nothing. Darkness."

"You can see the Phantom."

"Can't see through a bleeding brick wall, can I."

Tobias allowed himself a weary smile. With Jack Maggs, there was always an obstacle—a wall, a moat, a bridge—some impediment which must be crossed to enter the castle of the Criminal Mind.

"Then we'll take a brick out, Jack. We'll wear away the mortar and see what we can see."

"Not worth the trouble, mate. You take my word for it."

"Don't lie to me, man. You know where it is. You know what is on one side and on the other."

Jack Maggs curled his lip, but did not answer.

"Take out the brick."

"Take my word, Sir, it can't be done."

"Jack Maggs, I order you. Take out the brick."

"Damn you," cried the sick man, struggling in his bed. "Do not make me see what has been done."

Tobias leaned forward on his stool. "Show it to me," he demanded.

No answer. Then, suddenly: "Sophina. She is heart-broken."

This was not what the Magnetist was looking for. He already had some forty pages of copperplate, all of them concerned with Jack Maggs's love of Sophina Smith, and he did not, at this moment when he was dirty and weary and waiting for his fifty pounds, want to hear any more.

"Then Sophina will remove the brick from the wall."

"There is no wall."

"There is a brick wall right behind Sophina. Remove a brick."

But the Somnambulist was deep in his rut.

"Look how she takes Tom's hand. Look how he pretends to comfort her."

"Jack, the Phantom is lurking on the other side of that brick wall."

"I will not look. I couldn't bear it."

"Here's Tom. He has a chisel, he is scraping away at the mortar."

"He will make me look, the bastard. I'll shut my eyes."

"The brick is out."

The large man on the bed began to whimper, and brought his hand up to his face.

"Move your hands back from your eyes. Is it not the Phantom?"

And, indeed, Jack did reluctantly remove his hands, and open his eyes and stare hard at the dull rain-speckled window of the room. What he saw there, he did not say, but released a wail, so long and dreadful, that the writer, listening to it, bowed his head and shut his eyes.

56

The convict writhed against his magnetic chains. He sat up, straining forward, his dark eyes glaring bright as gin. Tobias had entered this transaction only to collect his fifty pieces, but now all thought of gain was put aside.

"Hold," he cried, and stood pluckily before Jack Maggs, his legs astride, his hand thrust forward as if to parry or to bless.

Jack Maggs seemed to look at him, but who could say what world he saw with those wild eyes?

"Hold now, Jack. Hold." The writer brought his soft palms to press down on the air between himself and his subject. As he pushed out his hands, Jack Maggs partially reclined upon his crib. Determined to insist on his mastery, Tobias came a half-step closer. Jack Maggs would not surrender entirely but lay propped on his elbow, like a great loaded spring. He was held, magnetized, though Tobias lacked confidence in the strength of this instrument.

The next moment made him fear the battle lost. Jack Maggs opened his wide mouth and cried not in pain, but in horror at some unseen thing. As a great *"No!"* burst from deep in his chest, he stood, not quickly, but as Gulliver might have, had he been better able to resist the ropes of the Lilliputians. When erect, his great high forehead touched the ceiling. He seemed to fill the room, blocking the light: it took every reserve of courage for Tobias to stand his ground against him.

"Down," cried Tobias Oates. "I command you."

He feared he had done something against the natural order, had unleashed demons he had no understanding of, disturbed some dark and dreadful nest of vermin. He tried to see, without removing his eyes from the subject, if there were some stave or poker with which to arm himself.

"In the name of Jesus Christ, I command you be still."

Jack Maggs paused, blinked.

"Quiet," Tobias cried. "You will be quiet."

The patient swayed, stooped over, in the middle of the attic, rubbing at his unshaven cheek.

"Now, you will lie down on your bed. And not raise yourself once more unless my voice commands it."

Jack Maggs then sat on the crib. He tugged off his boots and dropped them heavily onto the floor.

"Christ," he exclaimed, and then lay down, his hands still playing with his face.

Tobias reflected on how he was to lay this Phantom to rest for ever. He had by now long forgotten, if he ever knew, that this wraith was his own invention, a personification of pain that he had planted in the other's mind. He commanded the Somnambulist to describe the figure that haunted him. He could, of course, have himself described the ice-blue eyes, the cruel straight nose, the cornfield-coloured hair; but his purpose was to make his subject concentrate upon the Phantom, and then, by some violent strategy he had not yet imagined, to cast him for ever, like swine, into the sea.

Thus he pointed at the stain on the attic wall. "There he is, Jack, there he is."

Jack Maggs, for his part, resisted. He tossed his head and squeezed shut his eyes. He plucked at his cheek, digging into it with his straightened fingers as if his hand were a trencher and his flesh mere clay to dig into.

"Is he dark then, Jack?" asked Tobias, who knew Jack Maggs liked an argument. "Is he a black man?"

"Ah no," the convict sighed. "He is fair. Very fair."

"His skin is white?"

"He has my babe."

Tobias, weary and dirty, wished he could lie down, but he proceeded, calmly, to overcome this latest obstacle.

"Then take back the babe," said he. "Walk towards the Phantom. Stretch out your hands. He does not want the babe. He will return the babe into your arms."

"He is on the other side of the wall."

Tobias imagined that the subject was referring to the Phantom. "You have removed one brick," he said irritably. "You will now remove one more. If needs be you will demolish the whole wall in order to reach him."

There followed more childish banging of the subject's head, pulling at the cheek, etcetera. Tobias folded his hands on his lap and waited. When Jack Maggs was once more quiet, he asked, "Have you removed the brick now?"

The other man grimaced sadly. "It is a cess pit they throw him in."

"The Phantom is cast out?"

"My *babe*. My babe is dead."

"Where is your Phantom, Jack? Tell me again: how does he look?"

"Oh, he is a soldier of the King," the convict said bitterly. "He is a regular frigging beetle, but my poor dear little boy is laying in a ditch." Much to Tobias Oates's consternation, his subject began to weep uncontrollably. "Dear Lord, dear Lord. His sweet little cheek is cut open."

And there Jack Maggs lay, sobbing, his mighty legs drawn up to his chest as though he were a babe himself.

"Do not make me see it," he wailed, clutching at his own cheek, and dragging down on the flesh with his broad square nails. "Oh God, I wish I were dead, and that's the truth."

"Attend, Sir."

"Leave me, leave, let me be."

"I will repair your son."

"You cannot repair him. He is dead."

"We will close his wound. Please."

"Leave him alone, you meddling bastard of a man."

But Tobias Oates had received an insight. "Look, Jack, look, the wound is healed. When his wound is healed, yours will be too. It is the same wound."

"I want it."

"No, look and see the wound is healed. Your pain is gone."

"I want it," cried Jack Maggs, raising himself on his elbow and staring at Tobias Oates with such alertness that it was hard to believe he was still mesmerized.

"I want it, fool. It is all I have left of him."

57

The *tic douloureux* had been by no means vanquished, but the magnets had given Jack Maggs sufficient relief to enable him to scrabble under the mattress where, he now revealed, a great portion of his wealth was hidden.

He turned his back on Toby and hunched his broad shoulders so the writer might not see the extent of his treasure.

"On faith I give you ten," he called.

When he looked back his skin was still pasty, but some of his old rascality was again shining in his eyes. He spoke gruffly. "It's a hard bargain you've made."

Then he seized Toby's hand. "But, Jod's blood, you'll see me keep my word, mate."

He drew the startled writer very close, so close Tobias could not escape the stench of his sick breath. Toby's hand was clenched into a fist but Jack Maggs pried the fist open with the hooked fingers of his mutilated hand.

"On the morrow," said he, "we will meet the gent himself."

"He lives in Gloucester."

"Then to Gloucester we will go, mate. And when I have him, then forty more of these golden beauties shall be delivered to your hand."

And with that, he solemnly counted ten warm gold sovereigns into Tobias Oates's open palm.

Later, as his hackney cab trotted up Great Queen Street, the writer's fingers began to worry at these coins in his pocket. In the restless, ever-changing landscape of his mind's eye, he saw the circumstances whereby they might have found their way to him. As always, he believed in the scenes made by his imagination, thought them as real as anything in Great Queen Street. He saw a cabin in moonlight, a thrusting dagger, a fallen lantern, a fire blazing suddenly in the antipodean dark. These scenes led him, by and by, back to the novel of *Jack Maggs*. He began to rehearse the ways he might describe it to old Cheery Entwhistle.

He soon had himself immersed deep in the details of Jack Maggs's birth. He had learned, by medium of his magnets, that the infant Maggs had been thrown off London Bridge. Now he began to play with the notion that the convict was, like Richard Savage, a bastard son of noble parents. It was here he would start to tell the tale to Cheery Entwhistle. He saw himself pacing up and down the publisher's comfortable office while the old man sat with his hands folded contentedly across his waistcoated belly.

He came back from the depths of this fancy to discover that his cab had been a long time halted. He looked out the window and saw his cabby and the driver of an omnibus standing with fists raised in the middle of the street.

There was two guineas to be made here. He could write it in an hour. "An Altercation in High Holborn."

Add his sweeper boy (two guineas).

Add his canary woman (two guineas).

If he did not pay the grocer's or the butcher's bill, he might amass four hundred pounds by the time the deluge arrived.

The cab set off again, at speed. He took out his chap book and began to write, thereby achieving two hundred words by the time he closed the book again at Merton Street. Here he instructed the driver to wait, and ran up the cat-sour path to Dr Hardwick's door.

The doctor answered the door with a grey and unsanitary napkin in his hand.

"Dr Hardwick," said Tobias. "I have your fee, as I promised."

This information seemed to confuse the doctor.

"I am Tobias Oates."

"You are, are you?" said Dr Hardwick, and then wandered back up the hallway, leaving his front door ajar behind him. Not being invited to follow, Toby had no choice but to wait in the doorway, wondering all the while what sort of doctor would open his own door. On the evidence of the shadows, the old man was in the front room, walking hither and fro in the manner of someone conducting a search.

Some ten minutes passed, but when he finally returned to the front door, he still did not have the necklace in his hand.

"Here is a sovereign," said Tobias urgently. "I believe I am your debtor to the extent of five shillings."

Dr Hardwick looked with some surprise at the coin thus proffered. "How goes my patient?"

"The babe is well. I hope you can give me change, Sir."

This matter the doctor attended to readily enough, but he did not proffer any jewellery in return.

"I believe you have something of mine," Tobias said at last.

Dr Hardwick frowned. "Of yours?"

"Well then, of my wife's sister."

"Oh, you wish the girl's necklace?" The old man then began fumbling around his jacket pocket.

"It is not lost, I hope."

At this the doctor slowly drew the necklace from the fob pocket of his waistcoat.

"You show too much of yourself," he said to Tobias Oates, as he held the jewellery in the air in front of him.

"Sir?" said Tobias, blushing brightly.

Dr Hardwick lowered the necklace into Tobias's impatient hand.

"I trust you are as careful of your sister-in-law as I am with her necklace," he said.

Tobias could not believe what he had heard. He looked into the stranger's yellowish eyes, and saw the eyes staring boldly back at him. Beneath the man's discoloured whiskers he thought he saw the mouth move in some benign amusement. And, for a brief moment, he was tempted to unburden himself of all his woes, to seek a medical solution to that crisis which was presently threatening to destroy his entire world.

But then he observed a curl in the old man's lip, a steeliness in the eyes. He turned on his heels and returned to his cab.

58

Dear Henry,

I imagine you waiting and watching. I imagine you beyond the door, outside on the street, peering through the cracks in the curtains. I fancy that you are waiting to see what sort of cove your Da is. You are careful.

I also was a watchful lad. I watched Tom most particular, and I was not wrong to do so. Tom, at eighteen, had got tall and almost handsome. His hair had grown wild and curling, and thus did him the great service of hiding his ugly ears. All his spleen had concentrated in his ripe red mouth, where its meaning had become mixed up with appetite. This was a boy who liked to kiss, but there was also a conspirator's air to him, and a hardness, a fierceness in his eye.

—We are brothers, Jack, he would say, leaning over the famous carved oak table at the Swan with Two Necks. We don't need no outsiders to do our work.

By "outsiders" he meant Silas who, even whilst locked away in jail, still continued to control much of our activity and to take, according to Tom, the lion's share of the profits. He was not permitted to complain of this to Mary Britten, so to me he poured out all the bitter feelings in his heart. He would take me by the wrist and hold me hard. —You are not blood, but you are family. I would die for you, Jack, etc. etc.

This passion of his made me ill at ease, and even if I learned to counterfeit its equal—for he was very prickly and needful of my doing so—in truth I pitied him. And so, in looking down on him, I did not watch him as closely as I should have.

When I tried to have Sophina join with me in joking about Tom, she reproached me severely. —You should be shamed, she said, to have a brother who would die for you, and to make a muck of it.

In Tom, to her great cost, she heard and saw only what she wished were true. She did not understand the great animus he bore her Papa.

Tom was both secretive in his habits and careful with his tools, and this lucky combination gave him a great talent for house-breaking. He had become, now that he had stopped trying to escape the bonds of his apprenticeship, his master's great pet. This master had no idea that Tom Britten was a thief. Indeed, he boasted that there was no one in all the West of London who could make a dovetail so neat and fast. I do not doubt his claim was true. Tom told me once there was a way that lumber gave before him which felt like a beast surrendered. He made it sound a dirty thing.

Tom might well have gone on to have a useful, honest sort of life, but he was his mother's son and they were set on bigger things.

By 1806 we ate best brisket, chump chops, rolled roast beef from the butcher's shop in Upper Street, and Mrs Britten was the owner of two freehold titles, and her rooms were now attended by a better class of female who—if nervous to venture into Islington—were presumably relieved that they would see no one there they knew.

Now the Ma dressed in a get-up she had invented for herself, all in white with a queer white cap upon her head. She sold her bellyache sausages no more. Instead she advertised her Dr Britten's Cock's Spur Pills for Female Disorders. These pills she compounded from Ergot, a substance which gave all our hands an unpleasant fishy smell. Sophina and I spent many a morning counting the rough purple lumps into small brown bottles.

At fourteen, I had grown too big to fit into a chimney, but both

Sophina and I had got a mighty knowledge of old silver. Together with Tom, who had all the skills of his apprenticeship, we had elevated our thievery to a higher state than any Silas could have imagined.

Sometimes Tom might pick the lock, yet often a simple cut of his fret saw would make the key a cuckold to his finger. Sophina and I were not present when the entry was effected, though it is easy to see Tom feeling his way into the house with tarred string and wire ticklers and saw-blades fine as a human hair. He made less mess than a death-watch beetle, and when he was done the house would sit waiting for us, as easily opened as the pages of a book.

When he met us in our rendezvous to instruct us how we were to go about our entry, he would have his colour high. His movements would be quick but soft, and there was about him at once a great excitement and a heightened shyness. I saw how he cast looks at Sophina from beneath his long lashes, and how, in telling the story of his entry, he would seek to emphasize the risk. He wished to appear the real dog in the doublet. He did not speak to Sophina, or about her, but I was not blind to his strong feelings.

When he came to see us in the house in Islington, he would ignore us both. He would stay up late conferring with his mother, hunching with her over the dining-room table where they spent endless hours going through their "papers." What these were I could not say, although I do believe they included a sworn deposition relating to Silas's innocence, and the title of her two properties, although I never did see the other property—which she described as a "commodious gentleman's residence" in Notting Hill.

On Sunday afternoons the pair of them sat at the table drinking gin from yellow Venetian glasses, while they added up rows of figures and hissed secrets at each other. What these secrets were, I still have no idea. I cannot tell you if she knew that he had betrayed Silas, or if the whole thing had been done on her instruction. Anything you might imagine about that pair, you could not call impossible.

Sometimes Tom left early after some upset, but more often he was there long after Sophina and I had gone to sleep in our little room.

We were, for most of the time, exhausted, and not because we were walking half of London several nights a week—or not that only—but because we were charged with the care and cleaning of the household, and never was a downstairs maid worked harder than we were.

It was not so much the upstairs quarters which exhausted us, but that entire ground floor which Ma Britten had now devoted to what she called "my ladies." These rooms, where none might eat or sleep, where one could be thrashed for introducing a slice of bread and dripping, she decorated after her idea of a ladies' room.

Mary Britten was not an educated woman, and there was about her tall raw frame a great rude energy which might remind you more of a coster than a nurse, and yet she had a passion to be genteel, to walk St James's, to be admitted without question at Ranelagh, and she made this front room an altar to her passion, filling it with expensive flounces, and ruffles, with jardinieres, with doilies, and statues of dusky maidens whose outstretched hands could accommodate a lighted candle. And it is curious that I, who had certainly been in far more gentlefolk's houses than she had, did not think to quarrel with either her knowledge or her taste.

Sophina and I, of course, spent a great deal of time considering the very particular nature of that taste, for it was our task to clean both rooms, the pretty room and the plain room, as we called them.

The pretty room was a nightmare of oak floors (which must be waxed) and heavy rugs (which must be beaten). Lord help us if we did not have the skirting board shining, if insufficient elbow grease had been applied to the mantelpiece, if there were a residue of silver polish left upon the silver vase I had stolen from a farmer's house in Hampstead.

The plain room was at once easier and more difficult—easier in that it was free of flounces and curlicues, difficult in that we might here find blood in quantities enough to frighten any child, and discover things in muslin-covered basins that haunt me to this day. We said nothing about the plain room to each other, but emptied the contents of the basins into the cess pit at the back of the garden. We cleaned the plain room with soap and scrubbing brush, quickly, holding our breath.

To walk from these rooms up the stairs was like stepping behind the scenes at the theatre. Here was where we lived, and in quite a different style than previously. There was the large "cupboard"—in fact a small room with a window—where Ma ground up her Ergot and made her little pills: a painstaking process, for she moulded each small pill by hand, and one that made her tired and bad-tempered. There was the small kitchen with its fierce black stove on which we were forever burning ourselves. There was the room where Ma slept and in which, in a series of large boxes, she stored all the peculiar goods which had, before Silas's arrest, been kept in the net loft in Wapping.

There was a small "dining room" which also served as Ma's office, and here she kept, in the tin box, the titles, and mysterious other Certificates and Orders which she was forever checking.

We were both, Sophina and I, instructed to call her Ma, but did so knowing that we would be often reminded that we were not her children. When Tom came to visit, they would somehow team against us and, as they huddled over their papers, we did not think to calculate how much of the household income was produced by us, but believed instead that we had a roof over our heads only as a result of their whimsical charity.

When he came to the house, Tom did not look at Silas's daughter directly. And yet I was aware, even then, of the fierceness with which he did not look.

You would think it incredible that I, who knew his ways so well, would ever leave my pretty treasure undefended. But if I often did so it was because, my dear boy, I had already become Silas's son-in-law. Not, of course, that Sophina and I were married in a church, though we often talked of that, and longed for the day when we might suggest such a thing and not be beaten on account of it.

> *Amo, Amas*
> *I love a lass*
> *She is so sweet and tender*

We were then, as far as I can reckon, fourteen years old. And we lay under our counterpane at night, asleep in each other's arms, imagining ourselves safe, at least, in our heartfelt feelings for each other.

59

Henry, had you been able to hear Judge Denman make his ignorant speech to the jury about what a poisonous line of blood ran through my vermin veins, had you heard the phlegmy old lambskin list my misdemeanours, you might have imagined me so devoted to burglary that I had not a moment to spare between cock crow and midnight.

Sophina and I were worked hard, it's true, but more often as chars than burglars. When the Ma's floors were scrubbed and her banisters polished, time was often heavy on our hands and many is the fine summer's day we spent confined to the upstairs floor with no other amusement than to lie on the bare floor boards with a tumbler against our ears, trying to overhear the sad little dramas enacted in the room below our kitchen.

Silas in his penitentiary had more freedom than we did. He was permitted often times to stand at the open door of the prison in his fine grey tailored coat, and there, puffing on an Indian cheroot, pass the day with whomsoever passed by. But Sophina and I were forbid the little lane that ran down beside our home. Even hopscotch was denied us.

It is not so queer then that we looked forward to our burglary more than we feared its consequences. It was not our blood-line, or our criminal craniums, but our natural human desire for something other than the tedium of close confinement. Thus we waited to be called to risk, waited while the ground-floor voices murmured, while the blacksmith across the way set up his steady cling-cling-cling, while a housefly died noisily, buzzing against the green window glass.

The front-door bell rang frequently, but these were ladies for the Ma, and no business of ours. If there were a call for us, it would most likely come after supper when we were scrubbing down the kitchen tables.

—Come, my lovelies.

We would look up from our grey soap and our hard brushes, and see a cabby standing at the kitchen door.

—I am Uncle Dick, and I am here to take you for a little trot.

And in three minutes we would be dressed for the street and clat-

tering down the stairs, leaving the bowl of soapy water on the table for
the Ma—for she would never hinder us on our way to do our business.

Every Joe knows that the brotherhood of hackney drivers has a
calling in the criminal professions, but our Uncle Dicks and Handsome Micks were innocent, at least temporarily. No matter that
Silas himself had engaged them, no matter what skivers and mags-
men they might be on a Monday morning, on those sweet summer evenings they had nothing more criminal to do than to get us to
an inn.

They were, as Silas told us, base links in a chain of gold.

Likewise, Tom would break the door of the house, but never enter
it. Likewise, my pretty sweetheart and I would select the silver and
pack it in the hessian sacks, but take the sacks no further than the
kitchen door.

—You ain't breaking the law, Silas told us. You did not break no
lock, and you did not remove nothing from the premises.

It was a scheme, in all its very definite Divisions of Labour, which
would have met with the approval of Mr Adam Smith, but I do not
think that this was an author I ever heard Silas mention, although he
was a well-respected scholar and able to recite long passages from
the Bible and from Shakespeare.

Even in Newgate, he kept his books about him, and complained
often about favourites he could not accommodate in his cell. Alas, he
needed sufficient shelving for his port wine and his claret, for he
could not be without them either. Silas did not go short of comforts.
He always had a ham and two or three different pies, all nicely covered with muslin to keep the flies away. All this drove Tom into a
great frenzy, but I don't think I ever really believed that Silas's comfortable way of life was paid for by my labours. Indeed, I had come
to think of these labours as being for my own amusement. And as the
cab began, as it most-times did, to head towards the West wherein
the faint glow of the departed sun could still be seen, my heart would
be already pounding hard in my chest. My hand would soon go out
across the seat and find my sweetheart's. All around us, the drivers of
coaches, carriages, dog carts, phaetons, roared and raced their
mighty race, while we two children were like insects brought to fer-
vent life by a summer thunder storm.

As I had grown tall, Sophina had kept her own pace beside me, and when we sat opposite each other in the soft London light, our eyes were level, and each as hungry and curious about its opposite as our tangled hands. I sought those grey eyes in the gloom. What a heady blend of sagacity and recklessness I found there.

And hurt, also. There was much hurt my Sophina carried with her silently, hurt you would never guess unless you heard, as I often did, her crying by herself at night, and there was a certain wariness about her affections which had to be won over just when you imagined there was no more winning-over to be done.

But I said she was a beauty, so let me prove it to you: Sophina had dark luxurious curls and an oval face with such wise and gentle grey eyes and a wide, well-shaped mouth whose naturally serious expression was forever breaking in a most glorious smile. Her lips were soft—so soft I break my sentence to close my eyes and mourn them. And when we met with Tom at the inn, I was all impatience to get to the house, to get to the job, where I might kiss them.

Was this safe? For the most part, yes. It is much to Silas's credit that we were rarely called to any house where the danger of discovery was very great. Of course this was not necessarily on account of kindness, and one has only to think him like a fellow with a pair of good fighting cocks he does not want to lose too easily, to understand why he took great care in the gathering of his Information.

Twice there were slip-ups. Once we found a master by his fire when we expected no one home. Once we had a party return from Sussex when they had not been expected, but it is one of the wonders of great houses that their owners are forever closing them down, and these were the houses to which we were sent to do our "little spot of shopping."

Had we such a house—as Sophina and I said to each other—we would never sleep in any other, and it was our great fancy that the houses where we exercised our craft belonged to us, and thus, even in the selection of the silver plate we were to steal, we acted the parts of a lady and gentleman choosing which items to send to their country estate.

We were fast at our work, faster than those who depended on us could ever guess, and when we had filled our sack, and I had placed it carefully beside the kitchen door, I would mount the stairs and set off, in all that great house, to find my "wife" who had gone on ahead of me.

And who was in bed, of course, and waiting for me.

My dear boy, I pray I do not shock you with this tale or that you, in imagining us wild animals, will doubt me when I say, what innocents we were. Sophina was not one of those girls who bloom suddenly into womanhood. She ripened slowly in the London mist, and when I embraced her, I was a boy embracing a girl.

But a man too, for the man now who writes this embraces her still, and longs, thirty years later, for the smooth whiteness of her skin and all that great house around us.

'Twere the sweetest thing in all my life, to go burgling with Sophina and to flirt with the great dangerous web of sleep which came down to claim us afterwards.

60

On the twenty-eighth of July 1807 we were dispatched to a large gentleman's residence in Montpelier Square, an easy mark because of the lane-way entrance to its stables at the rear. We first met with Tom at the Golden Sheaf, a little inn in one of the smaller streets which lead into the square.

There we watched Tom fill his face with cold boiled beef and pickled walnuts. Finally, when he had washed all this down with ale, he pointed out the open window and showed us the house that had been selected for us. It was a tall, thin, four-storey beauty, straight and tall as a guardsman with all its iron work blacked and its brass work shining in the soft green summer light.

We waited for the dark to fall, and then left Tom sitting drinking his second tankard and playing solitaire.

A half an hour or so after we had gone inside, Tom heard a commotion down below and, kneeling on his settle, he looked out and saw a team of Bow Street runners "fair galloping" across the square, shouting at each other as they went. It seemed to him that they were heading towards the lane-way at the back of our house.

This alarmed him at first, but after he had watched the house a while and seen its windows remain dark, he went back to his solitaire. He had performed this vigil many times and was now accustomed to the long time it took us to select our merchandise. But when the clock struck midnight and the landlord wished to know would he like a room to sleep in, Tom paid his bill and went on out into the night.

He had a Mr Steelshank waiting in another inn nearby, and when the bag was ready he would call on Steelshank and tip him the wink. But now he began to imagine that the Robin Redbreasts had nabbed us in the kitchen, or the butler's pantry where—naturally enough— no light would have showed. If that was the case, they might be waiting in there now, and he could not send in Steelshank but neither could he make up his mind what he should do. He walked around the square two or three times until his activity was noted by a watchman who wanted to know what it was he was looking for. As the fellow raised his lantern, a hackney cab came into the square and Tom straight way hailed it and set off, not to Steelshank, but up to Islington where he set about the dangerous task of raising Ma Britten from her bed.

The Ma was a restless body who oft-times needed a dram or two of French Cream to get her to her sleep. Once that precious land was won, she did not gracefully surrender it, and when she was finally drawn up from the depths towards the light of Tom's lantern, she brought a foul mouth and an evil temper with her.

Now I was not, I am pleased to say, a witness to this event, but I spent enough years with the pair of them to now offer an honest sketch.

—You better not have lost them little varmints, said she, or by God, Silas will have the Push come looking for you.

—I ain't lost nothing, Ma, said he, I just did my job, and then the runners went into the house and now they ain't come back.

—You dunghill, said she.

—Ma, said he, don't call me that. I ain't a coward.

—Dung, she hollered.

She liked to call him that, call him anything that would make him red in the face and even more needful of her affections. So even though he were a big fellow now, and handy with his raw red fists, he was, as they journeyed out into the night, a whining little mutt around her great black skirts.

—You lose those little Nokes, said she, and I'll cut your bleeding ears off. Etc., etc.

She might call us Nokes, and worse, but the truth was she feared she was at risk of losing her golden geese, and although she was normally a very careful woman with a penny, she did not hesitate to pay for another hack to get her as far as Montpelier Square.

When they arrived at the back lane by the stables, Tom, being convinced that the runners were waiting there to trap him, gave his mother one more reason to call him a dunghill. She pushed her way ahead of him and walked into the house.

There, in the face of Tom's pleas that she do otherwise, Ma Britten lit a candle, located the kitchen, and there discovered the bag of silver Sophina and I had packed so carefully. That this valuable booty was still in its place was, to the Ma's mind, proof positive that the Robin Redbreasts had not been near the place. She jubilantly administered one or two fast clips across Tom's ears, and (having thereby calmed herself a little) set off to search the house.

Tom, however, had an awful terror of transportation. He tried to lag behind, and the Ma was forced to escort him by his ear up the stairs, and she did not let him go until, on a landing, she heard Yours Truly snoring.

God knows what Tom thought the sound was, but it did serve to send him into a dreadful panic.

The Ma demanded—Draw the curtains! But he had slipped away from her into the darkness, and she had to run the risk herself—as she was not slow to remind him later—of standing in front of the open window in a public square while she quickly drew the curtains. When this was done, she held the candle high.

—Nokes, she cried.

I woke to see her there, her hair all wild as if for bed, but dressed in the long dark skirts she favours to this day. She tilted the candle and a drop of hot wax spilled onto my bare stomach, then onto poor Sophina who leapt startled from her bed and stood in the corner, trying to cover herself.

—Out! Ma cried at Tom, who now was standing at the doorway, staring at our nakedness.

—Out! she cried again. Tom had gone, but I pretended not to know what she meant.

—Get out, idjeet! she cried, never once taking her eyes off poor Sophina.

It is to my eternal shame that I then deserted Sophina, and stood like a shivering child outside the door where Tom, having glared at me and shaken his head, was temporarily restrained from any more physical attack upon my person by his intense curiosity about what was being said inside.

—Stand! we heard the Ma say. Hands by your sides!

But then she dropped her voice, and the conversation inside the door began to sound like the conversations we heard through the floor boards of the kitchen. The questions, the answers, the tears. Only in its conclusion did this interview show Ma Britten's different relationship with the person whom she now interviewed.

—Five months! she cried. You stupid little bitch.

She had discovered, so I imagined, the length of time we had been man and wife.

61

Toby had been abroad a day and night. He had slept in a flop house, magnetized a criminal, retrieved a necklace, and drunk first claret and then brandy with Cheery Entwhistle.

He had sold the copyright to *Jack Maggs*. He had signed a contract for sixty pounds, and now, as he stood outside his house in Lamb's Conduit Street, he could feel the sticky dirt of London on his skin and taste its sulphurous corruption in his mouth.

A light rain was falling, scarcely more than mist, and it gathered on the outside of his curling hair like dew on a spider web. It ran down his unclean cheeks and thereby helped produce, in concert with a swollen mouth and shadowed eyes, a picture at once demonic and pathetic. He stood awhile in the shadows and watched his own household with a kind of dread.

As he gained the footpath he was able to look down into the kitchen and see Mrs Jones busy scrubbing down her table in readiness for the morrow. How he envied the old biddy the dull certainty of her day.

He let himself in the front door very quietly, only to be rewarded with her whom he wished most to avoid.

The girl was seated on the bench seat by the hat stand, clad only in dressing gown and slippers. Her hair was loose and falling on her shoulders, but still she came and recklessly embraced him, pushing against him with that darkest and most womanly part of her anatomy.

"Where is my wife?"

He drew her into the dark drawing room and sat her down opposite him at a small card table. Then, in the interests of propriety, he lit a candle.

"I have been waiting for you, dearest."

"Where is Mary?"

"In the nursery, but listen to what your Lizzie has been waiting all day long to tell you."

She then stretched out her free hand and touched his face. He could not help but flinch from her.

"Lizzie," he explained, "my face is dirty."

In reply she leaned across the table to kiss him once again. He saw then, quite clearly, the full curve of her breast.

"Toby—I plan to go away, by myself, to France."

"For Heaven's sake, do up your nightgown."

She did as he requested but in a teasing manner inappropriate to their situation.

She continued. "My French is really very good, as you have said yourself."

To France? He would not know how to effect such an adventure himself. She was but eighteen years old, and scarcely knew her way to the Royal Academy.

"Whom have you been speaking to?"

"I would be away but half a year."

The floorboards creaked upstairs.

"I would stay in a good Protestant house in Paris."

"Which house?" he whispered. "How could you find such a thing? Who would be with you?"

"I would be back by Christmas with the baby."

"No!"

"Oh, silly dear Tobias. I would not say that he was our own."

He looked at her with such alarm that she, in her madness, began to laugh. "I have already told Mary that I wish to adopt a foundling."

"You must do no such thing, do you hear me? My wife is one hundred times sharper than you imagine."

"No, poor Toby, she is one thousand times less sharp than you imagine. In any case, I told her this morning that I was resigned to being an old maid, but that I would adopt a babe of my own."

"You are treading on thin ice, girl."

"Do not be so cold with me, Toby."

"I am not cold. I am shocked that you should discuss this with anybody. What did my wife reply?"

"Well, you can imagine the scene, I'm sure. First she must drink her tea. Then she must contemplate the matter as if it were a frightful conundrum. In this case she was silent an awfully long time, but at last she said that she was sure that it was forbidden by the English foundling hospitals—to give their charges out to spinsters."

"She is correct."

"Of course she is correct, dear. She had considered it, don't you see? That is why she considers things. She has a terror of being wrong, especially in your company. I then asked her, did she think the French foundling hospitals would have the same proscription, and she said that she did not know, but that foreigners did the most peculiar things."

"Dear Lizzie, I will not give you up."

Lizzie frowned. "Of course. We will none of us give up the other."

"Mary would be the first to know it was your flesh and blood. Can you not see how we would insult the very foundation of her life?"

Whether Lizzie heard this or no, was not clear, for something he had said had obviously angered her, and now she stared at him so malevolently that he chose this moment to return her necklace. He laid it on the table, as evidence.

"I have been busy on your behalf," said he.

"On my behalf?"

She raised an eyebrow, then draped the necklace over her wrist. For a moment she twisted it to and fro, seeming to admire the way the stones reflected the candle light.

"So what would you have me do, Tobias?"

"It is a dark hour."

Lizzie was silent.

"That is all you have to offer?" She laid the necklace back upon the table. "It is a dark hour?"

"No," said Toby. "It is not all I have to offer. I have a plan, but first I must speak with Mary."

"You cannot discuss it with *me*?" she cried suddenly, a great temper erupting in her eyes.

"Please, Elizabeth. Please be a little quieter."

"And when might you have the time, Sir, to make the nature of your thoughts available to the mother of your child?"

He had no plan, of course. He had accrued one hundred and eighteen pounds and sixpence but no clear plan had come to him.

"I have a *wife*," he pleaded, "and tomorrow I must earn my necklace money by being a servant to the convict."

"But when will you reveal your plan to me?" She spoke loudly, carelessly. "How long do you plan to leave me alone with my mind spinning round and round?"

When Tobias stood, Lizzie remained in her chair, her shoulders rounded in despair.

"I will take care of this matter," he said. "You can rely on me."

And then he turned and walked up the stairs, where he discovered his wife standing on the landing, a peculiar expression upon her face.

"I go to Gloucester," he said.

62

Tobias took no change of linen with him on his journey to Gloucester. Instead he had brought his faithful yellow case, and in it he had carefully packed his cut-throat razor, his toothbrush, a quill, his work book and an ink bottle. Even before the coach had escaped the congestion at the turnpike, he had opened this ingenious portmanteau upon his knees, and made his travelling desk.

He uncorked his ink, set the bottle in the cavity made for this purpose, and there, in what de Quincey called "the great Mediterranean" of Oxford Street, he began the first chapter of *Jack Maggs*. He wrote in an ornate but graceful hand: not a wavering stroke to indicate that he was sitting in a coach, not a smudge or blot to suggest that this was a young man in despair, someone who felt himself to be moving only just ahead of the tide of his own disgrace.

He was not unaware that the subject of his tale was seated staring at him. Although Jack Maggs was in the far right-hand corner with his back towards the horses, as far away as he might be, the *True Briton*, as the coach was named, was no bigger than any other mail coach. That is, it was made exactly as the Post Office insisted, with the same cursed three feet and four inches from seat to ceiling, six feet and six inches on the horizontal diagonal.

Tobias wrote CHAPTER ONE, and underlined it twice. Then he began:

> *It was a dismal January day in the year of 1818, and the yellow fog which had lain low all morning lifted a moment in the afternoon and then, as if the desolate pile of rock and stone thereby revealed was far too melancholy a sight to be endured, it descended again like a shroud around the walls of Newgate Prison.*

"How do you do that, Sir?"

This from a clergyman, seated on his right. Tobias smiled, and dipped his quill again.

"I could not read with all this motion," said the clergyman. "But to write, Sir, that is certainly an accomplishment."

> *These walls, being made from Welsh blue stone, had not been easily broken by the quarryman . . .*

"I did once see a lass at Amersham Fair who could knit a scarf whilst cantering a pony around a field."

This from a farmer who had squeezed in opposite Tobias. He was a big square-headed fellow who could not get his knees anywhere they did not touch another passenger and who had seemed, until this moment, rather irritated on account of it. "Now that were something," he insisted to Jack Maggs, who responded by folding his arms across his red waistcoat.

The farmer then turned to the clergyman. "That were worth the penny, that lass."

"Indeed," said the clergyman. "But our companion produces an even greater entertainment, Sir."

"Oh, it were a *very* fine show," said the farmer. "That lass were no more than ten years old."

> *. . . and yet the fog, by virtue of its persistence, had been able slowly to penetrate the stone's dark, inhuman heart . . .*

"I do not doubt it, Sir," said the clergyman, "but I suspect the young lass is being over-shadowed, as it were."

"You'll not persuade me so easy, your Reverence . . ."

The clergyman had seemed at first to be a man with no big range of emotions, but now his mouth was very straight and his face exceeding red. Said he, "To tell the tale of Captain Crumley and Mrs Morefallen: why that must be a performance of some great difficulty."

Between the farmer and Jack Maggs there sat an old lady in a white cloak and faded red bonnet who had been quietly pecking from a pannikin of roasted wheat. Now hearing Mrs Morefallen's name, she looked sharply up.

"Mr Oates?" she said. "It is not Mr Tobias Oates?"

The farmer was then suddenly, and most noticeably, silent.

This occurrence was by no means usual, and Tobias, although puzzled to know how he was recognized, was inordinately pleased to feel himself esteemed by these strangers. Yet so deep was his certainty of his own imminent disgrace that he could not savour their love without calculating how soon, and how brutally, it was to be torn from him. He therefore took no bow, engaged in no conversation, and in this manner gave his fellow travellers the impression of a cold and arrogant young man.

The attention of the other passengers turned soon enough to the signs of May—bluebells, the plum blossom by the church at Hammersmith, the hare fleeing across the turnpike. Toby's eyes were on grimmer territory altogether.

> *There were a great number of women inside Newgate that year. They had been brought from all over the British Isles: petty thieves, murderers, all manner of wickedness crammed into that grim pile on Newgate Street.*

He was still at that same address when the coach passed the great Park of Lord Dingley. Here, the clergyman and the farmer got into an argument about the virtues of the fir tree, a matter which would not be easily or simply settled. The farmer began to shout, the clergyman to laugh in a high and unpleasant manner. Tobias hardly heard this and yet there was another, more silent element, which really did distract him. That is: Jack Maggs's gaze upon him.

He continued to write diligently, but now he was over-conscious of the other's stare. It was like a ray from an eye-glass, warm at first, but soon too hot to be comfortable. He brought his own hard stare up to match the convict's.

Time passed. One minute, two. It was a silent exchange yet such was its force that the conversation of their fellow passengers died away, and it was in the face of their attention that the convict finally retreated.

A moment later, it was as if nothing peculiar had occurred. Tobias returned to his labours, Jack Maggs looked out the window. Soon after they arrived in Hounslow, and the two travellers found themselves left alone in the coach for the next stage.

"What is it that you write about me?"

Tobias felt the colour rising up from beneath his shirt. "These notes do not concern you, Jack."

"I know you've been writing about me."

The convict then held out his hand toward the chap book.

"Dear fellow, this is not your business."

"Give me," insisted the other.

"No, Sir."

"Deliver."

Tobias hesitated and then, desperately, began to read out loud an item in his work book he had written late the night before.

> In the region of Camden Town there were once to be found many famous old eccentrics, but lately it seems that they have "passed on" whilst we have slept, and now even "John the Happy Hooper" is said by local people to have gone to Sweden to amuse the family of the King and Queen. But the Inquirer did find, in Shaky Row, she who is known in those parts as the Canary Woman.

"Deliver!" insisted Jack Maggs, and Tobias had no choice but to give up his work book, his finger indicating the passage he had read from.

He watched with his heart racing, as Jack held the pages to his hard-boned face.

"You see," said Toby. "It is as I said." But Jack Maggs doggedly read all six hundred words.

"It is an old woman." He did not smile, as the writer had rather hoped he would, nor did he relinquish the book, but held it stubbornly clasped in his lap.

"As I said, not you."

"You get a good laugh out of the old biddy, I must say." The convict opened the book again.

"She is a comic figure, Jack."

"I reckoned it were *me* that were the comic figure." He was turning the pages slowly now, and then he paused. He was staring down at the annotated plan of the Newgate cell in which Tobias planned to accommodate Sophina. On the right-hand page was the start of the chapter he had so recently composed.

"Come, Jack Maggs. My book, if you please."

Jack Maggs frowned, as if dimly perceiving the unhappy fate before him on the page. Then, as if brushing off a spider web, he pushed back his long black hair from his forehead, closed the book, and returned it to its relieved owner.

"To the Gods we are all comic figures," Tobias said.

"As flies to wanton boys are we."

Toby's heart was beating very fast as he tied up the red leather covers of his note book. "If you could look at my life from on high you would split your sides to see the muddle I am making of it."

He tucked the book back in its place inside the attaché. He screwed the top on his inkwell, wiped his quill clean, and returned these items to their respective places, and when he had secured one with a ribbon, and the other with a leather strap, he snapped the case shut.

"You are a chap what plans," said Jack.

"How plans?" asked Toby, although he was apprehensive about where any new conversation might take him.

"You have the one place for your pen, the other for your ink. I should have planned this better," said Jack. "I was famous for planning in the Colony."

It was the first time, outside of a trance, that he had acknowledged his past to the writer.

"Even before my pardon, I was known to be a chap what planned. I provisioned parties for exploration. I could make a list twenty pages long and not leave out an item. I thought nothing of provisioning that house in Great Queen Street from half the world away."

"What house, Sir?"

"Go on with you. You knew the house was mine."

"Buckle's house?"

"He didn't tell you? I am Buckle's neighbour, or should have been."

"You have the lease?"

"It is freehold, mate."

To say this shocked Tobias is to understate it. To think this criminal should own a lease while he should be forced to waste his time on Comic Romps and Brighton Fires!

"As I said, I provisioned it from far away. I had a bachelor, a solicitor in Gray's Inn. He sent me five score squares of wallpaper until I found the one I wanted."

"This house you let to Henry Phipps? The fellow we are seeking—he is your tenant then?"

Jack Maggs frowned. "My point is that I should have taken as much care with Mr Phipps as I did with the house in which he lived. But I put it off, see. I was a busy man in Sydney town, busy with my bricks from one day to the next."

"You were a brick-maker?"

"At the time of my conditional pardon, I was given a small grant to encourage me in my new honest life. It was a very poor bit of land, about twenty acres, all of them covered with vines and poisonous scrub. Beneath the scrub were solid clay."

"It did not serve?"

"You could not grow a cabbage, but you could, if you had the nous"— and here he tapped the side of his considerable nose—"make a brick as good as anything in London. That clay made my fortune, Mr Oates. It gave me a mansion in Sydney. It gave me the dosh to buy the freehold of the house in Great Queen Street. And then, as I said, I provisioned it. I bought the wallpaper, the china, the finest Oriental rugs."

"Oh, to stumble on such a landlord!"

"Mr Phipps wrote me very frank and respectable letters. I only regret I never took the time to be so frank with him."

"Because?"

"Because, mate, I cannot bear him to think me a common criminal."

He turned and looked out the window, leaving Toby surprised that so hard a man should give a fig for the good opinion of his tenant.

"I'm not your comic figure, Mr Oates."

"In what way do you mean?"

"This old soul with her canaries—do you have a tin box for her?"

"Tin box, Jack?"

"Like you made a tin box for me. The tin box in which you locked all the demons you extracted with your magnets."

"I have Behemoth and Dabareiel locked up safe and sound. I am not carrying them out on the high road."

"But do you have a tin box for your Canary Lady? That was my question. For if you do, you must have more tin boxes than a pawn-broker."

"I keep the canaries here." Toby tapped his own forehead and smiled. "In this tin box."

Maggs turned and looked out at the fields to the north. After a little while the turnpike became narrow, almost like a lane, and the hedgerows pressed in close upon the coach.

"All this," Maggs said at last, "I keep in *my* tin box."

"The country, Jack?"

"Aye," said the other wistfully. And then he shifted in his seat and sighed.

They rode thus for a while longer, the convict turning more and more toward the window.

"By this *country* you mean Buckinghamshire?"

"Look how the blackthorn grows," the other cried, as the untrimmed hedgerow lashed the coach.

"I took you for a London sparrow."

"And so I am, but look, damn me: hedge bells, ground ivy. You smell that smell."

"Is that violets?"

"Besides the violets, there's another baddish kind of smell."

"Can I smell Herb Robert?"

For answer, the convict bestowed on the writer a rare and candid grin. "My ma called it Jack in the Hedge," he said.

"The bad smell?"

He shrugged. "She were a strange woman, my ma."

Now Toby had already glimpsed this ma magnetically. He knew the pattern of her sword, but could not have yet drawn her hawk's eye, her handsome red hair, her startling white shoulder. She was shadow, passion, hurt, an inky malignancy in Jack Maggs's dreams, and now he sought to tease more winkle from the shell. "That could not have been so cosy, to have your mother name a bad smell after you."

Maggs turned away again, but when he turned back his eyes were bright, and it was not hard to see the boy in him, to imagine the orphan's hunger for affection.

"I don't believe she named me after nothing," he said. "She was from Bucks and that's what they call Herb Robert in these parts. But even if what you say were so, Sir, I'll tell you the truth: I'd rather be a bad smell here than a frigging rose in New South Wales."

And he was thereafter silent and sulky all the way to Maidenhead.

63

In Maidenhead, the *True Briton* filled up with a family of Harris, all of whom were set on going to the fair in Abingdon. There were five in total, the most senior of them being a grand old fellow with a white beard and a silver fob watch, which instrument the children got much amusement from finding and consulting. There was also a very comely Mrs Harris who sat with straight back and square shoulders, and sang hymns and ballads with her eldest girl. Lastly there was her husband Mr Harris, whose beard was more than equal to his father's, its fine growth covering the greater part of his broad chest.

From time to time, Mr Harris would amuse his children by undoing his broad leather belt and strapping the beard down upon his stomach. For some reason, mysterious to Tobias, this was regarded by all of the Harrises as a great joke, and the pater was entreated to repeat it constantly.

The effect of this family on Jack Maggs was not clear, for he had got himself in hard upon the window and, with his back to all the company, was either sleeping or looking at the passing scenery. But for Tobias, who had a tendency to exaggerate the goodness of people he did not know, the Harrises were a living reproach to his own miserable cupidity. He felt himself judged by their very Christian ordinariness.

What would they think of him to know how he had so shamed his own family?

In his misery, he also turned to the window as the coach, straining up a long slow hill, came through a grove of ancient lime trees. Behind the trees he spied a mossy Norman church, a vicarage, a garden, and the parson himself standing in the middle of his field of wheat. There was a breeze, enough to bend the wheat, enough to make the crab-apple blossom fall from the trees on the vicarage lawn.

He opened his chap book. He crossed out his entire first chapter. He wrote:

> *Many of M—'s companions could not stand the torture of banish-*
> *ment, and went mad on the voyage out. Sinners they may have been,*
> *but English sinners in their hearts. Whether plucked from village or*
> *the festering heart of the great Wen, they could not bear the prospect*
> *of never more seeing their beloved Motherland.*
>
> *M— would not go mad, but only because he carried with him the*
> *strong conviction that he would, no matter what Judge Denman read*
> *to him, walk once more in England's green and pleasant land.*

He was by now convinced that this was the last novel he would ever publish. He wrote full-steam, brazenly, daring Jack Maggs to turn around and snatch his book again.

At the crossroads at Wallingford he wrote the famous line with which, thirty years later, *The Death of Maggs* would finally begin:

> *As certain birds do declare themselves unto their intended, so the*
> *Murderer returned to court his beloved England, bold as cock robin*
> *in his bright red waistcoat.*

He then began to describe a storm at sea which he imagined as the heart of Chapter Two. On the edge of his own disgrace, he wrote about his belligerent subject with a sympathy he would never find again. In the dark face of the waves, in the cold foul air of the convicts' hold, he made a place beyond the reach of God Himself. There M— was pinned to the deck, his left wrist broken. Beside him lay a man named Harris with a sodden grey beard upon his cold and lifeless chest.

The coach stopped in Abingdon, which pleasant town he barely saw. It was not until the Harrises had departed the coach, when the shadows were lengthening and the *True Briton* was already labouring up the hills towards Farringdon, that he looked up from his own toils and saw himself again the focus of Jack Maggs's malevolent attention. Reluctantly he locked his book away, and engaged the fellow in conversation.

"Penny for your thoughts, Jack Maggs."

"Well, you already got my thoughts, mate," the other whispered in return, glancing at the other passenger: a straw-haired young gentleman who smelt strongly of both the tap room and the stables. Ascertaining that his neighbour was sound asleep, Maggs raised his voice to normal—normal, that is, with regard to volume, although not to tone, which was less respectful than before.

"Penny for my thoughts," said he. "That's awful rich, mate."

Then, with no explanation, he grabbed Toby's head and held it hard. He began slowly to pull the writer's face towards his own as if he meant to kiss him.

"How am I to get those thoughts back out?"

It is difficult to converse normally while having one's head pulled like a melon from the vine. Toby edged a little forward on his seat to ease the pressure. "I did not know you cared so much for them, Jack Maggs. You never took the time to read the minutes of our meetings. But when we return to London I'll give you the tin box and all my notes. And we will burn them together. Now kindly release me. You are hurting my ear."

Jack Maggs held him grimly. "Your notes are lies, mate. Your notes say nothing about me taking off my shirt. The truth is: you have had me reveal secret information in my sleep."

"All your secrets will be returned to you. Please let me go."

"Shut your gob."

Tobias suddenly understood how easily his life could be snuffed out.

"When I read you making fun of that Canary Woman," said Jack Maggs, with a quietness that in no way contradicted the violence of his dark eyes, "why, then it was clear as gin—you'd do the same with me. You'd tell my frigging secrets to the world."

Toby could not think how he should answer.

"How much will they pay you for a bit of fun like you have with that poor old biddy? One quid? Two? How much does it take to put her secrets in the gutter?"

"I told none of her secrets, Jack."

This Maggs answered by tightening his massive grip. "This is where my secrets are," he whispered. "Inside *this* box. The brain box. This is what we must break into."

Who knows what might have happened next, had not the guard sounded his bugle and the sleeping gentleman begun to stir. Then they were entering the yard of a village inn and the burly hostlers were shouting up at the coachman. Jack Maggs sat back in his corner like a wrestler between rounds, his arms folded across his bright red vest.

As they stepped down into the yard, Toby's heart was beating fast. He began to walk out into the High Street, but found Jack Maggs strolling close at his side. When he turned one way, Jack turned with him; and when he turned the other, he was beside him there also. At the end of five minutes of this perambulation, he had no choice but to return to the coach and hope there might be another honest citizen inside. It was not to be: the snoring gentleman had departed. No one had taken his place.

The coach returned to the turnpike. Maggs put his hands pacifically on his knees but continued to stare at his companion. This went on for some miles until Tobias could bear it no more.

"Well damn it, I am very sorry I have your blasted secret, Jack Maggs. I have no use for it. I wish I had never got it from you."

"If you had a very bad secret of your own," said Maggs, "it would take you out of danger."

"So now you threaten me."

"I do."

"Do you really think that wise?"

"I am not a wise man. I am a varmint."

"I have no 'bad' secrets, Jack Maggs."

"Well, that's a shame for you."

"You imagine I would give you the power to blackmail me?"

"That's the one I want," said Jack, in a much lighter tone. "By Jove, if you have a one like that, you can sleep like a babe all the way to Gloucester and know no harm will come to you."

Tobias wondered how he could be in danger when he was about to introduce Jack Maggs to his Thief-taker. And yet he was by no means certain of his companion's rationality. In Magnetic Sleep he had witnessed his torments and his rages, and it was not difficult to imagine Jack Maggs strangling him and throwing him from the coach. Indeed, as the darkness approached, he began to imagine himself stabbed, cudgelled, suffocated. He saw his broken, bloodied body in a ditch. He saw his work book torn, left to moulder beside the road. These visions remained in his mind's eye as vivid prophecies.

The road went over a stone bridge and entered a dark wood.

"You think me such a proper citizen, I'm sure."

"I don't know nothing about you, mate. I never formed an opinion."

"Then let me tell you, Jack Maggs, I have a secret twenty times as bad as yours." And then, as his heart thundered inside his chest, he found himself unburdening himself to his companion.

It was, in truth, a huge relief to do so.

64

Lizzie," said Mary Oates, "could you help me a moment with this little jacket?"

Lizzie Warriner looked up from *Castle Rackrent* and saw her sister struggling to dress her child. Mary, she decided, had no natural sense for how to clothe a body, even her own. It was not merely that her sense of colour had always been a little awry. Of that short-coming she was, at least, aware, and had developed a palette of grey and white and black in order to avoid the worst embarrassments, but poor Mary, no matter how she laboured, could not present herself to the world without a ruck or a rumple, and she could do no better with her child. She had laid little John out on the sofa and now, as she sat awkwardly beside him, was attempting to clothe him in a very beautiful embroidered jacket while holding his head clumsily with one hand. It was hard, so very hard, for Lizzie to look at this and not feel irritated. This was "Good Mary" and "Sweet Mary" whom everybody loved?

"Don't you think it still too big for him?" she asked at length.

"It is Aunt Bet's gift," said her sister simply.

"But what will Aunt Bet feel to see the arms rucked up so and the collar out around the poor chap's shoulders?"

"Aunt Bet has raised ten children on a clerk's income. I'm sure she will be pleased to see how much more use we will have from her thoughtfulness."

"I'm sure Aunt Bet can wait until little John is three months older. It will be a very handsome jacket then."

"Lizzie," said Mary, crossly. "Do you have other business to attend to?"

Lizzie put her book down and went to her sister's side. She put her arm around her shoulders. "Mary, dear good Mary, I am sorry. I know not the first thing about babies or their clothing. Besides, I am a horrid little beast as everyone has always known."

"You are not a horrid beast at all, dear Lizzie, but I do think you have been very sad all day."

Mary fussed further with the embroidered jacket and then lifted her son up for Lizzie to admire. "There darling, see, you like Aunt Lizzie. You will make Aunt Lizzie happy. There is nothing like a little one to make you happy in your heart, Lizzie. So often I am out of sorts or worried about one thing or another, and then I pick up little John and hold him to me and really, I swear . . . well, it is the best thing in all the world."

Lizzie took the baby from her sister and put her nose against the babe's soft downy little neck and breathed his milky soapy smell.

Mary sat on the sofa with her hands folded simply in her wide lap. "Why are you so sad, dear Lizzie?"

"Sad?" Lizzie brushed her eyes against the little fellow's short fair hair. "I am not sad, Mary."

"Yes," persisted her sister. "I think you are very sad. At first I thought it was because the doctor took your necklace, but then I thought it was because you fought with Toby. Did he speak to you of money? You know his father has been writing cheques again?"

"Where has he gone, Mary? I heard him leave the house very early."

"You should not be upset by what he says. He went to Gloucester with the convict."

"He has left *London* with him?" said Lizzie, very much astonished.

"You know how he loves to rush about."

"But how long is he gone?"

"Only two days."

"Two days!"

"Lizzie, you make it sound a life-time."

"Well it may be so," said Lizzie darkly.

"Whatever do you mean?"

"He is your husband, Mary."

"And whatever does *that* mean?"

"If he were the father of my child I would not permit him to travel so recklessly with a murderer. Why, poor little John, if something should happen . . ."

"Lizzie, nothing will happen. He is brewing up a story so he may sell it. We should not be too angry with him. Lizzie, you are crying."

"I am crying to think of poor little John," said Lizzie. "I am crying that anyone could be so careless of his happiness."

Mary was quiet then for a moment, and Lizzie saw the good slow soul was thinking.

"You are not thinking of our own papa, Lizzie?"

No, Lizzie had not been thinking of their papa. Their papa had never cared for her. It was Mary whom their papa had loved so.

"No," she said, walking up and down before the window with little John sucking on her neck. "No, I am thinking of Toby." She was so very angry. She stood at the window looking out at the beautiful spring day and the urchins from the stables playing cricket in the middle of the street.

"It would be a dreadful thing for anyone to lose their papa," said Mary. "Or their husband, for that matter."

Lizzie turned to look at Mary's sentimental little eyes.

"I am sad, Mary, I confess it. I really do think I should adopt a child. I think it would be very good for me. I'm sure it may be very hard to do in London, but why might I not go away? I could sell my necklace, Mary."

"Is it something in your novel that is making you talk of this? Do you remember when Mama forbade you to read any more on account of all the notions you were getting from your novels? You will have your own husband in good time."

"Can you see my future, Mary?" said Lizzie.

"Oh yes," said Mary blithely. "You will have ever so many children and you will have your own handsome husband and a splendid house and live next door and our children will all be friends and we will have Christmases together around a great oval table and Toby will perform his magic tricks."

"And my husband?"

"Perhaps he will perform tricks too. We don't know who he is as yet."

"I don't like him," said Lizzie. "I really do not see why I should not adopt a child."

Mary frowned. "Dear Lizzie." She patted the sofa. "Come, bring John and we will all sit together, and you can tell me the story of your book."

And so, indeed, Lizzie did, and spent a very strange, and oddly exhilarating, hour as she invented a variation on *Castle Rackrent*.

But when the hour was finished, her condition was not altered and there was no one who could tell her what it was that she should do.

65

Dear Henry,

I write this with the borrowed quill of Tobias Oates, the author of *Captain Crumley*. The paper inside the yellow envelope contains facts most damaging to that individual.

Henry, even if you presently abominate me, remember what you had from me, and in honour of my generosity, do the following: If I am arrested and charged on that man's Information, make a copy of the paper and take it to his wife at Lamb's Conduit Street which is just north of the Inns of Court. I don't know where his Pater lives, but believe he goes by the moniker of the *Fighting Bantam* and *John the Cock*. Find him too, and whatever members of his family or associates you can learn of. Then go to Fleet Street, go to whichever Tap Room is preferred by those Gentlemen of the Pen. Buy these gents whatever takes their fancy and Mr John Plasse at the Temple will make up your expense one thousand-fold.

If I am not arrested, let Justice prevail—burn the letter.

Me and this Oates are on our way to Gloucester, but where we are at this moment, I do not know. It is a case of Jack-be-nimble, for the night is dark, the coach hard as a rough dray and my dreams are troubled by a Phantom who stares at me and makes threats against me. This creature has been recently introduced into my sleep by Magical Arts. Perhaps you, with your education, will know how he can be drawn out again.

We are promised Gloucester by dawn. There we seek the famous Thief-taker who can find any man between London and Cardiff—all this on your account. I blame myself for the way I withheld my true history from you. I left a blank map for you and you have doubtless filled it with your worst imaginings.

This letter I will entrust the Thief-taker, and in it you will find the end of the tale regarding myself and Sophina. Much relief I hope you may find in the truth. Then you may lay these pages aside and say—Ah, is this the monster I was so afraid of?

I previously related how Sophina and I did fall asleep and were discovered by the Ma, and although a great deal were made of the *five months* etc., I had no idea that she was with child. I wrote this? I think so.

Sophina and I were hurried from the house as if in close arrest, and Tom felt himself obliged to carry the great hessian bag of silver plate upon his back. The Ma told him to give it up, but he was a good son and a foolish thief, and struggled with it through the dark streets until, by Piccadilly, we managed to wake up the driver of a lonely cab. Once we were, all four of us, squashed in together with the stolen goods, all of the Ma's poison was turned on me.

She told me that I was to be punished and was kind enough to de-scribe my treatment in advance of its execution. It was a new pun-ishment, and now she drew the picture exactly: Tom was to pull my arms through a ladder and keep me pinned there so she could wield the strop.

It was an hour before dawn when we arrived back in Islington. The sky was still dark but I could hear the cocks crowing, as they will, be-fore there was any need to do so.

Ma had me carry Silas's heavy ladder upstairs from the hallway. Then Tom helped me lay it on a slant against my bedroom wall, and then Ma made me lie against it while great hulking Tom—having sat himself obligingly on the floor beneath the ladder—pulled down on my arms so hard I feared they would be wrenched from my shoul-ders. I imagined I was being punished for being a filthy swine, but no one told me that I was to be assaulted for being the father of an un-born babe.

Ma, as I see now, was more concerned with business than our morals. She did not wish to lose her little girl-thief to motherhood, or me to Sophina. She needed both as servants to her cause. Thus she dealt with me in a manner very fierce.

Once she had me on the ladder, she hitched her skirts up in a style that revealed her white and muscled calves. She then retreated into the kitchen from whence she presently came running, and laid the strop down hard on me with an ugly grunt. Twenty times she did this, and though she were huffing and puffing at the end of it, there was not a stroke where she did not admonish Sophina to keep her eyes upon my humiliation, or to take her hands off her ears so she might hear my cowardly cries.

Then it was done, and Tom let go my arms. So caught up was I with my own shame that I did not notice Ma take Sophina from my room, had no inkling of what fate there was for her, but the moment I heard her cry to me—*Jack, Jack*—I sprang up from my rack with the intention of coming to her aid.

I have gone over this moment all my life, and in my waking dreams I have oft seen myself reach my beloved on the stair, and there I have imagined myself to punch the Ma—yes, by God, I did say punch, and sometimes stab and sometimes slash with that great sword. I have dreamed, over and over, the happiness of saving Sophina, of running out into the dawn street—our babe alive—into our fresh young lives.

In the half-light before that dreary dawn, I got only part way across the kitchen before Tom settled me. He came down on top of me with all his might and held me hard against the floor with my arm jerked up behind my back. I was a big boy, fifteen years old, but he was all of twenty and he sat atop my bleeding bum heedless of whatever pain he caused me.

—You dirty little scrub, he said to me. You rag-tag, etcetera. He pushed my head down against the boards and I can, to this day, feel that splintered surface against my cheek, hear Sophina's tearful voice in the hateful little room below. Much of the Ma's speech I did not hear exactly, but the following I did.

You want me to fetch Tom so he can hold you still?

Now I am going to tell you something which you may think unlikely—I imagined Sophina being beaten much as I had been.

You want Tom to come and look at you like this?

I did not see my beloved until the bright light of day came to the kitchen, and then she appeared, standing at the open door, and I— recently released by Tom and now sitting at the table drinking tea— looked up at her.

Her face was wan. Her hand was resting on her pinny. When she caught my eyes, she turned away and walked into our room.

I leaped up but Tom laid his hand on my shoulder.

—Now leave her be, you dirty little swine.

Still I would have gone to her, but he took me by the arm and, by virtue of his superior strength, was able to detain me at his pleasure.

—You come with me, Mr Mutt-sucker, said Tom, and thereupon did take me down through the house, down through the horrid little plain room, out towards the privy and the thistles to the brick wall, then along the little dirt track beside the wall, up and over a collapsing drain, and round the end of the wall. And here the smell was very bad—all kinds of excrement and rottenness.

Here Tom forced me to stoop and kneel beside the little drain as it pushed its way under the cheese shop. He kept me pinned, jerking my arm back a little now and then to remind me of the pain, and all the while he poked into the filth with a stick.

—Look here, he said.

I feared he meant to push me into the cess pit, and so was undefended against the real assault.

Thus, I looked.

—See, said Tom, it looks like a toad.

There lay our son—the poor dead mite was such a tiny thing. I could have held him in my hand. And on his queerly familiar little face, a cruel and dreadful cut.

Cannot write more at this time.

P.S. Went to sleep and woke to find Oates with hand familiarly on my knee. Says he, were you dreaming, Jack Maggs?

I told him, no, I weren't.

That were a lie—the Phantom above-mentioned had appeared to me. I saw *It* sitting opposite me in the coach. Yellow hair, long side whiskers, blue frock coat with gold buttons.

I said to *It*, is it you?

It replied, yes it was. Then *It* laid its hand upon my head and the hand so cold it burned me. I cried out, and woke to find the coach filled with strangers.

We gallop through the endless night, eleven miles the hour and candles sputtering.

66

I t was barely sun-up when they came to the crown of Burlip Hill, and all of Gloucester could be seen rising above a light low mist in the great dish of the Vale. The coach stopped, and the guard and driver entered into earnest consultation, at the conclusion of which it was suggested that the ladies and gentlemen might like to view the road ahead. If you yourself have viewed Burlip Hill, you will understand why, at half past five of a spring morning, Jack and Tobias and their fellow passengers decided to abandon the comfort of the coach and walk in ankle-deep mud down the road while the *True Briton* descended with all its locked brakes screaming against the wheels.

The slippery surface of Burlip Hill muddied the backside of more than one passenger, but Maggs impatiently galloped the slope towards his promised Thief-taker. It was, he observed, as pretty a scene as you would see in all of England—the land divided by hedges into fields and orchards, and the whole picture, with the Cathedral in the middle and the Morvan Hills of Wales in the distance, "was worth the price of twice the mud."

Of course, the ruffian was excited. His eyes were bright and everywhere about him. Twice he sneezed, loudly, and blew his nose like a trumpet at the dawn. Even as he loped down the hill he carried his three wrapped parcels—mirror, lemons, paper—as though the Thief-taker were ready to receive him at the bottom of the hill.

The writer, now contemplating his imminent disgrace, was in a darker mood entirely. He had in truth never met this Thief-taker. He had no address for him, only Dr Eliotson's assurance that messages left at the Bull would reach him. Eliotson, although perfectly respectable, was also given to both vagueness and naivety. It was a foolish and dangerous position he had placed himself in.

When the coach arrived in Southgate Street, it was Jack who found out where the Bull Inn was. He set off towards the Cross, carrying his parcels before him. Tobias—known for his brisk and energetic walk—was forced to skip to keep the pace.

Maggs's unbuttoned oil-skin, that garment he referred to as his Great

Joseph, floated behind him like a cape as he strode the streets of Gloucester, past Mercer's Entry, and down into Bull Lane where they found a very decent-looking little inn with a sign proclaiming ENTER-TAINMENT FOR HORSE AND MAN. It being so early in the morning, the tap room was empty, and there were chairs on tables, and the smell of soap fighting with the stale odours of the pipe and brandy bottle. The sound of pouring liquid, however, gave away the whereabouts of the landlord who was down behind the bar, seated on a three-legged stool, filling a line of bottles from a cask.

He was a narrow man of less than middle age, with a long hard face and a little slit of a mouth that was not hidden by his beard. He had the poached-egg eyes of a man who enjoyed the stuff he sold, and these eyes, blood-shot and a little yellow in the whites, considered Jack Maggs with some considerable astonishment.

"Jod's blood," said he.

"Now ain't this a treat!" said Maggs in a tone that seemed very jovial.

"I don't owe you nothing, Jack."

"I never said you did, George Conklin."

George Conklin looked sharply and briefly at Tobias, and returned his attention to Jack Maggs. "I'm Herbert Holt." He hesitated. "We are settled on that business. I don't owe you nothing."

"Aye, we're square, mate," said Maggs who now turned to survey the tap room: and a very neat and prosperous tap room it was, decorated with all manner of brass gew-gaws, and Toby jugs. It was the sort of house, Tobias felt, in which one would see solicitors and merchants gather to discuss their affairs, where you might expect to see a judge, still gowned and wigged, come to sit by the fire with his cheese and claret.

"If we're square, why're you looking for me?"

"I ain't."

The landlord, having accepted this with obvious scepticism, now transferred his attention to Jack's three parcels. "If you been talking to the silver again, I retired. I'm sorry, Jack. Don't take it personal. I sell nothing here but what is up and up."

"We're both gentlemen then, George."

"Herbert," he corrected.

There was then a longish period of silence while the landlord frankly appraised his visitor's attire. "I wouldn't wear a red waistcoat, Jack," he said at last. "Not in your position. A red waistcoat is going to catch the eye. It is like a rule of nature, that it is the poisonous things that got the stripe of red upon them."

"Bullshit, George."

"Herbert."

"Herbert, do you know a cove named Partridge?"

The long-faced man's mouth contracted. Silence.

"You know him?"

"Aye. Wilf Partridge. He who found the missing Duke. I knew him when he were a hedge creeper in Kent."

"They say he can find any cove in England once he sets his mind to it."

"They?" The landlord shrugged. "They say also he is a witch, or at least is married one."

"But you know him?" asked Tobias. "He is nearby?"

Herbert Holt glanced at Tobias Oates and then looked away. He bent and collected half a dozen bottles of spirits and silently stoppered them. "I'll get you the Private Room, Jack," he said at last. "But you'll not be staying in the house, and you'll use the back door when you leave. No, no need to pay me."

"Very generous, Herbert."

"Now you and your mate, listen to me," said Herbert. "This Private Room was given for a meeting of the Wanderers' Society, and that won't matter for the morning, but if you're still there at noon time they'll be none too happy. They wouldn't be happy to know I gave their room to a fellow in a red waistcoat. So it's best you lock the door from the inside, and don't let them in. If Partridge comes, I'll give him a key."

"No one's going to recognize me, Herbert."

"I recognized you, Jack. Very nice too, very nice to see you, but that's enough. You stay in there and don't come out for nothing. I'll send the boy to put the word around for Partridge, and you can pray he ain't in Bristol again, for if he's not here by evening, you shan't stay here, Jack, and no knife is going to help you. It isn't personal."

"Where there's no cheating, Herbert, there's no knife."

"I've got mates here, in the lane."

"You wouldn't shop me, George?"

"I couldn't be that civilized, Jack, if you take my meaning. I couldn't risk the association, like."

And with that the stringy landlord shepherded his unwanted guests through the tap room, down a half-set of stairs and along a corridor to a room which was, in spite of the gold-leaf letters on the door, a charmless hole. The windows were small and uncurtained; it had bare distempered walls, and furnishings consisting of nothing more than a long table and two mucky benches that appeared to have just been brought in from some barn where they had long been banished.

Tobias loathed the room, but he sat at the wobbling bench and slowly picked the dried mud from his boots and trousers. Jack Maggs stayed at the window, peering out into the dismal yard where, presumably, the horses found their entertainment.

Time passed slowly. It began to rain. The writer opened up his attaché case but his fingers were unpleasantly dry with the mud of Burlip Hill, and he could not bring himself to unscrew the ink bottle. Out of the window he saw an old man chop the head off a rooster, and the old man and a hostler stood and laughed while the headless bird ran flapping round the yard. The convict noticed the same event and his broad and powerful figure soon occupied the embrasure of the window, thus blocking out the light. The symbolism of this was not lost on Tobias. How deep had he sunk into the slough. One sin had led him to the next. Each danger spawned a bigger danger and now he was cast down into a room with a man whom he had cheated. He closed his attaché case and locked it. He had come a long way from his God.

At noon there was a rattling on the door knob, and both men looked up expectantly.

"Oh drat." They heard a woman's voice. "This is very very poor, you know. Very poor indeed."

Thus, in the space of an hour, the two men suffered the raising and dashing of their hopes by ten different visitors. The door was tried, rattled, but no one came in, not even a servant with the vittles Jack was convinced his "previous acquaintance" would send to them. They sat with their stomachs rumbling loudly, and when the key finally entered the lock it was hard to say what Tobias wished for more: the Thief-taker or his luncheon.

In either case he was disappointed. The door opened to reveal a clergyman, a black-clad fellow, with bushy brows sitting low upon his eyes.

"I beg your pardon," said Tobias, rising. "The room is taken."

Yet so confident was the visitor of his rights that he shut the door be-

hind him. He carried a big calico parcel tied under one arm and a black
and knobbly walking stick under the other.

"Wrong room," said Jack, hurrying forward so violently that Tobias
was reminded it was a fight about a private room that had his father in
jail for murder. He put his hand on Jack's shoulder to restrain him.

"This room is ours," cried Jack. He flung Toby's hand away and took
the intruder by the elbow.

To this assault, the clergyman raised an eyebrow.

"Mr Maggs?"

"Who says so?" demanded Jack.

"You say so, Sir," said the clergyman, and shook himself free. "If you
were not Mr Maggs, you would say, 'I am not Mr Maggs,' and that
would be that. If you say, 'Who wants to know?' you have admitted it.
Q.E.D."

Toby saw the tic quiver on the convict's cheek.

"Are you perchance a Wanderer, Sir?" Tobias asked.

He was answered by one more invader, a woman, who promptly took
a seat at the table.

"Not us," said she.

67

You are Jack Maggs," said the clergyman in a voice which evidenced
a rougher calling than his collar indicated. "And I am he whose
acquaintance you were so eager to make."

"*You* are the Thief-taker?" asked Tobias, much relieved.

"If you wish him to remain in your company, Sir," said the woman,
"don't never call him that." She was very plain and stocky with straight
grey hair cut in a brutal fringe. Now, in her chagrin, she was giving off
a strong odour of a cellar: earth, onions, something worse. "It were a
term used in ignorance."

Toby was not pleased to be talked to in this style by one so low-bred.
"Indeed, Madam?" He looked to her husband but found—to his considerable astonishment—that Wilfred Partridge expected an apology
for being called a Thief-taker.

It was then, so early in the transaction, that Tobias knew the Partridges for tyrants. *God help me if I ever fell under their power. Why, they would have me eating sawdust and picking locks for breakfast.*

But Jack Maggs seemed oblivious of Partridge's character.

"We apologize," he said. Toby was shocked to see how that pugnacious old body did bend itself so easily. "We had no wish to offend your Lordship." He reached urgently into his gunny sack and brought forth the wrapped papers, the mirror, the lemons, stacking them one atop the other.

Without abandoning his injured stance, Mr Partridge now contributed his own package to the table. It was a large oblong parcel about the size of *The Times*, but three or four inches thick.

"I am not a Lord," he corrected Maggs.

"If you truly can find any man in England," said Jack, "I will call you Duke or Baron."

"Plain Mister will serve me very well." Wilfred Partridge untied a knot and wound the string around his liver-spotted hand. Then he tied the twine with a loop and placed it on the bench. Next he peeled back several layers of wrapping: the first one calico, the next two coarse brown paper, the remainder, a yellow tissue like that often used by milliners. Finally, having tormented Jack Maggs considerably with his delay, he revealed a very learned-looking leather volume with a great deal of gold filigree on the cover and, on the spine, an artfully tooled crest. The scholarly appearance of this book reminded Toby of the company in which he had learned of Wilfred Partridge's name; this now softened him towards the fellow.

"I do believe," he offered, "we have a mutual acquaintance."

Wilfred Partridge considered Tobias Oates without interest.

"My friend, Dr Eliotson."

"There are many men of science," said Mrs Partridge, coldly, "who have studied my husband's powers."

"Mr Partridge is a student of Animal Magnetism. You studied with M. Labatte," Tobias addressed the husband. "Dr Eliotson wrote a paper on your Magnetic techniques. He was particularly impressed with the case of . . . who was it? You interviewed the witnesses Magnetically and then made the arrest yourself?"

"Eliotson?" the other responded moodily. "I don't recall."

"It is published in *The Zoist*."

"I am published everywhere," said Wilfred Partridge, opening his book to reveal, on the first page, a yellow newspaper clipping glued to the middle of a large white sheet.

"Did I not," Partridge brooded angrily beneath his heavy brows, "did I not find Emily Tudball who was taken from her mother's arms?"

"He did," cried his wife, pointing at a long glue-stained column of yellow newspaper:

EMILY TUDBALL IS FOUND.

"Did I not find the body of Lord Thompson when everyone said he was touring in the Pyrenees?"

"He did," announced his wife, and placed a close-bitten finger nail against the item:

LORD THOMPSON IS DEAD.

They had a long litany to complete between them and it took a good five minutes, and in all that Mrs Partridge did not vary her response by so much as a word.

"And how is it, Sir, that you work your art?" asked Toby once the case histories had all been recited. "Where do you stand on the issue of Magnetic Fluid?"

"No Magnetizer can doubt the Fluid," said Wilfred Partridge, indicating the leather-bound reports of his success, "but the Fluid stays in its puddle without the good faith of the subject."

"Faith?" cried Maggs. "By Jesus. We come from London. Ain't that faith enough to get the Fluids gushing?"

"Mr Partridge," said his wife, "requires a personal sign."

"I'm here. What more personal than that?"

Mr Partridge closed the book. "By personal," he said, "my missus is referring to two most personal matters."

"Money," said she.

"How much money?" asked Tobias.

"Fifteen on the table."

"Shillings?"

"Pounds."

Toby drew in his breath loudly, but the Partridges both kept their eyes on Jack Maggs, whose manner remained uncharacteristically amicable. "What was the second matter?"

"The second matter," said Wilfred Partridge, beginning to re-wrap his parcel, "would be an item, any item at all, however small, that is personal to the object of our quest."

"How *personal*?" asked Jack.

"Something that the party has laid his hand upon, Mr Maggs. Something that the surface of his skin has brushed across. A toy, a hairbrush."

Jack Maggs put his hand deep inside his Great Joseph, and brought into the light an extravagantly framed enamel miniature which he had kept hidden, mostly, in his trouser pocket. Now he revealed to the company an exceedingly well-bred young man in a blue coat, a white cravat. The character thus portrayed was most familiar to Toby, although he could not immediately place him. The young man seemed at once proud and companionable; although his light blue eyes were averted, his countenance was animated. The oval frame was silver and decorated, exotically, with stars.

"That's my son," said Jack Maggs proudly. "Mr Henry Phipps, Esquire."

This was the first time Toby had any intimation of Jack Maggs's very personal relationship with the tenant of the house in Great Queen Street. In the midst of his astonishment he was struck by the father's proud bright eyes as he offered the enamel portrait of his son to Wilfred Partridge.

He is waiting to have the lad admired, thought Toby.

If it was so, Partridge must have disappointed him. He did not look at the portrait at all but, having closely scrutinized the hallmarks on the gorgeous frame, handed the object to his wife.

"They all do leave a little of themselves," said she. Toby noted that she also looked carefully at the hallmarks. "They brush against it, they leave themselves behind."

"It is a good likeness."

"The question is, Sir, did he touch it recently? Was it in his possession?"

"The point is, Mum, I'm looking for my son."

Mrs Partridge slid the little portrait away from her. "If he hasn't touched it, it is of no use to Mr Partridge. We don't wants what he looks like. We wants where he is."

Tobias saw, or thought he saw, such a profound look of sadness on his companion's face that he felt compelled to take a lance against his tormentors. "Madam, you are making very little sense."

For thanks, his own man turned on him. "That's enough of that," said Jack Maggs.

"Wait," said the wife. "I can feel that you have something we can use." And produced, as if from nowhere, two small locks of children's hair. "His hair!" declared Mrs Partridge, her face now taking on a reddish sheen.

"Get out of my pocket," Jack Maggs cried, snatching the hair away from her. "That's private."

"That's the boy's hair," insisted the woman. "That's our man, Wilf. It's the son's hair. I won't be contradicted."

This was all uttered in a fierce and certain sort of way. Tobias was surprised to see that Maggs was, in some sense, cowed by it. There was a furtive, shame-faced air about him when he spoke again.

"Damn you. It ain't the one I want."

Tobias had no time to wonder at this information, for now the clergyman was rising like a warrior in his seat.

"You'll not *damn* my wife, Sir," said he.

The convict hesitated. Then he sighed, and sat slowly down, his head resting in his hands. "The hair don't belong to Henry Phipps," he said.

The clergyman now picked up the portrait from the table and carefully appraised it as closely as a jeweller. He passed it to his wife, who then placed the portrait against her ear, as if it were a seashell.

It was obvious to Tobias—indeed, it would have been obvious to a sensible child—that the Partridges were charlatans, but as the blunt-nosed little pick-pocket lowered the portrait from her ear, Jack Maggs waited humbly for her verdict. Tobias was touched, against all his expectation, by the eager way he leaned towards the woman. How sad, Tobias thought, the Somnambulist had become.

When the two Partridges begged that they might be excused to consult further in private, Jack Maggs suggested that he and Tobias Oates leave the room.

68

Toby drew his companion down into the dark end of the passage where someone had stacked some wooden saddle frames and then left them rotting on the floor.

"So, Master Maggs," he whispered, "what is your opinion?"

The convict's face had, on the whole, a rather frozen quality but his eyes were now glistening with excitement.

"They know their onions, that's for sure. The only thing against us— my Henry never touched his own portrait."

"Did you note the way they looked at it?"

"It weren't what they wanted."

"They each read the hallmarks first. Is the frame valuable?"

"I would not frame his portrait with rubbish, that's a fact."

"Jack, we are being swindled."

"It is not Partridge?"

"It is Partridge, yes."

"How swindled? No, I don't believe you. Trust me, mate, I know the game."

"And trust me, Master Maggs. This is mumbo jumbo. He cannot find anyone by placing a silver frame against his ear."

"It don't work?"

"It cannot."

Jack looked down at Tobias Oates, looked at him very hard. "But this is the same cove you vouched for."

"Now, Jack, that ain't quite it. He was vouched for by Dr Eliotson. And I am sure he performed the act my friend attributed to him."

Maggs's face contorted, a whole ugly spasm that passed from his eye down to his mouth. "You promised me I would find my son," he said coldly. His brows were down hard on his eyes. "That was our under-standing. It was for this, and only this, I wasted all my frigging time? Why would I make myself a fart-catcher? Why would I be a lackey to that ugly little wretch?"

Toby was afraid, but he stood very still and held the convict's eye.

"I'm sorry, Jack, from the bottom of my heart. I also have a son. It is not hard for me to understand your feelings."

This did nothing to calm Jack Maggs at all. Indeed it had the oppo-site effect. He began to drum a foot upon the boards. Toby took a half-step backwards.

"You understand nothing," cried the other, brushing roughly past him and coming back up into the passage-way. "You can hoodwink me into taking off my shirt, but you don't know a rat's fart about me." A great flood of colour had risen in Jack Maggs's face. "You steal my Fluid but you can't imagine who I am, you little fribble. What was that noise?"

"I do believe," said Toby, whose heart was pounding very hard, "that they've locked us out."

Uttering a curse, the convict literally spun upon his heel. In two strides he was at the door to which he administered such a mighty kick that it was brought screeching off its hinges and thus revealed, like a stage curtain raised through misadventure, the two actors in a state of some embarrassment.

That is, the Partridges had the window open, and Mrs Partridge already had one leg out into the court, and one blue-veined ham-bone showing to the room. Mr Partridge was by her side, his wide-brimmed hat back upon his head, the partially wrapped portrait still in his hand.

Jack's three parcels were still on the table, but the Partridges' bound volume was nowhere in sight.

Jack Maggs came across the room, moving with a grace his bulk had hitherto concealed. He moved like an acrobat, or a dancer whose steps, being much practised, appear more natural than they are. To be particular: he crossed the bleak little room crouched queerly low but with his stride undiminished, a contortion demanded by his need to withdraw a knife from inside his boot.

There was then a very loud explosion, and Tobias was confused about its cause until he saw a pistol fall onto the floor and smelled the distinctive odour of gunpowder. But even when the pistol lay revealed, he still did not understand that Wilfred Partridge had fired it at Jack Maggs.

Mr Partridge was sitting on the sill. Then Maggs stepped back from him, and Toby saw the blood on the Thief-taker's shirt and imagined he had been wounded by this pistol. Then he saw: Wilfred Partridge's throat was cut. His hand was holding the wound. Bright red blood streamed through his fingers, down his arm, across the face of the miniature portrait which Jack Maggs was now brutally prying from his hand.

Wilfred Partridge fell into the room. His head hit the floor very hard.

The convict turned, the bloody portrait in one hand, a rough black blade in the other. He looked Tobias Oates threateningly in the eye and thus they stood the two of them, the one with the power to take away life, breathing heavily, the other hardly daring to draw breath.

Toby thought: I am a dead man now.

It was then, facing the warrant he imagined in those dark brown eyes, that he spoke the words: "Come, Jack. Quickly. We must run."

69

J ack Maggs had bolted, she knew not where. He had departed as he
had first come in, in mufti. He had not spoken, not even waved. She had looked up from the kitchen window and seen him walk up Great Queen Street with his kit-bag across his shoulder. That night, after midnight, she went across the roof again, but the house was cold and frightening. She knew then: he had gone for good.

If the master knew his whereabouts, he was not saying. Indeed it seemed that Jack Maggs's departure had allowed all Percy Buckle's bot-tled feelings to spill out in a stinking rage. Mercy knew what her offence had been, and yet it could not be spoken of.

The master had seemed, in the shadow of Jack Maggs, a plain little thing, but in the quiet that followed the latter's departure she saw what a false perception that had been. Mr Buckle was her life, her safety. Her association with Jack Maggs had humiliated him to a degree she had been too intoxicated to see at the time.

Now he would not permit her to so much as pour his tea for him. Thrice she went to him unbidden; thrice he ordered her back to the kitchen.

She was ill. She could not eat. She assisted Miss Mott as she was or-dered, working with her back towards the light so the cook might not see the hot tears falling onto the liver she was preparing for dinner.

"Wherever he has gone to, dearie," said she, "it's better off for you."

"I don't know what you mean, I'm sure."

"If I was you I'd be running up stairs and taking the master a plate of that toast and cinnamon he is so partial to."

"He don't want no truck with me today."

"You get up there and get back in the master's good books or God knows what sort of life you're going to have."

She knew what sort of life. She knew it exactly. She saw the stinking little room in Fetter Lane. She saw the Haymarket, the vile dress with its gaudy ribbons.

"Go on, git." Miss Mott took forcible possession of her three-legged stool, and pushed its sniffling occupant aside. She took the knife from the maid's hand. "That other is a hard man. You can see it in his beak. He's not the man for you, girl. Go, wash your hands now. Make the master his toast, there's a good miss."

Miss Mott then took charge of the liver, lowering her little wire spectacles so she could see the veins the better. "Do what I say, and one day I might have the pleasure of calling you Madam. Fetch me the flour, that's a girl."

Mercy walked slowly down into the pantry. Her legs felt weak and wobbly, her bowels loose. She returned with a cup of flour. She watched as Miss Mott spread it across the table and dredged the slices of liver in it.

"Now bring me the loaf, Mercy, and I will cut it thin the way he likes it."

Thus Mercy called on Mr Buckle a fourth time. She knocked hesitantly on the snuggery door, and entered. He was at his precious bureau, quill in hand, but it was his eyes she noticed first, how naked they were: his hurt was plain to her now.

"A little bit of something," she offered. It was a way of speaking she was accustomed to use in their more personal moments together, and it was certainly a risk to use it now. But he did not immediately reject her, and she carefully set a small lace doily close by his ink bottle, then lay the toast in front of him.

"Shall I make a nice pot of Orange Pekoe for you, Sir?"

Percy Buckle stared mutely at the toast. The four slices were soaked with butter, sprinkled with ground cinnamon. They were laid one atop the other and sliced into lady-fingers.

"Is he gone for good?" he muttered angrily.

"I do not know, Sir. He did not say so, Sir."

She watched him nibble cautiously at his toast. Then she gave him her treasure. She had no other currency to offer: it was everything she had.

"If he ain't gone, Sir, I know how we could make him go. I have discovered where his Henry Phipps is hidden."

Mr Buckle finished his lady-finger and took a second. His appetite appeared to be returning.

"You did not tell him you had this information?"

"Oh no, Sir. I wouldn't do that, Sir."

"But how do you know such a secret, Mercy?"

"Well, it seems that Mr Constable visited Mr Phipps at the gentleman's club. He discovered that Mr Phipps is no friend to Jack Maggs, and so he did not inform Jack Maggs that Mr Phipps was found, not wishing to make him angry, Sir."

"Are you sure you did not tell Jack Maggs?"

"Oh no, Sir. Never. I would not want to make him angry either, him being a convict and all. He would be ever so upset to know he was hated by his son."

"His son!"

"He told Mr Constable that Mr Phipps was his son."

"But Mr Phipps is a gentleman!"

Mr Buckle's astonishment was so great that he seemed, for this moment anyway, to forget his umbrage.

"Good Lord," said he. "And hated by him? I do not wonder. A son, and hated. Hated by his own son. Son? It is beyond belief. The convict owns the house next door? Pretends to be my footman, but owns the freehold? So, Mr Phipps . . . his son. Why, I'd wager his fortune all comes from our Jack Maggs. It's convict gold, that's what it is."

"I couldn't say, Sir."

"And now this Mr Phipps, he doesn't like Jack Maggs?"

"No, Sir. He hides from him."

"Well, who can blame the gentleman? Dirty money. Thievery. Murder. Of course he would hide. He don't want Jack Maggs trampling through his life. But what if the rascal cuts off all his funds? Disinheritance: it may be on the cards, Mercy. It must be on the cards, by gosh."

"It's true that Henry Phipps hoped that Mr Constable was bringing him the title of a property."

"Then there you are," said Mr Buckle. "Then there you are exactly. That's his worry. That's a very big worry for a gentleman to have. Disinheritance. He fears he will lose his house, poor devil."

Mr Buckle then set upon his toast most hungrily.

"This Mr Phipps," he said, "could turn out to be a very dangerous person for our Master Maggs."

And with that he smiled at Mercy. She was back. She was safe. She would never be so foolish ever again.

70

Tobias could never have seriously imagined himself running away with Wilfred Partridge's murderer. Yet once the two men had passed a policeman in Bull Lane, no further moment presented itself when he could easily extricate himself, and so he continued to accompany Jack Maggs in the direction indicated by the other's elbow. No word passed between them.

Tobias did not look at his companion. However, he was almost neurasthenically aware of his force, his heat, his potential for further violence.

As they came down to the place where Westgate Street runs into the quay, they found themselves amongst a mob of foreign sailors who, crowding urgently around a seated officer, made a dense and rum-sour knot upon the cobblestones. Here was Tobias's chance, and he took it, slipping back amongst the sailors, pushing through them towards the peelers.

Yet at the very moment the bobbies came into view, he saw this was no freedom at all. It was in his interests to keep Jack Maggs out of the dock. If Jack were guilty of murder, Toby was guilty of being his accessory; if Jack were a bolter, it was Toby who had knowingly, criminally, harboured him. Of course he was a man of letters but he had been a Fleet Street hack himself and knew that, once he was in the dock, the Press would feast no less greedily on one of their own. He did not need to consider the explosive secrets Jack Maggs might add to this conflagration.

And so he turned his back on Robert Peel's men and quickly found Jack Maggs again. Reunited, they walked calmly down towards the Severn. There they leaned casually over an iron rail and peered down into the mist-shrouded river.

"Tide," said his fellow conspirator, very casual in his manner. "Ebbing," he said, pointing down at a willow branch drifting slowly to the south.

Tobias watched those light green leaves drag in the current, and felt an unexpected sensation, like cool water, running along his neck. He looked at Jack Maggs, who winked at him. Tobias watched the willow branch and, as it was swallowed by the mist, thought that he too might have his freedom, and a larger freedom than anything he had imagined when he had fretted at his pennies and his pounds on London Bridge.

He would flee!

He would flee wherever Jack Maggs fled. It was not his fault he had to flee. He had no choice but flee. He would flee anywhere he damn well chose. He might invent himself again, as Simon Winchester in Jamaica, or Cecil Gunnerson in Cape Town, or Phineas O'Brien in Boston.

Once he had glimpsed this possibility, a wild, conscienceless beast rose in his breast and turned his cheeks pink and his lips an extraordinary red. "We can take ship here, in Gloucester? If you buy my ticket now, I'll make the money later. You have my word—I can make the money."

The convict looked narrowly at the excited young man. Then, without further response, he hoisted his kit-bag onto his shoulder and walked slowly towards the end of the quay where a lock-keeper's cottage was perched between the basin and the river. Here, without explanation, he climbed its garden fence.

Maggs's hessian boots trampled lettuces, broke carrot stalks. Tobias took the same course. He put one hand in his pocket and jiggled his change while he strolled though a wicket labelled *Private*, and then along a pretty cobbled path (which was, on this fifth day of May, bordered with primroses) and thence to a steep set of steps leading down to the river.

From that giddy precipice, Tobias looked down on the sorry-looking little punt which was tied up at the landing. This was not the sort of ship he had had in mind. He looked across the silky surface of the Severn, and remembered that it was a famously difficult river with fierce tides and the dreadful Severn Bore which came rushing up from the sea on a crest six feet high.

He halted.

The convict gave a small blackbird whistle from the water's edge.

There was now a considerable distance between the two men, thirty steps. Jack Maggs came to the bottom of the wall and squinted anxiously up, as if seeing, for the first time, just how easily he now might be betrayed. To judge from the pinched look upon his worn-out face, he might have been staring at the gallows themselves, but Tobias had moved past betrayal, beyond the point where a small and sorry-looking punt could make him hesitate for long, and he was soon running down the mossy steps to the landing. Here he undid the rope, and stepped aboard.

"Now sit on the mid-thwart," said Jack Maggs.

The mist closed mercifully around them. The river sucked them slowly, inexorably, down towards the sea.

71

At first the journey was sluggish and malodorous. The mist stank of the tannery but it was also a good opaque yellow and hid their escape. In any case, they had not been travelling ten minutes before it became obvious that their pace was quickening, and soon the little punt was rushing forward through the waters at a speed its builder would never have anticipated. The broad square-nosed craft handled well enough, and Jack soon laid his pole down and allowed himself to squat near the aft-thwart and give his fellow traveller a wink. This period of rest lasted all of a minute, then the big fellow was on his feet again and squinting down-stream into the mist.

"What's that?" he asked.

"Is there a ship?"

"Listen."

Toby slowly became aware of a distant roaring.

"There may be factories along the shore."

"That ain't no factory." Maggs leaned forward, took his kit-bag and set it firm between his knees.

"There are tanneries. That's what the smell is."

"Get aft. Jod's blood, move your arse, man."

Toby reluctantly did as he was ordered. He sat on the aft-thwart beside Jack Maggs. The noise of rushing water—for such was clearly what it was—now filled his ears. Following Maggs's example he placed his yellow attaché between his legs and gripped it with his heels.

"Dear Lord—is this the Severn Bore?"

"Hang on, mate."

It was not the Severn Bore but it was the weir, and they were on the lip of it before the danger was apparent. Then the convict did something which later, in recollection, would touch Tobias's heart: that is, he put one strong arm around the writer's narrow shoulders and held him tight.

The punt was catapulted out into the air.

Maggs cried: "God save us!"

To hear such a cry, from one such as he, was enough to convince Tobias that his end was near.

He too cried out: "God save us!"

The drop was nearly three feet at that hour, and when the little punt smacked down, its nose bit into the foaming river and the waters engulfed the craft completely.

"Swim!" cried Toby.

But the older man held him tight until the punt emerged, still afloat, but with less than three inches of gunnel showing above the water.

"We're sinking."

"Bail! Give that to me!" Jack Maggs grabbed for the yellow case. "It's all we have to bail with."

The river was still turbulent and fast, and the square nose, being so low, seemed to invite the incursion of more water every passing second. Tobias therefore opened his lovely case, removed his soggy notebook and, having sadly consigned his quill and ink bottle to the river, offered the case to Maggs.

"You wish *me* to do the bailing?" Tobias was shocked to see the temper burning in his eyes. "I ain't your fart-catcher now, mate."

Tobias silently slid his wet notebook into his jacket pocket, and got busy with the bailing.

Thus they proceeded down-stream: Maggs standing guard with his pole and keeping the punt away from the shoals and banks, Tobias ruining his expensive attaché case with river water.

The mist stayed low but their noses soon told them that they had left the region of water meadows and that they were passing between new-mown fields. Tobias—having, by dint of much labour, reduced the water to ankle level—trailed his cramped hand in the silky cold water.

Maggs set down his pole and watched with satisfaction as the punt sat itself mid-stream and drifted. He observed the craft's progress for a moment, and when he was satisfied that it could find its own way a while, he took from his coat the enamel miniature which had cost the Thief-taker his life. This gore-stained object he laid on the aft-thwart of the boat while he carefully removed his great-coat, and then turned its bloodied pocket inside out. Drawing his dagger, he then cut out the pocket, and dropped it into the Severn like so much offal. Having carefully washed the dagger's dark blade, he dipped the portrait over the side and washed it also.

After a little time they drifted close by the bank, where they were confronted by the sight of a young woman and her old mother fishing for eels. When Tobias saw how they stared into the mist towards the silent punt, he raised a hand, and called, "Good evening." The girl waved back, but then the woman said something and the daughter's hand abruptly dropped.

Soon they were alone again in the mist, and Maggs, dipping his precious portrait in the Severn one last time, handed it across to Toby.

"Were it my purse he would have been welcome to it, but not my boy."

The frame was slippery from the river water, and it was difficult for the writer not to think of the blood that had so recently washed over it. The light was now rather poor, and yet when Tobias held the enamel up very close to him he saw what he had not noticed when examining it in the Bull Inn. The likeness had seemed familiar, he realized now, because it was George IV dressed as a commoner. The Order of the Garter was absent. He wore a plain blue jacket, not the uniform of the Prince of Wales Light Dragoons, but this little miniature was, to all intents and purposes, a copy of Richard Cosway's portrait which Tobias had viewed, only last year, at the Royal Academy.

"Were he to have stolen my gold watch, he would not have suffered so," said Jack Maggs, standing and picking up the pole which he then drove vigorously into the water. "But he were a foolish man to steal my son."

As the punt came forward he began to wield the pole regularly, bending his strong body effortlessly to the purpose.

"You have not seen your son in a goodly while?" Tobias asked carefully.

"To answer your question," said Maggs, jutting his chin, and gazing at Tobias a moment, "he ain't my son by way of having lain with his ma, but he is my son in every other way."

The little craft drifted around a rather sharp bend by a cottage, and for a moment Maggs was busy navigating with his pole, but even when he had piloted the craft into the next long stretch, he did not pick up the conversation and Toby, curious as he was, thought it wisest to remain silent. In any case, he judged it kindest to let the fraud remain.

"It were a rainy autumn day," Maggs said at last. "A cold miserable sort of day, with a bitter wind blowing low and hard across the marshes, and the off-side lead horse of my coach threw its shoe.

"That is how I met Henry. He were sitting in the smithy's forge, looking for that place by the vice where he could feel a little of the warmth and not suffer any of the rain. When our coach drew up, there he were. He were all of four years old."

It was almost dark now, although Tobias could still make out the outline of the smallish elms. If there was anyone on the banks with an interest in the fugitives, they were careful to keep their presence concealed.

"It were an honest everyday coach, with honest everyday citizens inside, but outside two wretches were held hard in chains. The first wretch was a poor mad forger from Hull who was trying to hurt himself by ripping at his arms with his bare teeth. The second wretch was me. We were, this mad man and I, in the care of two soldiers who took it in turns to be outside with us. They had spent all their food allowance on ale, and had no means to feed either us or themselves no more.

"My Henry had a pig's trotter. That was how I noticed him. And, oh, how I wanted that pig's trotter, Toby. I wanted it every bit as bad as you want your Lizzie. And I stared at him, doubtless, most fierce and wild. And what did he do? Why, first he ran away. But then, two shakes later, his little head appeared up amongst the baggage on the coach and he held out the very thing I might have stolen from him. When he saw my chains would not allow me to eat it without assistance, he did the holding for me, so I could gnaw each morsel off that bone."

"Very kind," said Toby.

"I'm much of your opinion," agreed the convict, "and brave. For all the time he fed me, the poor mad cove from Hull did gnash and moan enough to make a soldier nervous. Henry watched him, wary like, but he did not flinch from feeding me.

"When I had done eating, I asked the little chap where his daddy was, for I wished to pay him a compliment. Then Henry pointed over across the road where there was a small church yard and gave me to understand that his ma and pa both resided at that place."

"They were dead?"

"Passed away."

"Oh dear," said Toby. "Poor little mite."

"'I am an orphing, Sir,' said he. That is how he spoke it: *orphing.* 'And I am tomorrow bound to live outside of Harrismith with the other or-phings there.'

"I was in a emotional condition, Toby. I had, the month before, been betrayed by my brother Tom. I had seen my childhood sweetheart sen-tenced to be hanged. I had heard her cries and seen her struggle and kick as the turnkeys carried her away. I also was to be cast out of my dear England, not in a year or two as was the custom, but on *the very next tide.* I was feeling very bitter about my lot.

"Then I see this little boy just starting out on the journey of his life, a very kind boy, with all his God-given goodness still undamaged. And I thought, so must *you* have been, Jack, before you were trained to be a varmint. I was much affected by this, Toby. It made a great impres-sion. So when I finished my meal, I made this solemn promise to the lit-tle boy. I knew exactly what I said. I spoke it out loud: and promised anyone who would listen that I would come back from my exile and take him from his orphanage, that I would spin him a cocoon of gold and jewels, that I would weave him a nest so strong that no one would ever hurt his goodness. I would clad him in a scholar's robe and learn him his numbers and his letters, not only English, but Greek and Latin too, and I went on so long with my speech that soon even the mad man stopped his twirling and wrenching and sat still beside me.

"'There's mad,' he said to me. 'There's mad as anyone can find in a butcher's shop.'

"He never lived to see me get my pardon for he was stabbed with a bone knife that very night aboard the *Enterprise,* and all the clothes and leather shoes stolen from his body before his last breath was gone.

"But this boy"—Maggs retrieved the framed portrait from the writer's hand—"this boy has kept me alive these last twenty-four years, and I will not have him taken from me. Nor will I permit him to be placed in harm's way. I am his da. He is my son. I will not abandon him."

Tobias Oates leaned back in the craft and looked upwards. He real-ized only then that the mist had cleared: the sky was black and bright with stars, and he inhaled the acrid sweet perfume of hawthorn blos-som. The little punt slid through the velvet water towards Newnham.

The writer sat hunched over, staring into the blackness, remembering the horrid sound of the blood bubbling from Wilfred Partridge's throat, wondering about those two locks of human hair that must be, even now, inside the murderer's pocket.

It had been Jack Maggs's plan that they should continue down the Severn until they arrived at Bristol, and there was an unspoken understanding, or so Tobias imagined, that they would find a ship in that great port. But there are many sand shoals in the Severn below Gloucester and at around ten o'clock, still not having passed Newnham, they came into a stretch of water where the mist lay very dense and thick. Here they got themselves so badly stranded by the sands that Maggs announced he was frigged if he would go any further. As there was still a good two inches of water in the bottom of the craft, and neither of them had any wish to lie there, they tried to sleep leaning forward on their haunches.

It was very damp and cold. Tobias could hear water rats nearby, and it gave him no peace to imagine those wet grey furry bodies climbing aboard the punt and sniffing around his sleeping head. Somewhere nearby was a cow with a bell. He listened to it come close, then recede. He slept, only to be immediately awoken.

"Toby?"

"Yes."

"Are you awake, Toby?"

"Yes, Jack."

The boat tipped, and remained listing on the sand. Toby felt something on his knee. Imagining a rat, he struck out against it and barked his knuckles on something hard and cold.

"Careful," said Maggs. "That's good brandy I'm giving you, mate."

"Good man, Jack."

"Something to make the Phantom doze."

Tobias allowed his hand to be taken and fitted around a cool silver flask.

"Paint me a picture of him who tortures me, Toby?"

"I wrote down what you told me in your sleep, Jack. One day you will read every word of it. Every dream and memory in your head, I'll give them to you, I promise. You have had a hard life, my friend, and more than your fair share of woe. I would never make light of your misfortune."

"Yes, yes, very Christian of you, Toby. But what is his appearance?"

"Tall and fair-complexioned. He has long side-whiskers."

There was a long silence on the aft-thwart.

"But you have never seen this Phantom yourself, Toby?"

"Of course not. He lives within you."

"Then here's a strange thing. I never heard of this Phantom until I met you. I never saw him, asleep or waking."

"You lived with the pain the Phantom caused."

"What would you say if I said you planted him inside me?"

"How could I do such a thing?"

"I'm damned if I know. But he was not there before."

"Your Phantom is as real to your eighth sense as Silas and Sophina, and I did not put *her* there." Toby smiled. "I can vouch for that."

A moment later he was crushed. His head was banged. His breath pushed out of him. He lay pinned, half-winded, with the great weight of the convict's body on his chest, the deck and thwart pressing painfully against his spine.

"Don't never say that name again."

As Jack Maggs's heavy body shifted painfully upon his own, Toby felt the heat of his breath.

"You say her name, I'll . . . You must not do it."

Maggs's hand moved in the direction of his boot. Imagining himself about to be stabbed, Toby twisted his shoulders and bucked his hips.

"Help!" he cried. "Help!"

Jack Maggs then began to laugh. Indeed, he laughed so raucously that he not only released his captive but fell back rather heavily into the bow.

"*Help*," he cried in a weak, affected voice. Then he righted himself and came back once more to sit himself beside Tobias.

"*Help*," he whispered in the writer's ear, but not so unkindly, and soon Tobias began to laugh too, if rather cautiously.

"Do you take it as an insult that I was afraid of you?"

"Oh no, Tobias, I take it as very sensible indeed."

Tobias could feel the rough unshaven face lean towards him in the dark.

"I am with you, Jack."

There was a long pause during which there was no noise but the jangle of the cow bell in the dark.

"We are together till I find my boy."

So saying, the big man laughed and put his arm around the writer, and squashed him affectionately against his chest.

72

Three weeks earlier, Henry Phipps had been safe in his own dear house, breakfasting on salmon, and when he had opened the letter with the Dover postmark he had, naturally, not the faintest inkling that the rather common little envelope with its formal script would be such a harbinger of destruction.

Now his house was abandoned, his spring flowers uncared for, his most cherished valuables stored in a dank cellar on Blackfriars Road.

He stood at the window of his rooms in the club. He looked out at the bedraggled pigeons huddling on his window ledge, and beyond that at the dirty green roof of Covent Garden, and beyond that at what appeared to be a hawk circling slowly in the poisonous yellow sky.

He was, he thought, like a rabbit hiding in its hole.

As holes went, it was quite adequate, but he would never have suspected that the club to which he had been hitherto so attached, where he had enjoyed so many adventures and amusements, could be such a very depressing place to live.

There was nothing *wrong* with the rooms exactly, but in the morning light the green carpet was thread-bare and spotted, and the dark burgundy wallpaper was peeling at the joins, and the oval mirror was split on its frame. As he had, once again, made the mistake of breakfasting in, he had to endure that awful curry smell which seemed to affect everything that was cooked here.

In Great Queen Street, he had employed a splendid cook, an austere and handsome Cornish woman whom he had, of course, sent away. He had sent all the servants on leave, just on the quarter day—so he had paid them up until the end of June; and this meant overlooking several pressing debts, and required a meeting with the bank to discuss the account which was then overdrawn a hundred guineas. Whether this account would ever be "topped up" again was by no means certain. Today was the fifth, the day "topping up" would normally occur, but he was reluctant to call on his bankers for fear of discovering the procedure had been abandoned by his benefactor.

And thus he was sitting by his gloomy little window, with its forlorn prospect of the roofs of Covent Garden, when a knock came on the door. It was Magnus announcing that there was a gentleman to see him. As he was, to all intents and purposes, in hiding, this news produced a very queasy feeling in his stomach.

"What gentleman, Magnus?"

"I really could not say," said Magnus, exhibiting the closed and shiny countenance of a freshly tipped servant.

"Did he state his name, his business?" asked Henry Phipps, who had, after three weeks of close acquaintance, grown weary of Magnus.

"Yes, I would say it was definitely business," said Magnus. And waited, his eyebrows raised, as if he were a witty subject in charades.

"Inasmuch, Magnus?"

"Inasmuch as it could not be *pleasure*, Sir."

"What are you telling me?" asked Henry Phipps impatiently. "Is he rough?"

"Oh no, Sir."

"Is he a large man?"

"Oh no, Sir."

Henry Phipps placed his tea cup heavily upon the dresser.

"He's a wee chap," Magnus obliged quickly. "He would not worry you, Sir, if that's your meaning. He's just a wee wee chap, with his wee little legs and his wee little hands."

"Very well then," said Henry. "Thank you, Magnus."

"You never asked me his name, Sir?"

Henry sighed. A great surge of temper pressed up into his sinuses, and he bent his head, his hands pressing down beside his long straight nose.

"Very well then. What is his name?" he asked at last.

"His name is Buckle, Sir."

"Thank you, Magnus. I will be down directly."

Now Percy Buckle and Henry Phipps had been neighbours a good year, and on one or two occasions they had acknowledged each other whilst dismounting from their carriages, but that was all of the contact they had so far had. When Henry heard his neighbour's name today, it meant nothing in particular to him, and when he had brushed his hair one more time and buttoned his fourth button, he descended the narrow little staircase to the Lord Strutwell, hoping that the volumes of engravings had been locked away in their glass case. Indeed, when he entered the room, his eye went first to that case. It was safely locked.

Then, turning his attention to the visitor, he beheld this most peculiar little gent with his short legs and his expensive spats and his tailored coat and his thinning hair. Henry Phipps did not like ugliness. Did not like it in any form, in any thing. Now, as he looked at Percy Buckle, some small signs in his handsome face betrayed his feelings.

"I'm much obliged," said Percy Buckle, extending his hand.

Henry Phipps heard his accent and thought: *debt collector.*

"I don't think you recognize me," said Percy Buckle.

"No," said Henry Phipps, releasing the clammy hand. "Have we met?"

"We have a brick wall in common," joked Percy Buckle, then added, "and also an interest in a fellow named Jack Maggs."

Henry Phipps felt his breath stop.

"You are his friend?" he asked at last. He sat himself carefully in the leather armchair. "He sends you here?" His heart was beating very hard and all the old uncertainties of his troubled life came bubbling to the fore. His pulse was racing as it had raced the day he had been delivered at the door of Mrs Gummerson's orphanage.

"Oh no," said Percy Buckle, also sitting—or rather perching, for his legs were so short he thought it best to stay well forward—on the very edge of the armchair. "No, I fancy he would be very angry to see me here. As"—he paused delicately while his cheeks betrayed his anxiety with a most distinctive patch of colour—"as I believe *you* would be displeased to see Mr Maggs sitting where I sit."

Henry Phipps had so absorbed the notion that Mr Buckle was Jack Maggs's messenger, that it took him some time to understand that he was not: that, although his visitor knew Jack Maggs, he did not come to further Jack Maggs's interest in the matter. By the time he had reached this conclusion, Henry Phipps's shirt was soaked with perspiration, and he had more than once brushed at his fair hair with his hands, and more than once wiped his hands with his handkerchief. He now attempted to wrest some order from the chaos of his feelings.

"Let me ask you a question."

"No," said Percy Buckle, "let me ask you a question."

Henry Phipps blinked. "Very well," he said, surprised by the hardness in the other's tone. "If you wish."

"What have you done to protect your assets?"

"Sir!" Henry Phipps stood up. "That's damned impertinent." And he began to pace around the room. He did not know what was happening.

"Sit down," said Percy Buckle, "and quit the prancing."

Henry Phipps could not obey such a creature completely, but he did stand still.

"Your house is not your own," insisted Percy Buckle. "It is the property of Jack Maggs. I have seen the title again this morning, and as far as I can tell it is still in his name."

Henry Phipps had never inquired about this title, but once he heard this information, his worst fears were realized. Now this too would be taken from him.

"And if Mr Maggs is to get himself arrested, do you know what will happen to that title?"

"No," admitted Henry Phipps, and sat down in the chair.

"Why, it would be subsumed *nullus contredris*," said Mr Buckle, mumbling to obscure the fraudulence of his Latin. "It would be taken from him, as a felon, and auctioned by His Majesty—or Her Majesty as soon it will be. Were you not aware of this?"

"You are sure?"

"You were not aware," said Mr Buckle. "But now that you are, I assume you would do anything in your power to prevent him being arrested."

"Has he been arrested?"

"No, nor do you wish it. Nor do I, for reasons you need not know of. But, on the other hand, Sir, I see that you do not wish to play the part that he has written for you. You do not wish to sit around his fire eating cakes and drinking brown ale."

An involuntary shudder passed over Henry Phipps.

"You know he is attached to you?"

Henry Phipps slumped in his chair. He knew, in this instant, that his leisured life would soon be over. He had known this time would come ever since the day sixteen years ago when Victor Littlehales, his beloved tutor, had rescued him from the orphanage. Now this privileged tenure was ended and he must leave his house, his silver, his rugs, his paintings. He must be a soldier.

"I would imagine," continued the hateful little creature, "that there is a Last Will and Testament . . ."

"I understand I am his heir, yes."

"Well," said Mr Buckle, "then the news is not all bad." He took Henry Phipps's cup of tea, though it must have been luke-warm by now, sugared it enthusiastically and drank it with gusto. "Not all bad by any means."

Henry Phipps looked into the fellow's excited eyes and was made to feel most uncomfortable.

"May I ask, Mr Buckle, what is your interest in Mr Maggs?"

"It is a matter of the heart, Sir."

"Jack Maggs is your *rival*?" asked the other incredulously.

"He is."

"You would not mourn him, Mr Buckle?"

"He has betrayed my trust, which was very foolish of him." The little man looked him straight in the eye, and Henry Phipps was surprised to find himself pinned by the gaze. "There are people like Jack Maggs who see me, Sir, and they pity me, or make mock of me—well, I don't mind that, you know, I can see that point of view—but it is just a skip from pity to abuse, so I have found. And I will not be abused, Sir, not by anyone. And if I am to be humiliated in my own home, well then, that person will be punished."

"My, my!" Henry Phipps raised his eyebrows.

"You be careful, Sir. Do you hear me?"

This was a very different creature from the one whom the young man had first cast eyes upon. "Yes," he said. "I hear you."

"Jack Maggs has gone up to Gloucester, without informing me, but I found out. Yes, he has gone to Gloucester, trying to find you. I have not the foggiest where he sleeps in Gloucester. But I know, Sir, I have learned, the secret place he lays his head in London. And that's the point for you."

"And what would you have me do with that information?"

"Why," cried Mr Buckle, rising from his chair in a very energetic style, "I leave that to you, Sir. It is none of my business, but I do believe it is yours, for the house he sleeps in might easily be your own."

And with that he took his tall beaverskin hat, and carefully brushed it with the back of his hand.

Henry Phipps shook his hand once more, and when Mr Buckle had departed the club, he sat down in the chair alone, feeling rather cold and shivery.

73

Having heard Sophina's name on Tobias Oates's lips, having finally begun to understand the extent to which his secrets had been burgled, Jack Maggs became, by degrees, severely agitated.

He could not sleep, and as his mind tried to understand what had been done to him, a familiar dread slowly took possession of his being. As the punt lifted slowly off the sand, as the intensity of this feeling grew, he took his son's framed portrait from his coat and pressed it to his stomach with both his hands. And there he stayed, hunched over on the mid-thwart, hugging the image as he had on many nights before. Now he could feel the Phantom pulling with his strings inside his face, long lines of cat-gut knotted to his flesh. He felt the demon stirring in his belly and everywhere about him. He imagined that horrid half-smile upon his patrician face.

He did not know what was done to him, or how it was achieved. He rocked back and forth, stubbornly alone, waiting for the light.

When, at last, the yellowish light of dawn penetrated the mist, he found they were bumping around the shore of a "pill," or cove. His companion was still asleep, sitting sideways on the aft-thwart, his forehead resting on his drawn-up knees. Maggs leaned towards him. At first it seemed that he intended to shake him awake, but instead he executed the plan he had carried with him through the dark. Half-rising in his seat, he twisted his body and—with a thin, hard smile upon his face—inserted his three-fingered hand into the writer's jacket pocket; then, very slowly, he withdrew the note book. Once it was well clear of its owner, he sat down again and set the sodden treasure ever so gently upon his knee. There he sought that which was his.

The pages were very wet, and the ink in some places washed away, but he began his search from the beginning of the note book and very soon, on page three, he was rewarded: *M— would not go mad.*

His brows came down upon his eyes.

M— would not go mad, but only because he carried with him the strong conviction that he would, no matter what Judge Denman read to him, walk once more in England's green and pleasant land.

The hairs on his neck stood on end.

He had had that feeling in his gut before, that cold terror associated with the triangle. He knew his life and death were not his own. His forehead creased in a grid of criss-crossed frown marks. He turned the page.

Jack Maggs is a criminal who presumes to come home from Banishment, who, having accrued great wealth, buys the great mansion in which he will finally be burned alive.

He turned the page and found: CHAPTER ONE. Before the title, and afterwards: the sign of the Cross. All the following pages were vigorously crossed out.

74

CHAPTER ONE

It was a dismal January day in the year of 1818, and the yellow fog which had lain low all morning lifted a moment in the afternoon and then, as if the desolate pile of rock and stone thereby revealed was far too melancholy a sight to be endured, it descended again like a shroud around the walls of Newgate Prison.

These walls, being made from Welsh blue stone, had not been easily broken by the quarryman, and yet the fog, by virtue of its persistence, had been able slowly to penetrate the stone's dark inhuman heart and touch the skin of a young woman prisoner who had fallen asleep with her face against her cell wall.

There were a great number of women inside Newgate that year. They had been brought from all over the British Isles: petty thieves, murderers, all manner of wickedness crammed into that grim pile on Newgate Street. Here, in a small cell on the second floor, eight women waited for the Majesty of the Law to turn its weary eye on every one of them by turn.

There was a good thick palliasse of straw in the corner of the cell. This, however, had already been claimed for the sole use of a ham-legged female servant "without situation" who was said to have robbed and murdered travellers on the Turnpike at Bayswater. The rest of the women—one of them a mother suckling a new babe—made use of what straw had spilled from the palliasse in the battle for its possession. They did not speak to each other, though when the name "Sophina Smith" was called through the spy-hole they looked at each other to see who "Sophina Smith" might be.

She who had rested her cheek against the wall now stood, revealing the bloody injury which had made her seek that cold comfort: four deep scratch marks on her face.

When the door opened she stepped out. Chains were put around her wrists and ankles and she was led off.

This Sophina Smith was a very comely young woman. She had exceptionally fair skin, and coal-black hair which hung in pretty ringlets around her face. She was tall and stood erect. Although slender, she had a most womanly figure. It was this very comeliness which had so affronted the ham-legged servant who had scratched her face.

Being brought out of the side door of the prison, the young woman blinked, then lowered her head, walked ten paces, then was admitted through a second door. Thus she passed from Internment to Judgment, for she was now inside the Old Bailey.

She was brought first into a dark and dingy room, illuminated by a single soot-stained lamp. Here, in company with other women similarly shackled, she waited for an hour. Then she was called into court to stand before the Judge.

The court had heard many charges that morning: a mother had tried to drown her babe, a woman had pushed a red-hot poker into her husband's eye, but the charge against this prisoner brought a new gravity to the room.

Sophina Smith, it was now said, had used hammer and chisel to break into a house in Frith Street, Soho, the property of Gilbert Gunn, a solicitor, and therein she had stolen silver plate valued at one hundred and fifty pounds.

It was a figure high enough to have her hanged three times over.

"So," said the Judge, "what plead you to this charge?" He was a benign-looking man in spite of his lambskin, and although his mouth

turned down at the edges, an honest citizen might easily imagine him as an umpire at a county cricket match, holding the bowler's jersey draped around his shoulders. When his question went unanswered, he bore it with good grace, repeating himself in a tone that made the recording clerk smile slightly.

Yet the young woman could not be teased into speech. She stared up at the high, panelled bench, her pretty face contorted by a rather mulish scowl.

The Judge inquired about her injury. She turned her head abruptly so it was hidden from him.

After one or two more questions, the Judge finally lost patience. He slapped his hand loudly down upon the Bench. The prisoner flinched.

Everyone who sat in the court could see her fright. Now, finally, her eyes were bright with tears. She addressed the Judge in a whisper.

"Again. I cannot hear you."

The young woman spoke in a louder voice. She said that there could be no value in her testimony because she was a thief.

"Do you mean that you are a thief by nature or a thief as evidenced by these charges? If you are a thief by nature, that is not the concern of this court today. But if you are guilty of these charges then you must plead 'guilty.' If not, you must plead 'not guilty.' How do you plead?"

There were forty or fifty people in that court and every one of them understood that this comely young woman might be hanged for this offence. Thus her continued silence had a great effect on all of them; none more than upon a certain young man who had witnessed the proceedings with impatience from the very start. He was a tall youth, dressed in a "flash" style, with a green kerchief around his neck and a bright red waistcoat covering his chest. This wardrobe, in accompaniment with his rather bellicose expression, might cause one to suppose that he had been up to no good, and had profited from his wrong-doing. His hair was cut short and he was closely shaven, and there was nothing therefore to mask his raw emotion, to distract one from the restless anger of his eyes. Yet had his head been covered by a leather hood, he would have given himself away, for he continually twisted in his seat, leaning forward and then back, and when the young woman finally whispered that she was guilty, he leaped up to his feet and cried out that she was innocent.

Immediately the constabulary were after him, trampling over a little boy in their attempts to reach the heckler. He was big-boned, but he was nimble, and he leaped onto the bench behind. With one boot on the back of the bench and another between a parson's legs, he called to the Judge that it was he, Jack Maggs, who had done the crime.

By this time he was surrounded, and he stepped down to the floor, still very hot and passionate, trembling like a horse.

"Bring that ruffian to the Bench," said the Judge. Three constables, all of them shorter than their prisoner, brought the young man to stand before the Judge, who immediately declared him in contempt of court, and thereupon, without recourse to any other authority, began the young man's interrogation himself.

"Do you know this woman?" asked the Judge, and although the young man did not answer, the answer was obvious to all: he was hissing at the young woman and she was shaking her head back at him.

"She is my brother's wife."

"Ah," said the Judge, "you can speak. The malady does not run in the family?"

"Yes, I can speak," said the young man. "And I was also in that house in Soho and I can tell Your Honour that this young woman did not do nothing. It was her husband, Tom England, who broke the lock."

"And you, I suppose, are an innocent by-stander?"

"How can I be? It was I who packed the silver."

"Very well," said the Judge. "Then I will swear you as a witness."

At this, the woman in the dock began to rock back and forth. There issued from her a high and desolate keening that continued even as she was taken from her place and sat in the front row with a policeman each side of her. Then the young man, still trembling but straight-backed, did formally reveal his name and place of lodging, swearing upon the Bible that he would tell the truth. Then he grasped the top rail of the dock and looked down at the court. He looked pale, stunned by what he had done; his belligerence had faded.

"You entered these premises in Frith Street, Mr Maggs?"

"I did."

"You saw the silver taken from the chest?"

"I did."

"Who took that silver?"

"I did."

"Did anyone assist you?"

"Only so far as the door was broken. This was done, as I said, by Tom England, a carpenter of Pottery Lane in Notting Hill."

The clerk stood to whisper in the Judge's ear.

"Please explain to the court," said the Judge, very irritably, "why someone would break a door down and then call the police himself."

"Damn him," cried the witness, although whom he meant to damn was not made clear.

"Silence!" roared the Judge.

"Tom's interest is elsewhere."

"I fail to understand you. Who is Tom? How does this answer the question I have just asked you?"

"Tom England. His eye is taken."

"Jack Maggs, you will make yourself clear to the court."

"He has another Jill who takes his fancy."

"He has another woman, you mean?"

"He is tired of Sophina. He wishes to be quit of her, but she cannot afford to leave him and so he bent the twig."

"Bent the twig?"

"Set the trap, Your Honour. He put her in the house, then called the police, Sir. He wants her off his hands."

"Then you went ahead and stole the silver anyway."

"Yes, Sir."

"Do you know you can be hanged, Jack Maggs?"

"I do not care."

"You do not care?"

"It is over in a minute."

"You have sworn on the Bible, Jack Maggs. Do you not care what might happen to you when you stand before your God? Eternity is not over in a minute."

The young man seemed as hard as the streets he lived by, but not so hard that this did not give him pause. "Sir, I swear by God, I'm telling the truth."

"Do you imagine," said the Judge, "this court is like some street fair that you can work your wickedness and profligacy upon? Do you

imagine you can shout and lie before me and line your own pockets
when it is obvious to anyone who hears your testimony that you and
this young woman were partners in crime on that day? You, Sophina
Smith, were unlucky enough to be caught. You, Sir, were impudent
enough to imagine you could alter the course of justice. You shall
be taken from this place henceforth and charged with the crimes of
perjury and burglary."

"I'm telling the truth."

"Then you have confessed before these witnesses that you stole silver from Mr Gunn of Frith Street. But that will be dealt with at another time. Now," he said, "the prisoner will stand."

And then, on that foggy Wednesday afternoon whilst children
played with hoops, and their nursery maids flirted with soldiers in St
James's Park, the young woman named Sophina Smith was sentenced
to death by hanging and he who had tried to save her wept openly in
the dock.

75

Jack Maggs sat on the mid-thwart of the lock-keeper's punt with the
note book on his lap, and from his bent bulk there now emerged a
very peculiar series of sounds such as you might have imagined to be
made by an injured animal: a hedgehog or a mole.

Jack Maggs was weeping. He bent his body into a hard, tight ball. He
grasped his stomach and rocked to and fro. Then came the sound of a
squeaky wheel, very close by. The convict stopped weeping immediately. He sat bolt upright, staring with his red eyes into the wet mist.
The shadows of some elms were visible, nothing else. Chains clinked
together. Jack Maggs reached for the dagger in his boot. He withdrew
it with his right hand, while his high hawk's nose followed the progress
of the ghostly vehicle.

The cart (if that is what it was) passed by slowly, but even when it
could be heard no more, Maggs showed no intention of sheathing his
weapon. Rather he turned its cruel hooked tip toward the author of the
note book.

Tobias Oates continued to sleep with his forehead resting on his knees. Jack Maggs waved the knife across him. Then he paused, placing the weapon between his teeth, and kneeled upon the thwart. Without troubling to remove his great-coat, he lowered himself into the Severn.

The river at this point was some three feet deep, and it was therefore a simple enough matter to spin the punt around so that the sleeping author was presented to him back first. Maggs took the dagger in his right hand and he placed his left arm tight around the other's chest.

"You are a thief," said he quietly. "A damned little thief."

Tobias Oates woke up, struggling and splashing his heels amongst the bilge-water, but when he felt the blade up against his throat, he stopped. He lay as still as a fox caught in a snare, his speckled eyes staring straight ahead.

"Don't kill me, Jack."

"Shut your hole."

"You're cutting me!"

Maggs's coat floated out around him, like the skirt of some great antipodean squid. "You'll know when I'm bloody well cutting you." He turned the boat in the water so the frightened passenger was facing him.

"Why should I not kill you now?"

Tobias Oates glanced quickly towards the bank. If he'd had thoughts of running, he abandoned them for now. He remained huddled up on the aft-thwart, waiting for what would happen next.

"You stole my Sophina, you bastard."

Tobias felt in his jacket, but his note book was gone. "No, no. She cannot be stolen . . ."

"It were a very low scheming thieving thing you did, Toby."

"You read my note book, Jack? You read my chapter, is that it?"

"Oh, you wrote a chapter did you? With my name in it?"

"It is a memorial I am making. Your Sophina will live for ever."

"Don't say her name."

"I write that name, Jack, like a stone mason makes the name upon a headstone, so her memory may live for ever. In all the Empire, Jack, you could not have employed a better carver."

Jack Maggs did not answer, but some lessening of agitation on his part encouraged the writer to continue. "Your painful life . . ."

"You are planning to kill me, I know that. Is that what you mean by painful? To burn me alive?"

"Not you, Jack, a character who bears your name. I will change the name sooner or later."

"You are just a character to me too, Toby."

"Very funny, Jack."

"Funny? I have no reason not to kill you also, Toby."

"Except that I am flesh and blood."

"Did you ever see a man lashed, Toby? Did you ever see the parts of his back splashed across the soldier's uniform?"

"You would not be wise to kill me, Jack. Not now."

"But I am not a wise man, Toby. I am a vermin who made ten thousand pounds from mucky clay. I have a grand house in Sydney town. There is a street named for me, or was when I sailed. I keep a coach, and two footmen. I am Mr Jack Maggs Esquire, and I left all that so I might end up here today. You have cheated me, Toby, as bad as I was ever cheated."

And here he began, very slowly, to turn the boat around, with the intention, it seemed, of bringing the young man's neck once more within his reach. Tobias waited, staring all the while into Jack Maggs's unstable eyes.

"Spare me," he cried at last.

"Why would I spare you?" asked the other.

"Forgive me, Jack, but I know where your son is. I knew when I left London."

There was a long silence. Then Maggs spoke. "Oh, you are a very brave little chap, Toby."

"I am a wretched creature, Jack."

"Why in God's name did you bring me here?"

"The money."

"Are you not a clever man? Is not that the dart with you? Did it not enter that big brain box of yours that I would have paid you twice the price for you to take me to my son in London? Where is he?"

"I will arrange to take you to him."

"He has been in London all this while?"

"It does seem so, yes. I had a communication from your fellow footman. He has been so tormented by this secret, he knew not what to do."

"Why tormented? Why did he not tell me?"

"It was on the eve of our departure. It was only because of my desperation I hid it from you."

"What in God's name do you have to be desperate of? What would make you act so cruel as this?"

"I told you of my situation."

"Your wife's sister? Are you serious? Here you are writing the story of the death of Maggs, and you do not know how to take care of her condition? Take me to my boy, and I will give the pills to you."

"And my fifty pounds."

"To hell with your fifty pounds. I will give you what you need, which is more than you deserve. We'll stop off and get the medicine on our way into London. But let me tell you, if you do not find my boy, that is the end of you. Can you make a bargain like that? You are wagering me your very life."

"I can."

"Very well. Hand me your note book."

"You have it, I believe."

"It is on the thwart, beside you."

Toby picked up the book.

"Give it to me."

It was given.

"I forbid you now to write Sophina's name, now or ever. Do you understand?"

"Yes."

"Do you have your magnets with you?"

"No."

"You will not use your magnets. You will not write my name in your book. You will not write the Phantom's name."

"Yes."

Jack then hurled the book high out above the Severn. As it flew up into the mist, its pages opened like a pair of wings. At this moment a horn was blown very loud and there was a great thundering of hooves and wheels.

Tobias looked towards Jack Maggs, his face white with fright.

"Coach," said Maggs.

"Coach?"

"Stay!"

But Tobias had already jumped. He plunged down to his waist in water. Then, before Maggs had even let go of the punt, he was scrambling helter-skelter up onto the bank towards the road, wet sand clinging to his trouser legs.

76

If Tobias had not jumped into a rocky hole, his leg would not have twisted, and if his leg had not been twisted he might conceivably have made it to Newnham village before the convict caught him.

But his leg *was* injured, and thus he *was* easily felled, pinned down with his face pressed amongst the bluebells. And there he lay: winded, bruised, crushed beneath the convict's weight, as a wagon-load of hay rolled down the road, passing not six feet from where they lay.

Two young men in bright red smocks walked beside the load. One carried a long stave or quarter-staff across his shoulders. The other was unarmed, but he walked with such an easy yeoman gait that Toby never doubted he would fight in the defence of an honest stranger. Still, Jack Maggs's dagger kept him quiet and, like the hero of *Michael Adams*, he watched his liberators pass him by while all the time berating himself for his own cowardice: *He was crippled by that vision of the cut throat, the horrid mortal gurgling of the windpipe, the knowledge that his very Life could be drained as easily as from the bung hole of a keg.*

When the wagon had passed, Maggs squatted beside him, the black blade ready in his hand.

"Turn turtle," said the convict grimly.

Toby rolled onto his back and watched from the corner of his apprehensive eye as his captor cut a length of cord from his kit-bag.

"What are you doing, Jack?"

"Hands on your head."

"All I wished was to hail the coach."

Maggs brought the blade up to his bare neck, and Toby pressed his head hard back into the bluebells.

"Put your blasted hands on your head."

Toby did as he was bid.

But when he felt the other's fingers at his trouser belt, he brought his hands down to protect his privates.

"Please, Jack . . . No."

For answer he received a sharp sting on his thumb. He cried out with pain. Tears flooded his eyes. He felt the Australian undo his waist button.

Then the horrid hands were on the buttons of his flies. Numb with horror, he stared through his tears at the sky, the over-hanging trees. He felt the murder weapon slicing at his trousers.

"Now, put your hands into your pockets."

Toby imagined the cruellest consequences, but when he spoke his voice was level.

"You want your son," he said. "You would be wise to recognize that I am your only chance."

"Put your hands in your pockets, Toby."

This Tobias did, very slowly. He found the bottoms of his pockets cut away.

"Don't you move," said Maggs, dragging the right hand through the pocket and trussing it rapidly with cord. A moment later he had trussed the left.

"Don't pull on them," Maggs said.

Tobias did pull on them, and found his wrists to be manacled.

"Don't pull on them, if you don't want to get green rot."

And then, with the blade once again gripped between his teeth, he did up the buttons of the writer's trousers and helped him to his feet.

Toby looked at the brigand's face and saw that he was grinning around his blade. This obstacle to his mirth he very soon removed and laughed at Toby freely.

"Look at you. You thought I was going to cut off your gooseberries."

Tobias stood with his trussed hands deep in his pockets and was aware of being a very sad and sorry figure.

"See now," said Maggs, "you count your change, Toby. Make sure you've got your penny and two farthings." With that he hugged him, wrapping his arm tight around his shoulders and pulling Toby's face into his breast, thus forcing him to inhale what would always thereafter be *the prisoner's smell*—the odour of cold sour sweat.

"Come, Your Lordship," said Jack Maggs, "you can count your treasure all the way to London."

The two men then walked through the wildflowers to the road. The big man was still laughing, the smaller man was rather red-faced and grim-looking. He walked with his hands deep into his pockets, hobbling back towards everything he had hoped to escape from.

77

As her manacled husband was being helped aboard a coach in Gloucestershire, Mary Oates came down into the drawing room and was unpleasantly surprised to discover Lizzie, who usually liked to lie in bed till breakfast time, sitting at the window like a sea captain's wife, her placid hands atop her stomach.

"That little boy from Jones's shop will get himself run over," said Lizzie.

Mary did not comment. She settled herself in the low chair in which she liked to feed her baby, and in a moment she and little John had reached their usual accommodation.

"He is running his hoop across the street under the very hooves of the horses."

"Lizzie, are you waiting for Toby to return?"

The light was behind her sister, rendering her face in shadow, but there was no mistaking the false note in her voice. "Oh, is it today he comes, Mary?"

Mary did not deign to answer.

"It is today, Mary?"

This disingenuousness was so repugnant to her that Mary could pretend no longer. "You know as much as I do, Lizzie."

"Oh, I think you know much more, Mary. Look at how you have dressed."

Mary had already noted how her sister was dressed that morning— in her bright blue poplin, with her best lace shawl around her shoulders.

"I think that you have had word from him," Lizzie continued heedlessly. "Because you are wearing your velvet."

The notion that she should have to wear her best dress to win her husband's good opinion was so insulting to Mary that it was a moment before she could answer calmly.

"Perhaps *you* have heard from my husband, Lizzie."

"Oh Mary, you say the queerest things."

"Not near as queer as you," said Mary darkly.

She laid a white napkin on her lap and then laid the infant on it and gently paddled his back before setting him on the other breast.

"Mary, are you angry with me?"

"No, dear."

"What queer things were you referring to? Have I been babbling again? I know I do babble. I think perhaps I really should give up my novels. They give me very peculiar dreams."

"I was referring to no particular thing," said Mary, but those extraordinary conversations about adoption still burned bright in her memory. Had Lizzie not come back to this theme so repeatedly, Mary might never have noticed the way her sister sat with her hands resting complacently on her belly, or the way her bosom lately pressed against the bodice of her gown. These two symptoms had gnawed at her daily while every aspect of her sister's behaviour gave further indication of the true nature of her disease.

It was as if someone had died, but there was no death, just a horrible agitation she could reveal to no one. If she felt rage, it showed only on the itchy rash across her back. If she had tears, they were contained within the water blisters which had risen in the middle of these red weals.

She was a blunt woman, in many ways, but what she now knew, she would not name. What she was about to do, she would not look at.

She had carried the little newspaper advertisement for nearly a week, but even as she cut it out with her sewing scissors she did not admit to herself where it might lead her. This morning she had put on her best dress so that whoever she must now encounter would know she was, in spite of the circumstances, a respectable woman. She finished feeding little John, and buttoned her bodice. She carried her child towards the door.

"Will you come back and sit with me, Mary?"

"No, dear. I have an errand to run."

"If you don't mind, I'll stay and read."

"Yes, dear."

She took little John to Mrs Jones and, with no proper explanation of the formality of her attire or the nature of her errand, she walked out of the house.

She might have taken a hackney cab—her husband would never have hesitated to do so—and yet Mary Oates, ever mindful of the economic stress under which Tobias suffered, walked.

Mary Oates was from Amersham, in Buckinghamshire, and had lived in London only since her marriage a year before. On her husband's arm she had travelled to places as various as Limehouse and the Guildhall, but unless thus escorted, had been content to stay pretty much within the confines of her rooms. Thus to find her way to Cecil Street was no small expedition for her, and she had not got so far as Holborn without inquiring the direction of three different shop-keepers.

The day was clear and fine, although it was perhaps too hot for such a heavy velvet dress, or too warm to wear such a dress and walk so fast. In any case, the plump young woman finally arrived in the Haymarket very red in the face and out of breath, and allowed herself to be charged a penny for a glass of water by the owner of the coffee stand.

From the coffee stand to Cecil Street is no more than two hundred yards, yet Mary stopped twice more for directions before she came to that corner where the convict had stood on his first night back in London. From this point onwards their paths were so close that she must, from time to time, have brought her stout little heel down on the same spot of pavement where Jack Maggs's hessian boot had trod. As for attaining her destination, she was more successful than her precursor, for she not only got through the gate of 4 Cecil Street but to the brass knocker on its door.

Her knock was answered almost immediately, and Mary was confused to discover that the person who stood before her appeared to be both respectable and friendly.

"These are Mrs Britten's rooms?" Mary inquired.

"Indeed they are, Mum," said the maid politely. "You come on in. You come on in and rest your feet, Mum."

The young woman ushered her into a small room, decorated rather excessively with lace and flounces, and an almost violent looking wallpaper. There was a single window, large and arched, which was covered with two layers of white muslin. There was very little light from that source, but there were various lamps burning, and several ornate mirrors, and it was, as a result, a bright and determinedly happy little room. Three women were already seated here, though none looked up when

Mary Oates entered. This collective expression of shame went hard against the intention of the decorations, emphasizing the dishonour the latter were presumably intended to disguise.

Mary Oates sat in the chair she was offered and accepted a cup of tea. It was very good tea and Mary sipped it carefully. When she looked up her glance was not towards the other women but in the direction of the handsome marble fireplace and, above it, a rather troubling engraving which depicted Napoleon's army in grotesque and bloody disarray.

No more than ten minutes later, she was escorted along a hallway into a small plain room containing little more than a high leather couch and a straight-backed wooden chair. Here she was met by a tall, rather severe old woman in a starched white dress. The woman had a strong nose and chin, and piercing, angry eyes. She wore an extravagant tall white head-dress that reminded Mary of a painting she had once seen of a Dutch nun.

"And how may I assist you, dearie?" she inquired, raising her hands in a peculiar little greeting which might, in a church, have been taken for a blessing.

Mary felt very hot and itchy across her blistered back. She hesitated.

"What do you want of Mrs Britten, dearie?"

For an answer, Mary Oates held out the frayed little advertisement. Mrs Britten took it from her, and Mary, seeing how the fierce old lady held it between thumb and forefinger, was reminded of the way in which her grandfather had squashed caterpillars in his garden.

"These pills," said Mrs Britten, indicating the illustration in her puff, "are from a recipe given me by a Swedish doctor. Very good pills they are." She had a decidedly rougher voice than her initial appearance suggested, and although her features were handsome there was something of the fish wife about her hands, which were large and swollen at the knuckles.

"Very good pills," she continued seriously. "Except for just one wee shortcoming."

And here she winked, much to Mary Oates's distress.

"And the shortcoming is as follows: should you be so unfortunate as to take them when you was with child, then, oh dear . . ." She dropped the crumpled advertisement into the waste-paper basket. "Know what I mean?"

"I think so, yes."

"We are married women. We can be plain between us: you would lose the baby. You understand the shortcoming now?"

"I do."

A long silence followed while the old woman stared at her so hard, Mary could only look away.

"How far along are you?"

"I beg your pardon," protested Mary.

Before Mary could say anything further, the old woman had reached out and felt her stomach. It was a fast invasion, over before it had begun. Mary said nothing. What could a lady possibly say? She stood there like a goose, itching unbearably, blushing to the very roots of her hair.

"You come here for another lady?" Mrs Britten produced a yellow printed sheet. "Never mind. I have writ it all down, but the long and short of it is she must never, never, take these pills of mine if she is gestational."

From her pocket she produced a small porcelain jar which she placed in Mary's gloved hand. "Of course, she'd need to be taking one every morning and night for that to happen. Unless she did that, there'd be no danger."

"Every morning and every night?"

"Every morning and every night."

Mary felt another urge to scratch her back.

"As to payment . . ."

"Five guineas."

Mary looked up and found the old eyes staring at her implacably.

"The advertisement said three."

Mrs Britten shrugged. "Five is the price. Take it or leave it. Makes no diff to me."

"I've got no more than four," Mary fretted. "The advertisement said three guineas."

"Four will do." Mary Britten held out a weathered hand, thus revealing the name SILAS tattooed into the underside of her broad wrist.

Two minutes later Mary Oates was standing outside again. She set off back down Cecil Street holding the jar of pills tightly in her gloved hand. She arrived home without recalling the direction she had come.

78

As dark cumulus clouds spilled through the dirty air, stacking themselves high above St Paul's, Tobias Oates crossed the River Thames. It was seven o'clock on a May night, and the two men, having arrived in Borough at The Swan with Two Necks, were now passing over London Bridge in a hack. After thirty hours of travel, Toby's hands were still deep in his pockets, his wrists still bound together.

As their vehicle came into the West End, Jack Maggs leaned out the window whilst drumming his right foot upon the floor.

Tobias, meanwhile, was deeply troubled. He feared the poison they were about to buy. He feared Lizzie, and could not imagine how he would persuade her to take such a potion. There were many other strands of apprehension in the matted tangle of his mood, and they were knotted harder by the persistent pain in his wrists and the unholy pressure on his bladder, which pride had forbidden him mentioning to his companion.

The London they left behind had been a sunny place where daffodils grew in the window boxes. The London they returned to seemed hellish—broken cotton bales, cracking whips, an omnibus alight on St Martin's Lane—all the streets awash with a weary sulphurous kind of evening light that seeped into his very thoughts, and finally surrounded the image of the family he had come so close to abandoning.

His captor then brought his big unshaven face close, and Tobias could smell the cheap brandy on his breath.

"Soon be there, eh, mate?"

"Indeed." Tobias quickly turned his head away.

"All our trials will soon be ended."

"Indeed, yes."

"Miss Lizzie's troubles mended."

Toby shuddered at the damnable state to which he had descended: his very respectability depended upon enduring this insolent familiarity.

"We will visit Henry Phipps in the morning," he told the convict firmly. And once more looked away, praying to God that the footman had spoken true, for if Constable did not really have Henry Phipps's address, then Tobias was a dead man.

"It is a dream come true, mate. An old varmint's dream come true."

In spite of his previous vow to murder Toby, Jack Maggs had been unusually friendly to him throughout the journey, and now, as the convict leaned towards him, Tobias feared another embrace. But Maggs wished only to gaze up at the great sky, which was now, in the north, so very black and swollen.

"Isn't that a queer thing to go out of a cove's head?" said the convict. "When I was imagining my lovely English summers—and I did meditate on this subject an awful lot, my word—I would be suffering the mosquitoes and the skin-rot, to mention two of the least of my discomforts, but I would oft-times make a picture of me and Henry puffing our pipes comfortably in the long evenings. Do you ever make a picture like that, Toby?"

"On occasion."

"Sophina and me, it was the storms we loved to watch. Do you think the Day of Judgment might look like this, Toby?"

Tobias pushed himself harder against the wall of the coach.

"My Sophina always thought so. Look, she would say, how all our troubles are little things beneath that mighty storm."

Toby smiled weakly, sickened by this puerile philosophizing.

"See yonder clouds above Holborn," continued his companion. "Look at all the old men's faces in the sky. They'll rattle the windows, Toby. There'll be some fireworks with this one. But we'll survive it, you and me. Perhaps you may visit me and Henry when you've forgotten the pain in your wrists. Are they paining badly?"

"I can bear it."

"See, I'm as good as my word, for here we are almost in Cecil Street where Mrs Britten sells her famous pills. I'm surprised you never read her puffs. Well, I will be a moment collecting these items and I am sure you won't scarper, for if you should, I would have a very sad story to deliver to your wife."

The carriage stopped, and Jack jumped down. He was soon hammering on a black door with his silver-topped stick.

There was some brief dispute with a person inside, then Jack was admitted. Not three minutes passed before he was clambering back aboard to sit opposite Tobias once more, and the cabby was plying the whip *con gusto*. As they pushed violently into Cross Street, the convict's face was clearly very strange: the cheeks hard and hatchet-like, the eyes awash with such violent emotion that Toby began to fear that the potion had been refused him.

"All in order, Jack?"

Maggs delved deep into the pocket of his Great Joseph and produced a small white jar.

Tobias looked at his companion's trembling hands with some apprehension, but whatever drama had transpired behind that door he was never to know. Jack Maggs returned the jar into his pocket.

"I cannot produce your son tonight, you know that."

"But you *will* produce him, Toby."

"Yes."

"What time in the morning would that be, Toby?"

"Ten o'clock," said Toby decisively.

"Could you deliver my papers to Henry beforehand? It would be useful for him to read a little before we sit to have our yarn."

"I could not deliver anything before ten."

Said Maggs: "You know too much to lie to me again."

"I know the forfeit."

They travelled in silence until they had entered Lamb's Conduit Street and Tobias realized that Jack Maggs intended to disembark with him.

"Jack, I do think this matter with the lady is my own affair. It is not something to be done in company."

"I have business in your house, Toby."

"It is private business, Jack. You must trust me. Cut my bonds, I will not run away."

"First, we are to burn the contents of the tin box. Second . . ." Jack Maggs removed the cork from the porcelain jar and held it out so its contents might finally be examined.

Before they disembarked, Tobias had time to look inside the jar and see, not the clean white pills he had hitherto imagined, but some strange unsanitary little lumps of matter the colour of Virginia tobacco.

79

Henry Phipps had always been excessively afraid of thunder; so much so, that in those long-ago days of his wardship, his tutor had built the most fanciful fortifications against it.

This tutor, V. P. Littlehales by name (the same individual named in that famous case with Dr Wollaston), had conceived a most elaborate series of towers and trenches on the quarter-acre of meadow attached to their cottage at Great Missenden. To the extent that this maze had been pedagogical in intention, it had failed: Henry learned nothing useful of the nature of the elements. To the extent that it had been magical, its power was insufficient: lightning had twice struck the old oak tree at its centre.

Victor Littlehales had been a gentle but troubled soul and, if truth be told, very superstitious about lightning. No matter what lectures he delivered on Natural Law, the great sum of his instruction was that they were base beasts, naked before a vengeful, all-seeing God. The only comfort he could offer his pupil was the mortal cradle of his freckled arms, and even that he finally withdrew: Victor Littlehales abruptly and inexplicably disappeared from Henry Phipps's life on the eve of the young man's twenty-first birthday.

On the same humid afternoon on which Jack Maggs returned to London, Mr Buckle paid a second visit to Henry Phipps. His host on this occasion looked neither like a boy abandoned nor like a man afraid of thunder. He received the ex-grocer and his whispering lawyer in the uniform of a subaltern of the 57th Foot Regiment. He stood before them stiffly, his hands behind his back, and, in looking down at them along the barrel of his straight thin nose, gave the impression of being both impatient and sarcastic.

When the thunder first sounded in the distance, Henry Phipps squinted slightly, but otherwise showed no emotion.

Mr Buckle did not hear the thunder, being too preoccupied with his own agenda to notice very much else at all. Not even the military uniform surprised him, and it certainly would never have occurred to him that this commission had been purchased in a great panic not three days previous.

Mr Buckle and Mr Makepeace seated themselves side by side on the Chesterfield. Henry Phipps remained standing with his back to the windows, flexing his knees a little strangely.

"May I ask you your business, Mr Buckle?"

"I have come," said Mr Buckle, "to inquire as to your decision about your benefactor." He was about to introduce his companion, but Mr Phipps turned his back and abruptly drew the curtains shut. This disconcerted Mr Buckle, who felt himself somehow reprimanded. "Of course it is not my affair."

"True." Henry Phipps struck a match, and spent some moments fiddling with a lamp. "It is in no manner your business, and yet I would have thought it obvious I have a new benefactor."

"I have told no one, I assure you."

"No, you mistake my meaning. His Majesty has become my benefactor, Mr Buckle. As you see, I am now a soldier."

Now Mr Buckle appraised the uniform. Though no great student of the military, he knew enough to realize that the regiment was unfashionable, the rank lowly.

"No," he said. "This won't do."

Outside, the lightning flashed. Henry Phipps sat down quickly, and rested his chin in his cupped hand. "I am not going to be a dancing boy for a criminal."

"No, Sir. Indeed not. That is not what I wished, Sir. The opposite. Did you forget our conversation?"

"You seemed to imagine that I was corrupted by my comfortable life and would do anything to sustain it. But I would not lower myself to that, Sir."

"Nor should you, Sir. That was not my idea at all. It is for this very reason I have brought with me Mr Makepeace. Perhaps you have heard his name, Sir: he is a distinguished solicitor. Mr Makepeace has, at my request, studied the appropriate precedents."

"Precedents," Mr Makepeace whispered in agreement.

"Precedents which by their very nature must affect yourself. It is not too late, Sir. You are too good a man to be a subaltern."

"It is the case of the Crown *versus* Forsythe," continued Mr Makepeace in his distinctive whisper.

"What?" said Henry Phipps.

"In the best of weather, he is hard to hear," admitted Mr Buckle. "But always worth the effort."

"In the case of Mrs Forsythe," continued Mr Makepeace implacably, "who did kill her son. The Crown *versus* Forsythe. It is a case well known in the Inns of Court. It has that immediate advantage—you may mention it to anyone and be saved the time and expense of their going to look it up."

"I cannot hear you."

"It is Mr Makepeace's affliction," interrupted Mr Buckle, "that his voice box was damaged as a child. But it is to your advantage, Sir, for he comes the cheaper on account of it."

"It is of the Crown *versus* Forsythe that I speak," said Makepeace.

"Then speak, for God's sake," snapped Henry Phipps. The rain was now coming down very hard against the window pane, and Henry Phipps leaned forward in his chair and held his elbows in his cupped hands.

"The Crown charged that Mrs Forsythe had murdered her son in order to reclaim the ancestral home from which she had been cast out on the occasion of her husband's death. She was a very proud woman, and much attached to entertaining. Her son, as the heir to the property, was expected to take up residence in the Hall, and the mother to live in a dowager cottage on the estate. Nothing wrong with that. All quite in order. Then one wet night the son, it was alleged, broke into the dowager cottage with an axe, and his mother, allegedly mistaking him for a violent burglar, shot him through the heart."

"I do not have time for this," said Henry Phipps abruptly. He peered around the curtains, then sat immediately down again.

"Ask me the verdict," Mr Makepeace demanded.

Henry Phipps pointedly ignored him, and turned up the lamp.

"What was the verdict, Mr Makepeace?" asked Percy Buckle.

"English law has always held that you cannot profit from your own crime. A chap cannot inherit the estate of a person he has unlawfully killed."

"Unlawfully. That is your point, I warrant."

"Indeed it is," said Mr Makepeace. "The law has always held that reasonable force may be used in defending one's own home. Mrs Forsythe was found not guilty."

"It is too late for this," said Henry Phipps, but his manner was very sad, and when Mr Buckle advanced upon him, he seemed to have lost all will to resist.

"In a short while," announced Mr Buckle, "a criminal will break into your house." He then produced, from the depths of his tweed jacket, a large pistol. "You will shoot him through the heart."

Henry Phipps stared with horror upon this weapon.

"For God's sake, man. Are you mad?"

Mr Buckle continued to hold him with his eyes. There was a fixed sort of grimace, almost a rictus, on his face.

"You have a very nice house," said Mr Buckle, laying the weapon on a nearby table. "It is natural that you would wish to keep your hands on it, so to speak. If Jack Maggs breaks in your door with an axe, you are allowed to shoot him."

"Why would you think he would carry an axe?"

"What I know, I know," said Percy Buckle.

"You are certain he will come?"

"I have spoken to his travelling companion's wife. They are expected in London today or tomorrow. You should wait upon his arrival."

"I do not know the man."

"When you are a soldier, Sir, you will be called upon to fight many men you do not know, and for less reason than this."

"But he has done nothing to me that I should harm him."

The oil lamp sputtered, and went out. Mr Buckle could see the huddled dark shape of Henry Phipps not three feet from him in the gloom. He was all bent over himself, like a great round boulder that must be somehow levered off the hillside and sent plummeting onto the enemy below.

80

The rain had been heavy this last half-hour, but as Mercy let herself in through the kitchen door, it began falling in sheets, flooding the street and cascading down into the area. She leaned her dripping umbrella beside the door, and a small yellow rivulet began to invade the gloomy kitchen. It crossed the floor, making directly for Miss Mott, who was standing at the deal table not more than a yard away.

"I'm very sorry, Cook."

Miss Mott continued to sprinkle flour, and roll out pastry.

"I was running a message for the master."

There was a mighty clap of thunder. At this, Miss Mott raised her tightly braided head like a turtle.

"I was on an errand, Miss. It ain't my fault."

Mercy now cut her path wide around the cook.

"And where might you be off to now?"

Mercy hesitated. Then, as lightning flashed through the window, she set off briskly up the stairs.

"You come back here."

"I'll be back in a moment."

Whereupon Mercy ran. She left tracks of mud in all six ground-floor rooms without finding the object of her search. The house was unusually cold and dark. She took one of the small wax dips Mr Constable kept in a china bowl in the hallway, but did not light it as yet. She ascended the stairs to the second floor which was queerly deserted. The door to the snuggery was shut.

Please God, let Jack Maggs be returned.

She opened the door. Though it was very dark inside, she had the feeling of someone present. There was a small sound, clear above the sound of the storm: *tap, tap, tap*. She lit the dip and held it up.

A single sad sheet of paper lay upon the bureau. It was from here that the *tap* was emanating, like a whispering ghost. She touched the paper, then felt a sharp shock as a drip of water hit the back of her hand.

The roof was leaking. This is what she tried to explain to Miss Mott when the angry cook came to fetch her back to work. The box gutter was blocked again. It was what she told the master when he arrived, soaking wet, a moment behind Miss Mott. Indeed, she stood on his chair and held her finger up to the drooping fabric canopy. She showed them: the drip became a trickle running down her arm.

Then Mr Buckle sent Miss Mott back to her kitchen. He held out his wet hand so he might help Mercy down off the chair.

"He's back, ain't he?" he asked Mercy.

"Is he?"

She watched him as he brushed away the mud her shoes had left upon his chair.

"What are you doing skulking round here?"

"The roof's leaking, ain't it."

Mr Buckle took an altar candle from the bureau drawer; it burned with a smoky yellow flame which gave his face, wet from the rain, a strange and ghoulish appearance.

"You tell me where Jack Maggs is hiding or by God I'll make you sorry, Missy."

Although rain was now pouring through the ceiling, Mr Buckle did not seem to notice.

"I don't wish him harm," he said.

Mercy laughed incredulously.

For answer, he hit her. She did not see his hand but felt the jolt, saw the explosion of sparks inside the darkness of her skull.

She fell back, steadying herself against the paisley drapery. He knelt down with her, bringing the candle so he might peer into her eyes. She saw molten wax spilling onto her apron; she felt the snuggery curtains as wet as sheets upon the clothesline. Resting her cheek against them, she began to cry.

He was sitting upon the little ottoman from which she herself had watched Jack Maggs write his history. Mr Buckle's moustache was sodden, and his brown eyes glistened with tears. As the water cascaded through the paisley he patted down his side burns, as if to still whatever beastliness had been awakened in his heart.

"I'm sorry, Missy, very sorry. I can't bear the damage he has done to us. I swear to God I will never hit you again, only tell me: is he hiding in the house next door?"

The water had plastered his hair dark close upon his head, and she could see, through the wet poplin of his shirt sleeves, his dreadful ropy wrists. He made as if to touch her knee. She drew back into herself. He was vile.

"You must not leave me, Mercy."

"How could I leave you?"

She had a vision of the filthy water sliding behind the wallpaper, creeping down into the dining room below. She pictured all the house below her to be wet, spongy, beyond repair.

"Where would I go? You've ruined me."

"You will always be my Good Companion," said Percy Buckle with much emotion. "I have taken care of you, have I not? When you have been naughty, have I not forgiven you?"

"I was *not* naughty," said Mercy angrily. "And I never would have been alone with him if you had stayed with me in the snuggery. It was not my fault what happened."

"What happened?"

"Nothing happened."

"I'll kill him," said Percy Buckle quietly.

Mercy rose to her feet. "I know where you was just now," she said. "I know what you was up to. You went sneaking down to Covent Garden to talk to Mr Phipps."

Mr Buckle remained seated upon the ottoman. He placed his large hands on his bony knees. "Say you didn't follow me. That's all. Say that to me."

"I didn't need to follow you. I heard your wicked scheming before you put a step outside. You were plotting with that lard-bag from the Inns of Court again."

Percy Buckle cocked his head on one side. "My, my." He made a small round O with his mouth and then covered it with his hand. "You seem to have lost all of your respect."

"I heard what harm you wish to cause that man."

"You can have no idea what I intend. I never said what I intended."

"You just said it, then. You're going to murder him."

Mr Buckle did not deny this. "So, something did occur between you?"

"I kissed him," she responded fiercely.

"In my house?"

"Aye, I kissed him, and he held me here inside this very room. When you left me like the coward you are, I kissed him. And I am not sorry that I did."

"You are a very brave little miss," said Percy Buckle with a dangerous smile.

"Hit me again."

"No, Miss, I will not hit you."

"Then what will you do?"

Percy Buckle removed the key to the snuggery from his pocket, and held it out to her. "Why, I will present you with this key."

The water had eased off and was just dribbling down onto the desk. Mercy looked at the key lying in the master's hand.

"What is this?" she asked. "What would I do with this?"

"It's the key to the city," said Percy Buckle sarcastically.

"What do you mean?"

He dropped the key back in his jacket pocket. "You are dismissed," he said, and remained staring at her with his horrid smirking face until Mercy turned and left the room. She had nowhere to go. As she trod the dark staircase to her attic, she reflected that she was now worse off than when she first arrived.

She bolted the door behind her. She opened the window and climbed out onto the roof.

81

At the moment the two travellers entered that deep green drawing room, Elizabeth Warriner was sitting in a straight-backed chair by the window. She was wearing a dress which was very bright and luminous, like the whites in Henry Bone's enamel portraits. There was light also in her eyes and this, combined with the angle of her head, immediately bespoke a very intense kind of interest in her visitors, as if she knew that her fate was to be decided by the pair of them.

She placed her tea cup carefully on the sill and rose to meet them. Tobias then came to the fore. He approached her, his hands still manacled inside his pockets.

"Hullo."

"Hullo."

She was exceptionally agitated, and for a moment it seemed to Jack Maggs that she would rush into her lover's arms, but then he saw her gather herself in. She stretched out a hand to tug at the arm of her brother-in-law's travel-stained coat.

"Something is the matter with your hands, Toby?"

"No, no." His red lips twisted into a lopsided smile. "A little prank of Master Maggs. Where is my wife, Lizzie?"

"I rather think she will sit with Grandma Warriner until the storm is over."

"Yes," said Tobias Oates, staring at her expectantly.

"It will be a big storm," she said. "The sky is extremely dark. I have been watching it."

"You are not frightened?"

"Of the storm? Oh no."

"There is a spot of business I must transact with Master Maggs."

The girl looked briefly at Jack Maggs, but quickly returned her frank gaze. "Tobias, we really must discuss my trip to France."

"Yes, I will drink a cup of tea with you the moment this business is concluded. Is the pot fresh?"

"It is rather bitter, as a matter of fact. Mary insisted on making it herself. I tell her she is poisoning me, but she says it is from Rajasthan."

"Mr Maggs, come up to my office, and we will deal with the contents of the tin box."

While Jack Maggs judged the gentleman very hard for this off-hand behaviour with his beloved, he obligingly followed him up the stairs. It was not until they were both inside the writer's office that he took Tobias Oates roughly by the arm.

"Go back downstairs," he demanded. *"Kiss* her."

Tobias attempted unsuccessfully to shake himself free.

"She is still a girl," said Jack. "She is in a terror. Tell her you have the pills, and you will take care of the situation."

"Then release my hands, Sir."

"Do not give me orders, mutt."

"If you do not release my hands I cannot do as you wish, for I do not have hands to give her the pills."

Jack Maggs took out his dagger, and did that which was required. He cut roughly and watched while Tobias did up his buttons.

"Give her two pills, and when you have done that come back to me. If you run away or leave the house, I will have to hurt her."

Petulantly, Tobias rubbed the red marks on his wrists. Jack Maggs despised him for a sissy. "Go," he said. "Do it now."

"Why would you have me tread this path?"

"You would be a very stupid lad to argue with me."

"But is this not the very path that brought you and Sophina so much pain and anguish? Is this not what I hear you howling about each time the magnets touch you?"

Jack Maggs put his mangled claw upon his face, clamped his nose, his chin, his jaw, as if he were a dog whose life could be shaken from him. The convict's rage was very great, and he brought his vile cracked lips very close into the other's face.

"What else can she do? If she has your baby her life is ruined. This is the only path she has available."

"I cannot take it."

"It is not for you, Nokes. It is for her." And with that he pushed Tobias out the door. Half-way down, the reluctant writer turned and saw Jack Maggs's massive shadow on the landing.

He made a venomous, impatient sound, which Tobias would remember later as a kind of hiss.

82

It had always been Tobias's method to approach his subject by way of the body. When he had set himself the task of writing about Jack Maggs, he had first produced a short essay on his hands, pondering not merely the fate of the hidden tendons, the bones, the phalanges, the intercarpals which would one day be liberated by the worms, but also their history: what other hands they had caressed, what lives they had taken in anger. He began by picturing the newborn hand resting briefly on its mother's breast, and then he sketched, in the space of four pages, the whole long story leading towards and away from that "hideously misshapen claw." This essay he knew to be a jewel, and he had hoarded it like a clock-maker, setting it aside for its small part in his grand machine. Now, with his wrists raw and red from bondage, he had, to put it very mildly, lost interest in his subject: the Criminal Mind had become repulsive to his own imagination.

Yet it was the Criminal Mind which now controlled Tobias. It was at its directive that he must now, this instant, hold his sister-in-law in his arms. Under its orders he placed two pills in that tender white hand and spoke as confidently, nay, as reverently, as if they had been communion wafers. Yet even as he calmed Lizzie's fears he saw, in the pills' brown misshapen form, not the salvation he promised, but the excrement of something abominable and verminous.

Then came three loud thumps on the floor above his head. Returning to his office, he found the murderer, legs wide apart, demanding to be presented with his "secrets." He showed the writer no particular respect; indeed, he occupied his office wholly, the rank oil-skin odour of his coat possessing every corner of the room.

Later Tobias mourned the manuscripts he then so readily destroyed, for he very soon forgot how badly he had wanted Jack Maggs gone from his life. He might have contrived to hold back the best of his treasures,

but no, he jumped up and down on chairs and ladders, divesting himself of everything related to Jack Maggs. Here—pigeon-holed at "H"—
was the essay on the hands. Beside it, folded in four, were another two
pages labelled "Hair." This Jack Maggs received incredulously.

"This is my hair? All this about my bloody hair?"

"Yes."

"But nothing else?"

"That only."

There had been eight magnetic sessions in all, and the record of each
one was tied and bundled in good neat order as you see the clerks do at
the Inns of Court. Toby had to stand on his desk top, on tip-toes, to
reach, and then he threw them at their subject.

"All this is me?"

"One way or another."

Jack Maggs, for his part, untied each bundle and, although he did not
read everything, he did read a good deal, enough to cause a very great
embarrassment to show upon his face.

"My boy must not read this," he said.

"We burn it," agreed Tobias Oates. "We burn it now."

The thunder echoed in the streets. Wind and rain rushed round and
round the little garden.

83

Lizzie sat in her chair. She sat with her novel open on her lap while
she endured her terrible thoughts. Sometimes she read a line or
two, but there was not a word in *Castle Rackrent* that could not in some
way lead her back to her situation, to that homunculus which, being a
creature of her own heart and blood, must be at least dimly aware of its
fate. Did it not then, as she did, wait in dread, knowing that its last small
hope had been taken from it?

She could not feel the poor creature any more than she could feel the
presence of God or His angels, and yet she knew every moment of her
life to be ruled by its presence, and even as the storm descended upon
them and a mighty wind rushed down Lamb's Conduit Street, pushing
an empty wooden barrel before it, Lizzie sat with her hands resting over
her belly.

When she heard Toby's footsteps on the stairs, she felt no great expectation of comfort from that quarter. He had talked; she had listened. She did not blame him. She had done as he said.

But then she saw he brought that wretched convict back with him, and that the pair of them were carrying all manner of scrolls and piles of manuscript which they dropped, carelessly, before the fireplace. They did not look at Lizzie, or acknowledge her. Thus there was, in their general busyness, a kind of heartlessness.

Toby removed the fire-screen which she and he had bought together, one happy morning on Holborn in the early spring. Toby had always been afraid of fire, as if it would be the thing which would dash in and steal everything from him. How often, she thought, we defend ourselves against the wrong thing.

It was quite hot and close in the room, with the windows closed against the storm, but the two men were tearing up Toby's manuscripts, as if they planned to begin a fire. Now her brother-in-law knelt before the grate and Lizzie caught, in the cast of his mouth, a glimpse of his great stubbornness, his will. Why he was about to destroy his own creation was beyond her, but how she wished she might have a will like that, and not be sitting here now when she might have gone away on a ship to France.

The rattling of the window pane brought her attention back to the street, and there she presently spied a small bent woman attempting to cross the busy road. She was not an old woman, but clearly destitute. Her clothes were ragged, her legs bowed, and she had the panicky motion of a small creature that knows itself the prey of many larger ones. She was carrying some treasure in her pinafore, and there she was, like a beetle or an ant, determined to cross whatever obstacle chance put in her path. The rain was very heavy but the wagons were no smaller or slower on account of it. Lizzie watched the woman take a step forward, then one back, then forward and then, finally, the poor soul made a fast and desperate foray out into the centre of the road.

Here, with a brewery dray almost on top of her, she slipped and fell.

She had been carrying onions in her apron and now all these treasures went rolling out across the coal-black road. The Clydesdale's soup-plate hooves scattered the onions. The wheel of the brewer's dray passed by the woman's head. She rose hastily and began to gather up her onions.

Lizzie began quietly to cry.

On hearing the striking of a match, she turned. Toby was holding a match to the papers in the grate. She watched the fire catch. She watched the papers burn.

Then she saw that Toby had closed his eyes, and in that moment his face was so forlorn that she could easily see what great damage was being done to him as well. As the flames illuminated his familiar face, Lizzie saw, not stubbornness any longer, but a deathmask, like the one he had always kept in his office.

It was then she understood that her life had always been travelling towards this point. There was always to be this storm. The poor woman was always going to fall. This moment had lain there waiting since the day when Tobias had first come to court her sister at her father's house at Amersham.

Now the wind rushed down the chimney, blowing smoke into the room. Toby and the convict were arguing. Toby wished the convict to go to his home. The convict said that he would "damned well" stay all night. She did not pay them much attention. She was thinking that she had been a very selfish girl indeed. She had always known the hurt she risked doing to her sister, and of that she had been careless enough, but she had never considered the harm possible to that luminous young man who had appeared before her family's window one Sunday morning, dressed-up as a sailor, dancing a hornpipe. He had a boy's face, and sweet needful lips, but he had been, although the world had not yet seen it, a giant amongst men.

And she, Lizzie, had almost ruined him, and she could not bear that that be so. She laid her hand again upon that little mound, that soft roundness of her stomach.

The men's voices were softer now. It seemed the convict would indeed depart for his own establishment, and return here in the morning. A threat was made, a last match lit. She watched the final sheaf of papers flare, and saw the shrouds of blue and yellow as Toby stirred them with the poker. In the flames she saw ghostly figures, fictions rising amidst the skirts of flame.

When this last blaze had died away, the grate was filled with mourning: all those lines of gorgeous copperplate had become sheets of black crêpe which he now struck at with a poker. Whether they were struck in anger or merely from a desire to make them burn more efficiently, she could not tell; but if the latter, this intention was soon thwarted by the wind, which once again blew fiercely down the chimney and this time carried the black and broken paper out into the room. The men leapt back, coughing and waving their hands. The burnt papers rose, like black moths, as high as the ceiling.

Elizabeth Warriner, Tobias Oates, Jack Maggs—they all stood as the black ash fell around them.

84

Like I said, mate," said Jack Maggs, opening the door and stepping into Lamb's Conduit Street, "I'll be at your door at ten o'clock to-morrow morning."

"You trust me now, Jack?"

Jack Maggs shrugged. The pills Lizzie Warriner had now ingested would soon begin their work. Then Tobias Oates would be so fully oc-cupied, his hands might as well be tied.

"Are you not the least concerned that I might run?"

The other smiled grimly. "You tried that once already."

"Still, I might betray you."

"You're in too deep, mate. You'd get no benefit, no benefit at all."

For all this, Jack Maggs was by no means complacent. When he once again approached his property in Great Queen Street he in no way re-sembled the fellow who had got down off the Dover *Rocket*. Like a rat along the wainscot, he moved very quietly, melting with the shadows. He spied on his own house for a full hour before he crossed the street and unlocked its front door with a set of "ticklers."

While the storm had long since abated, the windows were heavily curtained and so, although it was only nine o'clock, the house was very dark.

As Jack Maggs closed the door behind him, he felt the presence. There was no unexpected sound, no foreign odour: the ground floor gave off that same satisfying beeswax smell as hitherto. Yet there was someone here, no doubt about it. And now Jack allowed himself to ac-knowledge that he had hoped it would be thus. Indeed it was this very prospect which had drawn him away from Lamb's Conduit Street when prudence should have kept him there all night. The hairs on the back of his neck prickled.

Cautiously, he stooped for his knife. He felt the rough sure grip of the handle which he himself had made with twine and tar. A convict's knife, it dated from before the time when he could have afforded the finest steel and ivory for the handle. He crouched now, a powerful shadow in the doorway of his own living room, drawing the blade in wide circles through the night.

Noiseless as a shade, he then moved forward towards the settle. He heard a small sniffle.

"Henry?"

There was a second sniffle.

"Henry, is that you?"

He struck a match, thus revealing a sad and sorry Mercy Larkin, huddled in a tartan cocoon upon the settle.

"Christ, that was a foolish thing to do." He sat heavily on a gilded chair, well apart from her.

"I'm sorry."

"I told you, don't stick your nose where it ain't wanted."

"I'm sorry."

"I told you long ago it were dangerous."

"You thought I were Mr Phipps." Mercy sat up and blew her nose. "I'm sorry if I frightened you."

"You could not frighten me, girlie. It would take more than you to frighten me." But he felt sick and sour with disappointment and he did not bother to hide his great displeasure.

"You was expecting your Henry?"

He slid his knife back in his boot. "None of your business."

"If that's what's got you in a snot, I can take you to him now."

"*You?*"

"Why do you look at me like that?" She folded up the tartan rug as if her departure were imminent. "Do you think I am such an idiot I couldn't find my way to Covent Garden?"

85

In Jack Maggs's dark and empty house, Mercy Larkin had prayed, *Dear God, forgive me for not visiting my mother. Dear God, grant me a position.*

Around herself she had assembled those few possessions which were her own: the cushions she had embroidered for her room, and the picture her grandma had painted of her poor mama, sitting below a Dutch windmill with a rag doll on her knee.

On and on she prayed, curled up inside Jack Maggs's tartan rug.

Dear God, please soften the Master's heart. Have him write me my references. Dear God, if that ain't possible, let Jack Maggs come back and let me find favour with him. God send him to me.

Then she fell asleep, and when she awoke, she felt the dark air moving across her cheek and heard, "Henry? Henry, is that you?"

A match exploded in the air above her head.

Lo: Jack Maggs.

He was wild and shabby. His eyes were red, his hair lank and greasy, unwashed and sprinkled throughout with ashes. The lining of his coat was torn, and there appeared to be a dark brown stain upon its hem. There was about him that bitter unwashed smell of a man weary from long labour.

"Christ!" he cried. "By Jesus, that was a silly thing to do."

Dear God, forgive his words.

He sat on a chair against the wall, rubbing at his cheek, gathering its flesh and pushing it up towards his temple. His bright red waistcoat was all speckled with mud. He was ever so cross, glaring at her from his red-rimmed eyes. And she was sorry, and sorry again, and sorry one more time, until she realized it was in her power to bestow on him his wish.

Dear God, I thank you.

"Why do you look at me like that?" she said, placing the folded tartan rug neatly on top of her embroidered cushions. "Do you think I am such an idiot I couldn't find my way to Covent Garden?"

"Henry Phipps is in Covent Garden?"

"He is."

His belligerence then washed away, and left in its place a kind of soft confusion. She felt a powerful urge to take his wild and knotted head and wash it in warm water.

"How came you by this information, Mercy?"

Mercy could not admit how long she had known this secret, but neither did she wish to begin to tell untruths again.

"Constable told me Mr Phipps was your son."

"It's true," he sighed. "But I ain't seen him since he was a nipper."

"Then he carries a picture in his heart of the last day he saw you."

"He was but four years of age."

"I too can remember when I lost my da, Jack Maggs. I remember the very day, and were he to come back to me, why I know my heart would burst. Sometimes I still dream he is alive. And in those few precious moments when I wake, I am happy beyond anything you could imagine. Surely it is going to be the same with him when he looks up . . . and there you will be."

Even as she drew this happy picture, she had that unclean feeling that always accompanies deception. She knew that she was sending Jack Maggs to break his heart, and yet she could not help herself, when she saw how benevolently he began to look upon her. It was what she had craved, dear God forgive her.

Jack Maggs lit the candles and gazed rather forlornly at a place above his mantelpiece. Mercy followed his gaze and found, inside that elaborate circle of gilt which framed a massive mirror, the prodigal father's soiled and care-worn image.

"You cannot go calling in those clothes," she said. "Here, give them to me. You don't want to frighten the boy."

He gave a long sigh, then divested himself as she indicated: first surrendering the long great-coat, then the four-button jacket beneath it, then the red waistcoat. Finally, he stood before her, his white shirt stained with sweat, wet on the back.

"You rest yourself now," she said.

Jack Maggs lay down as commanded, curling up his legs on the settle. At that moment she truly did love him.

There were shutters on the kitchen windows, and these Mercy closed. She lit the fire and stoked it high. She put on the kettle. She also set two flat irons on the hottest part, near the fire box. When the kettle was boiling she steamed the mud spots on the waistcoat. These ran in a fine spray, like the tail of a peacock across the breast, but by dint of careful sponging and judicious use of soap jelly, she soon had this first garment restored to its best crimson.

Her cheeks were flushed from the hot steam. She pressed the waistcoat, then hung it on the door knob. Miss Mott would not have recognized her diligence. Without so much as a teaspoon of sugar to refresh herself, Mercy laid out the oil-skin coat across the kitchen table and ministered to it with a stout scrubbing brush. It had been a handsome coat, with three wide capes on its shoulder, and she was pleased to make it seem so once again. One pocket had been ripped clean away, and although this damage was not obvious on the surface of the coat, there was some dark brown sticky substance below the pocket flap. This she sponged away. The other pocket was undamaged and housed the selfsame locks of hair she had found on an earlier occasion.

With these two mysteries in her hands again, she sat on a threelegged stool before the fire box and carefully interrogated them. She sniffed, but there was no smell to them. She picked at the woollen yarn with her nail, but could judge nothing from it.

"Mercy, what are you up to?"

She jumped. He held out his hand and she returned the locks of hair to him.

"I didn't mean nothing by it," she said. "I was just helping you."

"Is it not too dangerous for you to help me?"

"You refer to the Master? He has dispensed with me."

"Dispensed, Mercy?"

"I have been dismissed, Sir."

She was surprised to find how easily she could say it, and then she saw his brow erupt in a frown of such concern that it brought a sudden well of tears into her eyes.

"I don't mind," she reassured him. "I don't mind at all."

"What was your crime?"

"Go home to your babies," she said.

It was not what she had intended to say.

He blinked at her.

But it was obvious to her now. She saw it. Perhaps she had always known. "You have babies in the place where you have come from."

His mouth tightened in denial.

"My son is an Englishman."

"I meant your real children."

"I am not of that race."

"What race?"

"The Australian race," he said. "The race of Australians."

"But what of your babes?"

"Damn you, don't look at me like that. I am an Englishman."

"You are their da, Jack. They walk along the street, they think they see your face in the clouds."

"I made my promise to Henry before they were born."

"He looks at no clouds for you."

"He what?"

"He don't see your face."

At this, he shook her till her teeth rattled in her head.

"What do you know?" he roared, his face turning a dark russet red. "What . . . do . . . you . . . know?"

At which Mercy burst into tears and threw her head upon his broad chest. "I know what it is to lose a da."

He stood still and hard as a post a moment, but then he put his arms around her waist. The kettle began to boil. The pair of them swayed to and fro like a couple in a dance.

86

The spasm had passed, and Lizzie Warriner, now exhausted and putty-skinned, curled herself up amongst the discoloured sheets of the bed wherein she had suffered these last five hours.

Mary sought to push back the damp hair from her sister's brow, although this brought the sufferer no peace. Lizzie thrust the hand away, then pulled irritably at the tangled rope of sheet between her knees.

"I have been poisoned."

In response, Mary tucked her plump chin into her neck and looked sternly at her sister. Then she picked up and folded a yellow shawl that had fallen to the floor. She placed the shawl on the dresser beside a chipped brown basin which had been fetched with such urgency from the nursery. Now she covered the basin with a beaded cloth and placed it beneath the bed. "Come, come." She put her arm beneath the girl's slender back. "We will change the sheets again."

"No, Mary. You will only ruin your best linen."

At this Mary's face crumpled, and she fell upon her sister's neck. "Oh Lizzie, Lizzie, I do love you."

"Ssh, Mary. Please save your tears for someone better."

"There is no one in the world better. It is I who should be better. For it is I who have caused you such suffering."

"Rest easy in your mind, poor dear girl. The blame is hardly yours."

"I did not do it maliciously, I swear. But I have guessed your secret these last two weeks."

This revelation produced a most noticeable silence, broken only when the next spasm shook the girl on the bed and produced a loud high cry of pain. When the convulsion had passed, she tugged at her sister's sleeve.

"You knew of my condition?" she whispered. "How could you know? Who could tell you such a thing?"

"You will be well again soon. When the medicine has finished its work."

"What medicine do you mean?"

"Tablets, dearest. You remember the tea you complained of. You said it was so bitter . . ."

"Oh Mary, Mary," cried Lizzie despairingly.

"It is for the best, you will see," said Mary, beginning to fuss once more with her sister's hair. "Your secret will trouble you no more, my darling."

In answer Lizzie thrust her hand angrily away and looked out into the lamp light with the wild and angry eyes of an animal that her sister did not recognize. "You really should have told me what it was you planned."

In her mind's eye Mary Oates suddenly saw the horrid rouged face of Mrs Britten. She saw the drooping eyes, the great pitted nose, the manly hand with the name SILAS tattooed on its wrist.

This vision was disturbed by her husband, inquiring anxiously from outside the locked door. She opened it a crack to tell him there was nothing new to report. Although she barely recognized the fact yet, she had begun to hate Tobias. Later the roots of this emotion would penetrate the deepest reaches of her soul and make her into the slow and famously dim-witted creature who was commonly thought not to understand half of what her famous husband said, but for now the hate was only a small sharp seed, a pin prick in the corner of her heart, and she was far too worried to concern herself with it. Meanwhile Tobias paced outside the bedroom door, a model of "brotherly concern" and "propriety."

"Put your arm around my shoulder and I will slip the bottom sheet from under you."

"No."

"It will make you more comfortable."

"No, damn you!"

"Lizzie!"

Lizzie grasped her older sister by the wrist. "Listen to me, Mary." She stared so fiercely and frankly that Mary was ashamed. "Promise me," Lizzie demanded.

"Yes, dear. What shall I promise you?"

Lizzie's dark hair had long ago become unpinned, and now it formed a great tangled frame around her damp white face. "You must swear."

"Dear Lizzie, tell me and I will swear it to you."

"When I am gone . . ."

"Don't! You must not say such things."

"When I am gone, you will roll up my sheets. You will not look at them. You will burn them on the fire."

Mary looked at the vast amount of blood which was soaking into the mattress on which her younger sister lay, and was suddenly afraid.

"I will call the doctor."

"No," said the girl, lying back on her pillows. "It is too late for doctors."

"Tobias will fetch Dr Grieves now," said Mary. She would surely go to prison once the doctor discovered the sorry deed that had been accomplished that night. Soon all of England would know how she had put poison in her sister's tea.

"Promise me, Mary."

Mary called urgently for her husband. "Tobias!"

There was no answer. She flung open the door and found the landing empty. She ran downstairs but he was nowhere to be seen. Back in the sick room, Lizzie was writhing convulsively upon the bed. Mary held the basin ready for her sister to release the green fluid from her stomach. What was spilled into the bowl was laced around with red. When the spasm was done, Mary placed the beaded cloth on the top of the bowl, and wiped her sister's brow.

87

Mercy would have preferred to cut his hair in the kitchen, but no, His Majesty must sit in his grand room on his throne, dressed up once more in his cock robin waistcoat and his nice sponged jacket. You could see him as the Lord of his Manor, dogs at his feet, a fire blazing in the grate.

She tucked a sheet around his newly shaven chin and began to snip at his wet hair while he sat upright, formal in his living room. She had, cross her heart, no plan to be in the least bold with him. She would cut his hair and make him look nice for his visit. As God was her witness, she had no other plan, unless it was to be granted a position in his household.

"Keep still."

"I'm thinking." He blew out his cheeks. "I've got such bloody marvellous thoughts inside my head."

"What would you be thinking?"

"Could I ask you to run a message for me early?"

She put her hands upon the top of his head to hold it firm. "Well, I ain't employed by no one else."

"You could be employed by me?"

He caught her eye in the mirror. Once, in the cellar, he had looked at her like that. That time she had misunderstood him. She would not misunderstand him so readily again. She held his gaze a moment before returning to her work.

"Yes, Sir. It would be a great relief."

"I have certain papers that I want my son . . ." and at this word he glanced up to the mirror and smiled shyly at her. "I want my son to study these papers before we meet."

Never having observed this sweetness on his countenance before, she pitied him the cruel disappointment that awaited him on the morrow. She knew, God forgive her, what had happened when Constable had visited Mr Phipps. All Jack Maggs's great passions were to be dashed upon the cobbles of Covent Garden.

"I'd be happy to take your papers to Mr Phipps."

"Is he in the habit of rising early?"

"I know nothing of the gentleman."

She avoided his glance and applied the scissors to his hair. It was dense and strong like the hair of an animal; alien, yet somehow intimate. She pondered the question of whether she need confess her moment of indiscretion with Mr Buckle. She had told him Henry Phipps's whereabouts at a time when she imagined Jack Maggs had gone for ever. He was staring at her again. She felt her deception guessed at, and could not bear it.

"Is your wife a tall woman?"

He withdrew his gaze. Combing the hair down round his ears Mercy discovered that the top of the left ear was missing. It was not a clean cut, such as might be made with a knife, but a rougher, crueller kind of tear.

"You would not say *wife* if you knew the truth. You don't know nothing about what it was to be in that place. You would not be judging me. You would shoot a man you saw treat a dog as we were treated. You might blow his brains out and not think yourself a bad 'un for having done the business. As for me, Miss, I had no more wife than a dog has a wife. A girl like you cannot imagine what it was, to live in such darkness."

"You have no wife anymore?"

"You're a right little terrier, ain't you?"

She did not reply, but as the scissors flashed around him, he answered her.

"No, I ain't."

"Beg your pardon?"

"Ain't got a wife."

She knew she would do well to leave this subject alone, and yet she could not. It was not the wife particularly concerned her: it was those little children.

"Are your children with their mother now?"

"Oh ain't you ever the Miss Quizzical! There is two boys and two mothers. The boys are lodged with a mate of mine, a carpenter, and his wife, a good honest woman named Penny Sanders. It is a home they have known all their life."

"You left them alone?"

"No, not alone."

"But you were their *da*," she insisted. "You were their da, but you had an aim to find a better class of son."

"Jesus save me."

She snipped and cut. God make me calm, she prayed. God, stop this dreadful temper.

"Yes," said he. "I do hope I have found a better class of son. Yes, I most sincerely do. For his education, which is one thousand times as much as ever went into my brain box, cost me fifty pounds each year. I don't know why you look so angry, Miss. It is what every father wants— his son to be the better man."

"I ain't angry. What have I got to be angry about?"

She came now to the short coarse wet hair around his neck. His collar was loose, and as she snipped the hair close to the bare skin, the long, cruel fingers of the lash were visible. It was a shocking thing, to see those scars glistening like torture in the candlelight.

"I am not a hard man, Missy."

"Who lashed you, Mr Maggs?"

"He were a cockney named Rudder. A soldier of the King."

"Then it were the King who lashed you," she insisted.

"We were beyond the King's sight. Not even God Himself could see into that pit."

She cut the hair, staring down into the deep shadow inside his shirt.

"If I were your da, I would not leave you, Mercy."

"You ain't me da, though."

"No, I ain't."

"What are their names?"

"None of your business." He paused. "Richard," he said.

"Richard?"

"I call him Dick."

"How old is Dick?"

"John is six. Dick is ten."

"And while these little boys wait for you to come home, you prance round England trying to find someone who does not love you at all."

"You cannot know that, girl."

"I can," she confessed. "And I do."

88

Henry Phipps left his club with neither raincoat nor umbrella to protect his new subaltern's uniform from further rain. On the whim of Mr Buckle's lawyer, the self-appointed navigator of their little party, they set course for Great Queen Street by way of Russell Street and Drury Lane. It was not the sensible course, nor the most direct, but Henry Phipps followed, and said nothing which might question the lawyer's choice of route.

He was, as Edward Constable might have told him, a wilful and inhibiting man, but like many such individuals, Henry Phipps feared that he was weak of will, and as he followed Mr Makepeace, he brooded about that quality of character which allowed him to accept the direction of so poor a leader.

He walked down Russell Street with hands clasped behind his back, all the time looking with particular resentment at Mr Makepeace's posterior as it pushed against the confines of his mackintosh. In those ample haunches he saw evidence enough to confirm his fear that he would follow any damn fool rather than the dictates of his own common sense.

What that common sense dictated was that he bid his house goodbye and report on the morrow to his regiment. But the fact was, Henry Phipps had long neglected the call of common sense, and it was a stronger force, his passionate desire to ensure his own comfort, which held him in the company of a man who wished him to commit a murder.

In this turmoil of mind, he turned the corner into Drury Lane and, before he knew it, had set his new boots deep into foul yellow clay. The mud was past his ankles and up around the bottoms of his trousers.

"This was a damned fool way to come," cried he, staring down at the mucky ruin of his uniform.

"It is excavated for the sewer," whispered Mr Makepeace.

"I am perfectly well aware that it is the sewer." He withdrew his boots from the deep sticky clay and climbed up to the vantage of a broken brick. "Why would you come here when you could perfectly well walk up Long Acre? What possessed you?"

"I am more accustomed to Drury Lane," whispered Mr Makepeace.

"We'll clean you up, Sir, don't worry. You come to my house first. My housekeeper will call her troops out for you."

"Quiet." Henry Phipps's face in the gas light now clearly revealed that spleen which Edward Constable claimed to be so much a feature of his character. "I will lead the way."

"Very good, Sir—please." Mr Makepeace stepped back and, perching himself like a wet black biddy upon a pile of rotting lumber, gestured that Henry Phipps should move ahead of him.

Henry Phipps, however, did not move. He gazed instead down into that long pit the engineers had dug in the centre of the street. The trench was criss-crossed with new black pipes, and below this grid of iron was a further shadowy world of excavated arches leading to God knows what place. The sight induced in him a vertiginous unease which so paralleled the general anxiety about his life that he feared, even though he was some six feet from the edge, he might tumble into it.

He looked at Percy Buckle and found that gent nodding at him.

He looked back along Drury Lane, but it was a wild and unexpected landscape in no way like the Drury Lane he knew. Great wooden beams criss-crossed the street, like intrusions in a nightmare. Others had been propped against the walls of shops. These beams were joined together like inverted, lopsided A's, and something in their rude design brought to mind the gallows. A kind of fog now rose from the excavation, and in the penumbra of the gas light Henry Phipps imagined he saw a man's body hanging from a beam, suspended above the pit.

"You go," he said, much frightened. "You first."

He let the grocer squeeze past him, feeling, as he did so, the hard edge of the pistol case Mr Buckle carried concealed beneath his cloak. Then he followed suit, keeping close against the walls of the houses, avoiding the crumbling edges of the pit.

89

The yard at Moreton Bay had distinctive odours: of dry clay dust, of fetid tidal mud, of some antipodean plant which gave off an oozing stink like blackberry mixed with sweat. And although it is sometimes said that the experience of smell itself cannot be remembered any more than the experience of pain, Jack Maggs could remember these smells as well as he could the carolling of those so-called "magpies," and the squeaking wheels of the carpenter's dray and the bloody red colour of its timber planks which would, in the course of one wet summer, be devoured by white ants.

He could still see the small red button at the apex of the flogger's forage cap, the worn supple thongs which bound his wrists and ankles to the triangle.

There was a most particular smell hanging like bad meat around that cursed place, and small iridescent blue flies which crawled upon his face and nose. As the flies began to tease his skin, the wretched man would begin to build London in his mind. He would build it brick by brick as the horrid double-cat smote the air, eddying forth like a storm from Hell itself.

Underneath the scalding sun, which burned his flesh as soon as it was mangled, Jack Maggs would imagine the long mellow light of English summer.

The flies might feast on his spattered back; the double-cat might carry away the third and fourth fingers of his hand; but his mind crawled forward, always, constructing piece by piece the place wherein his eyes had first opened, the home to which he would one day return, not the mudflats of the Thames, nor Mary Britten's meat-rich room at Pepper Alley Stairs, but rather a house in Kensington whose kind and beautiful interior he had entered by tumbling down a chimney, like a babe falling from the outer darkness into light. Clearing the soot from his eyes he had seen that which he later knew was meant by authors when they wrote of England, and of Englishmen.

Now, all these long years later, Jack Maggs had become such an Englishman. Dressed in his red waistcoat and his tailored tweed jacket, he stood before what Tobias Oates might have called "a cheerful fire."

The face he turned towards Mercy Larkin was hardened by its time in New South Wales—it had been rubbed at by pain until it shone—yet there was in his dark eyes a bright and glittering excitement which even he, with all his schooling in the art of secrecy, could not hide.

When he had suffered pain, pain so intense he had begged for death, he had seen this woman with her dark tangle of hair, sitting with hands folded thus upon her lap.

Now he took the brandy bottle from the mantel and refilled her tumbler. He watched with approval as she drank, not daintily, but as one suffering from a deep and persistent thirst.

"To you, Miss."

"To you, Sir." She continued to toy with those locks of children's hair upon her lap. While he had insisted that the hair was not her business, it did not displease him that she was so stubborn. Tenacity was a quality he had good reason to value highly.

"What say you, girl? You will keep house for me?"

She drained the last drops of brandy, then looked him straight in the eye.

"I will keep house for your babes."

She stood up. Thinking that she intended to give him back the locks, he held out his hand to receive his property.

"They are in another country," he said.

But she gave him her left hand, retaining the locks of children's hair in the right, and so they remained, hand in hand, at once at cross-purposes and yet not.

"They are waiting for you," she smiled.

"Hark."

He withdrew his hand abruptly.

"It is the street door," she whispered.

In an instant he had the candles snuffed, but there was nothing he could do to staunch the fire which continued to burn brightly, throwing their two fretful shadows up onto the walls and ceiling.

Jack's hair bristled on his naked neck and, as the door swung open, he reached for the tarred twine handle of his dagger. A spectral figure entered the room, holding the candle high.

There, in the firelight, he beheld his nightmare: long straight nose, fair hair, brutal dreadful uniform of the 57th Foot Regiment. The Phantom had broken the locks and entered his life.

The apparition held a heavy pistol. Jack Maggs saw this instrument very clearly, yet he stayed rooted to the spot, his gaze fixed upon the spectre's uniform. The firelight flickered on that line of horrid buttons, each one embossed with the number 57. He smelt the bad meat smell of the yard at Moreton Bay, felt the soft supple leather bind his wrists and ankles again. He could see the great dull gape of the pistol's barrel, and the fire light twinkling on the bright brass hammer which was fully cocked. *I am to die before I meet my son.*

Then, suddenly, inexplicably, there appeared from the darkness of the hallway none other than Percy Buckle Esquire. He pushed violently at the Phantom's back so the creature lurched even closer to Jack Maggs, who was still staring, his mouth agape. "Take back your house, Sir. Defend your life against this burglar."

The dagger was ready in his hand, and still Jack Maggs made no move.

"Fire!" Mr Buckle stamped his foot repeatedly upon on the floor. "Fire, for God's sake, fire."

At this confusing juncture, just as the pistol was raised and pointed at Jack Maggs's heart, Mercy rose quietly from the shadows.

Jack Maggs watched paralysed as she walked softly towards the Phantom in her stockinged feet. In her right hand she still held those two precious locks of hair, but it was her left hand that he watched as she raised it, palm outwards, towards the barrel of the gun, as if by so doing she might catch the deadly ball; as if she were in truth a spirit, a force of nature equal but opposite to the malevolent being who now threatened to snuff out Jack Maggs's life.

90

Henry Phipps was ushered into his own hallway which seemed narrower and longer than he had remembered it. He did not feel himself a murderer, but an animal at Smithfield, hemmed in and hounded at all sides, with all his confusion magnified a hundred times by Percy Buckle, who was now pushing at his back with the point of his umbrella.

Gone was the mild apologetic little grocer who had first walked into his rooms at Covent Garden. In his place was this hissing, dark-shelled incubus whose alien and agitated presence strained the young man's already over-stretched emotions. Percy Buckle, without being aware of it, had already twice placed himself in mortal danger.

It was Mr Buckle who flung the door open to the living room.

"Fire," he cried, while the lawyer hovered somewhere behind them in the darkness.

"Fire!"—and pushed him forward into the room.

For Henry Phipps, everything in this present nightmare seemed to be happening very slow. He had all the time he required to look at the man who had written to him for most of his young life. He had always known Jack Maggs to be a convict, known him transported for "the term of his natural life," and Victor Littlehales, his Oxford tutor, had taught him how to gratify the needs of him who signed his letters "Father." They had laboured together on the replies until young Henry finally found his voice, and thereafter the role came to him easily enough. If the letters could be called "lies" they could also be called "comfort."

Henry Phipps had sung to Jack Maggs, sung for his supper. He had sung without understanding it was a siren song, without ever dreaming that this tortured beast might demand of him that which had been conceived only as a flight of fancy.

"Defend your house," cried Percy Buckle.

Henry Phipps had no choice. He raised the gun.

From the shadow by the fire, a young woman came towards him. Her feet were bare. She raised her hand towards the barrel.

91

At the instant Henry Phipps discharged the pistol, Lizzie Warriner died in her bed. Even though her pain ended, there was in that wracked body no suggestion of repose, but everywhere tension, angularity, distress. She lay in the midst of the rucked and tangled carmine sheets, her hand thrust into her mouth as if she were still biting it.

Tobias was not yet the bearded eminence he would finally become. On the night Lizzie died, he was a frightened, ambitious young man. His eyes were bloodshot, his red mouth contorted by spasms of grief. He wept upon his dead lover's pillow, and then on the skirts of his wife, although this lady, uncharacteristically, made no move to comfort him. Instead she sat upon the death bed, expressionless, heavy-jowled, the corpse's cooling hand in hers.

"Light the fire," she said.

"I will call the doctor."

Mary Oates bestowed on her husband a look of passionate antagonism. "You will light the fire, you foolish man."

"You are wrong," he said, although what exactly she was wrong about he did not say. It was clearly not the fire he was speaking of, for he soon took himself downstairs and managed to make a vigorous blaze of coals and faggots. Then he obediently performed that service which the dead girl had beseeched of her sister. That is, he made a pyre of her linen. Given that the fireplace was not large and the sheets were still, in some places, wet, it was not an easily accomplished task, but he persevered.

Throughout all this, he wept unashamedly. Mary, by contrast, sat woodenly in a straight-backed chair, the same chair in which Jack Maggs had first been mesmerized. When Mary did look finally at Tobias Oates it was with a gaze of such coldness that her husband quailed before it.

"You do me a great wrong," said he.

"We have both done great wrong," she said.

Later Tobias would think he had imagined this reply, but now he sat on his heels and watched Lizzie's very life blood burning upon the flames. In those flames he saw, as he would throughout his life, the figures and faces of his fancy dancing before him. He saw the wraith of their dead child folding and unfolding in the skirts of fire. He saw Lizzie herself, her face smiling and folding into the horrible figure of decay.

He could not bear it. Would not carry it.

He poked at the blackened linen and found in it one abhorrent face, that of the man who had led him to Mrs Britten's door, who had placed those dung-coloured pills where they would poison that precious life.

It was Jack Maggs, the murderer, who now grew in the flames. Jack Maggs on fire. Jack Maggs flowering, threatening, poisoning. Tobias saw him hop like a devil. Saw him limp, as if his fiery limbs still carried the weight of convict iron. He saw his head transmogrify until it was bald, tattooed with deep wrinkles that broke apart and floated glowing out into the room.

It was Jack Maggs who had done this, and in his grief Tobias began to heap up all his blame upon him. It was now, on the seventh of May, in the darkest night of his life, that Jack Maggs began to take the form the world would later know. This Jack Maggs was, of course, a fiction, and so it may not matter that Tobias never witnessed the final act of the real convict's search: never observed Henry Phipps raise that pistol with his trembling hand, never heard the deafening explosion, nor smelled the dark and murderous scent of gunpowder.

It would not have been lost on him that Mercy Larkin's wedding finger was blown away, and that when Jack Maggs came to her side, the pair were finally matched in their deformity. But the forces that made that famously "abhorrent" face inside the fire were different from those that drove the real Jack Maggs, who escaped London with Mercy Larkin that very night on the Portsmouth Mail. There is no character like Mercy in *The Death of Maggs*, no young woman to help the convict recognize the claims of Richard and John to have a father kiss them good night.

Dick Maggs was eleven years of age when Jack returned from England. He had twice been up before the magistrate, and little John, who was four years younger, had the same hard belligerent face, the same dark and needful eyes. It was not an easy role for Mercy Larkin, yet she applied herself to being their mother with a passion. She who had always been so impatient of the "rules" now became a disciplinarian. She brushed their hair and wiped their faces. She walked with them to school and saw they stayed there. It was she who moved the family away from the bad influence of Sydney. And in the new town of Wingham where they shortly settled she not only civilized these first two children, but very quickly gave birth to five further members of "That Race."

Jack Maggs sold the brickworks in Sydney. In Wingham he set up a saw mill and, when that prospered, a hardware store, and when that prospered, a pub. He was twice president of the shire and was still the president of the Cricket Club when Dick hit the cover off a new ball in the match against Taree.

The Maggs family were known to be both clannish and hospitable, at once civic-minded and capable of acts of picturesque irresponsibility, and it is only natural that they left many stories scattered in their wake. Yet amongst the succeeding generations of Maggs who still live on those fertile river flats, it is Mercy who is now remembered best, not only for the story of how she lost her wedding finger, not only for the grand mansion on Supper Creek Road whose construction she so pugnaciously oversaw and whose servants she so meticulously supervised, but also for the very particular library she collected in her middle age.

The Death of Maggs, having been abandoned by its grief-stricken author in 1837, was not begun again until 1859. The first chapters did not appear until 1860, that is, three years after the real Jack Maggs had died, not in the blaze of fire Tobias had always planned for him, but in a musty high-ceilinged bedroom above the flood-brown Manning River. Here, with his weeping sons and daughters crowded round his bed, the old convict met death without ever having read "That Book."

For this lack, Mercy compensated. She read *The Death of Maggs*, first as it appeared in serial, then again when the parts were gathered in a handsome volume, then again when the author amended it in 1861. Finally, she owned no fewer than seven copies of the last edition, and each of these is now (together with Jack Maggs's letters to Henry Phipps) in the collection of the Mitchell Library in Sydney. Of the seven volumes, six are cloth, one is leatherbound, and this last is signed: *To Mercy from Captain E. Constable, Clapham 1870.*

The Mitchell's librarian has noted on each index card the "v. rough excision" of that page which reads:

Affectionately Inscribed
to
PERCIVAL CLARENCE BUCKLE
A Man of Letters, a Patron of the Arts

A NOTE ON THE TYPE

This book was set in Caledonia, a face designed by William Addison Dwiggins (1880–1956) for the Mergenthaler Linotype Company in 1939. It belongs to the family of types referred to by printers as "modern," a term used to mark the change in type styles that occurred around 1800. Caledonia was inspired by the Scotch types cast circa 1833 by the Glasgow typefounder Alexander Wilson & Sons. However, there is a calligraphic quality about Caledonia that is completely lacking in the Wilson types.

Dwiggins referred to an even earlier typeface for Caledonia's liveliness of action—one cut around 1790 by William Martin for the printer William Bulmer. Caledonia has more weight than the Martin letters, and the bottom finishing strokes of the letters are cut straight across, without brackets, to make sharp angles with the upright stems, thus giving a modernface appearance.

Dwiggins began his association with the Mergenthaler Linotype Company in 1929, and over the next twenty-seven years he designed a number of book types, the most interesting of which are Metro, Electra, Caledonia, Eldorado, and Falcon.

Composed by ComCom,
an R. R. Donnelley & Sons Company,
Allentown, Pennsylvania

Printed and bound by Quebecor Printing,
Fairfield, Pennsylvania

Designed by Misha Beletsky